KILLERS

FORGE BOOKS BY HOWIE CARR

Hitman

Hard Knocks

Killers

KILLERS

HOWIE CARR

A TOM DOHERTY ASSOCIATES BOOK

NEW YORK

This is a work of fiction. All of the characters, organizations, and events portrayed in this novel are either products of the author's imagination or are used fictitiously.

KILLERS

A Forge Book
Published by Tom Doherty Associates, LLC
175 Fifth Avenue
New York, NY 10010

www.tor-forge.com

Forge® is a registered trademark of Tom Doherty Associates, LLC.

Library of Congress Cataloging-in-Publication Data

Carr, Howie.
    Killers / Howie Carr.
        p. cm.
    ISBN 978-0-7653-3374-2 (hardcover)
    ISBN 978-1-4668-0519-4 (e-book)
    1. Gangsters—Massachusetts—Boston—Fiction.   2. Organized crime—
Massachusetts—Boston—Fiction.   3. Political corruption—Massachusetts—
Boston—Fiction.   I. Title.
    PS3603.A77423K55 2015
    813'.6—dc23

2015020939

Forge books may be purchased for educational, business, or promotional use. For information on bulk purchases, please contact the Macmillan Corporate and Premium Sales Department at 1-800-221-7945, extension 5442, or write to special markets@macmillan.com.

First Edition: September 2015

Printed in the United States of America

0 9 8 7 6 5 4 3 2 1

To all my daughters

KILLERS

1

"DO YOU KNOW WHO I AM?"

I got the word about Sally Curto's nephew around 5:45 a.m. when he woke me with a telephone call to my apartment on Sparhawk Street in Brighton. I don't spend a lot of nights there, but some habits are hard to break, and one of those habits is never getting into habits, like sleeping in the same place every night.

"My nephew Tony," Sally said, in a whisper that was more like a croak. "He got shot this morning. Killed. On Parmenter Street. He was working the door at the barbooth game. Three guys with masks. I can't fuckin' believe it. Work my ass off all these years and this is the respect I get. It's all over the TV."

In the background I could hear a long, anguished female wail.

"I gotta see you," he said.

"Usual place?" I said. Then I heard another lengthy, mournful sound, followed by two toots on a car horn. Sally's ride had arrived.

"Usual place," he said. "I gotta get the fuck outta here."

Sally's real first name was Salvatore, as in Salvatore Matteo Curto. But as far as I know, nobody had ever called him anything but "Sally," except maybe his parole officer or his sainted mother, God rest her soul.

Sally lived in Nahant, but at that time of the morning, it doesn't take any time to get to Castle Island in South Boston. We both liked Southie for meetings, because neither of us is from there. Otherwise, it's a very overrated community in my opinion, and Sally's too. And spare me any nonsense about how brilliant Whitey Bulger was. The main reason he was able to take over the rackets in Southie was the brainpower, or lack thereof, of the competition. Sally and I have a joke about Southie hoods:

Q. What do you a call a Southie guy who moves from C Street to D Street?

A. A fugitive.

Anyway, I got to Southie first, and was sitting on the hood of my BMW when Sally arrived. He has two drivers, the older one they call George Graft; I don't know his real name, never asked. It's not considered good form. George Graft is supposed to look like some ham actor who played in a lot of old gangster movies. George Graft is also Sally's so-called bodyguard, which tells you a lot about how peaceful it's been around here for years now. George Graft couldn't punch his way out of a paper bag, and he has a license to carry, meaning he's never done time.

Sally's other driver is from East Boston, younger, fatter, at least 280 pounds, and I know he's done time, because he's got that con habit of always putting his hand to his mouth when he talks to you, in case somebody in the yard or in the sentry tower was watching him and trying to read his lips.

Sally called him Cheech.

Even though he was a lot younger than George Graft, Cheech was more old school. He always wore a raincoat, even in the summer when it was ninety degrees, and underneath it he carried a sawed-off shotgun. As far as I knew, he'd never used it, or been rousted with it, even though the cops had to know he was a felon in possession of a firearm, an illegal firearm at that. I don't trust guys who get passes from the law unless I know for a fact they're paying off the cops. If you're a wiseguy, it's not healthy to have other wiseguys thinking cops are taking care of you just because they like you, because the only reason they like you if you're not paying them off with money is because you're paying them off with something else, and snitchin' is the coin of the realm.

On the other hand, maybe Cheech was just riding his older brother's coattails. Hole in the Head was a genuine hard-bar, about the last one Sally had working for him. There was a story around that when they were kids, Cheech used to bring a pistol to the dinner table, because he knew Hole in the Head was likewise packing and was capable of going out of control at any moment, even at the dinner table, especially if Mama was out in the kitchen ladling out some more marinara sauce for her beloved bambinos. I figured Hole in the Head would be in the mix before nightfall.

Sally rolled up in a sleek Lincoln Town Car. Cheech was driving, which was a sign of how seriously Sally was taking this. He parked two spaces away from my BMW, and then got out of the car. I could see the outlines of the shotgun under his raincoat, on the right side. Cheech looked around menacingly to make sure nobody was coming at his boss—totally unnecessary at this time of the morning, but maybe he was trying to impress Sally, or overcompensating for having a tougher brother. Then Cheech walked back to the Lincoln and opened the front passenger door for Sally.

When Sally climbed out, Cheech nodded to him somberly, as if to indicate that he had reconnoitered the perimeter and found nothing amiss. Theatrical is what it was. Nobody I'd ever run into had ever mentioned Cheech capping anybody. If he was capable, he was keeping it a pretty good secret.

Sally was about five-eight, 260 pounds, sixty-seven years old. He too was wearing a raincoat, only his was over his pajamas, and on his feet were bedroom slippers. He'd left Nahant in a hurry. He shook my hand, then took a pack of Marlboro Lights from his rain-coat pocket, shook one out and lit up.

"You heard the details yet?" he said.

"Just what was on the radio, pretty sketchy."

This was the first time in a couple of years that the first words out of his mouth when I'd met him somewhere he'd driven to hadn't been a string of obscenities about how he'd had to look for a parking space on account of the bleepity-bleep-bleep *Herald*. Some broad reporter had caught him using a handicapped placard he'd paid a hack at the Registry $500 for. They'd plastered his fat-ass picture all over the front page for a couple of days and made him look like a real asshole. Now Sally, or his driver, had to look for a parking space like everybody else. Sally'd never gotten over it, or at least he hadn't until now.

"My nephew," he said. "You met him, right? At Tina's wedding last summer?"

"A good kid," I said noncommittally. If I had met him, he'd left no impression on me.

"He wanted to make some extra money, said he needed it for college."

College? Sally had a college boy working the door at one of his cash games. Sally ran at least one Las Vegas night per week for churches or charities. That's how he was breaking in his own son, Jason, or trying to. Inside a church seemed like a better place to start out a college boy than an after-hours barbooth game, although I would bet there wasn't a lot of cash in Sally's game anymore. These days the old-timers, which was all you'd have playing barbooth, tend to blow their Social Security on $20 or $30 scratch tickets, or maybe a trip to Foxwoods the first of the month, after the eagle shits. A stick-up guy could get a bigger haul knocking over the bingo game Wednesday night at Marion Manor, the old folks' rest home in Southie.

Sally took a drag on his cigarette and flicked it away, toward the seawall.

"I know what you're thinking, these kids ain't like us, they're soft. He's from Lynnfield—not Lynn, Lynnfield. Trees and shit, Lexuses, soccer, blond fucking cheerleaders. But what am I gonna do? He ain't really my nephew, you know. He's my wife's. If I don't use him she'll let me have it 'cause her sister's letting her have it. And now, I give 'em what they want and he's dead, and I ain't never gonna hear the end of it."

"I didn't even know you were still running a barbooth game."

"If I didn't, them old farts'd be bitchin' and moanin' all week at me at the social club down Salem Street. They oughta be home praying for a happy death, but instead they're on my ass, 'cause they got nothing better to do."

I thought to myself, this is a guy who's on the national La Cosa Nostra organizational charts that the Department of Justice shows off at press conferences in Washington. He's right under Rubber Lips in the New England Mafia. He's the "underboss," so-called, but when he's not taking a raft of shit at home he's taking it down the North End at his club. Mario Puzo must be rolling over in his grave.

"Sally," I said, "why didn't you have the kid doing something he couldn't get into trouble doing, running numbers or something?"

"Running numbers? How many guys you got running numbers, Bench? Numbers is deader'n dog racing. Or horse racing, for that matter. Besides, when was the last time somebody heisted one of our games? Gotta be at least ten years."

I knew what he wanted me to do. But he wanted me to volunteer. He'd lose face if he had to ask me. Not with anybody else In Town, as everyone in the Mob still called the North End, because he was "In Town," just like I was "the Somerville mob." But personally he'd feel embarrassed having to ask a younger, Irish guy for help, even a guy he's known his whole life basically, since I was a kid doing my first state bit.

But Sally didn't have many capable guys left. Just Hole in the Head.

"The reason I come to you, Bench, is because we're in this together now, I thought you ought to be the first to know. I mean, these ass-holes get away with this, nobody's safe. You still got that card game in Andrew Square?"

I did, with two guys running it named Salt and Peppa. If some junkie threw down on Salt, Peppa would shoot him in the back. Or vice versa. Nobody would figure it, a black guy on the same crew with an white guy. Peppa was a question mark. Stick-up guys don't like question marks. They find somebody else to rob, most likely a coke dealer.

But this was Sally's problem, not mine. I got my own headaches to deal with, guys stealing, guys getting sick, guys on drugs, guys beating up girlfriends, guys ratting each other out, the usual shit.

"I'm sure you got some people on this already," I said. "I don't want to step on anybody's toes."

"Please, who you kiddin'?" he said. "These guys I got now, most of 'em couldn't find their way off Hanover Street." The words were coming faster now, in a rush. "They lift weights, they think they're tough. They take steroids, they think they're mean. I don't need tough guys, I need intelligent tough guys. This is your problem too, you understand? They come after me like this, they'll come after you too."

"What about the cops?" I said. "They gotta be all over this one like stink on shit. It's a lot safer workin' a homicide down the North End than in Grove Hall. What are they telling you?"

"Cops." Sally spit out the words and his face got red. I knew what was coming next. Whenever he got really angry, something snapped in his brain, and suddenly the guy he was pissed at wasn't there any-more, even if in fact he was. Suddenly Sally would be screaming, giving you a message to deliver to . . . yourself. I'd been through this countless times, getting yelled at and threatened, once removed. I called it "going Sally." Now he was going Sally on me.

"Listen, you tell that fuckin' mick," he said, staring at me, that fuckin' mick, "he knows better'n to ask me about cops. Cops don't do shit, except come around at Christmas with their hands out. And he knows it. So you tell that fuckin' kid that by noon they'll be coming 'round his places, asking him if he knows anything. That's their idea of an investigation. That kid, he knows I got nobody no more, he shouldna oughta make me beg. This is like the fuckin' army, yes sir and no sir. You fuckin' tell him that. You tell him I said so."

I just stood there. The first time it happened, in state prison in Walpole, I was petrified. Of course I was only about eighteen years old. Now, I just waited for him to come out of his trance. Finally he blinked and shook his head and lit another cigarette. It was over. Afterward, I don't think he even remembered what he'd said, but I had never asked him.

He leaned in close to me. A tear ran down his cheek. This was something new. "Please, Bench, I can't take it, I ain't never gonna hear the end of this until these fucking punks are dead. And I don't mean disappearin' them, burying them down on Tenean Beach like you done with them ass-clowns from Charlestown. I want these motherfuckers' bodies found, hopefully fuckin' trussed, so's I can show my wife and my fuckin' sister-in-law the newspaper, with the pictures of their bodies on the front page. Drop 'em on the street if you have to, but what I really want is for you to fucking hog-tie 'em and leave 'em in the trunk at the long-term parking lot at Logan. I wanna see a quote in the *Herald* that says, 'They died hard.' You gotta pay some cop to say that, send me the bill, *capisce?*"

"How much did they get?" I asked.

"They got shit is what they got," he said, his voice rising again. "A million fucking drug dealers in this city they could be robbin' and they go after my game, which I'm running strictly for Auld Lang Syne." He lit another cigarette. "Listen, I'm serious, I wanna see the punks' car on the front page of the paper, and I wanna see the blood oozing out of the trunk, in color. Brown. Not red, brown, like it turned into pus, it was there for days, stinking up the garage, their faces turning into pudding. I want the cops saying somebody smelled the bodies—"

"Wrong season, Sally," I said. "The best I can do for you this time of year is 'They died hard.' Listen, I still don't get why they shot your nephew."

"They're fucking junkies is why. Who knows? Something went wrong. You know how it goes."

"But you don't believe that, do you, Sally?"

"Why do you think I called Cheech?" He was yelling again now. "If it's a robbery, they can get a lot more money than hitting one of my games."

"What color were these guys?" A very important question, and one that would never be answered on the radio or TV or in the papers unless they were white, which I doubted.

"Spics, more'n likely. They had accents, or the one who was speaking did. Sometimes they use guys fresh off the boat, can't even speak English yet."

Just like in the old days, but I didn't say that. "You think somebody's trying to send you a message, Sally?"

"Send us a message you mean. You're in with us now too, remember? Partner."

He had a point. That was the agreement we'd worked out, after the last "war," after all the wannabes were taken care of, mostly by what the newspapers called "the Somerville mob." Ever since then it was supposed to be one for all and all for one, and although we hadn't spelled it out formally, if the shooting started, I was the one for all.

As we walked, I suddenly heard someone running toward us from behind. It was Cheech. He had a cell phone in hand, the old-fashioned flip kind, not an iPhone.

"Boss," he said, "it's your wife. She wants to talk to you."

Sally looked over at me pleadingly. "Will you talk to her, Bench? Please. Tell her we're doing what we can."

"Sally," I said. "I thought we had an understanding. If we got business to discuss, we do it here, so nobody can record nothing."

Sally nodded and took the phone from Cheech. "Yes, dear . . . I'm with that guy we talked about . . . the one with the dead eyes, that's right." He looked over at me and shrugged. "Rossetti's of course, as soon as it's nine I'll call him."

Rossetti's was the Mafia funeral home in the North End.

"Don't worry, hon, tell Carmela we're working on it."

He handed the phone back to Cheech and waved him away. Cheech looked disappointed that he couldn't stick around and put his two cents in. But he followed instructions and lumbered off, looking slightly lopsided with the shotgun under his right armpit. The beach was deserted, so he had nobody to even scowl at, let alone blast. Meanwhile Sally lit a new cigarette off his old one.

"We don't need this shit," he said. "Not right now, not with the casino bill coming up and all."

They'd been working on it for years, the hacks at the State House, but this time it looked like they finally had the skids greased. Three casinos, one of which was reserved for the moribund racetracks in East Boston. The enabling legislation had already passed the House, and now it was pending in the Senate. Maybe we couldn't run things like the syndicate used to back in the good old days in Las Vegas, but with that much dough on the table, all we needed were scraps, the stuff on the margins. Laundry, the parking concessions, control of the booze and food deliveries through our Teamster locals, the hooker bars around the corner from the dice tables and the one-armed bandits, a little shylocking. . . .

For once the state getting into gambling might pay off for us.

Better than drugs, that went without saying. Drugs are a rat magnet; that's why the old-timers hated drugs, not for any moral reasons. The goombahs understood instinctively that the draconian mandatory-minimum sentences would turn everybody into snitches. Anybody could do three months in the House of Correction on a state gambling beef. But on Class B controlled substances the feds were locking up wiseguys and throwing away the key. Plus lately they're dropping the real f-bomb—forfeitures. If you were high up, like me and Sally, you needed buffers, at least two levels of buffers, because once your dealers start getting busted, they topple like dominoes, and your whole organization turns into a fucking deli, every last one of them standing in line, waiting to take a number to rat you out. . . .

Drug kingpins. That's what they would call me and Sally if they ever got the chance. Not to mention career criminals.

If we get a casino, maybe we can start weeding out the junkies. Maybe.

Just then we saw another car pulling up, a black Cadillac Escalade. It was Blinky Marzilli, another legend in his own mind. He fancied himself the East Boston captain. He jumped out of his car, ran up to Sally and first hugged him, then kissed him on both cheeks. Sally looked embarrassed. I was amused. I have a theory about these guinea greetings—the more emotive the hood is, the more likely he is to eventually end up in the Witness Security Program. It's like they're overcompensating, in advance.

I'd heard stories about Blinky, but nothing I could ever pin down. He'd been an "unindicted coconspirator" in a chop-shop indictment in Revere a couple of years back. One "unindicted coconspirator," you get a mulligan on. A second one, they put out a contract on you. At least I do.

Blinky had brought along his muscle, such as it was, another nitwit named Benny Eggs. I think he got the nickname because he has the IQ of a soft-boiled egg. He was sniffling, another bad sign in my book. I don't believe in colds anymore, not since cocaine came in.

As Benny Eggs looked on, Blinky shook my hand, then turned his attention back to Sally.

"From my lips to God's ears," he said, raising his left hand, "whatever I got is yours. I'll help you get those dirty motherfucking spics."

"Sally," I said, "how sure are we that these were spics?"

"That's what the dealer said. Charlie the Greek. He's been with me for years."

"I already got my spics out there beating the bushes." Blinky still lived in East Boston, even though it had tipped years earlier. The old white neighborhood was receding at the rate of two or three blocks a year, north toward Orient Heights and Winthrop. The Eastie state rep, an Italian of course, now wore long-sleeve shirts year-round so no one would see his tattoos. Two years ago he'd only gotten fifty-two percent of the vote in the primary against a guy named Ramirez. Eastie was on the verge of slipping into the past tense.

"I'm putting Vinny and his partner Fat Vinny on it too," Blinky said.

I know those guys. Let me tell you, if the killers were hiding in a meatball at Santarpio's, Vinny and Fat Vinny would find them for sure.

"We'll get 'em Sally," Blinky said. "We gotta get 'em. This here is a, a . . ."

"A provocation?" I suggested.

"Yeah, that's it, a provocation. You always come up with the right word, Bench."

"I caught up on my reading at Lewisburg," I said.

A couple of toothless tigers in scally caps were slowly hobbling towards us now. The only weapons they were carrying were canes, but I saw Cheech giving them the evil eye.

I looked at Sally. "We ought to get moving," I said, and Sally and Blinky nodded, after which Benny Eggs nodded. I couldn't see Cheech from where I was, but I had a feeling his trigger finger was getting itchy under the raincoat.

I watched them all leave, then sat down on a park bench and got out my cell phone. I called a detective I knew in Area A-1. I told him I'd meet him at Lupo's, a bucket of blood on Harrison Avenue in Chinatown, after the shift change. I asked him to bring along whatever he had on the murder, including photos.

"Pictures?" he said. "I don't know about that."

"C'mon, I just want to look at them, I don't want to keep them." He'd bring them. He was on my pad.

I got to Lupo's first and once my eyes adjusted to the darkness, I was sorry my eyes had adjusted to the darkness. Places like Lupo's are why people get phobias about germs. I ordered a Bud—in a bottle, hold the glass.

The detective came in around fifteen minutes later, a bulky manila envelope under his arm. He slid into the booth across from me and ordered two double shots of Old Overholt rye with a Heineken chaser. Apparently I was buying. He opened the envelope, pulled out the reports and the photos, and pushed them across the table towards me, after first checking to make sure there was nothing wet on the tabletop, or even worse, sticky.

"We get these homicides almost every other night now, you know," the cop said. "Only difference is, this dead guy is white."

"Pretty big difference, wouldn't you say?"

"I guess it is, if it's Sally Curto's nephew."

"Were they spics?"

"Who knows? They were wearing gloves, masks, somebody said they had accents, but what the hell does that mean nowadays? Could be Russians, could be Iranians, hell, they could even surprise us all and be citizens."

"Why'd they shoot the kid?"

"He mouthed off to 'em, near as we can tell. Found three packets of coke in his coat pocket. And some Vicodin and Oxys. He was so high he thought he was bulletproof, that's what the witnesses say. They're not going to tell Sally that, of course. One more thing: I believe he may have also asked the eternal question."

Do you know who I am? I shook my head. Working a door while you're snorting coke was bad enough, but then to try to pull rank on guys who've got the drop on you . . .

"I got only one thing of interest for you," he said. "One of the guns was a Walther PPK. We got the shell casings."

I took a swig of my beer. "James Bond's gun. I wonder where they stole it from."

"Reason I mention it is, it ain't like the old days, when guys got rid of a piece as soon as they used it, especially in a murder. Might keep your eyes open, I know we are. I wouldn't be surprised to see it turn up again. These illegals get a nice semi-automatic like that, easy to get ammo for, a real one too, not some Hungarian knockoff, they'll never get rid of it. They don't give a shit about anything."

"Why should they?" The former state attorney general had once said, "Technically, it is not illegal to be illegal in Massachusetts." She wasn't kidding. Anything goes wrong, some bleeding heart judge gives them bail and they're on the next plane out of Logan back to whatever Third World hellhole they came from until the heat dies down.

I caught the bartender's eye and motioned for another round.

"So is it spics?" I asked.

"In the Boston Police Department, we are only interested in apprehending criminals, not in the race, national origin or immigration status of said perpetrators."

"How much they get?" I asked.

"A guess? Not much over five thousand. The guys we talked to, the players, the dealers, all of 'em, the youngest one had to be seventy-five. Every degenerate gambler under seventy-five is on the Internet. The web ain't just for porn anymore."

"Tell me about it," I said. I'm a "brick-and-mortar" wiseguy, or used to be. Like every other businessman, I'm still trying to figure out how to "monetize" the Internet. The dirty bookstores and the Combat Zone are long gone, my best gambling customers bet offshore, and if you try to shake down your average shady run-of-the-mill hustler, they go running straight to the feds and quit the grinnin' and drop the linen, except the microphones are so tiny now they don't even have to take off their shirts to get wired, besides which there aren't any more wires anyway, just transmitters.

I studied the crime scene photos. The overturned tables didn't interest me. I wanted to see the corpse. He was wearing a tight-fitting jacket, another rookie mistake. If you're working the door, you wear a loose coat, at least two sizes too big, so you can keep at least one piece or even better two in your pockets so that no civilians even notice, only the bad guys. Sally hadn't imparted any of the tricks of the trade to his nephew, probably because he hadn't figured he needed to.

The kid had been shot in the head. His eyes were wide open, and so was his mouth. Maybe his last thought was, *I can't believe they don't know who I am.*

"Kid have a record?" I asked.

"Usual dipshit suburban stuff, continued without a finding, OUIs reduced to reckless—nothing like yours at that age, Bench."

"Yeah, the social workers always said I was precocious."

"I thought the word they used was 'incorrigible,' and I thought it was parole officers, not social workers."

"Same thing," I said, taking a sealed envelope out of my breast pocket and sliding it across the table to him. You never give cops cash; it makes them feel dirty, like you bought them. Somehow putting the cash in the envelope makes it okay.

"Sometimes," I said, "it pays to grow up in the city instead of the suburbs."

The cop nodded as he palmed the envelope. "Especially if you're planning on being a gangster."

2

A DIRTY JOB

It was shaping up as another banner year for Reilly Associates. And the banner said, "GOING OUT OF BUSINESS."

I was so broke that I was even considering scheduling an appointment with a crooked new Indian psychiatrist I'd heard about who was clearing ex-cops like me to go back on the job, years or even decades after we'd gone out on "mental disabilities." I had it all figured out: after I got the okay to go back on the job, I'd take a three-week refresher course at the academy, then go out to the range, fire one of the new weapons, take a fall from the recoil and refile for my seventy-two-percent tax-free disability, calculated at the new, higher, post-twenty-five-percent pay raise rate.

Of course I was going to have to move fast, because a scam like this goes around the world at the speed of sound while a new cure for cancer is still putting its pants on in the morning.

First things first though. I had some duties to attend to in the oppo-research end of my racket, I mean "business." I'd set the alarm clock for 6:30, because I had to meet the TV crew in Brighton at 8:30. I'd already given them the golf-course video of the mark we had lined up—the first deputy superintendent chief of the fire department, along with his car. The camera crew knew which golf course he was headed for—Woodland, in Newton. But I didn't want to take any chances on a screwup. This was a $3,000 job, maybe even more—a good score by my standards, which had been slipping lately.

I'm a private detective, so-called. Another description for my line of work is confidential investigator, and confidentially, business sucks. People say there's no such thing as bad publicity, but you can't prove it by me. I've got the kind of reputation money can't buy, and you wouldn't want to even if it could. I don't give out business cards anymore. If somebody's caught with one of mine on him, it just gives the cops probable cause to suspect . . . just about anything they want to suspect.

I know what they say in Hollywood: self-pity is not good box office. But after a while, the suck of it all just wears you down.

Today I was working for a guy in the Boston Fire Department who wanted to take out his boss, which would enable him to move up to first deputy. He could have just dropped a tip in an envelope with no return address, and sent it via snail mail to the "investigative" reporters in town. But that would be like putting a note in a bottle, throwing it into the ocean and hoping for the best. My client wanted results, guaranteed. He wanted a guy who could go directly to some reporter, in this case a TV guy, and make the pitch directly. He also wanted no fingerprints.

It's a dirty job, and somebody dirty has to do it.

So this morning I was a finger man. I had to point out the deputy chief. Today there was a new camera crew working, and God forbid they should videotape the wrong guy, and then confront some poor schmuck on his day off from a real job. They'd lose the mark and I'd be out three grand.

I drove my Oldsmobile out to Soldiers Field Road and parked at the edge of the parking lot on the Charles River across from Channel 4. Heard something on the radio about a murder in the North End, but I didn't pay much attention. Figured it was another

Yuppie walking alone at 2:30 in the morning like he was in Welles-
ley or someplace.

I'd been sitting there about ten minutes when a guy in a trench
coat and a scally cap came over and tapped on the window. He was
the investigative reporter—that's why he was wearing a trench coat.
Basically, he was Ron Burgundy. And now he was about to sternly
expose an abuse of the taxpayers' funds—a deputy fire chief who
took out an undercover car with "untraceable" plates to play golf
every morning. Untraceable means that if anyone like a hood ever
gets suspicious enough to run the plates with the Registry of
Motor Vehicles, they come back untraceable.

It's very convenient to have unregistered plates if you're trying to,
say, tail an arsonist.

They come in equally handy if you want to play a round of golf
on business hours, "on the city." The crack gumshoes of the "I team"
had been on this one for three days. On Monday the "hero jake,"
because jakes are all heroes, at least in the media, had driven the
car with the untraceable plates to a mall in Nashua, New Hampshire. On Tuesday, the jake—the fireman, or should I use their
preferred term, "firefighter?"—took it to his girlfriend's apartment
in Arlington. Wednesday he drove his twenty-one-year-old daughter back to college at Westfield State. Today, Thursday, he was back
in the 617 area code. Tee time at Woodland was 9:30. I'd checked.

"You got the other camera crew over there already?" I asked Ron
Burgundy.

"Just where you told us, Jack," he said.

They had more than enough video now. This was the day Ron
would confront the hero jake. Which was why the reporter was
wearing his trench coat. It was his trademark. It's every TV investigative reporter's trademark. The scally cap—his personal statement,
like Geraldo's mustache. The viewers were supposed to draw the
conclusion that he was Irish, from Boston. He was neither.

Some jobs I work on for weeks, and in the end, they don't pan
out. But this one had been like shooting fish in a barrel. The

untraceable plate had been issued to the arson squad, but of course they never saw it, if there even was an arson squad. The deputy chief pulled into the Woodland parking lot in Newton right on schedule. The first camera crew got him getting out of the car, then unlocking his trunk and taking out his golf bag. I took some video myself with my cell phone, just in case there turned out to be a crease in the tape or some other baleful act of God.

He was headed for the clubhouse with his bag of clubs over his shoulder when Ron stepped out from behind a tree with his second camera crew to ask the deputy chief why he was parked at a golf course outside the city during business hours with an untraceable license plate on his unmarked City of Boston car.

Back at fire headquarters, the guy who'd paid me $3,000 cash had already pulled the deputy chief's punched-in time card and made a copy of it, so he couldn't later claim he was taking a vacation day. I'd provided them with copies of the time card from the other three days too. I'm a "source," although more often I'm called "sources," plural. The story sounds more authoritative that way.

I must say, Ron Burgundy did a fine job with the ambush interview. He began with, "Excuse me, chief—" and the guy said, "You must have the wrong guy, I'm not a chief." Burgundy asked, "Who are you then?" And the jake gave the name of a Boston city councilor. It went downhill from there. Before he took off running for the clubhouse, the deputy chief's last words were, "I'll sue you! Do you know who I am?"

I think that may be the most-asked question in Boston, if not the United States. Do you know who I am? I know who I am. I'm somebody who would never ask that question, lest the person I'm addressing respond in the affirmative.

When I was working for the mayor and in the crosshairs of a federal grand jury, the media called me an "embattled cop." Then my case was nolle prossed, and I became "rogue ex-cop." If I don't drum up some more business soon, the next adjective they use to describe me is going to be "washed up."

I caught a ride back to Brighton with the TV crew. They were laughing, high-fiving each other all the way back. Once the job is done, it's like I'm not there, never was there. Reporters never like to admit that the only reason they get most "investigative" stories is because A is trying to take B off the board. In that way, reporters are no different from cops. Like I always say, there's a lot more snitchin' than sleuthin' goin' on.

When we got back to the TV station, I told Ron I'd send him a scan of the deputy chief's Thursday time card by noon, after which we shook hands. There was a bounce in his step as he walked into the station. This would take the heat off him for at least six months. Maybe a year if the *Globe* could be persuaded to pick up the story.

I drove back to my house in the South End and got on the phone to Katy Bemis. How's that old song go? We used to kiss good night but now it's all over. Double entendre—get it? There'd been a time when we'd been seeing a lot of each other, another double entendre, but somehow things had never been the same since she'd moved over to the *Globe* from the *Herald*.

"Hello, Jack," she said. "If you're asking, I've already got plans for the evening."

Have I been that persistent?

"Katy, I was just calling about a story. I got some pictures you might be able to use."

"What kind of pictures?"

I told her about the deputy chief I'd gift-wrapped for the TV station, how they'd be running with it tonight at six, and then I mentioned that I had some photos of the $100,000-a-year hero jake getting his golf bag out of the fire department car with the untraceable plates.

"You want me to do a follow-up to a TV story?" she said. "Are you sure you're doing this for me, or is it for the guy who hired you to blow up his boss? And who exactly am I supposed to say took this mysterious picture?"

"How about you caption it, 'Special to the *Globe*.'"

"They'll want to know how I got it, and who took it, and I'll have to tell them, and that will be that."

"Remember when I got you that picture of the hooker getting into the state senator's car on Marginal Road?" She'd been wearing a micro-miniskirt. Black whore with a blond wig. A he/she—excuse me—a member of the transgender community. "I don't recall getting the third degree from you that time."

"I was working for the *Herald* then." She sounded exasperated even by a reminder of her tabloid past. "Things are different at the *Globe*."

They sure were. She used to enjoy working with me. Now she treated me like I had fresh dog shit on my shoe.

"You know, Katy, that was a great story, 'The she-male and the solon.'" That was the front-page *Herald* headline. "It was stories like that that made your reputation, and I was the—"

"Jack, I've seen this movie. *A Star Is Born*. You're Kris Kristofferson, at least in your own mind, with a fake disability pension—"

"Fake? When it comes down to just two, I ain't no crazier than you." Another oldie but goodie.

"Do you get a bonus or something if you can get this untraceable license-plate story into the paper? *Cui bono*, Jack?"

Did I mention she went to Mount Holyoke? But I know Latin too; I went to Boston Latin.

"I was just trying to do you a favor," I said.

"Jack, I don't have time to fight with you this morning?"

"What's the problem? I'm just offering—"

"Look, Jack, I'm busy. Apparently you're not. If you want to get on my good side, put your ear to the ground and find out what's going on with this gambling legislation. I don't mean how they're going to vote on it, it's obvious the leadership's got the votes or it wouldn't be coming to the floor. What I mean is, who's spreading the cash around? It's gotta be cash."

"Maybe it's my clients spreading the cash around."

"Your clients are dirty, but they're nickel-and-dime dirty, this golf story being the latest example. If you were working for the casino guys, you wouldn't be trying to peddle me this 'exclusive.'"

"What about the time I gave you the story about Sally Curto having the handicapped placard?"

"You know, I've still never figured out who you were working for that time."

"Maybe I was just trying to help you."

"Please, Jack, I was born at night, but not last night."

"A line you got from me, by the way."

"Let's not start up again with what I 'got' from you."

I hung up and sat at my kitchen table for a few minutes. Then I got going. There were places to go, politicians to slime.

My next task was dropping off a copy of a police report on a ten-year-old drunk-driving arrest in the South End. The driver was now a first-term state senator from Worcester, a confirmed bachelor as they used to say.

In Massachusetts if you're arrested for OUI you have to tell the cops where you had your last drink, which in the solon's case was a gay bar called the Ramrod Room. The guy must have really been legless to give that up. Most times they come up with some tourist trap in Quincy Market rather than rat out their neighborhood joint, or a gay bar, or the place where they hook up with their gal pal. But the guy was a state legislator, which greatly increased the odds that he was below average in every way. The smallest caucus at the State House is the Mensa caucus.

This one was going to a reporter from Katy's old newspaper, the *Herald*. I'd shopped it to her first, for old-times' sake. But I knew she'd never bite. She said it was homophobic, and that there was only one person who I could have gotten it from—a friend of mine, an old-time Boston city councilor named Slip Crowley. He'd called a guy who'd called a guy. . . .

"I thought Slip was your friend too," I told her.

"I don't have friends," she said. "I'm a journalist."

What did the old boss of Columbia Pictures, Sam Cohn, supposedly say about Doris Day? I knew her before she was a virgin.

3

JUST SAY NO

I hate having anything to do with drugs. I'm serious about that, I really am. I mention this because most people think that if you're in the rackets these days, you're automatically a drug dealer. Maybe so, but that doesn't mean I have to like it. I wish it was like the old days, but nobody cares anymore about the afternoon card at Wonderland, or wouldn't, even if dog racing were still legal in Massachusetts, which it isn't.

It come out of the Mystic Projects in Somerville, and half my family is or has been, mostly is, on drugs. Mainly Oxys these days, but if they can't get the prescription "opiods," they'll go with the real thing, and I don't mean coke. Heroin, not religion, is the opiate of the masses. The other half of my family are drunks, except for the ones who are both junkies and drunks.

I was a pain in the ass when I was growing up, not having a brother or even an older cousin who could back me up when I got in a jam, and when you live in public housing, life is nothing but one jam after another. Don't get me wrong, I had family, but they were always either nodding off or passed out just when I needed someone watching my back. Maybe in the long run it was good for me, because when you're on your own from the start you learn pretty quickly not to let your mouth write a check that your ass can't cash.

Another thing I learned early on was that it was probably a good thing for me to lay off the sauce. Never touch the stuff myself. Except of course for the occasional wee small taste of the creature, say a morning Budweiser at Lupo's. But only if I'm buying for a cop or two.

Even though I'm basically a teetotaler, I have to be into the business of drugs, because otherwise I couldn't survive in my line of work, which is the rackets. If I'm not at least shaking down every dealer who's operating in my territory, somebody else will be. And it won't be long before whoever's shaking them down will have more money than me, a lot more. And if they have more money than me, they can buy more protection from the cops, and more guns, and pretty soon I'm not around anymore, in more ways than one.

That is of course a rationalization, but it's also reality. When I was a kid, pot was a new thing, just like the state Lottery. The state kept coming up with new games—scratch tickets, Powerball, Keno. And the wiseguys kept coming up with new drugs—pot sprayed with angel dust, cocaine, ecstasy, heroin, the "synthetic opiates" and now Mollys.

The amount of money wiseguys like me could generate from illegal gambling dwindled away to practically nothing beyond the NFL, while at the same time a new, even bigger source of income materialized. Some politician once said, "I seen my opportunities and I took 'em." That's what I did with drugs, and if I hadn't taken 'em, my opportunities I mean, somebody else would have.

So I'm into drugs, I admit it. I never get near the actual product, wouldn't think of handling it myself. Neither do the guys who answer directly to me—my buffers. They just handle the dough, to make sure I get my end before they get their end. But my buffers have other guys, tough guys, and they make sure nobody's freelancing. Whenever my guys find a new dealer operating in my territory, they tell him he has to join the organization. That's rule number one.

Rule number two is, they have to buy the shit from me—I mean, from my guys. I repeat, for the record I don't sell drugs. Can't stand 'em. Hate drug dealers. Ask anybody, ask Sally. . . .

Sometimes, in the beginning, when I was setting up my drug operation, the local dealers getting shaken down would come to me and tell me that so-and-so was leaning on them and could I do anything for them? Of course they couldn't admit what they were into because of my own well-advertised loathing of drugs.

So I worked out a routine. I'd tell them, hey, those guys that're after you, they're my friends, and if you got a problem with them, you'll just have to deal with it.

At least that's what I always said to the marijuana dealers. One day a guy came to see me, because some bad guys were looking for him, and he said he needed protection. Naturally he didn't know the bad guys were working for me. So we took a walk up the hill, just the two of us, and he admitted to me he was dealing cocaine. He explained how the business was set up, how much dough he was making, how much easier it was than moving bales of crappy sticks-and-stems low-grade marijuana that the customers were always bitching about. Until I took that walk, I had no idea how much money was involved in Class B controlled substances, but this guy was making more money than me. So I introduced this coke dealer to my buffers, and he taught them the cocaine business.

Afterward, I told the kid he was out. He was from the neighborhood, but he wasn't a wiseguy. He'd never taken a pinch, let alone done a bit. He wasn't capable. He'd moved into cocaine from a rock band. Sorry, kid, but those are not the credentials I am looking for. I want guys who've done time, who are as paranoid as I am. Sally wants intelligent tough guys, which I'm all in favor of, but if you give me a choice between intelligent and paranoid, I'll take paranoid, although sometimes I think if you're not paranoid, in any line of work, how intelligent can you possibly be?

Anyway, I couldn't be sure this kid would stand up. Nothing personal; I wasn't going to kill him or anything like that. I gave him

$20,000 severance and told him to screw—excuse me, I had one of my buffers tell him to screw. He knew better than to squawk. Lives in Florida now, I hear.

So I've got everybody organized, and nobody sells in my territory unless they are either buying from or at least paying off my guys, by which I mean me. My dealers know that if they hear about anybody freelancing, they should let us know, and we will straighten them out. You have to walk a fine line—you want to impress upon these guys the necessity of playing ball with us—me. But conversely you don't want to scare them so much they run away. That's how you lose a nice little revenue stream.

Sally Curto likewise claims he doesn't go near the shit. I tell him the same thing he tells me. We both know we're lying to each other but some things you have to keep off the record. We're partners, which means I'm also supposed to play by LCN rules, or at least pretend to, just like Sally and everybody else In Town does.

And now my In Town partner had asked me to handle a piece of business for him.

My plan was to make the rounds of what the *Globe* once called my "far-flung criminal empire." As always, I would be dropping in on them unannounced. I'm not much into scheduling sit-downs. Too many bad things can happen, like getting yourself set up for a hit. When somebody calls me and says he needs to meet me, I always say, "You know, I'm sure we'll bump into each other someplace." I'm like the Beach Boys, I get around. There are exceptions—Sally Curto, for one. If he calls, I meet him, wherever, whenever. But most of my guys, I don't want 'em to get in the habit of loitering in any of my places, the garage in Roxbury, my little dive in Allston, or the place where I spend most of my time, my bar on Broadway on Winter Hill, the Alibi.

Before I, ahem, acquired it, the Alibi was named the Gaelic Club, a name I found totally unacceptable. Do I really have to explain why? Plus, I don't go in much for all that Irish shit anyway. The Alibi just sounds more American.

Except for the ones who actually work there, like my manager Hobart, I discourage my guys from hanging out there. If you're loitering in the Alibi, you're not out making money. You're drinking my beer, on the arm. And if you're not out making money, you don't have anything to kick up to me, so what good are you?

Upstairs from the Alibi, I have my own "club." It's just an office, but I call it a club. You get to a certain level in the rackets, you're expected to have a social club. I invite guys upstairs to the club and they're scared shitless, don't ask me why. I try to be very sociable up there, not to mention everywhere else. But maybe my reputation precedes me, as they say. I have the whole building swept for bugs twice a week. The Somerville cops appreciate the work. My hourly rate's better than their paid details.

A couple of years ago I decided I needed a "hide," a place to stash cash and guns and other miscellaneous items. I hired a slimy old guy from Chelsea who does work for all the wiseguys—Marty Hide we call him. Marty Hide also builds hides on car doors, which come in handy if you're a convicted felon who can't legally carry a gun. The hide in my upstairs club is bigger than most—I had Marty Hide build a little freezer into it. It's got something in it that I've been saving for a special occasion. Maybe sometime I'll tell you about it.

Speaking of Marty Hide, after coming back to Somerville from Lupo's, I decided to switch cars. If Sally's hunch was right that there was something fishy about this hit, I wanted to be prepared. So I dropped the BMW off at one of our garages on the top of Winter Hill and took out my black Escalade. Years ago, during the Charlestown war, Marty Hide had built a compartment in the front door, big enough for one of my fully automatic HK MP7 "personal defense weapons," which I prefer to use for offense. Marty did a beautiful job on the door, and I'm surprised more guys don't have them built in. If someone's coming up on you fast on the street, a revolver's not going to do you much good. A PDW, on the other hand . . .

Anyway, this morning I was on the road in my Escalade, looking for information about last night's stick-up. It was early, but sometimes my guys show up before noon. The first place I hit was a small grocery store in Somerville, Magoun Square. It was mainly a gambling drop. The guy hadn't even heard about the hit but he did have an envelope for me, which I pocketed without counting. He was always good for the money; his store was too close to the Alibi for him to even think about skimming.

My second stop was a social club on Cambridge Street in East Cambridge. Used to be mainly gambling, now drugs—pills mostly. The windows were all boarded up, otherwise the metrosexual new Bostonians in the neighborhood would be wandering in, looking for local color like this was the set of *The Departed* or *The Town*. I banged on the heavy door and finally a red-faced guy with a potbelly opened it. He was holding a sixteen-ounce can of Milwaukee's Best in his hand.

"Little early, maybe, Mustard?" I asked him. My Budweiser at Lupo's didn't count. That was business, and I'm the boss.

"Hair o' the dog, Bench, hair o' the dog."

I regarded him more closely. I noticed his gut protruding over his belt even more than usual. The medical term I believe would be "distended." What made Milwaukee famous had made a loser out of Mustard.

I considered briefly whether to inquire, then decided that, as the CEO, I had every right to ask about an underling's health.

"You don't look so hot, Mustard," I said. "What's with the stomach there?"

"I got a problem, Bench."

"I hope it's not what I think it is," I said.

"It is," he said. "You been warnin' me for years, now it's finally happened. Cirrhosis."

I didn't know what to say, but I knew what to think. I was going to have to get a new guy in here, sooner rather than later. Poor Mustard. He'd always been in the Alcohol Hall of Fame, but now he'd passed the pint of no return. He was going out, the hard way. Maybe his brother could take over, but I had my doubts, because alcoholism runs in families. It sure runs in mine. I told Mustard I'd do whatever I could for him, up to a point. He understood.

Mustard had an envelope for me too, smaller, not good considering how many Oxys and Percs these guys moved. I made a mental note not to promote Mustard's brother. Alcoholism is genetic, but it can skip one sibling while striking down another. However, if one brother steals, guaranteed everybody else in the family does too. No need to do any scientific research on that. The empirical evidence is beyond dispute.

I must have hit six or seven of my places, mostly on this side of the river, but a couple more in Brighton and West Roxbury. I kept asking the same questions over and over, about stick-up guys, about who'd gotten out of prison recently and who was flashing cash or talking about scores or had suddenly gone into the loan sharking business. I kept getting the same answers, or non-answers. The guys I talked to didn't know anything, which was no surprise, because they tend to give stick-up artists as wide a berth as possible, especially those who think they can get away with sticking up Sally Curto's games. My crews have a motto, and it comes from the top:

"We don't want any trouble."

Despite not turning up any new information, the trip wasn't a complete waste of time. Usually I let other guys make the pickups, so this was good for me, checking on my not-so-far-flung dominions. Somewhat like Undercover Boss on TV, I once again learned how unimpressive my so-called gang is. I would not want to have to go to war with that army. Fortunately no one else's army is worth a damn either.

It was maybe three o'clock, and I was driving through West Roxbury when the phone call came. It was Sally again.

"They just blew up Hole in the Head! Got him in his car in his own fucking driveway."

"What happened?"

"I just told you, they blew him up. Some kind of remote-control bomb, dynamite, C-4, something, I don't know. I can't believe he's dead."

This time we met at the public beach in Nahant, Sally's hometown. What with his wife and sister-in-law and the rest of his family gathered together to mourn and plan the deceased nephew's wake, he couldn't get away to Southie, and we couldn't wait.

Hole in the Head and his brother Cheech came out of Jamaica Plain, and this never would have happened in the old days, because everybody in JP would have been watching the streets, and nobody could have gotten close to his car, even late at night. But now JP was full of new Bostonians, and Hole in the Head had moved to Swampscott. An old, familiar story: his new trophy wife wanted an ocean view, with respectable neighbors. Now Hole in the Head would be moving to an even quieter neighborhood—the cemetery.

Sally was pacing back and forth outside his car. This time he had Blinky Marzilli with him. Sally was a considerate boss. If your brother got blown up he'd give you the afternoon off, no questions asked. Blinky was wearing a well-worn leather jacket, bought when he'd been about forty pounds lighter, so it didn't cover the 9-mm he had sticking out of his pants.

Sally asked, "You find out anything yet, Bench?"

"Only thing I got is what kind of gun they used on your nephew," I said. "A Walther PPK."

"What the fuck—ain't that James Bond's gun?"

"Yep," I said. "Point being, it's not exactly a Saturday Night Special. Whoever used it probably didn't get rid of it, like we would. Chances are, it's going to show up again sometime. Then—"

"By then we may all be fuckin' dead!" Sally was yelling again. "If they can get to Hole in the Head, they can get to anybody. These ain't amateurs, obviously."

"Maybe, Sally, but these days most everybody's an amateur, one way or another. Maybe this guy learned how to build bombs in the service, but I can't see anybody we know capable of doing something like this."

Nobody except maybe me, but I didn't want to say that. Sally was skittish enough as it was and I didn't want to put any ideas into his head. One thing I've noticed over the years is how wiseguys usually get clipped by their friends. Sally was my friend.

"This may take a while," I told Sally.

"Bench, I ain't got that kind of time. They come out of the box, they hit my barbooth game and now they bomb my street boss, in less than twenty-four hours."

"They'll make a mistake. They always make a mistake. Then we'll get 'em."

"You sound like the fuckin' cops."

"Sometimes the cops can be right, Sally. Anything you got going right now, I'd double up the security. They seem to have your crews pretty well reconnoitered."

Blinky remained silent, his arms crossed, but he was frowning. He obviously thought Sally should be conferring with him, not me. Sally lit a new cigarette, again off the butt of the old one. I hadn't seen him chain-smoking like this in years. "Yeah, that's one thing I been meaning to ask you, Bench. How come they're hitting me, but not you?"

Here we go. I'd been waiting for this. He didn't want to hear the truth, that his guys were easier to reach than mine, because we'd been through that Irish gang war thing just a few years back. My crews weren't as sharp as they used to be, as I'd reconfirmed today, but they were mostly veterans. If they hadn't shot somebody, they'd at least been shot at. Either way, you tend to pick up certain habits. You drive home a different way every night, you don't drink in strange bars. If you're smart, you don't drink in bars, period. Real basic training-type stuff. But Sally was working with a peacetime army, draftees.

"Sally," I said, "I'll put some of my best guys on it. I'm gonna call in Salt 'n' Peppa."

Sally didn't care much for Peppa, and now he shook his head and looked over at Blinky.

"Relying on a guy named Peppa," he said, more to Blinky than to me. "What the fuck is this world coming to?"

I looked over at Blinky and asked him, "How's it goin' with Vinny and Fat Vinny?" It was a rhetorical question, and when he shrugged I turned back to Sally and stared at him. I didn't say anything. I didn't have to.

"Okay, I'm sorry," Sally said. "Listen, I'll take anybody you can spare. Couple more of these things, every punk in the city is gonna figure it's open season on me."

He mentioned three of his places—a club in Kenmore Square, a café on Tremont Street in the South End on the Roxbury line, and a bookie clearinghouse in Brookline. I told him I'd have two of my guys stationed at each place, but I didn't want any of his "soldiers" pulling rank and ordering my people around. Any bullshit, I said, and my guys walk. I glanced over at Blinky as I said it, to let him know this went for him too.

"No problem," Sally said. "We're partners. But you gotta find these guys."

4

A CAPABLE GUY

Kevin Caulfield reached out to me through a small-time lobbyist that I'd worked with at City Hall. Caulfield was the biggest lobbyist on Beacon Hill, with a suite of offices on the fifth floor of the building at the corner of Park and Beacon Streets, directly across the street from the State House. Last time I checked the secretary of state's records, he was reporting $800,000 a year in gross revenues. Key word: reporting.

Caulfield's go-between didn't want to tell me over the phone what the old man needed, but I finally pried it out of him. Caulfield and his clients were concerned about the two murders, although I didn't quite understand why. But I had enough time to make a few phone calls before I walked up to Beacon Hill.

It was 5:30 when the meeting convened. Caulfield's son, Terry, who used to work for the old mayor in City Hall, answered the door and escorted me into his father's outer office. We bantered about the old days; he was a decent enough guy and we'd always hit it off. His father, though, was a different kettle of fish. In his mid-70's now, Kevin Caulfield was one of these harps who'd made so much money he'd convinced himself his family had come over on the *Mayflower*.

Terry handed me some brown water over ice in a heavy crystal rocks glass. Veddy tasteful. Then he introduced me to a trim well-spoken Southerner in his late thirties, Clay Westridge. His business card identified him as "vice president, governmental relations" for the casino company that had spent $2 million this legislative session to push the bill through the legislature. A final vote was scheduled in the State Senate any day now. Also present was the casino company's "New England Director of Security," a former Boston FBI agent named Tom Taylor.

FBI—Fidelity, Bravery, Integrity. Or, as we called them in the BPD, Famous But Incompetent.

The office was all mahogany and leather and windows facing out over Park Street to the Common. Well-appointed, as they used to say. The old man had bought the building for peanuts back in the down-and-out seventies; it had to be worth at least $4 million now. The Caulfields even had their booze in decanters. Everything about the layout said: high fees.

Once everyone had shaken hands and sat down, Kevin Caulfield got right to the point.

He said to me, "You know who Mr. Westridge represents, and we represent him. Until today, we thought we had all the votes we needed in the Senate. Now this . . . gang war, or whatever you call it, breaks out. You know what this means? Every goo-goo in the legislature who was just looking for an excuse to vote against us now has one. They're claiming that if this is what we get before casinos even come to a vote, what will happen when we have casinos in the state, and especially one in the city? We've heard both papers are running editorials tomorrow, and it's already all over the radio talk shows. The quote-unquote reformers in the House are even threatening to move some kind of reconsideration vote to overturn the initial approval we got last week—that we bought, I should say, to be perfectly frank. All these years we've been laying the foundation for this moment, and now it's slipping out of our grasp again."

I said nothing. I sensed I might be looking at the kind of payday that could keep me going for at least a year. I could forget all about the Boston City Council off-year races next year. I could take a vacation to Florida. Maybe I could even play a round of golf at Woodland instead of lurking in the rough with my cell phone camera.

The old man, Kevin Caulfield, clipped off the top of a five-dollar cigar and then moistened it with his lips before he spoke again.

"What does the *Herald* call the legislative rank and file now? Sheeple, I believe it is. The phrase has caught on because it's so accurate. This current crop are afraid of their own shadows. They're simple, in the old meaning of the word. Simpletons. I see them at Anthony's, and I worry that some of them are going to wander away and fall off the pier into the harbor, and that's before they get drunk."

From his smooth cadence and perfectly timed pauses, I could tell this wasn't the first time he'd delivered this monologue. He hadn't even changed the name of the restaurant, even though Anthony's was going out of business in less than a month. His little spiel absolved him of his inability to deliver votes in the way he once could, while simultaneously placing the blame for his dwindling clout on somebody else, namely, the dumb-as-a-rock reps.

Not that there wasn't some truth to what he was saying. But nobody wants to hear from Alibi Ike. Personally, I would have thought it would be easier to do business now, when you only had to pay off the one or two guys who controlled the "sheeple." In this new top-down system, not even the committee chairmen had any clout. You didn't have to pay them off to move a bill out of their committees onto the floor. A whole layer of greedy middlemen with their hands out had been eliminated.

The fewer people you have to pay, the fewer potential witnesses. Plus, the five or six guys who ran the show had totally insulated themselves. Everybody used bagmen. One of the majority whips even had two bagmen, one Irish, one Jewish. That way, the marks got to deal with someone from their own tribe. It was all very cozy.

The casino vice president interrupted the garrulous old man.

"What Mr. Caulfield is getting at, I believe, is that every time there's another shooting or bombing like this afternoon in—Swampscott, is it?—we lose another five votes in the legislature. With the editorials and the liberals and the archdiocese, the politicians just can't take the heat. And we didn't have that much of a margin to start with, even after spreading a lot of money around, and I do mean plenty—and that's off the record. If they really stampede off the reservation, even the Speaker can't stop reconsideration, isn't that correct? You gentlemen live here, I don't, thank God, no offense intended."

Westridge looked over at the ex-FBI agent, who rolled his eyes and smirked. Taylor used to chase people like these state-rep-bribing lobbyists. Now he worked for them. He seemed to find the irony amusing, like the prosecutors who become high-priced defense attorneys in middle age. Private-school tuitions will do that to you. Clay Westridge had no doubt signed off on the invoices, so he knew how much Tom Taylor was costing his company for his supposed law enforcement expertise, and he wanted some answers.

"What I'm asking you, Tom, is why this is happening now?" He had just the slightest Southwestern drawl. "And to get right to the point, how can we stop it, right now?"

Taylor hesitated, so I decided to put my two cents in.

"It's pretty hard to stop a gang war once it gets going," I said. "Plus, Sally Curto's nephew and now his top gun just got clipped. That makes it personal." I paused. "I know the leadership has the skids greased on this casino deal, but is there anybody in the legislature who might have reason to try to deep-six the bill, maybe surreptitiously?"

Caulfield shrugged. "Nobody on the House side—the Speaker's going nowhere, so there's no point for anybody over there to try to kill it until next year so they can make a bigger score."

"Good Lord, I certainly hope not," said Westridge, "after all we've done for the House, especially the Speaker."

All the more reason for him to screw you, I thought to myself.

We have a saying around here: no good deed goes unpunished. I guess it's not in general circulation in Texas.

Caulfield scratched his chin. "The Senate though—the president's gone one way or the other, so—"

"Who's next in line?" I asked. Once upon a time I would have known the name of the next Senate president as well as my own. Now it was inside baseball.

"Denis Donahue," said Caulfield, caustically. "A very cute operator. Too cute by half. 'Donuts,' they call him. He's from Worcester, thinks he's the smartest guy in the room."

"In Worcester he probably is," I said.

"But I don't think he has the wherewithal to pull something like this off. He doesn't strike me as the type to have organized crime connections. And why would one faction go to war with the other to help . . . Donuts Donahue?" This time he said the name with even more distaste. Caulfield made his living kissing pols' asses. If he couldn't stand Denis Donahue, that was good enough for me. He had to be a real asshole. Donuts must have double-crossed Caulfield more than once.

Clay Westridge leaned forward. "Why now? That's the bigger question. From what I've been told, up until today, everything in the Boston underworld here has been comparatively peaceful for several years now. Sally Curto has more or less made this Irish fellow from Somerville, I forget his name—"

"Bench McCarthy," I said, "pronounced McCar-tee, like the old-time Irish."

"He's basically the number-two guy from what I understand. I've heard he was essentially a hit man in his younger days. Is that correct?"

"I don't know what you mean by his younger days," I said, glancing over at Taylor for confirmation. "He's only in his early forties now."

Kevin Caulfield harrumphed. "I'm very close to someone high up in the Boston Police Department—you fellows would know his name if I mentioned it. He told me, strictly on the q.t., that they have this McCarthy fellow for over twenty murders. Is that possible, Jack?"

Now I was the expert instead of the fed, and I wasn't even officially on the payroll yet. Things were definitely looking up.

"I don't know for sure, but twenty sounds like it's in the ballpark," I said. "He's from Somerville, so he got an early start."

Some guys love bullshitting their way through a subject they know next to nothing about, especially when they're trying to close a deal. That's not my style. For sure I wanted this job, but I didn't want to leave them with the impression that I was capable of accomplishing more than I actually could. That would lead to hard feelings and recriminations down the road, not to mention no future business from the Caulfields. I still have to live in this town, as much as I'd prefer not to, especially during the eight months we call winter, and I don't need any more enemies. Most of what I knew about Bench McCarthy I had read in the newspapers.

"I had McCarthy's jacket pulled for me this afternoon," said Taylor, the ex-FBI agent, who obviously enjoyed playing Mr. Big with all the connections. He was, after all, a G-man. "It seems that he was convicted of a truck hijacking at age seventeen, and he ended up in MCI-Norfolk. That's where he met Sally Curto, and while he was in there, McCarthy did some sort of favor for him."

"It's coming back to me now," I said. "There was some racial unrest or maybe a contract, and a black guy jumped Sally in the showers. Sally was about to get shanked when Bench—"

Westridge interrupted: "Why do they call him Bench, by the way?"

"The way I understand it," I said, "whenever he's indicted, he asks for a jury-waived trial—a bench trial, in front of a judge."

Westridge was leaning forward, paying close attention to what I was saying.

"See, Mr. Westridge, most wiseguys figure they got a better

chance with a jury. With twelve people, maybe they can get to one, if you know what I mean."

"But if you ask for a jury-waived trial," Westridge said, "then you must have the judge in your pocket, right?"

"One would think so," I said, "and I can tell you that except for fourteen months he and Sally did for contempt of a federal grand jury about five years ago, Bench has never been convicted of any-thing since he first got out of prison."

Westridge shook his head. "Are the judges in this state really that corrupt?"

Before answering, I glanced over at Kevin Caulfield for guidance. He frowned. As far as he was concerned, judicial corruption was some kind of dirty little family secret, as if nobody in Massachu-setts knows that in the halls of justice the only justice is in the halls. As my friend Slip Crowley always says, it's that ninety-eight percent of the judges who give the honest two percent such a bad rap.

I said, "All I can tell you, Mr. Westridge, is that Bench is in many respects a very formidable character."

"How did he happen to throw in with the Mafia?" Westridge asked. Again, I deferred, this time to the ex-fed. I wasn't on the payroll yet. But Taylor motioned for me to continue.

"When Bench takes out the black guy in prison, Sally knows he's 'capable.' After they both get out, Bench starts handling 'a piece of business' here and there for Sally, and it isn't long before he's kind of thinned out the Italians, if you follow me. Plus, Bench is building up his own crew at the same time—in Somerville, Southie, all the neighborhoods where there's still a lot of Irish, or were fifteen, twenty years ago. Neighborhoods, towns not controlled by the Mafia, that's probably a better way to put it. Then Bench had his own little war, against Beezo Watson's gang in Charlestown. McCarthy wiped them out too; several of them just 'disappeared,' including Beezo. My understanding is, a few years back he goes to Sally and makes Sally an offer he can't refuse—"

"Ah," said Clay Westridge with a smile, "a movie reference."

I nodded at the FBI guy and went on: "Just jump in if I get any-thing wrong, Tom, but the way I heard it is, Bench tells Sally, the city's teeming with bookies and drug dealers who aren't paying either of us 'rent' so why don't we just split 'em up? The ones Bench grabs first belong to him, and the ones Sally grabs first, he keeps. Sally figures, that seems fair enough, especially considering most of his top guns are either dead or in the can, plus he's like twenty-five years older than Bench so he's had plenty of time to set himself up. If he cuts in Bench, he doesn't have to worry about a war, plus he's got Bench with him if anybody comes after him. Lotta reasons to make the deal, so he does."

Clay Westridge furrowed his brow. He seemed brighter than your average vice president of governmental affairs. "Correct me if I'm wrong, but I thought most of the gambling now was online, off-shore."

"It absolutely is," I said. "As I said, this entire arrangement dates back at least a decade."

"So how does Bench make his money now?"

"A little of this, a little of that. Drugs, truck hijackings, he fronts money for guys just out of the can. He likes armored cars, at least if somebody else is going in with the gun and the mask. Heard he also made a bundle when that bank in Braintree was burglarized a couple of years ago. He got a piece of it, a big piece. Plus he's got a couple of bars and a garage in Roxbury, although that's mostly a clubhouse from what I hear."

"How do you know all this, Reilly?" Westridge asked, and Tom Taylor cut in:

"His brother's a wiseguy, Mr. Westridge." He smiled at me; he was supposed to be the expert, and after my soliloquy he needed to reestablish his bona fides. "Isn't that right, Jack?"

Westridge ignored that. He just wanted information. So I figured I should answer his question.

"My brother's doing a bit—a sentence—up at Devens. Federal

time. I told you, Bench likes to front jobs. He likes buffers. He set up a score my brother was supposed to be the driver on, a truck hijacking. Somebody tipped the cops."

"Your brother couldn't make a deal?"

I smiled wanly. "Not if he wanted to keep breathing."

It was Taylor's turn to lean forward. "I brought a few surveillance photos along, Mr. Westridge, so you can see what the two of them look like." He passed a manila folder over to Westridge, who studied the pictures carefully. Even though this gang war or whatever it was represented a major headache for him and his company, you could tell he loved this Mob stuff.

"So the little fat guy—that's Sally?" Taylor nodded. "My God, he looks like Danny DeVito. . . . And the younger, taller guy beside him in the windbreaker is . . ."

"Bench McCarthy," Taylor said.

"Doesn't really seem to look like a gangster," Westridge said, "not that I have a lot of experience. . . . Who's the hulking guy walking behind them? Now he does look like a Mafia thug."

"That's Philip Imbruglia," Taylor said. "The late Philip Imbruglia. He's the guy that got blown up this afternoon. He runs—ran— Sally's street rackets. They called him 'Hole in the Head,' because, as you might surmise, he survived getting shot in the head way back when."

Westridge nodded gravely and took a gulp of his drink. This was as much anthropology as it was governmental relations.

"Look at the next picture," Taylor said, and Westridge did. I leaned over to get a peek at it myself. It was several guys and a few cops standing around a compact car at night. They were outside a three-decker; it looked like Dorchester or Southie. In the driver's seat was the body of a man with his head thrown back, eyes wide open, his jaw slack. In his forehead you could see a gaping exit wound.

Westridge recoiled slightly, then looked at Taylor.

"Did Bench do this?" he asked.

Taylor nodded. "It's what the police call a 'cold case.'"

"I'm just trying to get the lay of the land here," Westridge said. "What's the current relationship between the Mafia and Bench? Mr. Reilly?"

"My understanding is that Bench doesn't have to kick up anything to Sally. He's the only one around here who doesn't. In return, I guess you could say he remains on call, if Sally needs him."

"You mean for contracts?" Westridge asked, using the movie lingo. I nodded.

"If Bench is so smart," Westridge said, "why doesn't he move the gambling to Aruba or someplace and get out of the spotlight? If he stays around here, he's bound to make a mistake."

"No doubt," I agreed. "But he hasn't made one yet. Not since he was a kid."

The old lobbyist Caulfield leaned forward across his desk to look at me. He had a wan smile on his face now. I was making him look good. I was the guy he'd brought to the table who knew more than Westridge's FBI agent. Points for Caulfield. But now it was time for the lobbyist to put in his own considerably more than two cents.

"Look," Caulfield said to me, "I don't suppose I have to tell you that we don't really care if they all kill each other off, but this is queering the whole casino deal, and our client has already got millions invested. We'll do anything within reason to stop the bloodshed."

"That's very commendable of you, I'm sure," I said.

"Are you being fresh with me, young man?" Kevin Caulfield said.

"No, sir," I lied. "I just think there's something you ought to understand before we go any further."

"And what is that, Mr. Reilly?"

"Well, I'm not sure anybody really knows who's been bumping off Sally's guys."

"Surely it must be this Bench McCarthy," Caulfield harrumphed, "trying to complete his hostile takeover of the Mob."

"That's the way they'd write it in a movie script, I guess, but sometimes it's not that cut and dried," I said. "I don't know much right now, but I made a few calls before I came over here. And I can tell you that Bench has been moving around the city all day, asking questions. He wouldn't be operating so openly if he'd just started a gang war with Sally. And if he'd started the war, he probably wouldn't need to be asking all these questions. Although I suppose he could just be doing it for show. They're pretty devious, these guys, especially when they're lining somebody up."

Clay Westridge said, "If he was behind these murders, he'd have gone 'to the mattresses,' is that what you're saying?" He was a gangster movie buff, no doubt about it. Assuming this could all be straightened out, it would make interesting cocktail party chatter in suburban Houston someday.

"Do you know either of these hoodlums?" Caulfield said. "Could you make an overture to them for us?"

"Sally I've met a couple times."

I didn't mention how, which was when I was at City Hall, picking up what you might call contributions for the old mayor. Like Sally, Bench was a cash contributor. His main base of operations was in Somerville, but he had the taproom in Allston and the garage in Roxbury, so he had to do the right thing by us if he didn't want any trouble, and of course he didn't. So Bench had our guys from ISD— Inspectional Services—on his pad. And their boss, the mayor, who was also my boss, insisted on his end. That was my job, collections. Everybody, not just gangsters, needs a buffer, and I was the mayor's. Plus, there was the familial connection to my dim-bulb brother Marty.

"I'd recognize Bench on the street, and I've had, uh, dealings with him a couple of times too, but I doubt he'd remember me."

"Well, then, could your brother make the approach?" Clay Westridge said.

"His brother is in prison, remember," Tom Taylor reminded him.

Westridge took a deep breath. This was not the kind of problem they brainstormed in the four-year program at the Harvard Law School/Business School, or maybe he went to SMU. I glanced over at the three of them. They all looked glum, probably wondering how they would be judged by the home office if I was the best link to organized crime that they could come up with. The old man's annual $100,000 retainer was on the line, maybe even the $300,000 salary of the vice president, governmental relations.

It had all seemed so neat and clean forty-eight hours ago. They had the governor, a lame duck, ready to sign anything in return for a couple of directorships down the road. They had the Senate president, preparing to run for governor, a race he would almost certainly lose. But until the primary, the Senate president would still need, first, cash, and after he was beaten and a lame duck, he'd likewise need the same thing the lame-duck governor was looking for: a golden parachute and a soft landing. The House speaker represented the district where Westridge's casino would be built, so he didn't need to be paid—not as much, anyway. Westridge and Caulfield were getting the hometown discount from Mistah Speakah, although eventually he'd get his end too.

But now all their scheming and dreaming was unraveling, and they couldn't believe it. They were at the mercy, apparently, of thugs. Blue-collar thugs, as opposed to white-collar thugs like themselves.

"Sir," I said to the old man, "may I inquire, just what sort of approach were you thinking of making to these parties?"

"To be blunt, I want to offer them cash to declare a truce, or armistice, or whatever, until the casino bill is signed into law by the governor." He looked over at Clay Westridge. "I know you can't say anything, you represent a publicly traded corporation, but this is what your firm has hired me to handle discreetly."

Westridge stared straight ahead. How would he ever be able to explain this to his board?

I said to Caulfield, very respectfully, "Do you really think it's wise, sir, to offer to pay them off before you've even gotten the bill passed, let alone broken ground on the casino? I mean, the only possible conclusion they can draw from such an offer is that they can shake you down at will whenever they want."

The old man nodded. He was calling the shots now, not Westridge. "Of course you're correct, but we'll just have to deal with that problem when it arises. I know you spend a lot of time up here on the Hill, but do you have any idea how long we've been trying to get this casino bill passed? We can't let some penny-ante racketeers sabotage the deal at the last moment."

The lobbyists always say "the Hill," and everybody else says "the State House." They seem to think saying "the Hill" makes them sound more connected. I think it makes them sound like poseurs, like if you're from D.C. saying "this town." I looked over at the three of them.

"You have to understand, if this really is a 'war,' I'm not sure you could stop it with any amount of money, but even if you could, who would you pay it to? Sally Curto's people got killed, and he's got Bench McCarthy out looking for who did it. If there really is a third party here, and I'm guessing maybe there is, then they can't quit until they find out who's doing this, because otherwise, they could be next." I paused and looked at Westridge. "Do you know what the word 'capable' means?"

"Why of course, it's—"

"No, I mean the wiseguys' definition. Capable means people who are able—capable—of killing somebody else, and getting away with it. Guys like Sally and Bench, they have to figure out who's 'capable' of doing this to them. They can't let this go on, because any crew this capable, they could kill them too."

Caulfield cleared his ancient raspy throat. "So what you're telling me, Mr. Reilly, is that you don't believe this really is a gang war?"

"Not at all, Mr. Caulfield. I just suspect, and that's all it is at this point, a suspicion, that this is not exactly the gang war you may think it is. Somebody else may be involved here, we just don't know who it is, and obviously Sally Curto and Bench McCarthy don't know either, or they wouldn't be beating the bushes like they are."

"Whoever's involved," Caulfield said, "we need this so-called war stopped. Do you want the job, Mr. Reilly?"

"I do," I said. "I'm just telling you up front, I'm not sure anything can stop this right now, until Bench figures out who's doing this and deals with it."

Kevin Caulfield took a puff on his cigar and glanced over at Taylor.

"What's your considered opinion, Mr. Taylor?"

"I think Reilly is possibly on to something. There's no record of any recent bad blood between these two organizations."

"That's my whole point," I said. "And that may be why it does have something to do with your casino bill. Apparently somebody's trying to sink this thing, I have no idea who, and neither do you, or you wouldn't have asked me to come here."

Terry Caulfield reappeared in the office doorway with one of the decanters and asked if anyone needed a refill. After we all shook our heads, Caulfield turned again to me.

"Mr. Reilly, it strikes me that you seem to think that figuring out this conundrum comes down not so much to Mr. Curto, but to his younger Irish associate. Am I correct?"

"Let me put it this way," I said. "I only know these people because of my brother, or mostly because of my brother." I glanced over at Westridge. "He's a half-assed wiseguy, a hanger-on. Lotta guys like my brother around. Most of the time they're just burping and farting, that and bragging. Taking credit for shit, pardon my French, that they know absolutely nothing about except what they read in the newspapers. There are guys in the can, believe it or not, doing time for crimes they didn't commit, but wanted everybody to think they did, so they bragged about it when they were drunk or high, and got picked up on a wire."

I paused to give them time to feel superior to ham-and-eggers like my brother.

"The point is," I finally said, "Bench isn't like that. As I said, he's a throwback. The reason he was in Norfolk when he stabbed that black guy for Sally is because even when he was a teenager, the cops knew he was trouble. When he was seventeen he shot a bookie in Medford. A contract hit at seventeen. The cops never could pin that one on him, so they 'liked' him for a hijacking and lugged him."

"He didn't kill him, though, did he?" said Taylor, glancing down at Bench's file. "The bookie, I mean."

"Bookie was wearing a Kevlar vest," I said. "Bench was shooting like they teach you in firearms class. Aim for the body, easier to hit. He's never made that mistake again. He learned that in the can, from Sally and the boys. Now he's a head man."

I smiled at my little pun. But Clay Westridge, the casino vice president, no longer seemed amused by my stories. "Now I know how your brother knows him, but how do you know this 'Bench'? Please, be specific."

But before I could answer, Kevin Caulfield spoke up. "I believe I can explain, Mr. Westridge, and please correct me if I'm wrong, Mr. Reilly. Mr. Reilly here used to work for the mayor of Boston, Mr. Westridge. The former mayor. As did my own son, Terry, whom you just met. And one of Mr. Reilly's duties was serving as a liaison, shall we say—"

"Mr. Caulfield is being diplomatic," I said, looking at Westridge. "What I was, in addition to being the mayor's driver, was a bagman, and his go-to guy at the State House, among other things. Point is, guys like Bench and Sally, if they don't want any trouble from City Hall, they have to pay all up and down the line. From the district police captain all the way up to the man in Parkman House. That's who I represented, the mayor. It's just overhead to these guys, like hiring a lobbyist in the state capital of whatever state you're trying to put a casino in."

Caulfield felt compelled to cut in again, lest his mark think he'd brought some kind of crooked cop to the table. "Mr. Westridge, what Mr. Reilly is saying is that he's more familiar with collecting money from Mr. McCarthy than giving it to him."

"So you do know him, you're not just somebody's brother?" The vice president didn't care how I knew him. He just wanted someone to make the connection. He wanted to protect his $2 million investment. Who could blame him?

He said: "You've spoken to him?"

I nodded. "Would he recognize me if I walked into his bar? Maybe. It's been five years. He wouldn't ask me how my family was, but he might know who I am. Might."

"Then I think you're the guy we want to make the approach, Mr. Reilly," Westridge said.

"Mr. Westridge," I said, "I don't know how things work anywhere else, but around here, you don't just walk into a wiseguy's barroom with $100,000 in cash. Let me see if I can make some kind of approach to Bench—I'm not promising you anything, but first let me see if I can get the lay of the land. I mean, for all we know, he could have already found the guys who did this, and if he did, then there won't be any more trouble, at least from them."

"You think that's possible?" the vice president said.

"Probably not, but it's worth a drive to Somerville. Now let's talk about my rates. I charge three thousand dollars a day."

I held my breath, but they didn't bat an eye.

Caulfield said dryly, "Your price has gone up."

I left soon after, with my instructions to reach out to Bench McCarthy. Terry Caulfield, who'd been listening in, walked me to the door while the others continued their deliberations.

"Three grand!" he whispered. "You've come a long way from City Hall."

"Not far enough," I said.

5

WHAT'S YOURS IS OURS

I bought the Alibi about five years ago. I'd worked there off and on since I was a kid. That's where I met my first wiseguys, selling six-packs of cold long-neck Narragansetts out the side door for six dollars on Sundays, back when Massachusetts still had blue laws. On Sundays, the Paul Revere Liquor Mart up the hill was closed. They had the coldest beer in town, that's what their neon sign said.

The Gaelic Club, as the Alibi was then called, was right around the corner from the old Brinks armored-car barn. They'd moved it out of the North End after the original Brinks job back in 1950. The guards were always dropping in after their shifts, getting bombed and swapping stories. The old owner never took advantage of the situation; he was just into reading Irish history and shit like that. By the time he decided to return to the Auld Sod, I was moving up in the element, and I fronted the money to a local wannabe to buy it. Even in Somerville, convicted felons aren't allowed to own barrooms, or at least they can't be the owners of record.

Once I took over, I made sure a few of my guys were always around, buying drinks for the armored-car drivers. We had broads for them too, if they were interested. And they could bet all they wanted, but unlike the women, they had to pay if they lost on their bets. We collected on those tabs. And if they didn't have the dough to pay off, well, we could always work something out.

Open under new management, the Alibi was the friendliest damn bar in town—at least if you drove an armored car for Brinks.

Some cops believe we use guards inside on armored-car robberies, but that gets messy, because they always fold under pressure. So you have to take them out. Maybe you shoot 'em in the head as you're leaving the scene, in which case you have to clip the second guard too. And shooting civilians—which is what guards are, because they sure as hell aren't cops—is not good policy.

But if you don't cap them on the way out, the feds immediately like 'em for the job, as well they should, and they start squeezing. Most of the crooked guards end up going straight into the Witness Security Program, and if that happens, you never see them again until they take the witness stand against you at trial.

Cutting guards in on a job just isn't worth the jeopardy when you can buy a few rounds of drinks and over the course of a few weeks the drivers themselves will spill every weakness in a route. It makes them feel like big shots. And after you've milked them dry, the guards who talked can't even remember what they said because they were so loaded. A hundred bucks worth of beer for a quarter-million-dollar job. Talk about buying an orchard for an apple.

Anyway, I had this guy in as my straw owner of the Alibi. Everything was fine until the guy decided he wanted to graduate from half-assed wiseguy to full-fledged wiseguy. I hate it when that happens. He began selling coke out of the bar. I let it slide until he started dealing keys. Then I thought he owed me a visit at the garage. He had to come clean and come with cash, and he came with neither. First he played Mickey the Dunce, and when I called him on that, he tried to stare me down. He was acting like he owned the joint.

Soon thereafter, one night after closing, a couple of guys wearing masks came in and ripped off five keys and $50,000 cash. They were my guys, of course.

I got a call from him the next day. He was wondering what had happened to his protection. I told him I was wondering what had happened to my end.

By then he was into the coke himself, and he decided to go along on one of the armored-car robberies. The cops were waiting for them. I just can't afford to have partners who are looking at heavy time, especially if they've never done time before. They found his body in the trunk of a rented car in the long-term parking lot at Logan Airport—two in the hat, as the old-timers say.

The Alibi's current owner of record is the wife of my older brother, who's been doing odd jobs for me, all legit, since he went into AA a few years back. He's the manager of record. He has a gun permit too. I see 'em twice a year, every Thanksgiving and Christmas. Their kids love me. Like Whitey used to say, Christmas is for cops and kids.

This day I made it into the Alibi around 3:00 p.m., after parking the Escalade in the back alley. I had business to conduct, so I went out onto the sidewalk to speak with everybody as they stopped by. A guy with a hijacking crew from Malden mentioned something about a load of flat-screen TVs; I told him to see my guy at a warehouse I lease in Everett. I never say anything incriminating, or at least I try as best I can not to. I always talk one-on-one, his word against mine, but just in case he's wearing a wire, everything is indirect. Nobody's name is ever mentioned. Out on the street I cup my mouth, like Cheech or an NFL coach on the sidelines, just in case the cops have got some lip-readers working with binoculars across Broadway.

The feds follow me everywhere, at least when they've got a hair across their ass. As a felon, I can't carry a gun in the car. A lot of the time I have a car that follows me, with two guys with clean records. They have the guns. I only drive the Escalade in times of emergency, like now.

I was basking in the early spring sunshine outside the Alibi when one of the local bookies showed up. I'd asked him to come by when he had some time. I never order anybody to do anything. But most times, the people I need to see do the right thing. This guy's name was Barry Weinstein and he operated out of an "insurance agency" on Broad Street in the financial district. He'd stopped paying "rent" to Sally, which was a mistake, because Sally asked me to speak to Barry for him. Sally didn't like Jews very much, and he was always worried he'd lose his temper and slap them around, or worse.

The way something like this works is, whatever I collect from one of Sally's guys, we split, fifty/fifty. Barry was about seventy, another guy shaped like a bowling ball, maybe five-five. I was leaning against a lamppost on Broadway when he showed up.

"Thanks for coming over, Barry," I said. "Like I told you, I need to borrow some money."

"You, Bench? You got more money than God. Banks'd lend to Bench McCarthy."

"God's tapped out too, Barry. I'm a little strapped. You read about that thing over at Logan Airport." The feds had grabbed fifty kilos of cocaine. I had nothing to do with that load, but it had been in the papers and on TV. He'd remember it. "That was my load. I need a new stake to get back on my feet."

Barry was skeptical. "What about Sally, he can't help?"

"Sally? C'mon, you know Sally, he tosses around quarters like they were manhole covers."

That much was true. When we first partnered up, Sally told me he'd drive the car for me if I needed to whack somebody. The only thing he told me never to ask him for was a loan. "Neither a borrower nor a lender be," that was his philosophy, but not quite in those words. He wasn't much into Hamlet.

"No offense, Bench," Barry said, "but how do you pay me back?"

"How do I pay you back?" I said. "What kind of question is that?"

"Again, with all due respect, it's the kind of question that follows after Barry asks himself the first question, which is, why does a guy like Bench need to see Barry Weinstein?"

I find it irritating when somebody speaks of himself in the third person.

"Look, I been watchin' you, Barry. I'll be honest, Sally tells me you've gotten a little behind. That puts you in play. If you ain't with Sally, you're with me, and I need somebody I can send people to who get a little behind. You know how skittish some people get when they're in arrears to somebody like Sally. They're worried something bad might happen to them."

His nostrils flared in anger, and I could see that Barry had also gotten behind on trimming his nose hairs.

"Are you threatening me?" he said.

"Not at all," I said. "Forget I even mentioned it. You don't have to do nothing for me. But just remember that next time you get in a jam and somebody comes looking for you, you ain't gonna have me watching your back. Or Sally either."

"You're saying I need a shoulder to cry on?"

"Everybody needs a shoulder to cry on, Barry."

"Okay," he said. "You're right, I do need a shoulder to cry on. I got this guy, he's always been good for the money, never a bit of trouble, but now he's behind, forty large. Says he won't pay. Got a new wife, she tells him he don't have to pay."

"Well?" I said.

"I need somebody to put the fear of God into him," Barry said. "I know Sally wants his money from me, but how can I get Sally what I owe him if this other guy won't pay what he owes me?"

I recognized a guy in a car headed down Broadway. He honked the horn and I waved back. It gave me time to think how to let Barry down gently.

"Barry," I said, "I thought we had a deal, you and me and Sally."

"We do, Bench, we do have a deal."

"And what's your understanding of that deal?"

"I could have gone with you or Sally, but I picked Sally, 'cause I know him longer, but once I made my choice, he told me, I'm not supposed to ask him for any help collecting from deadbeats. Or you either, that goes without saying, I suppose."

"And yet here you are doing just that," I said.

"Well, yes, I guess I am," Barry said.

"And why is that, Barry?" It was strange, addressing a guy old enough to be my father as if he were some wayward kid. "Why did Sally tell you he doesn't threaten anybody with any strong-arm stuff anymore?"

"Because, he said, whenever a wiseguy threatens a civilian nowadays, the bum goes running to the FBI."

"Correct," I said. "This guy who owes you forty, if I go to him, he's going to agree to pay me, only the next time I see him, he'll be wearing a wire. More'n likely the feds'll be rolling videotape too. The best possible scenario is I get arrested and have to pay a lawyer at least forty large to get myself a continued without a finding. The worst possible scenario is I go to prison for attempted extortion. You wouldn't want to see your good friend Bench go to prison for attempted extortion, now would you, Barry?"

"Of course not," he said.

I was getting tired of talking to Barry.

"Barry, do you understand the kind of relationship guys like me and Sally have with guys like Barry Weinstein?"

"I don't follow you, Bench."

"Maybe you can follow this then. What's ours is ours, and what's yours is ours. Do you understand now, Barry?"

He looked worried, but standing out on Broadway, he was restraining the urge to run away. I was staring at him now, putting on my best mean face. I've been told I have a pretty good mean face.

"Barry, here's the deal. You owe Sally forty large. I'm his collection agent. And since you've been pissing me off here, I'm going to fine you another ten grand, which means you owe me fifty thousand."

"Fine me?" he said. "I never heard of such a thing."

"Then you're not going to pay me?"

"I didn't say that, Bench."

"Because if you don't, Barry, I am going to kill you."

"Hey, Bench, you know what? I think we got a deal here."

The problem with bookmaking is that you eventually become a loan shark. It's the nature of the racket. You're dealing with degenerate gamblers, and they're always broke. So you lend them money. If you don't, they'll find another bookie who will. Then they run up a tab with that guy until he finally cuts them off and then they just run to another bookie.

This wouldn't be such a headache except that very few bookies are muscle guys. They're the kind of guys who got their lunch bags stomped on in high school. They got pocket protectors in their stockings for Christmas. They can't collect what they're owed.

Now they're hanging out with gangsters, or so they think, and they lap it up. They start dropping your name to their marks to impress them. But the deadbeats are their problem, not mine. I protect bookies from other wiseguys, not from their own piss-poor choice of customers. But they never stop asking, which is why I now have a guy who sits in a booth at the new A&A Deli on Com Ave in Brookline handling the Jewish bookies. He settles up with them every Monday. We have his booth swept for bugs once a week, every Monday morning, by the Brookline cops. We always use local talent, that way there's never any hard feelings. My guy is of course Jewish himself, from Brookline, like most of the Jewish bookies now, except for a handful who still operate out of the bars on Fifth Street in Chelsea. Those guys may be the last Jews in Chelsea; the Young Men's Hebrew Association under the Tobin Bridge is now an Iglesia de Dios.

I have another guy in Cambridge who handles the bookies from North Cambridge. He's Irish. So's the guy in Quincy. Sally has the Italian districts, or what used to be the Italian districts, before the Brazilians and the Guatemalans moved in.

We charge 'em on a monthly basis, for "protection." I'm not their layoff guy, I'm not their partner, I'm the taxman. I take my end, and I get it first. Win or lose, they pay. If Sally wants to be in business with them, handle their layoffs, that's his call.

After Barry left I wanted to sit down with the guys who ran my poker game in Andrew Square, Salt and Peppa. Salt was tight with Peppa because he came out of one of the last white families to move out of the Orchard Park projects in Roxbury. They were both capable. After I heard about Sally's nephew, I had asked them to stop by. We went inside the Alibi and sat down in a booth in the back, near the jukebox. I put a few quarters in and punched some random buttons, to create a little ambient sound just in case.

"Gotta be even more careful than usual," I told Salt, who ran the crew. There's always gotta be a boss, even if it's only two guys working.

"You don't think maybe we ought to shut down for a few days?" Peppa asked.

"Nah," I said. "That would send the wrong message, that they're in our heads." I thought for a moment. "Notice anything out of the ordinary lately?"

Salt answered. "Few more cop cars lately, wouldn't you say, Pep?"

"Yeah," Peppa said. "Even before Sally's kid got killed. Kinda weird, almost like the cops knew something beforehand."

I stared at Peppa. "I wish you'd told me this before now."

Salt answered for him. "You don't spend much time in Southie, Bench, not that I blame you. Them cops got more freedom from headquarters than most of the other districts. Probably because of all the politicians livin' over there."

I asked, "You're takin' care of our friends every month, aren't you?"

"Couldn't operate no other way," Salt said.

"Okay, just don't let anybody catch you flat-footed. It's our turn to get hit one of these nights."

"We watchin'," Peppa said. "I got two of my boys in a car across

Dorchester Street from the game, in case anybody comes outta there fast."

"What about guns?"

"Got another car behind them, with some good solid citizens in it, white citizens, guys with permits, you dig?"

You dig? Sometimes I couldn't figure out if Peppa was putting me on with that seventies *Superfly* dialogue, or if he was serious. Maybe I should start calling him "Jim," like the Mafia guys with Richard Roundtree in *Shaft*.

"If I was checking us out for a heist," Peppa continued, "I'd be giving us a wide fuckin' berth. Too many eyes, too many guns."

That's what I had figured. I just wanted to make sure they weren't getting lazy.

They got up and after we shook hands, I noticed the guy standing in the front door of the Alibi, mid-forties. He looked a little like an undercover cop, except he wasn't dressed as well.

But I didn't make this guy for a cop. Any cop I knew—that is, paid—would just walk over. And if this were an official inquiry, he wouldn't hesitate, and he wouldn't be by himself. He was scanning the room, so I knew he could only be looking for me. He made me but was smart enough to walk over to the bar and sit down. I called to my manager, Hobart, who was wearing an old-fashioned butcher's apron. He walked over to my table and leaned in, close to my face.

"See that guy over there at the bar," I said. "You recognize him?"

Hobart slowly looked around, then turned back. "Never seen him before."

"He looks familiar. But he ain't Somerville. I'd remember him if he was local. Must be from Boston."

Hobart smiled. "Maybe he's another one of those guys, read about you in the paper and now he wants to get rid of his wife and he figures you'll do a hit on the arm for him."

It's happened before, more than once. This guy, though, didn't have that furtive, beaten, henpecked look. He also didn't look like he had $10,000 cash in his coat pocket, which was what the last guy had who asked me to kill his wife. I told him, let me give you some free advice pal, you want a hit man, just go down to your nearest State Police barracks and turn yourself in, 'cause they're the only ones you're gonna find in a bar who are willing to take a contract from somebody they don't know. I always tell the poor bastards the same thing: it's cheaper to keep her.

Hobart said, "You want me to tell him to screw?"

"Nah," I said. "Let him make his play. Sometimes I think I don't talk to enough people anymore."

"Sometimes I think you talk to too many," Hobart said. He was referring to Peppa. That was something he and Sally shared in common. Neither of them liked blacks. I'd tried to explain to Hobart that these days it was good to have a few blacks around. Somebody wants to cap me, maybe he'll think twice, wondering if he wants to have to worry for the rest of his life if every black guy he sees coming at him on the street is one of Bench's guys. You've got to look for every edge you can.

To which Hobart always replies, "You can't fix Negro."

I halfheartedly read the *Herald* for a while, but the guy just sat there at the bar, sneaking an occasional look over at me. I got tired of the *Herald* and had started in on the *New York Post* when the guy made his move. He took a last swig of his beer, then got up and began slowly walking toward me. Every eye in the place was on him. Hobart, at the next table, reached into his apron pocket, just in case. The guy didn't look like trouble, at least not gun trouble, but you never know. He reached the table and stood in front of me.

"Hi, Bench," he said. "You may not remember me—"

"I don't."

"My name's Jack Reilly, I used to be a cop in Boston, worked for the mayor—"

Now I remembered him. He was a bagman. He used to come around to my place on Columbus Avenue, Dapper's, before I burned it down. Then he started showing up at the garage. I paid City Hall a grand a month, which didn't include the district cops and the building and zoning inspectors. Reilly was a cop, which was why whenever I duked him the grand, I always wondered how much of it actually ended up in the mayor's pocket—$700 or $300? You give something to a cop, he thinks it's all for him. That's just the way it is. I don't know who I'd use for a bagman if I needed one, but it sure as hell wouldn't be a cop.

I looked up at Reilly. He was waiting for me to offer him a chair. He'd be waiting for a while longer.

"Yeah, sure, I know you," I said. "Didn't I read something about you, Jack? Something about a wire?"

"The feds got me picking up a donation from another cop—"

"Cash?" I asked.

"Of course, that's why I was the one making the pickup. He wanted a promotion, that's what he said. That's what the feds told him to say. They wanted to flip me to go up against the mayor, but I stood up."

"Do any time?"

He shook his head. "I got nolle prossed. I had a good lawyer."

"It's easy to stand up if you're not looking at time, you know what I mean, Jack?"

"Well, in retrospect that's true I suppose. But at the time, when you get that target letter, you never know how it's going to shake out, do you?"

A good answer, delivered like a pro. But I still didn't show my hand.

"Listen," he finally said, "can I sit down? I have something I want to run by you."

"You can run it by me standing up." I looked over at Hobart, motioned to him to come over, and then turned back to this Jack Reilly. "First, though, I just want to check something, if it's okay with you, Jack."

He nodded. He understood. I always wonder about guys who've been caught on wires, even if they had a good lawyer. I'm suspicious, just like with "unindicted coconspirators." Maybe they got used to being taped. Maybe it was all a setup by the cops, to keep them on the streets with a short leash, very short. Hobart gave Reilly a quick frisk, pits to tits, and told me, "He's clean."

I told him he could sit down now, and he did.

"What do you want, Jack?" I asked.

"You know the casino bill that's coming up for a vote?" he said. I told him I read the newspapers.

"I'm working for some people who want it passed," he said. "Vote's very close right now. And, well . . ." He paused. "Every time somebody else gets killed, a few more of the reps get cold feet."

"And this concerns me how?"

"These people that have been killed, they worked for Sally?"

"You'd have to ask Sally," I said.

Reilly took a deep breath. "I don't know Sally."

"And you think you know me?"

"Not really," he said. "But my employers really want to put a lid on this thing, at least until after the vote."

"Who are your employers?"

"Some concerned citizens. They'd really like to see everything quiet down, at least until their bill gets signed by the governor."

I smiled. "You want to put a lid on a gang war so you can get a bill passed? I guess you don't know much about gang wars, Jack."

"What my employers figure is, and I'm just passing on their thoughts, is that you and Sally are having a war to figure out who's going to shake down the casinos once they're built. These guys who are voting, they're state reps, from the suburbs mostly. They can't take this kind of heat."

"What's your pitch, Jack?"

"The shooting stops, we make it worth your while."

"Just me, or Sally too?"

"Whatever it takes to stop it." He paused for a moment. "Look, I know how stupid I seem walking in here with no introduction or nothing. But I'm just an errand boy, you understand? I told them this was a fool's errand, but they're from the South, they're business-men, they're squares."

"And you're not?"

"I'm broke is what I am."

"How much they offering me?" I asked. "How much if I can stop it?"

"I think they'd want some kind of guarantee."

A guarantee? I had to smile again.

"They want something in writing, do they?"

"You know what I mean."

"No, I don't, Jack. I really don't. Tell me."

Hobart glanced over at me, scowling. I don't think he could be-lieve I'd been talking to this bent cop for as long as I had.

"You got this money with you now?"

"No, of course not. They just wanted me to sound you out."

"Okay, Jack, you've done that. You go report back to your busi-nessmen from the South that I'm thinking about it."

"What does that mean, exactly? 'Thinking about it'?"

"It means I don't usually talk to people who just walk in here like you did, but I made an exception in your case, and I want to do a little checking."

"On me?"

"On everything."

"What can I tell my people?"

"Tell your people I'm doing a little checking."

"When do I see you again?"

"When I have something to tell them. Or when you have some cash. Now screw."

6

EX MARKS THE SPOT

I screwed.

A lot of people might have been taken aback to get that kind of brusque brush-off. But I didn't take it personally. To take something personally, you really have to believe something's on the level. I've been around too long to entertain such delusions. Bench was just playing his role—tough guy gangster. And I was playing mine—messenger boy. And I was already ahead of the game, having gotten paid up front.

On my way back to the South End, I called Kevin Caulfield to fill him in. He didn't seem disappointed either; at least he had something to tell Westridge. I don't think he'd been expecting much anyway. He was another guy who wasn't operating under any illusions that anything was on the level.

I was glad for the business, but despite my alleged dodgy reputation, I don't play in the same league as Bench and Sally. I'm just a State House hustler, and they're wiseguys. Caulfield might have been able to come up with somebody a little more "in the element" as they say, but there's a danger in dealing directly with wiseguys. They have a tendency to go rogue, especially if you give them cash. You could hand somebody $20,000 to deliver and then you'd never see them again, or if you did, they'd claim somebody ripped 'em off before they got to the Alibi and could you please give 'em another twenty large, no hard feelings? And no, they didn't get a good look at the guys who robbed them. Everything with these guys is a scam, they're even worse than politicians.

Caulfield was using me because he and I played by the same rules—State House rules. I had to answer to him, just like the guy who frisked me had to answer to Bench. Caulfield told me to keep making calls, see what I could turn up, and they'd keep paying me. Sounded like a plan to me, especially the part about getting paid.

Once I got home to Shawmut Avenue, I made a call to a House chairman who owed me. He'd paid me well for services rendered, but I'd gone above and beyond the call of duty. He'd been pinched in Boston for drunk driving, survivable in most years, but this particular cycle he'd just split up with his wife and he'd been running against a fresh-faced young selectman.

The cop who'd pinched my guy was a real blister, and I soon discovered why he had such a chip on his shoulder. He'd tried to move up to the State Police, but he'd been bounced out of the academy at New Braintree for reasons I was never able to ascertain. So he'd come crawling back to the BPD, which is allowable under union regulations, and soon was testifying in all manner of gun and drug cases, not to mention the occasional OUI.

When the lawyers first get a cop on the witness stand, or when he swears out an affidavit for a search warrant, he has to stipulate under oath how long he's been a cop. For two years, since he'd come back to the job, this guy had been claiming he'd been on the job with the BPD "continuously since 2007."

Well, no, he hadn't. He'd been out for those three months in 2010. In other words, he had been working "continuously since 2010." A defense lawyer would call it perjury, I'd call any and all of his subsequent testimony impeachable, and an assistant D.A. would say simply, "Your Honor, the Commonwealth moves to dismiss all charges."

Well, that information got the charges dropped against my guy. Then the story got picked up by the defense bar, and it wasn't long before the Department of Correction had to spring a few dozen really bad actors who were doing time on this cop's testimony. The *Globe* harrumphed for a couple of weeks about the "corruption" in the department, the lying cop got bounced to the harbor patrol (where he wouldn't have to testify anymore) and I was persona non grata at J.J. Foley's all that summer.

You might have thought I'd have gotten a medal or a citation or at least a ribbon, if not from the *Globe* then from the ACLU, for my courageous gumshoe work that resulted in the return of all those fine upstanding drug dealers and drive-by shooters to the street. But apparently they looked me up on Wikipedia and . . . nothing to see here, folks, move along.

You know my old saying. No good deed goes unpunished.

Fortunately, though, at least one person remembered what I'd done for him, the state rep, who'd been reelected after all and was now Mister Chairman. I gave him a call and told him I needed a debriefing on the casino bill.

He explained to me how the various do-gooders were still trying to move reconsideration on the bill, and were trying to recruit more votes by throwing in all kinds of amendments, most of which involved handing out phony-baloney hack jobs for "addiction services" and "community outreach" in the affected cities and towns.

The leadership was closely examining every amendment, with an eye towards finding some particularly odious ones that they could present with some alarm to the casino lobbyists, who would then shower them with yet more money, to prevent the amendments from being attached to the main legislation.

Some of the amendments had undoubtedly been written by the legislative leaders themselves and given to the more compliant rank-and-file reps to actually file. The whole legislative process was nothing more than a giant conspiracy. If they'd ever put any of these bills or amendments in the mail, the feds could have charged them all with attempted extortion and mail fraud. It was only a matter of time—say, the swearing-in of the next Republican U.S. attorney—until all these reps and lobbyists were indicted for wire fraud (i.e., sending e-mails).

Anyway, my guy couldn't get away from the State House, but he said he could meet me outside the House chambers. I got a cab and was there early, so I decided to watch a little of the debate. It was as dreadful as ever, guys in bad suits and worse haircuts yelling "Point of order!" at each other like it really mattered.

I was working on a medium-sized headache up in the spectators' gallery by the time my guy made eye contact with me and motioned me outside. I went downstairs and we took the elevator to his fifth-floor office, the walls of which were covered with about a million photographs of himself with high school athletic teams and Kiwanis Clubs and congressmen who weren't ever going to have a courthouse named after them, even in Worcester. I asked him about the casino bill.

"I thought it was a done deal three days ago," he said. "Now I'm not so sure. Both papers are going crazy about how the gang violence, so-called, shows that the state doesn't need another vice."

"Is gay marriage a vice?"

"What?"

"Never mind. Look, tell me, who stands to benefit if the bill gets killed, and don't tell me the gangsters."

"Well, see, the thing is, the leadership's been pushing it, of course. Especially across the hall." That meant the Senate. "The bill as it stands now is basically theirs. But if it all starts over again next January, then everybody's pretty much on equal footing again."

Which meant every would-be casino operator and their lobbyists could be shaken down once more.

I asked him whose fingerprints were on the current bill. He didn't have any skin in the game—nobody was paying him off—so he hadn't exercised his customary due diligence in ferreting out the real beneficiaries of the legislation. But what it seemed to boil down to was that the state had been divided into three districts, with each district getting a casino. The Senate president, Mick Carberry, had personally drawn the lines to put Foxboro in its own district, along with the Indians who were guaranteed a casino. Boston had its own district—the mayor and the House speaker both wanted a casino at Suffolk Downs. The third district was almost all of the western part of the state, all the way east into Bristol County. Nobody cared as much about that one.

It was gerrymandering at its finest, and most of the big publicly held casino corporations had gotten screwed, blued and tattooed. They'd hired the wrong lobbyists, many of them former legislators, who'd robbed them blind. That's what always happens, and the further away from Massachusetts the companies' headquarters are, the more the local lobbyists charge. That includes Caulfield.

The casino interests pushing Foxboro seemed to have played their cards right. They had teamed up with the Indians and put all their eggs in Carberry's basket. Now he was running for governor. Senate presidents never win statewide fights, but hope burns eternal, as the mayor of Boston has been known to say. Money would not be a problem in his doomed campaign.

Mistah Chairman walked over to his little dorm-room-sized refrigerator and returned with a Bud Light for me and a Diet Coke for himself, now that he was in the program. I pried off the cap and gulped from the bottle and pondered the situation.

"So a lot of people would like a mulligan on this thing, right?" I said, as much to myself as to him. "Big-money people."

"Not just the casinos and the lobbyists," Mistah Chairman said. "How about everybody in the legislature who feels like they missed a big payday?"

"Present company included?"

He shrugged. "Kinda risky, if you ask me. I mean, what's going on with these shootings and bombings? I smell cops, and that means rats. There's easier ways to make a buck."

Mistah Chairman was one of those rarities at the State House. His near-death experience with the OUI and the selectman had chastened him. Most guys, if they skate on something heavy, they figure it means they have nine lives. They run even more wide-open than they did before they got lugged the first time.

"If the bill gets killed because of this alleged gang war," I said, "then it starts all over again next January?"

"As do the payoffs," he said.

"And whether Carberry wins or not—"

"He won't—"

"Agreed," I said. "So the new Senate president will be—"

"—Denis Donahue, also known as Donuts, and by the way that's Denis with one 'n'—"

"Because he didn't have time to steal the second one. I know the joke. So you're telling me he's the one who has the most to gain, monetarily, if he can put a stake through the heart of Carberry's bill."

Mistah Chairman nodded. "The Speaker's got his casino, in Boston. There has to be one here. Nobody gives a shit about the Indians, but they're pretty much guaranteed theirs, in Foxboro. That leaves one slot open."

Which meant Denis Donahue was the guy I needed to keep an eye on. He was from Worcester. I used to have an aunt from Worcester. I always thought she had some kind of learning disability, but then I realized it was just that she was from Worcester. Not a deep gene pool out there. In the kingdom of the blind, the one-eyed man shall lead. That was Denis "Donuts" Donahue, the one-eyed man.

"Donuts can't directly go up against Carberry, can he?" I asked Mistah Chairman.

"No, he can't. But he can wring his hands and commiserate with him if the bill starts taking on water because of the 'war.'"

"Anything else I need to know?" I asked.

He shook his head. "Donuts is pretty much what you'd expect

him to be, a garden-variety snake in the grass, your basic turd in the punch bowl."

"You like him a lot, huh?" There seemed to be a pattern emerging here.

"Oh yeah, here's something. He has season tickets to the Red Sox. I mean, good seats. Front row, right down the first-base line. Doesn't use them himself every night, but you can tell who he's doing business with by who gets 'em."

"You got the exact seat numbers?"

He shook his head. "Just scan the first row and you'll be able to spot 'em. If you're indicted—"

"You're invited. Yeah, I think I can figure out who's in those seats."

I thanked Mistah Chairman for his time. It was warm for early spring, so I decided to save the cab fare and walk home. Once I got home, I cracked open a real beer, a sixteen-ounce Ballantine Ale. Then I popped three Vicodin, turned on the satellite radio, sat down and waited for liftoff. I was trying to figure out how I could approach Denis Donahue when the phone rang.

"What's going on with Sally Curto?" It was Katy Bemis. If they ever name a street after her, it'll have to be one way.

"Why are you calling me?" I said. "I thought we were *finis.*"

She laughed. "*Finis*, huh? That's a hoot, you using Latin."

"I keep telling you, I went to Boston Latin."

"So you say. I've never checked, and I think you told me once your ex-wife got the yearbook in the divorce settlement."

"Katy, as much as I enjoy what the movie reviewers would call the rapid-fire Hepburn-Tracy-style banter between exes, I do have other things to do."

"Like what?"

"Maybe I have a date."

Now she really laughed. "With who? Slip? Gonna catch a few wakes, go by Waterman's and steal some dimes from a Chinaman's bier?"

"A Chinaman?" I said. "That's not very PC. You'd never even been to a Chinese wake at Waterman's until you ran into me and Slip."

"And it's something I've been meaning to thank you for, believe me. What's the old Bob Hope song? 'Thanks for the Memories.'"

"Actually, I was thinking of Rod Stewart. To paraphrase, 'I know you're thinking that she must be sinking or she wouldn't get in touch with me.'"

"Okay, you're right. I do need something."

"Don't tell me the *Globe* doesn't have any sources other than yours? And how would it look if you had to tell them that when you were at the *Herald* you sometimes took tips from a guy who won a photo finish with a federal grand jury."

"Are you carrying a foreign load, Sunshine?" Another local-color expression she'd picked up from me. What must her family in Wenham, especially Uncle Dudley, make of her jaunty urban patter every November at Thanksgiving dinner?

She said, "I figure you must be on something. Most of the time you wouldn't tell me or anybody else if their coat was on fire."

"You called me, Sunshine. Feel free to call some of your other sources. I'm not stopping you." I stood up and walked to the refrigerator to get another can of Ballantine.

I knew she must have heard the "*pssst*" when I popped the top. But she let it slide. For someone whose father ate lunch every afternoon at the Somerset Club, she was very pragmatic, especially when she needed information.

She said, "Can't we get along, Jack? Some men, they even go on vacations with their ex-wives. You haven't talked to yours in ten years, and now you barely even talk to me, and all we were was—"

"I wasn't the kind of guy you could bring to a *Globe* party, was I? That's the bottom line, isn't it? I helped you get over there, but once you were there, I didn't fit. White. Irish. Catholic. Heterosexual. From Boston. Want me to think of some more reasons you had to drop me?"

I heard a deep sigh on the other end of the line.

"I've told you a million times, they don't care if you're Irish. They really don't. You've got this ancient James Michael Curley chip on your shoulder about something nobody else cares about anymore. The fact that I went over to the *Globe* had nothing to do with . . ." Her voice trailed off again.

I thought about asking her how she was getting along with her new boyfriend, who had a trust fund, used "summer" as a verb, had a family "cottage" on Nantucket, a Yale degree and a closet full of bow ties that he wore to his job as metro editor, whatever that meant. I was pretty sure he'd never covered a fire, let alone set one. Metro editor—did that mean he was a metrosexual too? But the Vicodin had kicked in. I was more comfortably numb by the moment.

"What do you want, Katy? Go ahead, ask." Then she could go back to her boyfriend and tell him how she'd just been talking to one of her lowlife sources, whom she couldn't name of course, to maintain an air of mystery about her extraordinary talent for enduring the foul breath of the plebeians while hobnobbing with those beneath her on the socioeconomic totem pole.

"I'm just wondering if there's a gang war about to break out," she said. "What do you hear? Is Bench making a move against the Italians?"

"How would I know?" I asked her. "You know me, I'm just a dirty cop with a phony disability pension."

"So what were you doing at the Alibi this afternoon?" She'd always been able to surprise me, and now she'd done it again.

"The Alibi? Isn't that Bench's place over on Winter Hill?"

"Yeah, and you were there. We had the place staked out, wanted a shot of Bench. I'm right now looking at a photo of you walking in. You didn't even pull the collar on your coat up around your neck. What were you doing there?"

"Would you believe me if I told you I had a thirst so great it would cast a shadow?"

"Yes, I would, considering how well I know you. But I also remember you don't much like hanging around wiseguys, so I'm guessing there had to be some money on the table for you to make the drive over to Somerville."

"You got me," I said. "There was money involved." I said no more.

"Well?" she said.

"Well what? As you pointed out, we're not married, never have been. Ain't no spousal privilege here. I just don't like my business bein' spread all over the street."

"Did you talk to him, Bench I mean?"

"I would ask, are we off the record, but I know the answer to that is always no, no matter what you say."

"Spare me the lectures on journalism ethics. Just answer the question. Did you talk to him?"

"In a manner of speaking, yes. I talked to him, and he . . . well, he answered. In a manner of speaking."

"And the subject of the conversation?"

"I walked in, and he was behind the bar, and I looked over the draft selections, and then I said, 'I'll have a Harpoon IPA,' and he drew one for me, and I said, 'Much obliged, pardner,' and he said, 'That'll be four bucks.'"

There was a pause on the other end, and then she said, "Very funny. I guess you want your name and picture in the paper tomorrow as having visited the Alibi."

"I'd prefer you didn't do that, but you're gonna do what you're gonna do."

It went on like that for a while. I was trying to think if she could do any legwork for me, but right now I couldn't think of anything. I finally told I'd see her around the campus and hung up.

7

DITTO'S DILEMMA

I own a commercial building off Warren Street in Roxbury, bought it cheap off an old-line wiseguy who was retiring and moving to Florida. There was a $12,000 lien on it for unpaid city taxes, and $3,500 in overdue water and sewerage bills, all of which I paid, and the guy threw in three silencers to sweeten the pot. The price was $5,000. Setting up the real estate trust that owns it, since I can't very well have it in my own name, cost me another $1,500.

The old-timer ran a half-ass garage out of there, and the word is that during the Irish gang wars, he'd settled up a few scores there, with acetylene torches and the like. That was before my time. But I kept the garage going, with the old mechanic, a guy named Rocco. He was used to having the element around, and we do a steady business. A lot of our work is insurance—we don't fix the cars, we wreck 'em. I used to run that racket on consignment—if you got $5,000 in claims, I'd take ten percent, $500. But I was working with too many cops, and you just can't trust them guys on insurance fraud any more than you can trust 'em on anything else.

Now I charge a flat rate. Five hundred bucks. Getting the accident report is up to them. If they need an appraiser, I'll provide one for them. That's another $500, which I whack up with the appraiser. If that seems high to you, you haven't been to a new-car showroom lately. Think sticker shock.

But the garage is short money. What I like is having a place in the city. It's not what you'd call prime real estate, obviously, but I'm not in it to turn a quick buck. It's a half-acre, a good-sized lot in Roxbury. There's always been a four-foot-high brick wall around the lot, and up above that I've got eight feet of barbed wire with razors all around the top. You'd have to be an Olympic pole vaulter to get in. I used to have dogs patrolling the property, pit bulls, rottweilers, etc., but the locals shot them for sport through the front gate.

Now I have two new ones, Tyson and Atomic Dog. Neighborhood names for neighborhood dogs. I keep them inside nights. Rocco cleans up their shit every morning when he comes in at 6:30.

I called a meeting for 4:00 p.m. of all the Boston and South Shore guys except the dealers. I like to give them a wide berth. They report to Salt and Peppa. I have a piece of a couple of bars in Quincy, and some independent layoff guys who pay me for "protection" just like the bookies. I'm a silent partner in another gin mill in Weymouth, same deal with the bookies there, although their daily receipts are less than Quincy. The Chinese moving into Quincy has been a boon. Most of them still bet with their own kind, but once the Chinese assimilate enough to start betting pro football, Quincy will be a real gold mine.

To me, meetings are a big waste of time, so this was a somewhat unusual occasion. I have a state cop from the Old Colony barracks that I use for sweeping the garage at least once a week, just like I use Somerville cops at the Alibi and Brookline cops at the new A&A. Gotta spread my business around—goodwill means a lot in this line of work. I know, my policy is no serious business is ever discussed either inside a building or a car. But sometimes you get careless, or there's an exception, like today, when you need to talk to everybody at once. I didn't have time to go door-to-door.

They drifted in one by one, talking among themselves, until I finally called the meeting to order. I reminded them of what had happened over the last day or so.

"We don't know who's doing this, or why," I said. "Anything you hear, I want to know about it, immediately, no matter how reliable or otherwise you think the information is. Considering they've already killed two guys In Town, and one of them was Hole in the Head, this is serious business. You ain't just looking for money when you blow somebody up. You're trying to deliver a message."

"What's the message?" one of the guys asked.

I shook my head. "You find out, be sure to tell me, and we'll both know." I paused. "Everybody here, I'm gonna have somebody from the Alibi with you nights until further notice. Salt 'n' Peppa'll handle that end of it. Talk to them if you got any questions." I looked out at the fifteen or so guys. Middle-aged mostly, maybe two or three under forty. Most of them had beer bellies, and red faces. Donald Rumsfeld used to say, "You go to the war with the army you've got." I remembered how that war turned out. I was not reassured.

"Any questions?" I asked.

Ditto Foley, the front man for my bar in Quincy on Adams Street, raised his hand.

"So you really got no idea who's behind this, Bench?"

"If I knew, don't you think I'd be doing something about it?"

That was the end of the meeting, but Ditto lurked around, watching me exchange small talk with some of the boys. He waited until the crowd had thinned out and then he finally got me one-on-one.

"I need a favor, Bench," he said.

I shook my head. "Can't it wait?" I said. "I got my hands full right now. Sally is fuckin' fuming."

Ditto is Good People. He's one of five brothers who came out of Mission Hill. They always struck me as cop material, but they'd all had a lot of problems early on, so now they worked as security guards at various places around the city. You can imagine how valuable they are to me—schedules, keys, guard uniforms, etc. Being of a certain age (they came up in the seventies), the Foley brothers are also quite proficient with fire, if you know what I mean. We call the youngest brother Frankie Flame.

So I knew I was going to have to listen to Ditto's story.

"It's my son, Bench," he said. "I wouldn't ask you otherwise, but he's all jammed up."

I sighed. He wasn't going to take no for an answer. I told him to come into my back office. I shut the door behind us. I knew his son by reputation; he was no damn good, all strung out on steroids, always getting into barroom brawls. Ditto told the story quickly and concisely. That was one of the things I liked about all the Foleys. They didn't waste my time, or anybody else's.

His son had gotten into yet another knock-down drag-out, at one of those so-called sports bars down in the Financial District. A place I tried to give a good leaving-alone to—Charlestown and Southie crackheads, Oxy dealers stacked up on top of one another, the only ones who have any teeth are the ones who'd done enough time to get free dental work in the can. So Ditto's kid, with the proud Irish name of Eamon, had gone nuts and broken the jaw of the son of a retired Quincy cop. The cop was now demanding $25,000 to make the case go away.

"What do you want me to do, Ditto?" I asked.

"It ain't right, Bench," he said. "This fucking cop is dirty, and his kid's no fuckin' good either." He noticed that I was looking at him askance. "I know, I know, my kid's an asshole too, but compared to this other kid, he's fuckin' Little Boy Blue. Every time this punk kid gets pinched in Quincy, the father gets his cop pals not to show up in court until the judge throws out the case."

"How many times's this happened?" I asked.

"Enough so's the kid's starting to think he can get away with it up here in Boston too."

"Oh, he does, does he?" I smiled. "Has he got any other cases coming up in Boston anytime soon?"

Ditto smiled and nodded. That was when I noticed that he had a manila envelope with him. He fumbled with the clasp, pulled out a wad of dog-eared, Xeroxed police reports and court filings and pushed them across the table at me.

"You know my brother-in-law's a half-assed lawyer, he pulled all these papers for me. Look at 'em. This kid's got at least five pinches in Norfolk County, Quincy mostly. Beats up his girlfriends, possession with intent to distribute, bouncing checks, stolen credit cards, attaching stolen license plates . . ."

I was thumbing through the papers. "Ditto, they even got him on a couple of chew 'n' screws."

That's what we call walking out on a restaurant tab. Another name for it is dine 'n' dash. It's real high-school Harry stuff, most guys outgrow it about the time they start getting laid regular. This shitheel was twenty-five years old. I kept rifling through the papers until I found what I was looking for—one of the Boston pinches. I pulled it out and scanned it—OUI. It looked like it hadn't been broomed yet.

"I see a drunk-driving coming up in Dorchester," I said. "Anything else in Suffolk County?"

Ditto's face lit up. He knew this stuff by heart. See, I have a presence in Norfolk County, but I try to maintain what you might call a low profile. In Suffolk—Boston—and in Middlesex, which is Somerville, that's where I can wheel and deal. Costs a lot of dough, but the alternative is endless cop harassment.

Ditto separated out the Boston cases for me—three were still open—and told me where the ex-cop drank in Quincy. Fortunately, he was a drunk and he worked the third shift as the security officer at a trucking company terminal. I knew the bar he hung in every morning. I was a friend of the guy who owned it. In other words, he took bets for one of my bookies.

"I give this cop a check yesterday for five grand," Ditto said. "More 'n enough, I'd say. He says if I don't get him another twenty, he'll make sure Eamon goes away."

"I'll see what I can do, Ditto."

It was dusk by the time I got back to Somerville. There's a nice new athletic club in Union Square, and I'd gotten a charter membership on the house. Had my own personal locker. I did a half-hour on the stationary bike, then went upstairs and lifted a few weights, no set pattern, just whatever struck my fancy, upper body mostly. I was thinking about who was killing Sally's guys, and when they were going to start killing mine. I showered, changed into some casual clothes I leave in my locker, and headed over to The Middlesex Room in Magoun Square. I owned a piece of it, and I liked to hang there in the early evening before it got too loud.

The Middlesex Room was where the young gash in Somerville congregated—the kind of women who liked hanging with, well, guys like me. I had my pick of the local talent, although for a few years now, I'd been running around with a hot ticket named Patty Lamonica. She'd just turned nineteen. I even knew her parents. She'd dropped out of Somerville High as soon as she turned seventeen, had gotten in with a bad crowd and now I was keeping her on the straight and narrow. Or so I told her parents. I'd even gotten her a job in Teele Square, in my real estate lawyer's office, as the receptionist.

My plan was to stop by the Middlesex Room for a drink or two—I couldn't take much of the KISS-type music anymore. Then I was going to head over with Patty to my place around the corner from the bakery in Ball Square, which was the nearest thing I had to a permanent address.

It was still early when I arrived. Ninety percent of Somerville's population has turned over since I was a kid, but you'd never know it from the Middlesex. It was still 1978 there. Saturday Night Fever every night, even Tuesday.

Patty was sitting with a couple of her gum-chewing big-hair girl-friends, wearing a miniskirt and the traditional fuck-me pumps. She had the largest bust by far—I'd paid $5,000 for her "enhancements."

I gave her a kiss on the lips and then sat down. Most nights, I'd have given her the eye, and her friends would have taken the hint and drifted off. Tonight I was content to zone out, at least for a few minutes, listening to the female gossip. I motioned to the bartender for a round of drinks, and the girls all smiled. They had no idea what was going on in the world—not unless it appeared on Facebook.

I just sat there, half-listening, thinking about my own problems. I still didn't have a clue who was after me—or Sally. There wasn't much wiseguy competition left, Sally and I had seen to that, with a generous assist from the feds. But if this went on, pretty soon Sally's suspicions would center on me, and despite our "partnership," I was still very much the junior partner, in terms of age and manpower. As long as none of my guys got hit, I was the number one suspect—excuse me, person of interest. Isn't that what the cops say now?

If Sally ever started suspecting me, that would be very bad, for both of us. I was better than anybody he had, but he had more guns than I did.

The worst thing is, ninety percent of the time, it's your friends who kill you. The better the friend, the more likely he is to whack you. There's only so much time you can spend looking over your shoulder before you sprain your neck.

I took a deep breath and tried to relax and enjoy the scenery at the Middlesex Room. They were all good-looking girls—the pretty ones always run together, I've noticed. But Patty was by far the class of the field. She was wearing a low-cut blouse designed to flaunt her new cleavage, and a short leather skirt that showed off her tight but ample Italian ass. Yes, watching her was taking my mind off my problems. I decided it was time for us to leave.

Ball Square—Sally always got a kick out of that name. Growing up in the All-American City, I never even thought about the double entendre until he asked me one day if I ever took Patty over to "Ball Square," and then started laughing. I guess I'm slow on the uptake.

I leaned over to whisper in her ear and she looked back at me with what they call bedroom eyes. She smiled and nodded.

The valets at the Middlesex knew me, so my Escalade was waiting for us right out front on the curb. I won't say I wasn't paying attention, but it was Patty I was paying attention to, not business. And that's when you're at your most vulnerable, when they catch you flat-footed. Most guys get clipped within a mile of where they live—that's a fact. And here I was on my home turf, on the main street—Broadway—less than a mile from my condo in aptly named Ball Square.

Once we were in the car, Patty playfully started pawing me, teasing me about whether I'd laid in any decent champagne. I told her I was planning on laying something else. She asked me if we were going to Florida anytime soon, and as I was telling her probably not for a while I saw a car coming up fast behind me on Broadway. I glanced back—the one night I needed congestion, nobody was around.

The car was closing fast. Patty was saying something about liking the TVs on Jet Blue when I told her, as calmly as possible, to get down on the floor. She immediately dropped to the floorboards. I saw another car headed east on Broadway, and I drifted over toward the double yellow line, so the hit car couldn't get beside me on the driver's side. That didn't stop them, though. They closed on me from the right side, a dangerous stunt if somebody suddenly pulled out of a parking space on the north side of Broadway.

"Stay down, Patty!" I said, as I sped up to about forty and opened the hide to get my PDW. I knew it was loaded and the lock was off—otherwise it was no good, because I wasn't going to have time to do anything but fire. In the rearview mirror I could see an automatic rifle barrel pointing out of the other car's back window. I wasn't going to have much time. I heard a shot and suddenly all the lights on the dashboard were flashing like a pinball machine.

"Hang on, Patty," I said, and then I slammed on the brakes.

Surprised, the driver of the car behind me kept coming. I put the gun on automatic, and as the car passed us on the right I fired right through the Escalade's front passenger window, raining glass down onto Patty. If I'm lucky, I get the driver. If I miss, the car keeps coming, and the automatic rifle takes me out.

The guy who shoots first almost always wins, or at least that used to be the rule of thumb. But nowadays, if you're using an automatic weapon, it really doesn't matter if the other guy fires first if you're the better shot. The bad guys' car, an old Ford Taurus, undoubtedly stolen, lurched to a halt. The driver was slumped against the steering wheel, blood pouring out of a gaping wound just above his left ear. The guy in the backseat with the rifle seemed frozen, so before he thawed, I fired another burst at him through the back passenger window of my Cadillac. The bullets made a neat line of holes in the Ford's rear door, the rifle dropped onto the pavement and the gunman slid out of sight.

I floored the Escalade, but it was sputtering, and smoke was coming from under the hood. The guy with the rifle in the backseat had done a much better job ventilating the Escalade than he had ventilating me. I was less than four blocks from my condo in Ball Square but I wasn't sure I could make it. I put the pedal to the metal and I still couldn't top fifteen miles an hour. Patty was sobbing, still curled up on the floorboards, her hands covering her head.

I'd have preferred to turn around and get the Escalade into one of our garages at the top of the hill, where the glass could be replaced very quickly and Rocco could come out from Roxbury to try to put the Escalade back in working order, if possible, which I doubted.

But the important thing now was to get away. I momentarily wished I had a throw down to drop at the scene, but quickly thought better of it. Sometimes it's better to play it straight, or at least as straight as you can.

Once I got the Escalade into my own garage, I tried to calm Patty down. She was crying hysterically. Her face and arms were covered with spots of blood where the flying glass had nicked her. Until now she'd only seen the upside of being with a wiseguy—the occasional fur coat from a hijacked load, the best tables with no waiting at the best restaurants, the new cars with dealer plates every six months. She'd never been around during a war.

Inside, I stripped off her clothes and pushed her into the shower. Then I looked through my medicine cabinet and found some Oxys. I turned off the water and picked her up and carried her to the living room—there was no lust, believe me. I just didn't want her to cut her feet on any random shards of glass that had dropped off my clothes. She was still sobbing as I toweled her off and bundled her into one of my bathrobes. Finally I got her settled down on the couch with a glass of gin over ice. I was going for the quick knockout, but she was too excited.

"Why were they trying to kill us, Bench?" she asked.

"I wish I knew," I said. "It'd make it easier to find them."

"Did anybody see us?"

"I hope not."

"I'm scared, Bench. What if they're still coming after us?"

"No need to worry about that," I said. I came over to the couch, leaned over her and kissed her on the forehead. "Try to get some sleep."

"I wanna go home, Bench."

Home was maybe three blocks away, on the other side of Broadway and Powderhouse Square. But the Escalade was wrecked, and besides, all of Broadway would be crawling with cops for hours to come.

"Not now, baby. I have to get another car. I gotta call Hobart and have him bring over a new one, and then I'll drive you home. How's that, hon?"

She smiled sweetly. "Okay, Bench. Just don't leave me here alone."

I turned on the radio and put it on some smooth jazz station, then went around and checked to make sure all the shades were drawn. My kitchen opened onto a patio, and when I bought the condo, I'd had the sliding glass doors removed and replaced with steel plates, just in case. That way I could sit at the kitchen table in the mornings and make my phone calls. I missed the sunlight, but I didn't want to go out like Bugsy Siegel.

The first guy I called was Hobart. He was at the Alibi. He'd heard the sirens but sirens are nothing special in Somerville. We had a guy, one of our bookies, who was in tight with City Hall and the police department, kind of our own personal "vice president, governmental relations." I told Hobart to call him and have him make discreet inquiries about who was in the hit car. That would give me more to work with tomorrow.

After that, I told him, get me a car—not a boiler, but a properly registered vehicle—and to have somebody follow him in another one. Also, he was to call me just before he got here, and I'd come out and get the keys and then he could get a ride back to the Alibi. We'd worry about the Escalade later.

I considered whether to call Sally Curto. He ought to know, but on the other hand, if he'd had a hand in it . . . Then I reconsidered. Having your nephew and your street boss clipped is a pretty tough way to establish an alibi. It was 10:30, which meant he was probably drunk in the North End somewhere, but I dialed his cell phone number anyway.

"Sally," I said, as I heard loud, boozy talking behind him, "be sure to watch the late news tonight."

"Don't play games," he said. "Tell me what happened."

"Not on the phone," I reminded him. "I'll see you tomorrow at six. The usual place."

8

A BUST OUT SOLON

I can't say much good about this endless recession, but it has helped one part of my business—bankruptcy investigations. For turning up sold-gold dirt on somebody, the only thing that beats a bankruptcy filing is a federal pre-sentencing report, and once a pol has reached that stage in his career, when he's about to be packed off to prison, the only ones still making money off him are the lawyers handling his appeal.

Anyway, in the boom years, a rep's $60,000 salary wasn't that great, unless you were completely unemployable, which most of them are.

Nowadays, though, that sixty large is looking a lot better, especially when you factor in all the perks—the per diem for driving into Boston from the district, the federal income tax write-offs if you live more than fifty miles from the State House, the kickbacks from your one or two aides, the campaign account out of which you can pay most of your personal expenses . . .

All of a sudden, there were more contested legislative races, and a lot of the challengers, who often brag about their experiences in what we call the Dreaded Private Sector, just happen to have a recent bankruptcy filing on record in the Brooke Courthouse. Which of course is why they're running. They want to bury their snouts deep into the public trough.

I don't keep records, for obvious reasons, but I'd say I pull at least twice as many bankruptcy files as I did five years ago. Let me put it this way: I now give Christmas presents to the clerks up on the sixth floor of the courthouse. One Lottery season ticket per person.

I charge my clients a grand per bankruptcy file, but it's simple work, Xeroxing, and my clients don't have to dirty their hands by signing out the jackets. Actually, they could access the files easily enough themselves if they had PACER, but not many of them know that, and I'm not telling, although eventually I'm going to have to get PACER myself and save some money on downtown parking. Anyway, bankruptcy filings are a nice little side operation, and my clients always prefer to pay cash too, which is tidier for both parties.

I'd spent the afternoon pulling records for three of my incumbents. I was getting ready to leave when it suddenly occurred to me: as long as I was here, why not see if Denis Donahue had a jacket? Just a shot in the dark, but the lack of a second "n" in "Denis" made it very unlikely I'd run into a case of mistaken identity. And I didn't.

It appeared that three months ago, Donuts couldn't have afforded a box of a dozen assorted Honey Dew donuts. He owed child support, he was behind on his mortgage, his credit cards had been cut off, a couple of New Jersey and Connecticut casinos were chasing him and behind all of them came the usual local unsecured creditors—tradesmen, utilities, the cable company, the lawn service, even the *Worcester Telegram* newspaper . . .

This guy was a complete deadbeat. And it was a telling commentary on the collapse of the local newspapers that no reporters had yet picked up on this. Ten, even five years ago, the Boston papers would have routinely checked out court records to see if any of the legislative leadership had filed Chapter 7. Or somebody, probably me, if I had the right client, would have tipped them off, or sent them a Xeroxed package of the documents in an envelope with no return address.

But what was even more significant than the debts was the fact that they had all been discharged, less than a month ago. I did some rough calculations and the payments came to some $300,000, give or take a porn movie or two in the Presidential Suite at Trump Towers in Atlantic City.

Granted, Donuts was next in line to the Senate presidency, but that was still eight months off. And that kind of front-runner money generally trickles in slowly, finally gushing into a torrent as the moment of succession arrives.

I told the clerk I was going to have to copy this one last file. I was enough of a regular that he could groan that it was 4:15, fifteen minutes before closing time. And I was enough of a regular that I could slip him a double sawbuck and tell him to calm down.

He smiled and calmed down.

9

THE HR DEPARTMENT

Sally and I were sitting on a bench at Castle Island. It was another foggy morning. Fifty feet behind us, smoking a cigarette, was Blinky Marzilli's boy Benny Eggs. When I was starting out, all these guys were in their twenties. Now the youngest of them looked like they were in their late forties. The talent pool had dried up.

"Nice shooting last night, kid," Sally said to me. He seemed in a better mood, now that I was no longer a suspect. "Lucky the cops don't have any witnesses."

"There's no luck involved. That's what I pay 'em for. I don't care how many stones they look under, as long as they don't turn over the one I'm hiding under."

"I assume you got the names they ain't releasing 'til they, what-tayacallit, notify the next of kin."

I took a piece of paper out of my pocket and read aloud to Sally.

"The driver was Emilio Cortez-Rodriguez, also known as—do I really have to read all these aliases? Illegal alien. East Boston, Chelsea and Revere addresses. Twenty-eight years old. Guy in the backseat—a white guy from Winthrop. Michael Cortese, former

Probation Department employee. He's in critical condition, two slugs in the pancreas. Doubtful he makes it."

"Cortese, you say. I know some Corteses in Winthrop, but this kid, I can't place him. How old you say he was?"

"He's thirty-four."

Sally shook his head. "Probation Department. Makes no fucking sense. Former probation officer? Who the fuck quits a state job?"

"Maybe he got fired?" I said. Suddenly I had a question for my new friend Jack Reilly. This was hack shit, his kind of thing.

"Motherfucker," Sally said. "I wish I knew somebody to ask about this kid."

How about Blinky Marzilli, I thought to myself. Through Blinky, Sally still ran Eastie, at least nominally. After the last big heroin bust in Eastie, the feds had a press conference with an organizational chart of the Mafia crew, and at least a third of them were Hispanic.

"I still can't believe it," Sally said, "the spics having the stones to come after us."

Why wouldn't they, when they outnumbered In Town in East Boston maybe five to one? What bothered me about this job was the white shooter working with the illegal ex-con. I know I got Peppa on my crew, but we speak the same language. We're both Americans. I never heard of white guys working contracts with illegals. Drugs sure, but contract hits—never.

"What about the car?" Sally asked.

"The usual. Stolen license plates. It apparently belonged to another illegal in Everett. She has one of those 'zero' registrations on it that the Registry gives out to accommodate the newcomers to our land. She'll get a fifty-dollar fine for court costs, and a continued without a finding."

"You mean they don't deport her?"

"C'mon, Sally, where you been? We fuckin' celebrate diversity here in Massachusetts." I paused. "What we gotta do is figure out who these two were working for. I assume you got some guys beating the bushes on that."

"Assumptions are the mother of fuck-ups," he said. "Who am I gonna send over there? I don't even have lunch in Maverick Square no more. I can't believe what they done to the place—"

"We're down to two scenarios now," I said. "Number one, somebody hired them to whack me so it'd look like a war between us. Number two, they want to get rid of both crews so they can move in. Whoever 'they' is. You got any ideas, Sally?"

He looked around over his shoulder at his so-called bodyguard, who was lighting a new cigarette off the old one. Chain-smoking was back in a big way with In Town. Sally turned back around to me and lowered his voice.

"I told you, I'm short on good help. I'm counting on you, kid, nobody else can do it."

He was right about that, but what he didn't say was, nobody else would touch it with a ten-foot pole. Overhead, a jet taking off from Logan practically drowned out our conversation. Probably a couple more of Sally's "soldiers" were on it, heading south to Florida until the heat died down. After last night, Patty had more experience being under fire than anybody in any of Sally's crews.

"Sally," I said once the plane's noise died down, "I can't take care of nothing until I know who's coming after me. Are you absolutely positive this ain't a guinea thing, you'll pardon the expression."

"Hey," he said, "we don't use spics."

"You sure about that?"

He slumped down. "Okay, correction. I don't use spics. I can't speak for nobody else. I grant you, that other guy there, that friend of mine in Worcester, he did. That's why he's doing two hundred years. The spics ratted him out. I tell Blinky a million times, watch yourself, they're no fuckin' good, but he says, who else am I gonna use? Any Americans over there have kids, first thing they do is get the fuck out, move to Saugus, Revere, Winthrop, anywhere except maybe Chelsea, which is even worse, if that's possible."

He shook his head slowly, sadly, and shook another cigarette out of his pack.

"Who the fuck is gonna send a white kid to a public school in Boston? Which is why there ain't no white kids hanging out on the corners no more, or maybe you ain't noticed?"

"I've noticed."

See, our way of life is over. It was never what it was made out to be in the movies, but now it's nothing. I see young guys, not many but a few, they want to be the next Dutch Schultz or Al Capone. Idiots is what they are. I don't care, I'm just passing through. I don't blame Sally's guys getting the fuck out of Dodge before the shooting starts. There's nothing left here worth getting capped over. I have to stay, just like Sally. It's the old rule about captains going down with the ship.

As much as I possibly can, I now avoid the day-to-day wiseguy stuff. You just never know who's a rat anymore. Drugs are the worst, of course, but these snitches are reporting back to the cops about every goddamn thing. I still go to wakes and funerals, because I'm expected to. But any social events, forget about it. As hard as I try to avoid everybody, I still run into wiseguys who want to talk. They try to tell me something, they got something going, do I know anybody needs some work? Later, when something goes wrong, because it always goes wrong, Sally or the guy's uncle will start asking questions, wanting to know who knew about this score? If I don't know nothing, nobody can suspect me of ratting them out.

So whenever somebody leans over and whispers in my ear, like he's gonna pass on some good gossip or a hot tip, I put my hands up. 'Please,' I say, 'I don't want to know.' There's only one thing I'm interested in anymore: if somebody gets hit, I want to know who did it. Because I absolutely have to know who's capable of doing that kind of wet work.

Myself, I'm capable. Very capable. I know, it's supposed to be up to other people to say how tough you are, but I'm just quoting everybody else, trust me on that. See, what my job boils down to is basically human relations. In corporations, HR handles the job searches, hires the headhunter firms, figures out which health insurance to buy and so on. But let's face it—there are two major reasons why companies have HR departments. The first is so they'll have some place to dump all the incompetent affirmative-action hires where they can't get into too much trouble. The second, and more important reason for HR, is to have a group of people who know how to fire bad employees while making sure the company doesn't get sued.

In the rackets, nobody gets fired. Sometimes they get run off, but that can be risky too, because if they fucked up here, chances are they're going to fuck up in the next place they end up. And then they get to thinking about what they know from back in Boston that they could trade up, and how they might be able to snitch themselves into the Witness Protection Program if they can point the finger at somebody else high enough up in the rackets.

So we frown on people leaving town. Like Don Corleone, we like to keep our friends close and our enemies closer, until someone from HR—that would be me—can work out a severance plan, if you know what I mean.

Another thing I do is, I put shit on the record. That means, I tell Sally what I'm doing. He isn't exactly my boss, but I still have to answer to him. He's number one, and I'm number one-A. So if I'm going to talk to a cop, I tell Sally. I don't want nobody running to him behind my back and whispering in his ear, 'I seen McCarthy talking to a fed.' Guys have gotten hit for less. I also let him know if I'm going down to Lewisburg, or Otisville, to talk to a guy.

This is the kind of shit I'm always thinking about when I talk to Sally.

"You hear anything about a grand jury?" I asked him.

"All I ever hear about is some fuckin' grand jury somewhere," he said. "Boston, Worcester, Providence, you wanna talk to me, get in line, motherfuckers."

"This is a new one," I said. "They're pulling in guys that're doing federal bits. They're asking them about this problem we got."

"You got some names to go with that?" Sally paused. "No, I take that back. Don't tell me no names."

It's a funny thing, sometimes the cons inside know more about what's going on outside than we do. They get visits from the cops and prosecutors all week, and from their girlfriends and assorted wiseguys every weekend. And when they do get subpoenaed to come back to Boston to testify before some grand jury, they have to make sure they have a story that will stand up, or they'll be in deep shit when they get sent back to their home prison. You don't want to be known as a rat inside. This is why the feds have set up their own separate rat prisons, if you don't quite rate the Witness Protection Program. Tough places to do time, from what I hear, because everybody's trying to rat out everybody else. A lot of foreigners in there—Russians, Israelis, Mexicans. Can't trust 'em. A guy once told me, those guys'd stick you with life to get a day off their sentences. So you can't talk—about anything.

Sally Curto took a drag on his cigarette.

"You know, I always dreamed of the day we'd have our own casinos in Boston. Figured we'd all be rolling in dough. Our own unions shaking down the owners, skimming the parking receipts, loan-sharking, all that shit, and we never would have had to even go inside the casinos and give all them retired FBI agents they'd have working security fucking hard-ons when they caught us on the surveillance cameras."

I nodded. "Lot more dough in casinos than in those Las Vegas nights."

"No shit, and the worst thing about those Las Vegas nights is, we're being robbed blind by the civilians. With casinos, we wouldn't have to worry about that shit, 'cause we'd be the ones doing the robbing."

"Maybe it still works out that way, Sal."

"Maybe," he said. "But we ain't off to an auspicious beginning.

Somebody's using us for target practice to sink the whole deal, at least that's the way I see it."

"You know what they say, Sally. Information is power. Right now we're real short on power. That's why I'm heading out this weekend. You don't wanna know where."

"Damn right I don't. Just keep me informed." He flicked his cigarette into the harbor. "On second thought, don't keep me informed."

10

IMPERSONATING A KENNEDY

The place was familiar—J.J. Foley's. The time, not so much—
10:30 a.m. Morning drinkers are a depressing, sad-sack lot. But at
least I didn't have to worry about anybody reporting back to the State
House that I was sitting down with the attorney general's top political operative/fixer/bagman, a former *Herald* reporter named Typo
Rivard.

Typo hadn't been a bad legman—feeding stuff to the rewrite
guys back in the newsroom. But when the old system withered away
and he had to start writing his own copy, he quickly ran into trouble.
The problem was, he would take a drink under extreme social pressure, pressure that for Typo usually started before lunch. By late
afternoon, when he was knocking out his stories, he was always
carrying at least half a load. He started fucking up his copy, basic
totally avoidable errors like whether a suspect was released on bail
or not, or how a vote had gone in the legislature, etc. Papers hate
to have to run corrections.

Finally, he came up with the bright idea of blaming all the errors
in his copy on typographical errors down in the composing room.

That worked, up to a point, until the *Herald* went to computers, and he was in effect setting his own type.

Soon thereafter, Typo made the move to the dark side, as Katy and her friends called it. He became a flack for a politician.

I presumed the sit-down had been called to discuss the rather mysterious auto accident involving the lieutenant governor two nights earlier on I-190 in Sterling. At 5:20 in the morning. Seventeen miles from his house. He said he'd been out looking for a cup of coffee and an early edition of the *Herald*, which was odd, considering that he no doubt had Internet service that would have enabled him to read the paper online at his house at any time after midnight. He was driving an unmarked State Police Crown Vic when he hit a patch of black ice. Or so he said. He had told reporters he was driving at the speed limit, but the State Police later estimated he'd been doing 108 miles per hour. Suddenly the lieutenant governor's nickname was Crash.

The joke was Crash was lucky he hadn't been charged with impersonating a Kennedy. Still, there was one difference between Crash and a Kennedy. When the cops arrived, he demanded to take a Breathalyzer, which he passed.

So he wasn't drunk at 5:20 in the morning. That left only two other possibilities, one of which (girlfriend) was bad, and the other of which (boyfriend) was worse. Unless of course you believed his second explanation, that he had decided to survey the damage from a recent ice storm—at night.

The governor was a lame duck—one reason casinos were on the table—and the lieutenant governor was one among many Democrats running to succeed him. Typo's boss was also being "urged" to run, as Typo told the papers, off the record, like it was some kind of state secret.

I got to Berkeley Street first and grabbed a sparkling water and lime—I'm trying to cut down on my pre-noon drinking—and read the *Herald* while I waited for my connection to arrive. The governor, the lieutenant governor, the public safety commissioner and the

State Police colonel were all refusing to release Crash's cell phone records, which would have shown who he was talking to when he suddenly floored it, either consciously or otherwise. Naturally the pols were blaming the stonewalling on the State Police. The staties, who are renowned for putting the fix in, were claiming that the phone records couldn't be released for the traditional "security reasons." Both newspapers had already appealed the decision to the secretary of state, another ambitious State House lifer who likewise wanted to run for governor.

"Jack Reilly, as I live and breathe." It was Typo Rivard. He was over sixty now, and hadn't graduated high school, forget college or law school. But every statewide officeholder was cut a little slack—allowed one or two guys on his payroll whose only job was getting the political grunt work done, no questions asked. Typo was the A.G.'s guy. He made $120,000 a year, more than anyone else in the office except his boss. His job description was "special assistant attorney general," which raised a few eyebrows, especially since it got him into Group 4 retirement group—along with police and other first-responders—where he could retire with a full boat anytime he wanted after the age of fifty-five.

Say what you will, despite his lack of formal education, Typo was undoubtedly the leading expert in the A.G.'s office on drunk-driving statutes, quite an accomplishment considering how many prosecutors and state cops the A.G. had working for him.

"Looking good, Jack," he said, lightly tapping me on the arm. "Looks like you've lost weight."

I smiled. "C'mon, you can't shit a shitter, Typo. Sit down and tell me what you want, as if I didn't know."

He frowned. "Is that brusque tone anyway to talk to someone who goes back with you as far as I do? I remember when you worked for the mayor at the State House."

"And I remember when you worked for the *Herald* and got a story that would have proven very embarrassing to us, and all you wanted in return for spiking it was a job at City Hall for your girlfriend."

Typo laughed, sat down and took a sip of his brown water—he wasn't trying to kid anybody about his drinking. "You know, Jack, I was never cut out to be a 'journalist' any more than you were cut out to be a 'cop.'"

"Typo, I'd love to bat the breeze with you, but I got a busy day, so let's get right to it. We're here to talk about Crash, because if this wasn't something that smelled really bad, you'd be handling it yourself. Has he got a girlfriend, or is he queer? I'm guessing the latter. Am I right?"

Typo banged his fist on the table. "By God, that's what I like about you, boy. Cut right through the bullshit! No politically correct euphemisms. Of course he's gay, or that's our working supposition anyway. You know how many middle-aged heterosexual men can't sleep at night—sleep apnea, perhaps, so they get up at night and drive and drive to a local rest area where they can meet their fellow insomniacs—"

"I didn't read anything about a rest stop."

"Nor will you, unless you and I putting our heads together can figure out how to pry that incident report out of the State Police's sticky little paws. To put it in a nutshell, pardon the pun, there's a pickle palace up there in Sterling, behind the twenty-four-hour rest stop. Lot less suspicious to be there, with two or three all-night restaurants or doughnut shops. A lot easier to cruise in than your traditional old dark 'rest areas' where they lock up everything at sundown. The local inverts have taken to congregating out behind the McDonald's, in their cars. Lotta complaints lately apparently, so C Troop had been sending a car around, just to scatter 'em. God knows you can't arrest 'em anymore, they got more rights than illegal aliens, especially if they're in drag."

"That's what I don't understand about this whole thing, Typo. Given the modern-day Democrat electorate in this state, wouldn't Crash be unbeatable if he came out of the closet?"

"You might think so, but on the other hand, he has to think about all the others of his, uh, stripe. How much is too much of a good thing, even in Massachusetts? Besides, it's one thing to come out on Gay Pride Day or in an op-ed piece in the *Globe*, and another thing to get busted for deviant sexual behavior."

"'Deviant?'" I said. "No such thing anymore. Sodomy's legal."

"Okay, open and gross. Lewd and lascivious. Whatever. You know what I'm talking about."

There used to be another statute on the books—being abroad in the night. It had taken on a whole new meaning in this day of transgender rights, or would have, if it hadn't been struck down as unconstitutional just like every other beautifully vague law I used to roust assholes with back when I was on the job.

"Anyway," Typo continued, "Crash sees the State Police car, panics and takes off at a hundred eight miles an hour and spins out."

"I read most of that already in the papers. Everything but a believable explanation."

Typo paid no attention to my interruption as he went on telling the story, or what he knew of it.

"All the trooper sees is a dark car speeding off south on I-190. Originally he did put it in the report that he thought it was the same car as in the rest stop, but the brass made him take it out. At the behest of the usual suspects in the Corner Office."

I shook my head. "This is not going to be easy."

"That's why I have come to you. As you know we have our own crew of staties, plainclothes, detectives, and they assure us that the guys in Area C swear he was at the alfresco bathhouse."

"Isn't he married?"

"And your point is?"

"Doesn't he have kids?"

"Adopted, from Russia."

"I can't see getting this into the papers."

"Who said anything about getting it into the papers? We just want to get him out of the governor's fight."

"This'll take time. It won't be cheap."

And then Typo said the magic words. "Money is no object."

11

CLASS OF '038

It's a hell of a thing when you have to drive four hundred miles to a prison in Lewisburg to find out what's going on in Boston. But that's just the way it is—the cons in there have a grapevine better than anything on the street. Maybe because everybody on the street is too busy robbing and stealing—and getting high, basically trying to make up for all the lost time from their earlier bits, which is why it usually isn't too long until they're back inside, once again swearing that when they get out it'll never happen again.

The fact is, if you're a wiseguy, you know you're going to have to do time sooner or later. And when you finally do get lugged, how the hell are you supposed to pass the time, except by keeping tabs on what the other wiseguys inside are doing.

It's all part of the prison paranoia. Which is another reason it sucks so much to be back, even for a few hours. All the way down, all I can ever think about as I drive are the three numbers—038. Those are the last three numbers on your Bureau of Prisons ID if you're from Boston. When I got out I swore I'd never be 038 again, but you've heard that one before, right? So far, though, I'm doing okay.

The guy I needed to talk to was Bobby Bones. He used to be on my crew when we were kids, robbing armored cars. The jeopardy got to be a little too much for me, but he tried to keep the crew going, until one day in New Hampshire when they killed a guard. Last time I checked the BOP website, he's eligible for parole in 2054, when he's eighty-six. Now that's a bit. After I drifted away and started working for, and then with, Sally, Bobby Bones added his brother Billy Bones to the crew. Now Billy too was doing what amounted to life, at Otisville, in upstate New York.

That's why I had to talk to Bobby. He and his brother had the two big Northeastern wiseguy holding pens covered. Bobby would know who was being shipped out to Boston to testify in front of any new grand juries. Once I knew who they were bringing in, I'd have a lot better idea of what the feds were up to, and that might give me a lead as to why somebody was trying to take me and Sally off the board.

At least I hoped so, because it was a large pain in the ass to have to drive down there. First of all I had to set it up to Bobby over the phone. Of course he can't call me, because I'm an ex-con and a "career criminal" and I have "OC" (organized crime) stamped on my BOP jacket. Plus, I'm not a relative, so I have to call his sister Lori in Charlestown to set up a call. His sister the junkie. Which means I have to bring her a few packets of methadone, which I have to pick up from Salt and Peppa.

I have no idea what Lori's drug of choice is, but apparently she uses the methadone as a kind of chaser. Bobby Bones tells me, don't give it to her too early in the day, she's not supposed to take nothing until she feels bad. I'm guessing she feels bad as soon as she wakes up if she doesn't have some crack or Oxys or heroin or whatever she's on. As a matter of fact, I'm betting the last time she ever felt good, anytime, was when she was in high school, maybe thirty years ago.

Anyway, he can't call until 7:00 p.m. at the earliest, and I ain't spending the day sitting in the front parlor with Lori. I mean, she didn't look all that great when she was seventeen, and if drugs can ruin Lindsay Lohan, you can imagine what they do to a Charlestown project rat. But Bobby Bones always asks, did I cut the little pink fuckin' pill in half, and I always have to lie and say yes.

When she finally gets him on the line, I have to politely tell Lori to get the fuck out of the room, please, and she cops an attitude, so while I'm talking to her brother, I have to throw her another packet of methadone.

Then I have to make sure that my cousin from Malden, a stick-up guy named Gonzo Ronzo, is still there at Lewisburg, because he's the one I have to be visiting officially. Unless you're a lawyer, you only get to visit relatives. So I want Bobby Bones to just drift over while I'm talking to Cousin Gonzo Ronzo, because it wouldn't look good if the feds thought I was catching up with a guy from my old crew.

Plus I had another problem. The shooters had put two bullets in the crankshaft of the Escalade. It was going to take Rocco days to get it back in shape, because he was having to work out of the garage in my condo, since we couldn't very well tow a bullet-riddled SUV through Somerville, Cambridge and Boston all the way back to Roxbury.

I called my car-insurance guy in Davis Square. He's connected, and he reads the newspapers, so I didn't have to tell him much before he figured it out. He offered to total it, no questions asked, which would have been a big favor ninety-nine percent of the time. But he didn't know about the hide. That was a real custom job to begin with, but the bigger problem was, I haven't even seen Marty Hide for two or three years. The word was he'd relocated to Miami, a good late-career move for sure, considering all the work he could get down there from the local Tony Montanas. He's probably even building hides on their yachts.

Good for Marty Hide, but bad for me, because I needed to get down to Lewisburg fast, and I couldn't be carrying a gun under the front seat. All these years later, they could still violate me.

There was only one thing to do. I called Patty and told her we were going out to dinner in the South End, one of those chi-chi joints where eighty percent of the customers are gay, and zero percent were born in Boston.

As soon as the waiter sashayed away after delivering our drinks, Patty narrowed her eyes.

"You must want something, Bench, if you're taking me to a nice place like this."

"C'mon, honey, relax. I just feel bad about the other night. That's all. Go ahead, drink up."

"That's another thing. You don't like me drinking, now you're trying to get me drunk. I'm not as dumb as you think I am."

She was wearing fishnet stockings and a mini-skirt. These guys in here don't know what they're missing.

"Stop staring at me like I'm a piece of meat," she said. "What do you want?"

I tried on a smile, but it didn't fit. "How'd you like to go to Lewisburg with me for the weekend?"

"Oh, great. What's my second pick, Brockton?"

"Please, Patty, it's not that bad."

"That's what you said about Otisville too, and it was so fucking cold I swear to God I saw a polar bear."

"Patty, c'mon. You know, we haven't spent a nice romantic weekend together in quite a while."

"And we won't have one in Lewisburg either. There's nothing to do there, Bench. Your fucking cousin Gonzo Ronzo always grabs my ass like I'm on the Red Line at rush hour."

I tried to look hurt. "Babe, you're practically related to Gonzo Ronzo."

"Like hell I am," she spat out. "You only want me to go with you so everybody'll be checking me out while you're talking to Bobby Bones."

She was right about that. If you bring in a broad, it becomes a family thing. Everybody gets to hug each other. That's when Gonzo Ronzo tries to grope her. But I did need "Mrs. McCarthy" for diversion. If you brought in a broad that looked like Patty . . .

"You only got to stick around an hour or so," I said, "and then you can leave and go shopping."

"Shopping. In Lewisburg. Oh be still my heart. Can I use my Cracker Barrel gift card?"

I took that as a yes, however grudging.

"Thanks, babe." I motioned the waiter for two more drinks. "I need you to do one more thing for me tomorrow."

Now she was really giving me the evil eye. She said nothing. The silence stretched on. We were staring at each other. She was daring me to say something.

"I need you to get a gun permit," I said. "The Escalade is in the shop and I can't find Marty Hide."

"So I have to get a gun permit?"

"It's no big deal. I already got it lined up. Hobart'll drive you up to New Hampshire tomorrow, the course is two hours long, and then he'll buy you a piece. I want you to keep it too, you never know these days."

"Let me guess, it'll be the same kind of gun you have in the Escalade."

"I wish, Babe, but PDW's are hard to come by on short notice. I'm thinking a six-shot thirty-eight revolver, Smith & Wesson. Real basic, nothing exotic. They're not gonna hit us on I-95. This is just in case we have to do a little walking around in Lewisburg. Anyway, we got a police chief up there in New Hampshire, he'll write you up the permit tomorrow. No waiting, no red tape."

"How can I ever thank you, Bench?"

"Lotta broads would like a license to carry, you know."

"Yeah, about as many as would like to spend a weekend in Lewisburg."

12

ALL ROADS LEAD TO WORCESTER

Walking back to my house from Foley's, I got lucky. My cell phone rang and it was a cop from District D-4, Roxbury, a guy I went to the academy with. I'd helped him out once, on the arm, getting some sneaky shots of his bride with a weightlifter who was out on disability from the Fire Department. It didn't stop the divorce, but it ruined her relationship with the kids, which was all he was really looking for.

And they say cops are crooked. Cops got nothing on "jakes." And I love the way their funerals are bigger than JFK's now. Actually, with all the new building codes, you end up with a dead jake about once every five years. Most of the time firefighters get killed nowadays, it's because some illegal alien welder working without a permit set the building on fire. But I digress. Anyway, I'd called the cop who owed me a favor for catching his wife in the sack with the hero jake and asked him to let me know if anything turned up on the Curto hit. Less than twenty-four hours later, he called me back.

"We got the gun from Parmenter Street," he said. "Just got the ballistics back. You know the Blanchard's on Mass Ave?"

A big liquor store on the South End—Roxbury line. Always had a police detail, for obvious reasons. Every stick-up guy and junkie in Boston left it alone, for that same obvious reason. Everyone except one, apparently.

"An illegal tried to stick up the place yesterday. I saw the surveillance video. He practically nodded off with his hand in the cash register. He was so stoned he didn't even see the cop coming."

"Anybody I know?"

"The cop or the perp?"

"Very funny," I said. "Was he using the same piece he used on Sally's nephew?"

"Negative. He walked in with a twenty-two, not even loaded. The gun, I mean, he was plenty loaded himself. After we grabbed him, we found the Curto piece in the trunk of his car, which was stolen, which I know comes as a terrible shock to you."

"Let me guess—he didn't have an valid inspection sticker either."

"We got him for affixing stolen license plates too." I heard raised voices behind him. "I'll call you back," he said, and hung up. I clicked on the cell phone to find out the number, and all it flashed was 617, the area code. Balls. I couldn't call him back, I'd have to rely on him to get back to me. That could be ten minutes, or a week.

I was home, working on my second Ballantine Ale, when my phone rang again.

"I'll make it quick, we got a double homicide on Blue Hill Ave," he said, and I resisted the temptation to ask him what else was new?

"He must have bought your gun as a throw down. A Walther PPK. Gun like that, had to have a history, right? Especially if a junkie was selling it. You'd think he'd at least ask whoever sold it to him where it came from."

"Like they'd tell him the truth."

"You got a point there. Anyway, the gun was on top of the spare tire, no attempt to hide it. Complete fucking moron. You want the perp's name?"

He gave it to me. José Cruz—there couldn't be more than a million of them in Massachusetts. But the address was a surprise—Worcester.

"How did he get a gun that was just used in the North End?" I asked.

"You tell me," he said. "It gets odder. He makes his one call, and five minutes later, we hear from his probation officer. Who is also his brother."

"Really?" I knew the Probation Department was crooked, but this was just plain sloppy. The way it works in probation is, if you're a P.O., your best friend takes your brother, and you take your best friend's brother. Same as the legislature with girlfriends, you hire Mistah Chairman's squeeze and he hires yours. I asked him for the brother's name, it was Pablo Cruz. Like the crappy seventies band, only they spelled it "Cruise," I think.

I said, "You're kidding me, right?"

Worcester is the Chelsea of the 508 area code. There are worse places than Worcester. There have to be. I pondered for a moment, then remembered who had the most to gain at the State House if the casino bill did a Dixie. Senator Denis "Donuts" Donahue of Worcester. And then I remembered who was in the car that got shot up in Somerville the other night—another probation officer, this one suspended.

You know what I need for Christmas—an iPad. If I had one, I wouldn't have had to even get up from my table to walk over to my laptop to check out the website of the Office of Campaign and Political Finance to find out if Pablo Cruz was one of Senator Donahue's contributors. But hell, it didn't take long even using a Hewlett-Packard. Pablo Cruz, whose employer was the Commonwealth of Massachusetts, had maxed out to the senator for the last three years.

I had my first lead.

13

HARD TIME

When I was in Lewisburg on the contempt beef, I did a lot of reading, mainly biographies. I read one on Jimmy Cagney, and for some reason I've always recalled what he said about Joan Blondell—best ass in Hollywood. I was curious, so when I got out I bought a couple of her old movies on DVDs, and Cagney was right.

The reason I mention this is because that's how I regarded Patty: best ass in Somerville, make that Boston. But damn, she had an attitude, probably because she knew how to strut her stuff. She was a great broad when things were going well, but you wouldn't want her beside you in a foxhole. Now that I think about it, I remember another line from some book I read in the can: "Adversity often brings two people together, but not when they are of opposite sexes."

These teen moms in the projects, they routinely carry their homeys' heat in their purses. I doubt any of them are busting their baby daddies' balls over it either. And let's face it—Patty had a lot better life than her fellow teenagers. She didn't have to drop a new little bastard every year for an extra $110 a month on the Electronic Benefits Transfer card.

But that didn't stop her from copping a major attitude on me.

Anyway, I rented a new Escalade while she and Hobart were in New Hampshire buying the piece, taking her lesson and getting the permit. They got back around 8:00 p.m. I was sitting by myself in the Alibi, paying some bills as she stomped in in her high heels, Hobart following sheepishly behind her.

"Look at my hands!" she said, thrusting them in front of my face. They looked fine to me.

"They took prints of every one of my fingers," she said, "like I was some kind of criminal or something."

"That's what they do when they give you a license to carry, baby," I said. "It's the law. What's the big deal?" I looked at Hobart and he shrugged.

"You know what else they told me?" she said. "I can't carry the gun in the car, unless it's taken apart."

"That's bullshit," I said. "Tell her, Hobart."

"I did. But she don't believe me. The chief told her she had to carry it on her person. I tried to tell her, her 'person' includes a purse."

Hands on her hips, her eyes narrowed as she focused her ire on Hobart. "Since when are you a fucking lawyer?" She turned back to me. "I've seen Hobart go out with you on collections. He wears a holster."

"Patty, he wears a holster because he doesn't carry a purse. Right, Hobart?"

Hobart just rolled his eyes.

"I'm not wearing a holster," she said. "I don't work out three hours a day to have some piece bulging out of my Spandex."

I thought about telling her she should have bought an ankle holster, but I wanted to go have dinner and I didn't feel like two hours of hot tongue and cold shoulder. You know how it is. They never say something once when they can say it a hundred times. I finally got her calmed down and took her into the North End to Bricco for dinner, then back to my place in Ball Square—no jokes please. We got a few hours sleep and we were on the road by 3:00 a.m. I wanted to be there when visitors' hours started at nine.

One thing I've learned over the years, both inside and out, is that if a guy comes in by himself to talk to a con, the screws will keep an eye on him. They figure he's up to no good, and they're almost always right. Bring a broad in, and they relax. Bring a good-looking broad in, and you might as well be invisible.

Hubba hubba hubba, as the GI Joes say in the old World War II movies. Va va va voom. What a pair o' gams, and what a pair of everything else. That was Patty, a Betty Grable for the twenty-first century. That was her job, that and the gun, just in case. I wasn't lying when I told her we didn't figure to get whacked on the New Jersey Turnpike. But you can't assume anything. Like Sally says, assumptions are the mother of fuck-ups.

Patty was muttering as we got out of the car in the prison parking lot. She knew what was in store. There's supposed to be a female C.O. to handle the pat downs at the metal detector, but there never is. So she had to sign a five-page waiver, including initialing the bottom of each page, agreeing to be frisked by a male guard. Then she got the usual thorough examination/groping from an unshaven C.O. reeking of fortified wine. Finally we made our way down the hall to the visitors' area, which is an open room.

Gonzo Ronzo was waiting for me, and it wasn't long before Bobby Bones drifted in.

It always amazes me, whenever I'm down there, how many guys I see that I served time with. Mainly New York LCN wiseguys. Before I sat down, I had to pay my respects to them, including the traditional kissy-face. Thank God Sally doesn't go in for that kind of stuff, maybe because we see too much of each other to waste time with the goombah nonsense. I introduced Patty all around, and even though most of them had met her before, a lot of them wanted to tell me again how nice it was that I had taken up with a sweet Italian girl. As I made my rounds, Gonzo Ronzo and Bobby Bones were following us, or should I say Patty, with their eyes.

I finally pulled up a chair across from Gonzo Ronzo and Bobby Bones. After a while, Gonzo Ronzo got up and drifted away, towards

Patty. I didn't have time to worry about that—I'd be hearing about it all the way back to Somerville anyway. I just wanted to find out what Bobby Bones knew and then get the hell out of there. I filled him in on our problem.

"Me and Sally don't even know who's coming after us," I said. "I come down here, I need to find out, is there something going on I don't know about?"

Bobby looked at me for a second, then said, "You heard about the grand jury?"

"Bones, I'm always hearing about a grand jury. What's going on with this one?"

"You ever talk to that rat motherfucker Peanuts Merlino?"

Peanuts Merlino, a fucking no-good quote-unquote made man from East Boston. I remembered him from Walpole, when I was a kid, doing my first bit. He was shooting heroin, inside, even then. Years ago, Sally Curto had told him to stay on his side of the tunnel, in East Boston, or Sally would have him whacked. An empty threat, probably, but Merlino never showed his face on Hanover Street, as far as I knew.

Peanuts was also a free man, as far as I knew. But here in the can, he was apparently number one on the Hit Parade. This is why I come down here all the time.

I said, "Merlino's a rat? He's, like, the underboss of East Boston, after Blinky."

"He's another fucking Whitey Bulger is what he fucking is," said Bobby. "They say he's been wired for twelve years. He was wearing a wire all them years they was having that gang war in Eastie. He must have ordered at least a half-dozen hits, did more'n few himself most likely. And the fucking feds had him wired. I heard they even paid the monthly bill on his cell phone."

This explained a few things. Merlino had come by the Alibi about a year earlier, chatting me up. First he starts in with the usual shit, "Bench, do you remember when?" I don't remember nothing, especially if the statute of limitations hasn't run out, or if it's something there's no statute of limitations on. He asked me, did I want to make some easy dough? Is the Pope Catholic? But like I told you, I never deal with junkies under any circumstances. He told me anyway that he needed an arbitrator, I guess you'd call it. A mediator. Someone who was respected, to settle some beefs. Didn't make any sense, him coming to me instead of Sally, but the feds probably put him up to it, figuring I'd bite. I told him he'd have to clear it with Sally, which was my polite way of telling Peanuts to go fuck himself.

"You never did nothing with him, did you, Bench?" Bobby Bones said.

"I wouldn't tell that no-good rat bastard shit if his mouth was full of it. But what's this got to do with me getting shot at by Dominicans and crooked P.O.s in Somerville?"

"Everybody over there in East Boston is done for. Peanuts has been wearing a wire and doing business with all them guys all those years. They got guys on tape bragging about scores they'd forgotten they ever done. And this ain't no rumor either."

"I don't get it," I said. "How can he still be walking around if everybody knows he's wearing a wire?"

Bobby Bones smiled. "He ain't walking around no more, Bench. That's the point. Merlino has fucking vanished—you can take that one to the bank. They know he's gone 'cause there was one dealer in Day Square that owed him fifty grand, and he had it ready for Peanuts, and Peanuts didn't show up to collect."

This was where Sally's feuds worked against him. When he got pissed at somebody, if he didn't have him whacked, Sally would never speak to the guy again. I don't know how many guys he's told, don't ever set foot on Hanover Street or I'll stick your hand in the toaster. Sometimes these guys come to me, ask me to intercede with Sally, trying to make things right. Not once has he ever relented. When you make Sally's shit list, you've made it for life. So half the wiseguys in the city aren't speaking to him, so he doesn't get enough information about what's going on out on the street, and what happens is big fucking hairy two-legged warts like Peanuts Merlino develop right under his nose.

And Blinky's. I blamed Blinky more than Sally, actually. He should have put all this shit on the record.

"Has Blinky got a problem?" I asked, but before Bobby Bones could answer, I felt a tapping on my shoulder. I turned around and saw Patty.

"Honey, can I have the keys to the car? I wanna go shopping."

I handed over the keys and didn't even ask her when she was coming back. I wasn't thinking about anything except what a jackpot Sally's Eastie crew was in if Bobby Bones knew what he was talking about, and I had no doubt that he did.

I said, "Blinky don't tell us nothing about this."

"If somebody you'd been running with for twenty years had flipped, and he had you on tape, would you want anyone else to know about it?"

Obviously not. If you were Blinky, the best thing that could happen is that the wiseguys that Peanuts hadn't recorded would start moving in on your rackets. The worst thing that could happen was guys like me and Sally would decide to turn you over to Human Resources, because if you were going down, obviously you couldn't be trusted.

"Are you sure about this?" I asked.

Bobby Bones said, "The reason I hear about it is—you remember that kid, the Fonz, Peanuts' nephew?"

The Fonz was in for attempted extortion. He'd been collecting bad debts for one of his uncle's bookies, and he'd left a death threat on some mark's voice mail. I'm not saying he's the only guy who's ever done something that stupid, but most times, it gets straightened out, or pleaded out, before it goes to trial.

Bobby Bones said, "The Fonz checked out of here last week. He had some song-and-dance about a state grand jury after some motorcycle gang up in Beachmont that was running a meth lab and he was just gonna take the contempt citation 'cause it's concurrent on the extortion beef. He tells us they're sending him to Otisville to throw him in the hole. Like he's a fuckin' martyr, a stand-up guy, but that's bullshit."

"How can you be sure?"

Bobby Bones grinned again. "My brother Billy's got someone in records up in Otisville there. I asked him to check, just to satisfy my own curiousity. The Fonz ain't gettin' thrown in no hole, he ain't even going to Otisville, he's going into WITSEC. He's cooperating."

Gonzo Ronzo had drifted back over. He was still standing up, listening to us talk.

"This is worse than I thought," I said. Everybody who was any-body in Eastie appeared to be in jeopardy, which usually meant they would be ready to take some chances. They had to lay in some dough—not for lawyers, nobody paid for their own lawyers anymore. What was the point? If the feds get you on tape, you have a better chance of hitting the Lottery than beating the rap. It's better to save the money and give it to your family. Indigent is one of those words that no wiseguy ever heard of until maybe ten years ago.

Nowadays, when you get pinched, the first thing you say is not "I want to make my phone call." The first thing you say is "I'm indigent."

Bobby Bones shook his head. "If Peanuts was wired, Bench, and I guarantee he was, it'll be a giant cluster-fuck for all you guys up there. It's almost enough to make me glad I'm in here for another thirty-two years. Almost."

14

A TOUGH STREET KID FROM LINCOLN

Even though I'm in politics, sort of, I don't buy the *Globe* anymore, me and 300,000 other former subscribers, and 450,000 on Sundays. Why support assholes who are trying to destroy me, and everybody like me? But I still read it, online, at least the stories they don't charge for. If they try to force me to sign up for the "free thirty-day trial," I'm outta there.

I always read the *Herald* first, but this morning, after making quick work of the "feisty tabloid," I went over to bostonglobe.com. Nothing much struck my fancy there either, until I saw the headline on Ted McGee's piss-poor column: "Underworld mayhem: casinos' first casualties."

So now it starts, the public-relations war against the casino bill. The *Globe*'s reasonable-doubt-at-a-reasonable-price columnist was making the pitch against casinos, on the grounds that the hoodlums were already littering the sidewalks with victims as they fought for control.

"The EMT looked down at the crumpled body of the young Dominican curled up in a fetal position on the floor of the front seat of his stolen SUV on Winter Hill in Somerville.

"'Another gang war,'" the EMT was saying. "'Comes as regular as clockwork around here. And this time you know what it's about . . .'"

As always, the EMT—or cop, or hero jake, or whoever—had no last name. This time, he didn't even have a first name. Because of course there was no EMT. Ted McGee was a fraud. He wasn't a tough street kid from Boston; he was from Lincoln. He also wasn't a Vietnam vet and he wasn't a reporter; he was a shakedown artist. He was so damn authentic he called Boston Beantown at least once per column.

I went back to the column, where the EMT was delivering more salt-of-the-earth Joe Sixpack wisdom.

"'These pols on Beacon Hill don't care what happens on the streets. They've never been on the street.'" Neither had Ted McGee, as far as I could tell, unless maybe it was Brattle Street in Cambridge. Now it was time for some hard-boiled narrative to break up the made-up quotes, probably lifted from an out-of-print paperback collection of Jimmy Breslin or Jimmy Cannon columns.

"This double-slaying had all the earmarks of Bench McCarthy's mob." Funny, the way I'd heard it, the Dominican and his P.O. pal had been chasing Bench. "Bench is a guy who operates out of a Winter Hill bar, the Alibi, where the first shot is on the house and after that you have to use your own bullets." If he were still alive, Johnny Carson could have sued for plagiarism. "They are merely the latest victims in what will be a long and bloody struggle to control the pols' latest misguided boondoggle to generate more revenue. A few days earlier, Sally Cuarto, the plug-ugly who rules the North End with an iron fist, saw his nephew gunned down at an after-hours card game. Then his consigliere was blown up. This war is just getting started."

Sally Cuarto? The tough street kid from Lincoln couldn't even spell the underboss's name right? And nobody on the city or the copy desk picked up on it? You can bet the *Globe* never misspells Barney Frank's name.

I had almost reached the bottom of the page. That meant it was time for the nameless EMT to return with one final, jarring pearl of wisdom.

"'Nobody'll see Bench now until it's over. He's gone to the mattresses.'" Now he was lifting a line from *The Godfather*. "'There will be a lot of mothers wearing black, a lot of funerals in Beantown before this casino war is over, but what do the solons care? All they're looking for is their next payoff.'"

In other words, the "solons" were a lot like Ted McGee himself. I poured myself a second cup of coffee and called Katy Bemis on her cell phone.

"What do you want?" she began pleasantly.

"I want to know what the fuck is going on with Ted McGee's column this morning."

"That's Ted McGee's job, to make people ask what the fuck is going on with Ted McGee's column this morning."

"I know that EMT and he claims he was misquoted."

"Very funny," she said. "You know as well as I do there was no EMT."

"That's what I mean. How the hell does he get away with it?"

"What are you, the *Columbia Journalism Review*? He's been doing this for thirty years. You must have some dog in this fight, and his name is Bench."

"Not really," I said without much conviction.

"I mean, I never knew you to care much one way or another what was written about you or anybody else, especially by the likes of Ted McGee."

"I just got an idea," I said. "You want to go to the game tonight? My treat."

"I have a saying. Beware of Jack Reilly bearing gifts."

"What's that supposed to mean?"

"It means I don't trust you. What are you after?"

"If I show you something at the game tonight, will you help me out?"

She paused before continuing. "Jack, you seem to forget how well I know you. I remember helping you out one time, and it almost got me killed."

"And it got you a job at that fine newspaper working with such distinguished scribes as Ted McGee."

"What do you really want?"

Now it was my turn to pause. She knew what I really wanted was to have her back, but I couldn't admit it. I could handle my own sleuthin' at the State House, but cutting her on this story was a way to maybe start repairing the relationship. Working stories with her had been my entrée into her life to begin with, and maybe if I could show her I was on to something . . .

"The pregnant pause is duly noted," she said. "I assume you're trying to think up a good story."

"Why don't you just come to the game with me tonight? What have you got to lose?" I thought of adding, certainly not your virginity, but she didn't seem to be in a playful mood this morning. I told her I'd meet her at the Eastern Standard in Kenmore Square at 6:30. I offered to pick her up at the *Globe*, but she just sneered at my suggestion. Luckily, my Oldsmobile didn't take it personally.

15

A MATURE INDUSTRY

I've got money problems. Not cash-flow problems, which would mean things would be okay once I tracked down a few deadbeats and put a gun to their heads and asked them if they wanted to play Russian roulette with a full chamber.

No, my problem was the rackets were coming apart at the seams. They already had come apart at the seams. In the financial pages they call these "secular" as opposed to "cyclical" changes in an industry, a mature industry if you will, in this case the rackets.

As I've told you, I'm into drugs, but I keep them at arm's length. I need buffers, and the buffers cut into my end. But I can't operate without buffers, because otherwise drugs are too fucking risky. Can't trust anybody, especially once they get into sampling their own wares.

Unions are gone too, at least the kind of unions I grew up with: Teamsters, longshoremen, ironworkers and such. Nobody unloads ships anymore except with cranes. Then they put the loads on flatbed trucks. It doesn't matter how quickly you can cut the fifth wheel, you still can't get inside a cross-country load with anything less than a bazooka.

Nowadays the only real unions with any dough are in the public sector, like the Service Employees International Union, most of whose members are either illegals or hacks. From pinky rings to nose rings in less than one generation.

Gambling ain't what it used to be either. The Lottery runs numbers nowadays. Football's okay, but it's only sixteen Sundays a year, plus play-offs, and unlike the daily handle at the tracks, you can't fix games. Or at least I can't.

I used to be a stick-up guy. That's how everybody starts. I don't count burglaries. In my neighborhood, even the National Honor Society students did B&Es. They were a gateway crime, you might say, to armed robberies. From the start, I planned every one of my stick-ups down to the most minute detail. One time Bobby Bones and I took a bank in downtown Malden across the street from a freight rail line. Every morning at ten, a mile-long freight train rumbled through the downtown, cutting off the bank from the police station for four minutes. Exactly four minutes. That was all we needed. You could check it out with the Malden P.D. It's still an open case.

Problem is, for every job like that there's ten others where every fucking thing goes wrong. It's like they say about war, once the shooting starts, you can throw out all your plans. I used to front armored-car jobs. But no more, because you need so many guys, and these days at least one of 'em's bound to be a drug addict, or have an itchy trigger finger, or both. You're a hundred yards away sitting in a crash car and some Oxy zombie gets jumpy and starts shooting and your life's over. Just ask Bobby Bones.

I don't even bother hijacking local trucks anymore unless they're carrying smokes or electronics, and even then I usually subcontract the heists to the kids from Southie. Everything has gotten too risky. I had a convenience store once in Union Square. I figured I could use a free load of groceries to cut down on the overhead, so we followed this truck out of the warehouse in New Bedford every Tuesday morning for weeks. Everybody's a creature of habit, and every haul this truck driver pulled into a truck stop on Route 24 in Randolph for a piss and a cup of coffee. Simple—we didn't even have to hit the driver over the head, or pretend to. Just wait 'til he got inside, and then hot-wire the truck.

It went smooth, perfect in fact, until we got the truck back to the garage, pried open the back and saw . . . two backhoes. Oh sure, I unloaded them eventually, but what I'd really needed were those dry goods. I finally sold the grocery store to an Indian.

So I've got the "Irish" rackets all locked up, for what that's worth, and it ain't much these days. Sally's got a guy he needs straightened out, I straighten him out, and he pays me "expenses," because we're supposed to be partners and all that. Then there's the Alibi, the garage and my little place in Allston.

In the cellar of the Alibi, I run my own Filene's Basement, where I stock the stolen goods sold to me by the younger hijackers, the ones who haven't figured out yet that, if you put it into hourly terms, trucks aren't worth grabbing anymore. Fencing stolen stuff is okay, but you end up giving away half the stuff. The fucking cops are the worst, of course. Get a load of furs and suddenly every cop on the job has not only a wife but a girlfriend. The Southie and Charlestown crews I buy from don't even grab furs anymore; it's not worth it to them. The cops broke up the fur-theft trade not by any great police work but simply by stealing so much stuff off the hijackers and the fences. Now the cops have to buy their own fur coats. Serves them right, the greedy fucks.

I figured I'd be okay once football season started, but for the time being, I needed cash. So I called a loan shark. I could have gone to Sally, I suppose, but that would have altered the balance of power. I already told you Sally's tighter than a frog's ass. Loan-sharking's another racket that ain't what it used to be—how can you compete against Visa or MasterCard? There's a few old-time loan sharks around, and I was on my way to meet one, Henry Sheldon. He'd started out in Roxbury, but had followed his clientele south to Weymouth years ago. He now operated out of a strip mall in a tired neighborhood where approximately ninety percent of the population was originally from Southie, Dorchester or Roxbury.

I pulled into a parking space in front of his office and walked in. He was the only one there—not much security considering he was supposed to have at least $25,000 on him at all times, which he was going to lend to me today.

I sauntered into his fly-specked storefront office and grabbed a chair in front of his desk. He was seated behind it, telephone in hand, haranguing a deadbeat client, threatening him with physical harm. It was an empty threat. Reddington had no muscle and he went maybe 320 pounds on a five-eight frame.

"Don't make me get ugly," he yelled into the phone. Too late Henry—not to get ugly, I mean. He was about fifty, a sparse comb-over matted across his skull by sweat. He smelled like he'd already made his first trip of the day to the mean shebeen two doors down.

Sheldon had a cigarette dangling from his mouth. After hanging up, he rose and leaned across the desk to shake my hand. His was clammy.

"Bench," he said, "I don't see you as much as I used to."

I shook my head. "Weymouth's not really my neck of the woods."

"And Roxbury isn't mine anymore either."

"I got guys who handle Weymouth for me." And they're such good earners, I'm sitting in Henry Sheldon's office, hat in hand.

"Bench," he said, "remember the—"

"Henry," I said, "I don't do 'do you remembers'? Nothing personal."

"I understand," he said, smiling, showing off some cheap MCI-Norfolk dental work from his last bit. "Do you talk about the paper? 'Cause you're in it this morning."

He tossed the *Globe* over to me. I'd gotten a couple of calls on my cell phone driving down, but the guys who had phoned me weren't exactly rocket scientists, and they hadn't been able to convey the gist of the piece. As soon as I saw the Ted McGee byline, I knew it had to be bullshit.

Some reporters are okay. Or so I've been told. Most of 'em, in my opinion, ought to be picked up as common nightwalkers. I can't believe the shit they print, and I know where it all comes from, the police reports. As far as I can tell, they fucking believe that just because something's in a police report, it's true. Or maybe they realize at least half of it's bullshit, but they don't care, because it's a public document, so they don't have to worry about being sued. As if any wiseguys were going to sue them anyway.

I read the column over quickly and tossed the paper back on the desk. I said nothing. What's the point of refuting bullshit from some guy who doesn't even know how to spell Sally's name? James Michael Curley used to say, "Never complain, never explain." Words to live by. But Henry kept staring at me.

"So what's going on?" Henry asked.

"Henry, I don't do—"

"Yeah, yeah, I know. You don't do 'what's going on?' questions." He picked up a pack of cigarettes, tapped out a smoke and lit it. Then he reached into his top drawer and took out a thick business-sized envelope. Inside was the twenty-five grand, in one-hundred-dollar bills, judging from the heft of the envelope.

"Want to count it?" he said, and I shook my head.

"Vig's three points a week, which is—"

"Seven fifty," I said. "I know. I went to Somerville High."

"You know what they say about Somerville. You learn how to add, but never how to divide." He chuckled softly.

"Is that what they say, Henry? About Somerville, I mean?"

"Look, Bench, I didn't mean nothing by it, it was just a little joke." This guy was petrified of me. I liked that. "Just like asking you those questions about McGee's column. It's just, when it's in the papers—"

"Henry, you asked me a question, you got a right to an answer. The answer is, everything in that column is complete bullshit, and that includes the 'the's' and the 'and's.' The cocksucker is just trying to stir up trouble, is all. That's all you need to know. Your money's safe. I'm not going anywhere."

"Was that you that the spics shot at on Broadway?"

"They're dead, aren't they?"

"One of 'em is, or so I heard," he said. "I thought you were going to say, I don't do 'was that you' questions."

"Henry, you're right. You know what? I don't do 'was that you' questions."

Henry Sheldon stood up. Jesus, he'd gotten even fatter lately. He hadn't worn a belt for years, but now even the suspenders couldn't hide his gut.

"I don't mean to seem like a shy or anything, but how are we going to work these payments out? Maybe we could set up a time every week that I can come by the Alibi." He saw me grimace; having a sweaty fat guy coming around looking for money from me every week wouldn't be good for business. My business, that is. It'd be great for his, being able to drop my name all over town.

"Okay, okay," he said. "I get it. You don't do meetings."

"It's easier that way," I said. "I'll be around. We'll run into each other. I'm good for it. You know me."

"I do," he said. "I do indeed."

16

"I'M A GIRL WATCHER"

Katy had insisted on driving her own car to meet me at the Eastern Standard. I guess she was afraid I'd exercise my seductive powers on her to lure her back to my love nest on Shawmut Avenue to show her my etchings, after which I'd use her for my own unspeakable ends.

Like we hadn't ever . . . never mind. If she wanted to drop forty dollars for parking in Kenmore Square on a game night, it was okay by me. These days you need a home-equity loan to go to a Red Sox game. It's been a long time since a bleacher seat cost three bucks. It was back when my father started taking me to games, come to think of it.

While I waited for her at the Eastern Standard, I was sitting by myself at a sidewalk deuce nursing a twelve-dollar martini. The maître d' who seated me had pulled out the chair on the right, State House side, but I wanted the other seat, so I could face back toward Beacon Hill. It gave me a much better view of the local talent strolling into the park. It was still May, too cool for the really good girl-watching, when they're wearing next to nothing. On the other hand, the coeds were still in town, so the average age was a little lower, and the butts a little tighter, than in July and August.

I'd been girl-watching for about ten minutes when Katy arrived. Tight-fitting slacks, a low-cut blouse under a dark jacket, and her light-brown hair swept straight back under a Saks Fifth Avenue headband. I've never seen a Yankee dress as stylishly, or as provocatively, as she did, but as she would be sure to tell me, how many Yankees did I know anyway?

I smiled and stood up. She sat down and looked bored as she stared at the backs of the throngs of fans filing by on their way into Fenway.

"You never change, do you, Jack?" she said.

"I don't know what you mean," I said.

"Sitting out here checking out the babes. You don't mind paying an exorbitant amount for a drink if you can see the scantily clad teenagers prancing by."

She reads me like a book. "There'll be more scantily clad in another month or so. It's a little cool for May, don't you think? Still sweater weather at night."

Katy gave the waiter her order and then took a deep breath.

"Okay, Ace, now tell me why you wanted me to bring my binoculars along?"

"We're gonna do some sneaky stuff. I remember when you used to like to do sneaky stuff. Now I'm not so sure. Sometimes I think you'd rather be seen at a time for Elizabeth Warren at her cheese shop in Harvard Square than take in the Olde Towne Team with your old—"

"My ex," she said firmly, as my eyes wandered toward a twenty-something brunette wearing practically nothing, a harbinger of sweltering summer evenings to come. Suddenly I felt a sharp pain on the right side of my face. Katy had slugged me with her $400 Gucci purse, and I could already feel the throbbing welt that the buckle had left on my cheek.

"Don't you ever, ever look at another woman like that when you're with me." My face stung. It wasn't the first time she'd slapped me for "lookism," as they say at Smith College. But this one didn't sting like a slap from an ex, it felt like the way she used to hit me when we were in a fever hotter than a pepper sprout. For a second or two I was actually seeing stars. It hurt like she still cared.

"I thought you were the one who always said, 'Fifteen'll get you twenty,'" she hissed. "Now finish your damn drink and let's get out of here, you damn perv."

We had great seats, upstairs, in a box shared by two law firms that each used to have one of their own before the economic tailspin. The only person I knew was the waitress, Donna, and all I needed from her was a couple of Häagen-Dazs chocolate bars in the sixth inning. Katy and I got settled in the top row, right under the heater, so the dropping temperatures weren't a problem.

I had her binoculars out as soon as we got there and started scanning the seats along the first base line. No one showed up until the bottom of the first inning, a fashionable arrival time for the Beautiful People. Let's face it, unless it's the Yankees, who really cares who the Sox are playing? You're only there to watch the Sox, and be seen yourself, of course.

I scanned the two middle-aged guys making their way to the seats and smiled. I handed the binoculars to Katy and told her to scan five seats down from the home plate edge of the Sox dugout.

"Ted McGee," she said. "So what?"

"You know whose seats those are?"

"I have a feeling you're about to tell me."

"They belong to Senator Denis Donahue. Also known as 'Donuts.' Are *Globe* columnists supposed to be taking two-hundred-dollar seats from crooked hacks?"

"Maybe he bought them."

"And maybe my family came over on the *Mayflower*."

"How do you know they're Donuts' seats?"

"A burning bush told me."

She was still peering through the binoculars. "Who's the guy with him?"

Katy handed the binoculars to me. I put down my beer and trained them on the guy sitting next to the columnist. He looked familiar. It took me a second, but I finally made him—Drew Amato, the commissioner of probation. I told Katy and she frowned.

"He's supposed to be dirty, isn't he?" she said.

"His first name is 'commissioner.' What do you think?"

"Wasn't one of the guys who got shot in Somerville an ex-probation officer?" she said, her interest growing.

"They've fired a few P.O.s, some others are suspended with pay." I always love that. Suspended with pay—also known as a vacation. "At least that's what I read somewhere. Supposedly somebody was selling P.O. jobs."

She took the binoculars back from me. "They're having quite the animated conversation."

That they were. And I don't think it was about the Green Monster. Shit, I wished I were better at lip-reading. Times like this it was good to have a guy like Bench McCarthy around. They said he was a master at reading lips; that's the kind of skill you pick up when you're in Walpole at age eighteen.

I looked over at Katy. "You still think your boy McGee is on the level."

"I never said he was on the level. I said that just because he wrote an anti-casino column doesn't mean he's in the satchel."

"How about going to the game with the commissioner of probation?"

"What do you want me to say?" she said. "He's a columnist; I'm a reporter. He was a finalist for the Pulitzer Prize once."

"Until they found out he was piping the columns."

She took a deep breath. "Look, Jack, why don't we both just take the night off? These are great seats." She squeezed my forearm. "Not everything has to be a conspiracy, you know." She smiled at me. I hadn't seen that grin in months. I immediately forgot Ted McGee and Drew Amato and didn't think of them again until the next morning.

17

VISITING HOURS, 2-4, 7-9

I had to put in an appearance at Hole in the Head's wake. It was, of course, at Rossetti's in the West End. Rossetti's went way back, and I couldn't count how many wakes I've been to there. Sometimes even for guys I'd taken care of myself. That was when an appearance really was mandatory.

Years ago, the Rossettis bought the building right behind their funeral home, and then knocked down the abutting building's back wall and connected it to the funeral parlor. Since then all the wise-guys would get dropped off in back and come through the other building and avoid all the feds in wingtips and the TV cameramen loitering outside the front door wearing those stupid lanyards.

Must be ten years now that we'd been coming in the back, and the feds still hadn't figured it out. Filed away somewhere in the J. Edgar Hoover building in Washington, D.C., they've probably got 209s and 302s, stating authoritatively that the Boston LCN no longer attends wakes of their deceased members. Now that I think about it, why are all these G-men called "special agents"? What's so special about them?

Normally I would have driven myself, but I didn't like the ominous drift this thing had taken. Leaving a car somewhere, especially at night, can make you a sitting duck. Sometimes they slash your tires, so you can't get away, and even if you make it back inside the car, you're an easy target. So I had a kid from the garage give me a lift, and as I got out I told him to drive back to Roxbury, lock the gates tight, keep somebody else there with him at the garage on overtime, and wait for me to call him for a pickup.

I opened the back door to Rossetti's and was greeted by JoJo Rossetti, the older brother. They were a political family, like a lot of funeral home owners used to be. JoJo had been the state rep, and he'd done federal time with me and Sally in Lewisburg when we were doing our time for contempt of the grand jury. JoJo had been in for assaulting a DEA agent, I still have no idea why, because I never asked, and he never told me. After JoJo got out, the voters in their gratitude promoted him to the Governor's Council. I always thought that was only fitting and proper, that at least one of the eight politicians who has to vote on state judgeships should be an ex-con.

JoJo smiled when he saw me and even took the cigarette out of his mouth. He still calls them "racks," not packs.

"Mr. McCarthy," he said, pronouncing my name correctly. "How's your hammer hangin'?"

"I been better," I said. "How's the family taking it?"

I heard a long moan from the larger parlor, followed by a female scream. JoJo rolled his eyes.

"What a mess," he whispered. "I thought the bodies that get left in the trunks at the airport in the summer were bad, but those ain't nothing compared to this here. I ain't seen nothin' like this since I got back from 'Nam."

"You're telling me it's a closed casket?"

"Closed? Bench, there ain't nothing in there but . . . body pieces. You ever hear the phrase 'empty suit'? That's what in there, an empty suit. Nothing left, the cops said whatever they used was more powerful than dynamite. They think it was maybe C-four."

"That's military, isn't it?"

"That's what they told me," Rossetti said. "I'm telling you, whatever it was really got the job done. I had to call the family to send over a suit, just to make them think—"

I'd heard enough. I got the picture. I asked, "They're in the front parlor?"

"Follow the screams."

Or I could follow the scent. Diego the Florist had done an excellent job, as usual. We all used him—he understood Mob protocol, but this one had been a little tricky. Sally always sent the biggest arrangement, since he was the boss, but Hole in the Head had been number two. Then came Blinky Marzilli, at least nominally. I usually ordered the fourth largest wreath.

Diego had sounded relieved when I called earlier in the day to inquire about my wreath.

"Who-sa I make number two now?" he asked.

"Blinky's," I said. "That's the way Hole in the Head would want it."

"You really think-a so?"

"How the hell do I know? Just make mine third—no, fourth biggest, after Cheech's. I'll defer to the grieving brother."

"'At's another thing, Bench, now you bring it up. Cheech, he no call. What you and Sally want I should do?"

Not even sending a wreath to your own brother's funeral? But that was Cheech for you, tighter than a frog's ass, wouldn't pay a nickel to see a volcano. Still, not sending a wreath to his brother's wake would push Sally over the edge. In the interest of peace (and quiet), I told Diego that if Cheech didn't call in an order, just send over the usual and put it on my tab.

"What if he ask who paid?"

"You know him better than that, Diego. He'll figure somebody took care of him because he's a big shot."

Now I was slipping into the viewing room. No line, there couldn't have been more than fifteen people in the room. Hole in the Head had more enemies than that, wiseguys who should have shown up just to make sure he was dead. I shook Cheech's hand and he made the introductions to the family. It was Hole in the Head's ma who'd been making all the noise. She was no more than five feet tall, maybe 180 pounds, dressed all in black. She was definitely old enough to remember where she was when she heard the news about Pearl Harbor. I arrived just in time to hear her let go with another screech.

"My Felipe," she screamed. "He was-a the best boy! Philip, I love you! I'll see you in heaven! Philly, why'd it have to be you?" She shot a withering glare at her surviving son; talk about putting the "dis" back in dysfunctional. "They hadda blow you up, Philly, them dirty cock-a-suckahs, they was afraid-a ya." She paused to gulp some air, then started in again.

"PHILLLLLLIIIPPPP!"

Cheech leaned over and grabbed her by her flabby, age-spotted upper arm. He got in close to her face and hissed: "Jesus, Ma, calm down. He murdered half of Boston."

That set her off again. I averted my glance and looked over at the bank of wreaths. Sally's said, "From the boys." Mine said, "From the boyos."

I kneeled at the casket, crossed myself and pretended to pray. If there is an afterlife, nobody's prayers were going to help Hole in the Head. I stood up and made my way to the family. I took Ma's hand and introduced myself.

"Mrs.—" Then I drew a blank. I couldn't remember Hole in the Head's last name. I looked over at Cheech.

"Mrs.—" Cheech stepped up behind me and whispered in my ear, "Imbruglia."

"Mrs. Imbruglia," I said. "Phil was an inspiration to us all."

"He was-a the toughest guy in Boston," she said.

Well, the meanest anyway. I was trying to think of something else to say when I felt a hand on my arm. It was Sally, in a suit about two sizes too small for him. His face was flushed, either from booze or from his too-tight shirt collar.

"C'mon," he said, more softly than he normally spoke, perhaps in deference to Mama. "Let's go upstairs." He nodded in her direction. "You'll pardon us, Mrs. Imbruglia?"

"You just find them motha-fuckahs blew up my boy," she said, staring at the casket. "He shoulda been the boss, not you—then you'd be lying in there. In pieces."

Sally turned, tightening his grip on my arm, as Cheech excitedly pushed aside his mother and then bumped his brother's casket in his haste to get to Sally. He grabbed Sally's arm.

"Sally," he said, in obvious terror. "She don't mean none of it. We all love you."

Sally pulled his arm away from Cheech's grip. "Forget about it," he said. As we walked up the stairs, he said to me:

"You think it's easy?"

When we reached the top of the stairs he guided me toward a door that opened into a room I knew well. Downstairs was for family, upstairs for wiseguys. Again I noted the small turnout—no more than ten or twelve people, average age close to seventy. There was only one other non-Italian in the room, a real old-timer named Tommy Callahan. He sold me my first machine gun, a burp gun actually, when he retired from the rackets. Somebody later used it in Framingham to kill a strong-arm guy who'd snatched one of Sally's bookies and buried him alive. I've been told the Framingham cops still keep the piece in working order, even fire it on the police department range every six months or so.

As usual, the Rossettis had set up a small service bar in one corner of the room, tended to by an amiable young guy in a suit who looked vaguely like JoJo. I walked up to him.

"Anisette all right, Mr. McCarthy?" he asked, mispronouncing my name. Anisette is not one of my favorites, but when in Rome . . . I took the tiny glass and slid to the side so Sally could belly up.

"Fuck that wop shit!" he snarled at the kid, whose smile instantly turned to terror. "You got any American booze? I want some vodka."

It was not exactly a celebration of life taking place. Usually, if the wiseguy had died a natural death, all his pals would be recounting his glory days, like the time Tommy Torch got his eyebrows singed while setting fire to Larry Baione's pig farm in Franklin. Or the day the dearly departed Danny Dot had so terrified an old Jewish bookmaker with a baseball bat that the guy actually shit his pants in the old G&G Deli on Blue Hill Ave.

Sally and I stood silently with our drinks near the door. Tommy Callahan was the only one even trying to keep up his end of the patter. He was telling a story about how he "knew a guy" who was the wheelman on Hole in the Head's first hit. He was standing on a running board of an old Packard shooting at somebody called "the Syrian" who was running down Columbus Ave on a snowy night, trying every door to see if he could find sanctuary inside, with Hole in the Head emptying a .44 at him . . .

Sally cupped his mouth with his hand and then whispered to me: "A Packard? Tommy's softer than a sneakerful of shit. Let's get out of here."

I shrugged and we left Tommy in mid-sentence. We walked down the hall and into what appeared to be JoJo's office. Once we were inside and Sally had shut the door, he reached into his pocket and took out what looked like a smartphone. He pressed a button and a green light began flashing on the side. He motioned for me to sit down as he walked around the room, pointing the device at one wall after another.

"Mind if I was ask what you're doing?" I finally said.

"Checking for bugs," he said, holding it up proudly. "I just got this."

"Where? Out of a Crackerjacks box."

"Just so happens I bought this off a cop, smart guy."

"Now I know it came out of a Crackerjacks box."

Sally's upper lip curled. He slipped the device into his pocket.

"Do you think this is fucking funny?" The fact that he said "fucking" rather than "fuckin'" meant that he was really pissed. "Do you realize I gotta problem?" The slightest pause. "We gotta problem. If you're driving a different car the other night there, one that don't have that special hide, you're downstairs right now in the parlor in a box next to Hole in the Head."

"Sally, believe me, I never forget it when somebody shoots at me. By the way, and I'm not giving you the needle, but where is everybody?"

His nostrils flared, and I realized too late the mistake I'd made. He was going Sally on me again. Suddenly he was screaming.

"Listen, next time you see them motherfuckers, you tell them dirty rats, nobody runs out on Salvatore Matteo Curto. Fuckin' every flight to Lauderdale and Fort Myers had to be jam-packed today with them yellow fucks." He was tapping on my chest with his index finger, hard. "Yellow fucks—you tell 'em that's what Sally Curto called 'em. I says, Youse guys, when I tell youse we are going to the mattresses, I don't fuckin' mean the mattresses in your condos in Deerfield Beach, or Palm Beach Lakes, you treacherous wannabe college-boy cocksuckers. Youse fucks, we used to shoot guys for dealin' drugs, now youse are making more than the Jew bookmakers, a lot more, but most-a youse never even made your bones—"

He was breathing heavily now. Sally really needs to do two things. Number one, take off about seventy pounds, and number two, stop watching the *Godfather* movies over and over again. I was waiting for him to threaten to have the deserters "sleep with the fishes," but suddenly it was over. He took a couple of steps backwards, then stumbled heavily into the swivel chair behind Rossetti's desk. When he fell into it, the chair rolled back and tipped over, dumping Sally on the floor. He was embarrassed. He got up slowly, dusted himself off, and I could see tears in his eyes.

"I'm going nuts," he said. "I can't take it. I'm too old for this shit."

"Tell me about it," I said.

"The thing is, I . . . don't . . . know . . . what . . . they . . . want." He said it that slowly. "If we don't know what they want, how can we figure out who they are? I understand musclin' in, that's how we all came up, right?" He regarded the swivel chair warily, then slowly, very carefully sat back down in it. "But now, we ain't musclin' nobody.

Niggers, spics, gooks, motorcycle fucks with their meth labs, it's live and let live. Even them whaddaya call 'em, hipsters, wearing pajamas and those fucking godawful wispy-ass goatees down there in the Seaport District, selling Mollys, whatever the fuck they are. But the point is, it's an open city, every man for himself, am I right?"

"Absolutely," I agreed.

"So what do they want, Bench? Can someone fucking please tell me that? When you get right down to it, what have we got that anybody would want? You got a garage, a barroom or two. I got the towing service, couple of contracts with the city, a few apartment buildings. It's all legit. You know how the wiseguys in the movies always say that they're 'businessmen'? Well, that's what we are. Mostly, anyway. So why do they want to kill us?" He paused for a moment. "You makin' any progress?"

"Other than staying alive, you mean?"

He nodded thoughtfully but said nothing. He was stumped.

"I went down to Lewisburg over the weekend," I said, and he snorted.

"You talkin' to Bobby Bones again? That guy's a junkie, you told me so yourself."

"He's clean now," I said. "He told me some interesting stuff. You ever talk to that guy there, Peanuts, works for Blinky?"

Sally's face curled into a snarl. "Peanuts? I told him I'd chop his balls off if he ever set foot on Hanover Street again. You know that."

"Well, Peanuts has disappeared."

"Good!" Now that the ice in his drink had melted a little, Sally took a long swig of his vodka. "I hope somebody clipped him."

"Bobby Bones thinks he's joined the program."

"No fuckin' way. Blinky would have told me. Besides, how the fuck would Bobby Bones know something like that?"

I explained about Peanuts' nephew, the chop-shop story that didn't add up and his transfer to WITSEC, and how Peanuts had missed a meeting with a dealer who owed him fifty large. Now I had Sally's attention.

"You think Blinky's flipped too?"

"All I know is what I'm telling you," I said. "What you do next, that's between you and Blinky."

I don't get involved in intramural Mafia squabbles. If Sally says he wants something done, that's different. But until he tells me otherwise, I'm staying out of it. One thing I learned a long time ago: don't go around asking a lot of questions because somebody might get the idea that you're looking to find out some answers.

But now Sally was interested.

"What does Bobby Bones think?" he asked.

"I thought Bobby Bones was a junkie."

"Don't be a wise guy. What's the scuttlebutt inside?"

"Well, they're pretty sure they've flipped Peanuts' nephew—the Fonz—he doesn't have any juice with anybody. So they had to be moving him out of general population for some reason, and there's only one anyone can think of."

Sally's brow was furrowed. "Why didn't Blinky tell me this?"

"You tell me, Sally."

"Well, I tell you one thing—Peanuts and Blinky couldn't both be wearing wires. Don't make no sense."

"Did it make sense to have both Whitey and Stevie as Top Echelon rats?"

"I don't believe it."

"Okay, don't believe it. But somebody who knows us pretty good has gotta be tipping these guys that're shooting at us."

Sally stared down into his empty drink. Normally, I'd have gotten him another one by now, but I wanted to finish this conversation. I wanted it all on the record, in no uncertain terms, about what I knew, and what I had told him just in case everything went south later on.

Sally looked up at me. I was waiting for him to say something. Finally he did.

"I'm not hitting Blinky."

"I didn't say you should. All I'm saying is, watch yourself around him."

What I didn't say to Sally was, if you do get hit, for sure Blinky runs to Providence or New York and puts the finger on me. And the feds'll figure out some way to back him up—leaks to the papers, most likely, lining me up for a head shot. That way, the two guys who aren't rats—me and Sally—get taken off the board, and Blinky slides in, all the while snitchin' out everybody else on the commission.

"Look," Sally said, shaking the ice cubes in his empty glass, "once we get this other thing straightened out, we'll worry about Blinky."

"What makes you think the two aren't related?"

Sally put his glass down and took a pack of cigarettes out of his coat pocket. He looked about a hundred years old. He politely asked me to go get him another drink. I was just standing up when suddenly we both heard a light tapping on the door. Sally and I both snapped to attention. He pulled a .38 out of a shoulder holster inside his coat that I hadn't noticed. The safety was off and he pointed it at the door.

"It's me, Sally. Liz."

Liz McDermott was Sally's girlfriend. Or had been, until she turned thirty and started putting on weight and her teeth started falling out from all the meth and every other damn drug she was doing. Five years ago, she looked like my younger sister. Then she looked like my mother. Now she resembled my grandmother, who's been dead for fifteen years. She used to be a hot mess. Now she was just a mess.

You've heard of someone who looks like ten miles of bad road? Liz McDermott looked ten counties of bad road.

"Fuck," Sally muttered. "Just when you think things can't get any worse . . ."

"Let me in, Sally, I have to talk to you."

He sighed deeply. Sally got a girlfriend because he couldn't stand his wife, and now he couldn't stand his girlfriend, but he couldn't get rid of her anymore than he could get rid of his wife, because if he tried, she'd rat him out to Mrs. Curto. Not that Mrs. Curto didn't know what was going on, but the rule was, you didn't rub your wife's face in it. Liz understood the rules very well.

Sally nodded at me and I walked over to the door and opened it.

"Bench," she said. "I was hoping you'd be here."

Her breath reeked of booze. Sometimes she was sober, but less and less often. Not much more than thirty-five years old, her black hair was now shot through with gray. She didn't care. Any money she spent keeping her hair touched up was money she couldn't spend on getting high. Her eyes were glassy, unfocused. She was stoned out of her mind. She was wearing a ten-gallon cowboy hat.

Sally didn't even bother to try to hide his contempt.

"Who'd you steal that from?" he said, gesturing at the hat.

"I bought this down Newbury Street," she snapped defensively.

"The last time you were on Newbury Street, I had to send somebody down to District Four to bail you out."

She daintily touched dirty hair that was spilling out from under the hat, as if she were preparing for her close-up.

"You shouldn't be here, Liz," Sally said. "This is family."

"And I'm not family?" she said, putting down her purse, opening it and removing a tiny nip bottle of something clear, maybe schnapps. The smaller the bottle, the bigger the problem. She emptied it in one gulp, smacked her lips and underhanded the bottle into the trash can.

"You're not family," Sally said. "Get that straight. I can't believe JoJo even let you in here."

"I just want to help."

"You want to help? Then go kill yourself. *Capisce*?" Sally shook his head. "You was raised on Commercial Street, I'm gonna say something to you in Italian: *Fatte a cazzo e me.* You know what that means, Liz?"

"'Mind your own business'?"

"Wrong! It means, 'Mind your own fuckin' business.'"

Well, close enough, I guess. Besides, it wasn't my place to correct Sally on his Italian.

Sally looked at Liz with pure disdain and took a wad of bills out of his pocket. "How much?" he said. "Just tell me how much you want? If I give you what you want, will you get the fuck out of here?"

"I got a problem, Sally."

"So do I," he said. "How much?"

"The lawyer wants another thousand." A couple of days earlier, she'd been arrested in one of the new high-rises in the Back Bay. She'd been emptying out one of those $3 million condos when the owners returned. Liz had told them she was the new maid. Then she lay down on their couch and passed out. She'd spent enough time in Framingham to know she didn't want to go back to the women's prison.

"A grand?" Sally was peeling off bills. "Like I really believe you, Liz. How much shit can you buy with a grand?"

"Sally, that's a rotten thing to say," Liz said. "You never appreciated me." She glanced over at me. "Ain't that right, Bench?"

Sally didn't look up as he continued counting the bills. "Leave him out of this, he's got nothing to do with this here problem."

"So now I'm a problem?" she said, looking at her boyfriend. "You used to tell me I looked like Ava Gardner."

"You still do," Sally said, managing a little smile. At first Liz did too, until she realized the dig.

"Oh, I get it. Ava Gardner's dead. That's so funny I forgot to laugh."

I stepped between them. "Look, Liz, you got what you wanted, we got business to discuss here."

"Oh yeah," she said. "You think I don't watch the news? I know what's going on. Somebody's trying to kill you guys." She looked at me. "I still like you, Bench, you're a gentleman, but him—"

That was it. Sally's nostrils flared and he was having a Sally, the second one in less than ten minutes. I'd never seen them come so close together. He threw his cigarette at Liz and she stepped clumsily aside to avoid it.

"You tell that fuckin' whore," he said, pointing his finger right in her face, "that I've about had it up to here with her bullshit. I'm through bailing her out, I'm through paying for her abortions, I'm through putting her in them sober half-way houses in East Boston as part of the plea deals in the BM-fuckin'-C. Fuck that! You tell her that—fuck her and the horse she rode in, and for the sake of the fuckin' horse I hope to fuck it's a fuckin' Clydesdale she rode in on, she's gotten so fuckin' fat."

She just stared at him, her mouth open.

"You tell that no-good cunt, if you want to be somebody's girlfriend, you gotta stay in shape, and nobody ever stayed in shape doing every fuckin' drug in the world, and what's even worse, when she fucks now, it's like fuckin' a dead body, 'cause she's usually nodding off when I hop on top of her. You tell her she ain't the only slut in the North End."

Now Liz was scared. She made a sudden move toward him, but I pulled her back. Interrupting Sally in the middle of a Sally would be the worst possible thing to do. It was like he was possessed; if he was interrupted maybe he'd never come out of it, like in some made-for-TV horror movie, I forget the name of it.

"Shhhhhh," I said to her. "Let him come out of it by himself."

She put her arms around me and cooed, "Oh, Bench," but I pushed her away. Sally was right about her; her days as the siren of Salem Street were way behind her. Sally was breathing heavily now. That meant he was coming around. Finally he blinked and shook his head. Then he saw Liz and he grimaced.

"You got your money," he told her. "Now get the fuck outta here."

Her head down, she slinked out of the room without a word and closed the door softly behind her.

"If she ever goes to Rosa," he said, "I swear to God, I'll, I'll . . ."

By which he meant I'd get the contract.

"Don't sweat it," I lied. "The cops got her cold on this last beef. She'll be gone soon enough. She ain't gonna be bothering nobody from Framingham."

Sally shook a cigarette out of his pack and lit up.

"Christ," he said. "I wish to fuck it was 1973 again."

Poor Sally. He was going to have his wish come true about the time I got Tommy Callahan's burp gun back.

This time when the cell phone rang at three in the morning I was sleeping at my condo just outside Ball Square. Patty turned on her side fitfully, so I grabbed the phone and tiptoed quickly into the living room. I didn't even have to look at the number to know who was calling.

"They hit the check-cashing place on the Lynnway—killed my guy Vito, shot him in cold blood, no fucking reason," Sally Curto was yelling so loudly that I had to hold the phone away from my ear. "You tell that Irish prick I gotta see him right away."

I glanced out the window into the parking lot. There were a couple of light poles—it was, after all, a "luxury condominium"—and I could see that a steady rain was coming down. No Carson Beach meetings this morning.

"How about the garage?" I said.

"The garage?" he said, in surprise. He doesn't like talking inside. Neither do I, for obvious reasons.

"It's okay, Sally. I got the guy coming in today with the equipment, first thing in the morning." Sometimes the trooper wasn't too punctual about getting over, but I knew he would be there today. While he was there, he wanted us to total his car for him. It was a professional courtesy for our friends in law enforcement.

"He'll be there right at eight," I said. "Tell me what happened."

"Two guys walked in, just before closing. Americans. Wearing ski masks. Don't make no sense, in the first place, it's a check-cashing place, not a bookie joint or a bar. At the end of the day they got less money then in the morning."

"And less security."

"Yeah, that too."

"So your guys called the cops?"

"Of course they called the cops."

"Which means it'll be on the news this morning."

"Yeah, so what are you getting at?"

"I don't want to talk on the phone. Drive into the third bay, it'll be open at eight. I got a couple of ideas."

Sally came by himself, another sign of how agitated he was. Or maybe what I'd told him about Blinky had sunk in. No Blinky, no Benny Eggs—maybe Sally was coming to his senses. When he drove inside, I shook his hand and guided him past where one of my tow trucks was smashing into the cop's Lexus sedan. The cops used to burn their old cars in the Allston rail yards, but the feds had run a sting out there a few years back, and then Harvard bought the land and put some real security on the gates. It had been a big break for my business, and for my relationship with the local constabulary. My garage had no windows. It was the perfect place to commit insurance fraud.

I'd told the statie to sweep my office first, so Sally and I could speak in there. Once we got in I flipped on the all-news radio station and turned it up high, just in case. I took Sally's overcoat, got him seated in a chair across from the desk with an ashtray for his smokes, and then sat down in my office chair.

"Sally," I said, "I been thinking about this a lot. I don't think we're dealing with wiseguys here."

He looked confused. "Who the fuck else would it be?"

"Hear me out," I said. "You used to do stickups, right?" He nodded, a little warily. He enjoyed "do you remember" conversations about as much as I do. "What's the best way to do a stickup?"

"One guy, of course."

"Of course. That way, no one to whack up the pot with, no one to rat you out."

Sally frowned. "Some guys, they do their first one with another guy. That way, they can't back out if they get cold feet."

"You ever get cold feet?" I asked. "I mean, even when you were a kid."

"Fuck no."

"Me neither. You either got it or you don't, that's the way I see it. You go in by yourself. Unless it's a bank or an armored car, of course." I was never actually in the car on any of my armored-car jobs. I just lined 'em up for Bobby Bones; I never went out on the heists myself. The jeopardy was just a little too much. But I did banks, and I almost always used four guys on a job. Three inside and one outside, the driver. Most guys'll tell you, the best guy to use as the driver is your brother, because if it's your brother in the car, it cuts down the odds that he's going to leave you high and dry. There's nothing worse, coming out of a bank, no car, and all you've got in your hand is your dick. Too bad for me, I didn't have a brother who could back me up. That's why I used my cousin Gonzo Ronzo whenever possible.

I said to Sally, "You don't need two guys to take that check-cashing place of yours. Besides, what's the point of icing one of the clerks but not the other one? There's no point in icing either of them, because they sure as shit ain't calling nine-one-one if it's just a robbery, right? But if you gonna hit one of 'em, don't you hit the second one too?"

"Bench, I keep telling you, we're dealing with junkies here. Nothing has to make sense."

"Listen to me," I said. "It makes perfect sense—but only if you're trying to make the news. One guy's dead, that's news, two is more news, but if you want to keep the story going, you need a witness who can talk about the shooters in ski masks blah-blah-blah."

Sally fumbled for a cigar in his overcoat. "What are you driving at?"

"Look," I said. "This ain't about starting a gang war between us. That's not what they're trying to do."

"Who's 'they'?"

"—I'll get to that, but hear me out first. Everything they've done is for the news splash. Sally Curto's nephew gets hit, Bench McCarthy gets clipped on Broadway—that's what they wanted, and what the fuck was that all about, by the way? Did that make any sense? If they want to take me out it'd be a lot easier to get me with a rifle walking out of the Alibi. Fuck, you're always telling me I'm becoming a creature of habit, right?"

"What I told you was, that's how your uncle Buddy got it." He lit up his stogie and took a long drag. "But that's ancient history. All I want to know is, who's behind this, and when are you going to kill them?"

"Sally, I wish it were that easy. If it were, I'd already have taken care of it. Somebody's using us as pawns." I was trying to go slow. Sally may not be the swiftest gazelle on the savanna, but if you lay it out, point by point, he gets it. This, however, was above his pay grade, I don't care where he is on those DOJ LCN charts. I was about to take it to the next level.

"Sally," I said, "did you read the *Globe* yesterday?"

"Fuck the *Globe*. They ruined the city with their fucking busing."

"Listen to me. Sometimes people use the *Globe* for their own agendas, you know what I mean?"

His eyes narrowed. "Go ahead."

I opened my top desk drawer and got the copy of Ted McGee's column out and pushed it across the desk. He took it in his stubby fingers and slowly lip-read it. After about a minute he looked up at me.

"I never read such a load of shit," he said, and then he stood up, started pointing at the wall and began yelling. He was going Sally again. This was getting to be a problem. In peacetime, this maybe happened once a month. Now he was folding under the pressure.

"You tell that no-good motherfucker I want him over the Dog

House tonight, and I don't mean no fucking maybes either. And on top of everything else, you misspell my name, you drunken Irish motherfucker."

He was shaking. He was talking directly to McGee, who needless to say wasn't there. "You, you rat cocksucker, are you trying to get people killed? What the fuck you think you're doing? I'll fuckin' tear your black heart out, you dirty piece of shit." Sally took off his porkpie hat and threw it at the wall. I heard a knock on the door; one of my drivers wanted to know if everything was okay. Obviously, this kid hasn't been around the garage very long. Most of the guys had heard these kinds of rants from Sally at least once or twice. I went to the door and handed the kid a couple of twenties and told him to go buy a round of coffee for the garage.

"Black for me, regular with two sugars for the other guy," I said, nodding in the direction of Sally, who had quieted down somewhat but was still muttering a steady stream of obscenities in the direction of the wall. Before I could shut the door one of the pit bulls, Atomic Dog, got inside and jumped up on Sally and started sniffing his crotch.

"What the fuck is this?" Sally bellowed, batting Atomic Dog away. "Is this dog queer or what?"

"It's a female, Sally. She loves you."

Sally scowled, but when I told him maybe he should take a load off, he reluctantly sat back down. Atomic Dog curled up at his feet. He reached down and stroked her head. Tyson was going to be jealous when he saw this.

"This motherfucker McGee, I got a good mind to drop him where he stands," he said. "Just hit him in the head. Bap-ba-beep-boop. You understand American?"

"Sally," I said patiently, "whoever's paying him to write this shit, clipping the asshole would just be a bonus for them. Guy'd be a hero, he can't testify that he ever took a payoff. They'd name a scholarship after him at BU." I shook my head. "No, we gotta play this thing cool."

Sally took a long drag on his cigar, which was now wet and all bent at the non-lit end. "Are you telling me that somebody's actually paying him to write this shit?"

"That would be my guess. This guy McGee has been for sale for years. He's the one who kept writing 'Whitey kept the drugs out of Southie.' And I'm also thinking that the same guys who are paying off McGee are paying the people who are trying to kill us."

Sally leaned forward across my desk. "Why?" he said. "Only place we're big shots now is in the papers. Why go to all this trouble to take out two guys that ain't got two nickels to rub together?"

It wasn't quite that bad, especially for Sally. He was twenty-five years older than me. He'd come up near the end of the golden age of wiseguys, and he got in a few years running the numbers—back when they called it nigger pool—before the Lottery killed off just about every kind of gambling except pro football. Sometimes, after a few drinks, he'd brag about how much dough they used to make, him and the Angiulos. For me, it was more of a struggle. Cripes, I was on the hook to Henry Sheldon for twenty-five large.

"Sally, you notice in that column how McGee isn't really interested in us getting shot, he's worried about sinking this casino bill."

"Fuck casinos—nothing there for us except crumbs. Wish there was something big we could grab but it's not 1975 anymore. We go in there, try to talk to whoever gives out the licenses, the feds'll have the office wired. Closed-circuit cameras too. Might as well be on TV. Hell, we probably would be on TV, that same night most likely."

"You know that, and I know that. But if they can make it seem like we're having a war for control of casinos, then maybe they can stop them."

"Who's 'they'? I ask you that before, you don't tell me. Who is 'they'? I thought everybody was for casinos now."

"Not everybody, apparently. I'm guessing 'they' are the people who don't have the juice to get the licenses right now. I don't know exactly, I'm not inside. But don't you see, Sally,—if all of a sudden a bunch of bodies start piling up, it looks like the wiseguys are fighting it out and this is the future if the state legalizes casinos."

Sally considered this for a moment. "Didn't I read somewhere that to get one of them new gaming licenses, you had to post a bond to guarantee to put up a $500 million casino?"

I nodded. "Something like that."

He looked around my windowless office, which hadn't changed since the previous owner opened the garage back in 1957. There was even an old Pep Boys girlie calendar from 1961 that no one had ever bothered to take down.

He smiled. "Does anyone really think either of us got collateral for a half-billion loan from a bank for a casino?"

"That's my point. If you think this thing through for about ten seconds, you realize it's bullshit, us fighting over something we couldn't come near affording, even if we could pass the background checks, which we can't."

"Yeah, but my nephew's just as dead."

I thought for a second. Then I decided to bounce something off him. That's not quite the right way to put it. I wasn't seeking his counsel; I was seeking his consent. He's the senior partner, even though I do almost all the wet work now, what little there still is, or was, until this week.

"You ever hear of this guy Jack Reilly? Used to be a cop, was a bagman for the old mayor?"

Sally put his cigar in the ashtray on my desk. I could smell it from where I sat.

"How old's this guy?"

"About my age, a little younger maybe."

"He hang out in the North End?"

"Fuck if I know, I'm from Somerville."

Sally scratched his head. "I think maybe I knew his mother, way back when. Lived on Richmond Street, I think. Married an Irish guy, a cop maybe?" His lip curled up a little. "Why you askin' me about this guy? We got assholes trying to clip us."

"This guy, he comes around the Alibi the other day, asking questions."

"Asking questions?" Sally likes strangers asking questions about as much as I do.

"Yeah, he was interested in talking. First I make him for a cop—"

"How many times I gotta tell you, never talk to a cop. I don't give a fuck, all they wanna do is be able to identify your voice in court. 'Yes, sir, I know the defendant, I recognize his voice, I talked with him at the Alibi.'"

I'd heard this lecture a million times. Maybe two million.

"Sally, I told you, he ain't a cop. He almost got indicted, he was shaking down some other cop for a promotion, they got him on tape I think, but he was too cute for 'em."

"Well, I like that."

"The other thing is, I know his brother. He's done some work for me."

"Capable?"

I shook my head. "Not that kind of guy."

"Stickups?"

I shook my head again. "Trucks. He's just a guy hangs around. Marty, Marty Reilly. Not a bad guy. He's up at Devens right now."

"So what'd he want, this guy, your friend's brother?"

"Not sure. We didn't talk much. I asked him, 'Do I know you?'"

"Good."

"Sally, I learn from you." He placidly accepted the compliment, didn't even realize I was giving him the needle, gently. Irony has always been in short supply on Hanover Street.

I said, "The more I think about it, though, the more I think he's on to this too."

"You mean us getting shot at?"

"I mean casinos. See, he works now for pols at the State House, City Hall, crooked pols mostly."

"I didn't know there was any other kind."

"So I'm figuring, maybe he's gotta couple ideas, wanted to bounce them off me. I'm thinking maybe—"

"No," Sally said. "No civilians."

"Sally, he ain't exactly a civilian."

"Plenty guys at the State House almost got indicted, that don't mean you wanna be sittin' down with them. Them guys don't stand up."

"Who does, Sally? These days, I mean?"

Before he could give me another lecture, there was a rapping on the door. The kid brought in our coffee. We waited until he was gone before resuming our conversation.

"Sally," I said, "lemme talk to the guy. We're clay pigeons out here, and we don't even know who's using us for target practice."

Sally frowned. "You ain't going to pay him, are you?

"Are you shittin' me? I'm a wiseguy."

Just then Atomic Dog stood up, looked up at Sally, raised her hind leg and pissed on his pants. Sally closed his eyes and gritted his teeth as he considered this latest indignity. He finally opened his eyes and looked first at Atomic Dog, who had again collapsed in exhaustion on the floor, and then at me.

"I guaran-fucking-tee you," he said, shaking his wet trouser leg. "What just happened to me never happened to Jerry Angiulo."

18

LAST CALL AT ANTHONY'S PIER 4

Mister Chairman, Senator Denis Donahue of the Worcester, Franklin and Hampshire district, was having a time at Anthony's Pier 4. One yard per person, $500 per "sponsor," and $5,000 per table.

I got my ticket from Kevin Caulfield. As a lobbyist, he can only contribute $250 a year to any politician, as opposed to non-lobbyists. This was another of those marvelous reforms so beloved of the newspaper editorial boards. It saved the lobbyists $250 per hack, although of course if you really needed to duke somebody some cash, there was always some secretary in your office to make up the $250 deficit. And if it was really important . . . well, that's what they all had guys like me for. Guys like I used to be, I mean.

Old Man Caulfield wasn't in a good mood when I stopped by to pick up my ducat. Ted McGee had written another column in the *Globe*—a "special," on the front page. The way it was written, it sounded like he'd been there when Sally's collector got hit. As usual, plenty of dialogue, no last names. At the bottom of the piece, McGee reassumed his omniscient voice and lectured the squares in the suburbs who didn't know he was making it all up. He told them how this "carnage" would continue as long as the cancer of gambling loomed over Our Fair City, the City on a Hill. Fucking guy grew up in Fitchburg, and all the rubes thought he was a Townie or some such shit.

"He's killing us," Caulfield said.

"What's the head count on the vote?" I asked.

"It's not coming to the floor, if that's what you mean." In other words, leadership no longer had the votes. From the tone of Caulfield's voice, it wasn't even close.

"Any way to save the bill?" I asked.

"That's your job," he said glumly. I could see he didn't think I was up to the job, but I didn't take it personally. Probably no one could pull it out now.

I said, "I went to the game last night."

"Really?" he said. "Let me guess, it cost you fifty bucks to park and you're pissed at the mayor."

"That goes without saying," I said. "But I thought you might be interested in who was sitting in Donuts' seats."

He looked up at me. Now he was interested.

"The Pulitzer Prize winner himself."

"McGee?"

"None other. And sitting next to him was the commissioner of probation."

"Drew Amato? That's Donahue's guy, his cousin."

"Really?" I said.

"You didn't know that? I thought everybody knew that."

"I don't get around much anymore."

It was the usual Pier 4 time, maybe my last, now that I thought about it. The old joint was closing in about a month; more high-rises going up in the "Seaport District" formerly known as Southie. Anthony's upstairs function room was crawling with lobbyists, legislators and assorted other hacks. I'll tell you how shady the crowd was: I broke my own iron-clad and passed out four business cards that actually had my own name on them. It was a great "networking" opportunity for low friends in high places. There's always a few veteran legislators looking down the barrel of a primary challenge, and that's where I come in. Inside the Beltway, they call my job "oppo research." I just call it digging up shit. Which is what I was doing at Pier 4, but most of the payroll patriots just assumed I was trolling for new business. Let 'em think that. It was better that way, plus I was killing two birds with one stone.

I gulped down a couple of gin and tonics, hold the tonic, to loosen up and then lingered around the back of the room. The only time I left was to go downstairs to the main dining room and grab a couple of Anthony's famous hot popovers for old-time's sake.

The sun was setting over the harbor and I'll have to admit, the view was spectacular. I was going to miss this place. Anthony Athanas, the owner, had been a miserable old prick, but when he built Anthony's Pier 4 he was way ahead of his time, right down to the huge parking lot.

It was around nine when they flashed the lights in the room and I saw a florid-faced guy at the podium, asking for quiet in the room. I knew him from Fenway Park. It was the probation commissioner, Drew Amato. I suddenly wished I'd brought along Katy Bemis. If she'd seen this, she'd have been totally onboard.

"You all know why we're here tonight," he said, as I noticed the two beefy guys standing behind him, their hands clasped in front of them, like they were his bodyguards, as if a probation commissioner needed bodyguards for anything but effect. On the other hand, maybe they worked for Donuts. He didn't need bodyguards either, he needed bagmen, but these guys were much too conspicuous to be picking up cash. They looked like state cops on steroids, or do I repeat myself? As your bagman, you need someone nondescript, someone like, well, like me.

Amato began: "We're here to pay tribute to our good pal, the

Leader, who has done so much for all of us here, who never hesitates when any of us need a favor."

I was growing slightly bilious. Favors? He had everything but a rate card for those so-called favors.

"Some of us may need an increase on our line item in the budget." This was for the hacks. "Some of us may need an outside section inserted into the budget in conference committee." This was for the lobbyists. They could put anything in an outside section, tack it on at the end of a budget along with hundreds of others, with no fingerprints, and with any luck no one would figure out for months what they'd done—a land-taking of some prime public real estate, a fake pension, a ninety-nine-year lease, putting fifty-year-olds on the State Police despite the age requirement. In other words, something you wouldn't want to see splashed on the front page with your name in the headline. An outside section was so much easier than actually having to get a bill passed—and cheaper too, because you only have to pay off one guy, in this case Donuts.

"People outside the building, you know what they say about us. They don't understand the true meaning of public service." A few uneasy chuckles followed. The commissioner didn't appear drunk, so maybe it was some kind of inside joke, this gag about public service.

"Public service is about giving your word, and keeping your word." Now he was back on track. God, how they loved to talk about giving their word, and keeping it. Almost as much as they loved to reminisce about who they'd stabbed in the back. "And that's what our friend is all about—keeping his word. If the Leader tells you he's going to do something for you, you can take it to the bank." Preferably an offshore bank, where Donuts would be depositing your money.

"This is a watershed year in the history of our Commonwealth." Aren't they all?

"Powerful interests, out-of-state interests, are attempting to change the culture of our state." God forbid that should happen.

"They want to turn our city into a gambling mecca, with all of the social pathologies that gaming will bring in its wake." More chuckles, but fewer than before, because most of the crowd was in on this casino play. Surely Donuts couldn't be going rogue on them at this late date, could he?

"But there is one man who stands athwart these nefarious forces." Athwart? Nefarious? The commish was pushing it now. One of the bodyguards frowned slightly. Or maybe he was just confused by the big words.

"Denis Donahue knows that if casinos are the answer, then we must have asked the wrong question. He will do his best to halt this blight before its malignant tentacles begin strangling our state." Somebody must have written this shit for the commissioner, I was sure of it now, even if I couldn't see any notes on the podium. On casinos, Donuts was galloping off the reservation. Everything was starting to fall into place. "My friend, your friend, the man we have gathered together to pay tribute to tonight, knows the high price he may pay for his principled stand, but as we have all heard him say on more than one occasion, 'I answer only to the people.'"

Eventually, it'll be twelve people he's answering to, along with a few alternate jurors thrown in for good measure. Was there a reporter here? Or perhaps the FBI had bugged the room. I hoped they were enjoying this as much as I was. Especially the part about paying tribute and high prices.

"But you don't want to hear from me. You want to hear from the man himself, the majority leader of the Massachusetts State Senate. Ladies and gentlemen, I give you our dear friend, the man whose word is his bond, Denis Donahue."

Donahue approached the podium, and gave the commish a bear hug. He whispered something in Amato's ear, and Amato nodded in the direction of his two plug-uglies, who peeled off to the side. If anyone was taking photos, especially newspaper pictures, Donuts didn't want those two behind him. I wondered why.

The senator stepped to the podium, and bowed in mock appreciation of the applause, which I'd rate somewhere between tepid and average. Apparently the tickets bought access, not enthusiasm. This was incumbent money here tonight. The only thing they believed in was being with the winner. You wouldn't call it a tough crowd exactly, but it was jaded.

Donuts looked like a majority leader straight out of Central Casting: average height, just the hint of a potbelly, expensive suit that somehow didn't hang quite right on him. My guess was Shrewsbury, St. John's Prep, Holy Cross, Suffolk Law. I wondered how many times it had taken him to pass the bar exam.

Donuts continued to hammer on the theme of Good Government and Reform. It was like listening to Ted Kennedy on temperance, or Bill Clinton on marital fidelity. Cognitive dissonance, I believe they call it.

"As always, my friends, I remain only a phone call away." Preferably on a burner, an untraceable prepaid throw down. And don't forget to use whatever code has been agreed to in advance. "But as important as I consider service to my constituents, and you are all my constituents, everyone who is here tonight, this year I find myself embroiled in what I can only describe as a crusade." The Third Crusade of 1204, when they looted Constantinople. "I refer of course to the scourge of casinos which the commissioner has just described so eloquently." A couple of the younger lobbyists standing a few feet away from me near the door took this opportunity to duck out. They'd paid their respects, and their cash, and if they wanted to hear this shit they could find themselves a First Communion breakfast in Wakefield on Sunday.

"What a fine capital city all of us here in the Commonwealth can be proud of. I can recall when this boulevard, Northern Avenue, was best known for its gangland killings." Me too. I still remember the day Whitey Bulger shot two guys in broad daylight outside an upholstered sewer called the Pier. I was in the seventh grade.

"I ask you, my friends, why would we put all that we have accomplished in jeopardy? Why would we roll the dice?" A couple more lobbyists ducked out. Donuts was losing the crowd, fast. Did he think he was addressing the annual meeting of the Knights of Columbus at the American Legion Post in Clinton?

I know I wasn't the only one in the room who was puzzled by the direction of this peroration. Wasn't his boss, the Senate president, still officially in favor of the casino legislation? Hadn't he introduced this bill Donuts was now calling a "scourge"? Dissent was no longer tolerated in either house, and yet Donuts was trashing his boss' big payday.

I mean, I understood jumping ship, trying to line up the next big score, but the brazenness of this play, in front of hundreds of lobbyists at Anthony's, was breathtaking. Donuts was revealing himself as one of those pols of whom it was said, they would steal a hot stove without gloves and then come back for the smoke.

Now he was saying, "Fortunately, those of us in this room tonight are not alone in our struggle against these malign forces. In the General Court, our allies are too numerous to mention." Let's just call them unindicted coconspirators.

"And in the media, some courageous tribunes of the people have stepped up." Now he had my attention again.

"One of them, I'd like to recognize here tonight. Ted McGee, the columnist for the *Globe*, a man who will someday be described as a Pulitzer Prize winner." Only if they start giving out Pulitzers for plagiarism.

"Ted has almost singlehandedly made the state aware of what lies ahead if we allow these unscrupulous merchants of vice to operate unimpeded." You know, like the State Lottery Commission already does.

"Ted, raise your hand—let's have a round of applause for our good pal in the Fourth Estate."

I saw a hand go up. It was clasping a highball glass. So McGee was a brown-water man, and something told me he had been even before the bourbon renaissance. The applause was even more restrained. One of the two thugs now standing off to Donuts' side started working his way along the wall toward the door. Obviously, the speech was drawing to a merciful close. I made an instantaneous decision to tail Donuts' car when he left.

Chances were, he'd just duck down to one of those new upscale bars like the Whiskey Priest. Good name, but I'd never been there. Even from the outside, it looked pricey. Either that, or he'd jump onto the Turnpike Extension west in Chinatown, headed home to Worcester, in which case, I'd just turn around at the Allston tollbooths. Nothing ventured, nothing gained.

I ducked out of the room and watched the thug head down the stairs. I followed at a respectable distance, nodding to each picture on the wall as I went by. Spiro Agnew, Ted Kennedy, Frank Sinatra and a whole host of other local celebs you've never heard of, guys with charming nicknames like Nicky Pockets, the Corrupt Midget and I'll Take a Buck.

No valet parking for Donuts. His car was in a handicapped space, right up in front. A Crown Vic. No legislative license plate for Donuts either, he was too cute for that. People throw shit at you if you have one of those. He might have a three- or four-digit plate, but that was probably on his wife's car, or the one at his summer place in New Seabury, around the corner from Bob Kraft.

My guess was he had an untraceable, like the deputy fire chief I'd bagged a few days earlier with Ron Burgundy. That was the true status plate, although of course you could never brag about it. They say you can be either a successful poisoner or a famous poisoner, but not both. Same with untraceable plates. If people know you have one, they can trace it back, can't they, and give you tickets for parking in all those handicapped spaces and fire lanes. I used to have one of those plates myself, back when I was a contender.

Anthony's weeknight dining-room crowd had thinned out considerably, so I could move my late father's old Oldsmobile into a space closer to Donuts, where I could watch him as he left. I hadn't done a tail in a while, but traffic was light and I was pretty sure his driver wouldn't be paying attention.

I got into my Olds and turned the key in the ignition to get some heat circulating. That was when I saw a shadow pop up in the rear-view mirror. Then I heard the voice from the backseat.

"I thought you'd never get here."

It was Bench McCarthy.

19

DONUTS' DETOUR

The way he jumped, you'd have thought Jack Reilly thought I was going to cap him.

"Jesus fucking Christ," he yelled. "What the fuck are you doing, hiding like that?"

"You oughta lock up your car, Jack. This is the city. Lotta criminals lurking around here, from what I hear on the news. Didn't they teach you that in the academy?"

Reilly was still breathing heavily. I think he was more embarrassed than anything else. For not locking the car, maybe, or for freaking out, which was only natural, considering how I'd surprised him, in the dark.

"What do you want?" he finally said. There was exasperation in his voice. "Last time I saw you, you told me to fuck off."

"That was then, this is now. Listen, can we go somewhere and talk? You're a Foley's guy, right?"

"How come you didn't just call me?"

"I don't like phones, Jack."

"We could have just met somewhere."

I shook my head. "I'm not a big meetings guy. Especially lately." I paused. "Mind if I come around and sit in the front seat?"

Reilly was looking intently out the windshield, towards the front door of Anthony's.

"Jack, are you waiting for somebody to come out?"

"Yeah, I am." He looked up into the rearview mirror. "Come on around, I think we're going for a ride here in a minute or two."

"A ride, huh? I like taking rides. Who we gonna go see?"

I opened the back door and came around the back of the car and jumped in the front seat. I extended my hand and Jack Reilly took it. He seemed a lot calmer now.

"You know a senator named Donuts Donahue?" he asked me. "I wanna see where he's going from here."

I'd been in the backseat for about forty-five minutes, inhaling the musty old-car smell, cheap cigars and mothballs and stale beer. That afternoon I'd had one of my younger guys stake out Reilly's house in the South End, and he'd tailed him over here to Anthony's and sat on him until I could drive over myself.

It's good to run into people, if you know what I mean. If you catch somebody off guard, you may find out whether or not he can stand up under pressure. If I'm going to be running with a guy, I like to know how he deals with a wild card turning up, especially a faceup wild card like me. Some guys, you can't peel them off the ceiling for hours. Others get pissed, I mean really pissed. Jack Reilly, though, was taking it pretty good. My guess was he'd been surprised more than a few times and it didn't take him long to figure out that on a scale of one to ten, this was about a minus-three in the danger department.

I said, "This guy Donuts, does he have something to do with what we were talking about the other day?"

He looked over at me and smiled. "Who wants to know?"

"C'mon, Jack, you can trust me. I'm not like the others."

He ignored that. "Look, they're going to be coming out soon. You wanna ride along or not?"

"I'm game," I said. "You want me to drive? I've probably done more of this kind of thing than you."

"I was a cop, remember."

"But not that kind of cop, or so I hear."

He shook his head. "This kind of tail I can handle. Look, he's coming out. Shit, that's Amato with him."

I didn't know who Amato was. But I recognized Donuts from television. He was a regular at the St. Patrick's Day breakfast at Halitosis Hall in Southie, which I still watch out of habit. A bad habit. Donuts especially—he was about as funny as a crutch. He was wearing a Chesterfield topcoat. He was accompanied by a middle-aged guy without a coat—was that Amato? With them was a younger guy who handled himself like a wannabe. Hair combed straight back into a ponytail, kept his right hand in his pocket, like he was carrying, which I very much doubted. Like Sally, he probably watched way too many gangster movies.

We watched them get in their Crown Vic, Donahue and the other guy in the back, and the ponytail kid in front, driving. When they reached the end of Anthony's long parking lot, the Ford turned right, towards downtown. It cruised past the Whiskey Priest, which was when Jack spoke again.

"Good," he said. "I was afraid he was going to stop in there to count his cash."

The Crown Vic turned right again, onto Atlantic Avenue, and wound its way around to the Callahan tunnel.

"East Boston?" said Jack Reilly. "I didn't expect this."

"Airport maybe?" I said, just to keep up my end of the conversation.

"I have no idea."

At the end of the tunnel, instead of heading for the airport, the Crown Vic turned toward Maverick Square, cut past Santarpio's, and then headed left on Bennington Street.

"I bet I know where they're headed," I said.

"Where?" He looked over in curiosity.

"A place called the Python."

"Mafia?"

"Once upon a time, maybe. It used to be called Santo's. It's Spanish now, everything over here is, until you get to Orient Heights."

Reilly was keeping a steady five or six car lengths behind the Crown Vic. It was a leisurely tail. He turned to me and said:

"What makes you think they're going to Santo's—I mean, the Python?"

"A couple of guys I ran into in Somerville, I heard that's where they hung."

Jack Reilly thought for a second. He was pondering the past tense of hang—"hung."

"Are you talking about those two guys that got shot in the car on Broadway a couple of nights ago?"

I didn't say anything.

"It'd be a helluva thing," Reilly said, "if the next president of the state Senate walked into a bucket of blood like that."

Up ahead I could see the neon sign for the Python. There were a couple more beer signs in the glass windows. When they burned out they'd be replaced with ones that said "CERVEZA." The fact that the glass wasn't boarded over meant that the neighborhood was no longer in play. No need to worry about getting machine gunned by a passing car full of guineas pissed about getting pushed out of their own neighborhood.

The Crown Vic pulled into a bus stop directly in front of Santo's and Reilly drove past. I watched everyone get out, including the driver. Reilly made his first left turn and then backed out onto Bennington and took the first space he could find. He was right behind a low-rider with the hood up, and a couple of tattooed illegals staring into the engine. As soon as they saw us, they shut the hood and walked off down a side street.

"Drug sentries," Reilly said needlessly. "Maybe they thought we were cops."

I laughed. "In this piece of shit? I mean, no offense, but what

junkyard did you steal this out of? They don't even make Oldsmo-
biles anymore, do they?"

"They don't make Crown Vics either."

I let it go. "What do you want to do now?"

Reilly gave me a puzzled look. "We go in and check it out, of
course." He opened his door and had one foot out onto the pavement before I grabbed his right arm.

"Hold on," I said, grasping his arm tightly. "Are you crazy? Walking in there alone doesn't make any sense."

"I didn't know I was alone," he said. But he pulled his left leg back
inside the car and closed the door. The roof light went out and we
sat in darkness. He looked at me quizzically.

"C'mon," I pleaded. "You don't want to tip your hand."

"I don't mind walking into strange bars. I do it all the time."

"So I've noticed," I said. "But let's think about this. You're not
even carrying, are you?"

"Aren't you?" he asked.

"I can't," I said. "I'm a convicted felon."

He snorted. "Please."

"Please, nothing. If I were carrying there'd be another guy here
with me. A guy with no record."

"I didn't realize you were such a law-abiding citizen." Now he was
starting to get fresh. I think I liked him better when he was scared
of me.

"Look, it's your car so it's your call, but why do you want to stick
around here? I mean, we kinda stick out. We're Americans."

"Yeah, but it's dark, and we're in an illegal-alien car."

"You got a point there, but the bigger question is, why bother to
let them make us, now that we've confirmed our suspicions."

"We?"

"Yeah, we. You came to see me, remember? I think we share a
mutual interest in this . . . this matter. I'm assuming you're working
for somebody, so you want to turn up some information for your client. My interest is, me and my friends, we don't like getting shot at,

especially when we don't know why they're shooting at us. Speaking of which, that's another good reason for moving along. It's harder to hit a moving target."

Reilly didn't say anything for a second or two, but he finally turned the key in the ignition, then put the Olds into gear and pulled out onto Bennington Street. He didn't say anything for a couple of blocks before he spoke again.

"You guys really don't know why they're shooting at you?" he said.

"I have my theories," I said.

"Me too. Let's hear yours first."

"Like I said, you're the boss. You're driving." I scratched my head, trying to figure out how much I should tell Reilly. My general policy is, what you don't say can't hurt you, but I didn't figure anything here was top secret. This was just theorizing.

"It seems pretty clear," I said, "that somebody's trying to make it look like there's a gang war going on."

"And there isn't?"

"C'mon, Reilly, you're smarter than that. There hasn't been a hit around here for years."

"What about in Somerville the other night?" Reilly asked.

"That? That was self-defense. Or so I'm told. I think that's even what the cops said in the papers, didn't they? They found guns in that car, rifles. Rifles that had just been fired."

Reilly turned right towards the tunnel entrance. "So why would they start shooting people?"

"You tell me. I'm not even sure who 'they' are. You're the political guy. Seems to me I heard there was a casino bill up at the State House. Maybe somebody's trying to make it look like the element's running out of control, and that it'll only get worse if they start licensing casinos."

"Who'd want to do that?"

I sighed. "Look, I've told you what I think. Now you tell me what you know."

"I don't know anything," Reilly said. "All I know is, the pro-casino people had the votes to pass the legislation when the shooting started, and now they don't."

"Well, there you go."

Maybe the shooting was over, if they'd gotten what they wanted. But we still had some scores to settle with them, me and Sally, whoever they were. Still, something told me there was more to this than Reilly was letting on, or maybe knew.

Reilly said, "I probably shouldn't be telling you this—" which meant he was about to tell me whatever "this" was.

"You know Sally's nephew who got shot the other night?" he asked.

"Yeah." Now I was really paying attention.

"The BPD's got the gun—it was a Walther PPK. Did you know that?"

"No, Jack, I didn't." Okay, I lied. The important thing was, his information was good. That fact hadn't made the papers.

"Where'd it come from?" I asked. "Where'd they find it?"

"In some junkie's car. He was trying to rob Blanchard's down the Roxbury line, stoned out of his mind. The cops grabbed him and went outside to his car and they found it in the trunk."

"No shit." This was news I could use. "What color was this gentleman?"

"Spanish," Reilly said. Being from the South End and having worked at City Hall and the State House, I guess he had to be politically correct.

"The most interesting thing of all," he said, "was that when they let him make his one phone call, he called his probation officer, who is also his brother—"

I interrupted: "Who works for that front-running cocksucker who just walked into Santo's with the senator."

"Bingo," Reilly said. "I just gave you a lot of stuff you didn't have, didn't I? I think we could turn up more, working together."

"I'll think about it, Jack."

"Where's your car, back at Anthony's?" he asked, and I nodded.

He doubled back around onto Northern Avenue and I pointed out the Chevy Blazer I'd driven over in. He pulled alongside it and we sat there in his warm Oldsmobile.

"I wonder who owns the Python," he said.

"Somebody who's in with the people who are trying to kill your casino bill, obviously."

Reilly said, "Why would somebody with that kind of dough hang out at the Python?"

"C'mon, Reilly, these aren't the guys with the money, these are the guys who are taking the orders from the guys with the money. Even the senator. Especially the senator. I mean, are you putting up the dough for the casino you're trying to help get built, or are you working for some guys who are working for some guys that have the $500 million for the casino?"

Reilly shook his head. "Hard to track guys that hang out at the Python back to the big boys. Lotta buffers."

"Of course," I said. "That's how the system works, you should know that, being a former buffer yourself. There's always got to be a fall guy waiting in the wings. Or in this case, at the Python."

Reilly still seemed to be trying to figure out his next move.

"Listen," I said to him, "you do a little sleuthin', and I'll do a little sleuthin', and maybe we'll get together again and compare notes."

"How will I know—"

"You'll know," I said, opening the door. "When I need to find you, I'll find you."

20

LUNCH WITH DINTY MOORE

I asked Katy Bemis to see what she could find out for me about Senator Denis "Donuts" Donahue. Even when I worked at the State House, back in the days when I was straightening things out for the old mayor, I never paid much attention to anybody who collected a per diem of more than $10 a day. The per diem is what the legislators get for the expense of commuting into Boston. Believe it or not, they get paid for coming to work. Or not coming, as the case may be. It's run on the honor system, wink wink nudge nudge, and the reps can grab between $10 and $100 a day, depending on how far away they live from Beacon Hill.

Anyway, the more a guy collects in per diems, the more time he spends driving, which leaves less time for stealing. There's an old saying at the State House: "When the boys from the suburbs go home, the boys from Boston go to work."

It's true, if you include the adjoining cities as Boston—especially Somerville, Chelsea, Revere and Cambridge. Donahue, though, was from Worcester, a $35 per diem. But he had to be pretty good, if he had the votes lined up to become the next president of the Senate.

Katy must have been intrigued by my request that she pull the files on Donuts, because after a little cajoling, she agreed to join me for lunch at Meg's on West Broadway in Southie. It used to be a good place to meet her because it attracted a strictly lunch-pail blue-collar crowd, unlike Amrhein's across the street, where the more upscale hacks and hoodlums hung out.

Now, with the gentrification going on, the Meg's breakfast crowd was a bit more chi-chi, or so I'd heard. I never ate breakfast in Southie; I hate being the one who finds the body in the alley and has to call 911. But by noon the yuppies are all at work in the skyscrapers, and it's the old crowd, very few of whom would recognize me or, more importantly, Katy. The *Globe* loves the hoi polloi, but only in the abstract, on the editorial page. Actually consorting with the riffraff—that was as unthinkable as the married lesbian *Globies* sending their gaybies to Boston public schools.

I got to Meg's first and grabbed a table in the window, so I could keep an eye on the Amrhein's crowd across the street, mainly for shits and giggles. Then I went up and ordered the blue-plate special, corned beef hash. Katy sauntered in about five minutes later, saw me, slung her Gucci bag over the facing chair, and went up to order her food. Another reason I like Meg's—it's refreshing to see Katy Bemis with a tray in her hands. A couple of minutes later she sat down across from me.

"I hope you don't mind I didn't wait for you," I said.

She eyed my clean plate with distaste. "I see you went with the Special Du Jour too," she said.

"Corned beef hash," I said. "Dinty Moore's finest."

"They told me it was homemade," she said.

"They tell that to all the girls from Wenham."

She took a few bites without saying anything, then pushed the plate aside and dug into her bag. She took out a file folder full of printouts and put it on the table. I felt somewhat embarrassed, having to ask Katy to fill me in on anything at the State House, but if you're not around somewhere every day, you can lose touch quickly. I still knew everybody from the city, and everybody who'd been around when I was working on Beacon Hill, but Donahue had been a backbencher when I was the mayor's fixer. He'd moved up fast, after the feds wiped out the Senate leadership a few years back in a scandal involving racetrack dates, or maybe it was no-bid state computer-software contracts, or perjury in a gerrymandering case . . . the scandals all run together after a while.

The key here was, it was an election year, and the governor wasn't running for reelection. An old-time governor's councilor used to say, "Lame duck is my favorite dish," and it still is, for everybody. There was a going-out-of-business sale sign on the front lawn of the State House, just like at Reilly Associates, except that underneath their "GOING OUT OF BUSINESS" sign, there was another one that said, "EVERYTHING MUST GO!"

The outgoing governor was peddling judgeships. Instead of reasonable doubt at a reasonable price, in a lame-duck year the lawyers themselves were seeking reasonable retirements at a reasonable price.

Construction contracts were big too. This governor was trying to "straighten out" the so-called curve at the Allston tolls on what was no longer officially called the Turnpike. No one had ever noticed there even was a bend in the road until the governor's rubber-stamp Pike board decided to fix it, which would triple or quadruple the value of the land underneath it, which had been sold to Harvard University eight years earlier, during the prior administration's lame-duck session. That former governor was now a vice president of Harvard, for $350,000 a year.

I had told Katy about Donuts' time at Anthony's, and how he had basically thrown the casino bill under the bus, after his boss the Senate president had been pushing it for years.

"I called around this morning," she said. "The word is they all think the bill is dead for the year, so the president cut Donuts and everybody else loose. They're all free agents, they can tell anybody they're going to vote whichever way they want, unless it comes to the floor, in which case, they still have to vote with the leadership. But that's moot, because they don't have the votes. Don't be surprised if the Senate president calls a press conference today to announce he's withdrawing his support."

"And here I thought a man's word was his bond at the State House."

Katy smiled in spite of herself. "The polls have flipped since the shooting started; he knows which way the wind is blowing. Besides, he's been paid off already. He gave it his best shot. It's not his fault what happened. Now he's got to worry about himself. It's up or out. The pro-casino money's not going to do him any good if he's out of office and there sure won't be any more money coming in if he's gone."

"What about Donuts?" I asked.

"I guess," she said, "he was just testing out his new stump speech in front of a friendly audience."

Katy was explaining this quite clearly, no BS, her green eyes flashing occasionally as she used to good effect one of the simple phrases she'd picked up from me, like "up or out." I'd been a good teacher, perhaps too good. She didn't seem to need me anymore, for political tutoring or anything else. But as they say in Hollywood, self-pity is not good box office, and I'd have plenty of time for feeling sorry for myself later.

"Tell me about Donuts," I said.

She took a legal pad out of her file folder and glanced at her hand-written notes.

"Well," she said, "he's from Worcester, and I seem to recall you teaching me something about pols from Worcester."

"It took him three tries to pass the bar exam?"

"Actually, four." She smiled in triumph.

"What's his tie-in to the probation commissioner?" I asked. "Other than kin."

The tie-in was this: the judges and the legislature had always battled for control of the hack jobs in the judicial system—court officers, assistant clerks, probation officers, chief probation officers, etc.

The legislators always figured that they should have the upper hand, since they had to run for their jobs every two years, whereas the judges made close to $100,000 more a year than legislators, and they had lifetime appointments. The judges were immune from those rare Republican landslide years. So the legislature decided to effect a hostile takeover of the Probation Department. The shiftless judges could still get plenty of P.O. jobs for their equally shiftless friends and relatives, but to get them the judges had to go hat in hand to the legislature, just like the reps had to clear their court-officer job lists through the judges. One hand washes the other, you scratch my back . . .

Thinking about the courthouse hackerama reminded me of an old State House joke.

Q: What do you call a lawyer with an IQ of forty?

A: Your Honor.

To control Probation Department patronage, the legislative leadership needed a commissioner they could control, a front man. A guy from Boston would raise eyebrows in the press; he would automatically be assumed to be at best a hack, at worst a white-collar wiseguy.

At this point Donuts stepped forward and nominated as commissioner Drew Amato—a chief probation officer who had the added advantage of being . . . Donuts' cousin. Katy beamed as she told me that; she was proud of her little tidbit and far be it from me to say "I already knew that." Being from Worcester, she continued, Amato, like his cousin, was presumed to be too lame to represent a serious threat to anyone. Donuts and his cousin might be hot stuff in Worcester, but anybody from east of 128 could roll them, no problem, or so the leadership figured.

This legislative takeover of probation had occurred about four years ago, and since then the hacks had been running amok. The judges, greedy pricks that they are, wanted more, and not only did the legislature tell them no, they cut the budgets of a couple of the more vocal judges to put an exclamation point on their refusal to share the wealth.

None of this was exactly a state secret—almost every new connected probation hire was snidely reported in the *Herald*, although the *Globe* didn't deign to even mention such low-rent effluvia. Presumably the Globe editors didn't want to embarrass their fellow travelers in the judiciary. It was all so incestuous among the Beautiful People, and Katy wanted so desperately to pass muster with the PC Police. She'd even taken to calling sex-change operations "gender reassignments."

"Let me guess," I finally said. "Finally, a delegation of distinguished jurists, most of whom drifted into Massachusetts from New York, went to see the capos di tutti bow-tied bum-kissers of Morrissey Boulevard, all of whom blew in from the Hamptons and Park Avenue."

"It's always 1953 to you, isn't it, Jack?"

"More like 1853. You're familiar with the Know Nothings, I presume?"

Her great-great-great-great-grandfather had been the governor back then. Oh, how her ancestors had despised Roman Catholics. The Yankee mobs burned convents back in those days. I still have the sign above my mantel that I bought years ago at the JFK Library—"No Irish Need Apply." God, how Katy had hated that sign.

"Now I'm starting to remember," I said. "*Globe* runs a big Sunday story putting together all the little *Herald* stories about the probation hackapalooza, and the judiciary is shocked—*shocked*. And the very next day a blue-ribbon commission—a Pabst Blue Ribbon commission—is set up, and now the feds have a grand jury investigating how Amato's wife and daughter got jobs at the state Lottery after he ran a time for the state treasurer with about a hundred of his P.O.s there."

She nodded. "And of course the Lottery jobs are the ones everybody wants because they're union and you can't be fired if the treasurer runs for governor, which they always do, including this one. And he's going to lose like all the other ones."

So between the grand jury and the blue-ribbon commission,

Amato was going down for the count. Even if he wasn't indicted, he was going to be fired. He needed a soft landing, and what could be softer than a sinecure at one of the new casinos? But as the number two guy in the Senate, Donuts couldn't deliver much. Even as majority leader, he was still basically a coat holder, until he ascended to the throne.

If, however, this year's casino bill suddenly imploded, which it now had, then it would be up to Donuts to pick up the pieces next year. The King is dead, long live King Donuts.

The guy who had been arrested with the gun that killed Sally Curto's nephew—he'd been on probation. He was from Worcester. He'd used his one phone call to reach out to a probation officer who happened to be his brother, who was duking a grand a year to Donuts. It's a small world, isn't it? Plus, one of the two guys who'd opened fire on Bench on Broadway in Somerville—he'd just gotten out of the can too. And the guy in the back seat was a fired probation officer.

Everything was falling into place. But I still couldn't figure out how they knew which places to hit, although I had a feeling Bench McCarthy might be one step ahead of me on that piece of the puzzle.

I hurriedly got up from the table.

"Hey," said Katy, "where are you going? What is this, the old dine 'n' dash?"

Yet another line she'd picked up from me. I reached into my pocket, pulled out a double sawbuck and threw it on the table.

"I'll be in touch," I said, heading out onto West Broadway.

Slip Crowley, my old pal on the Boston City Council, got his start on the Boston Licensing Board. He'd been the driver for a winning candidate for governor, and he'd begged for the job of chief secretary, the guy in charge of patronage in the Corner Office. But

Slip had turned out to be a little rough around the edges for that position—he was always demanding cash from strangers who wanted jobs, even Republicans.

So the governor gave him something where shakedowns were just part of the overhead and no one would ever complain—the Boston Licensing Board, which handled all the liquor licenses in the city. All these years later, Slip still had a few people up there. Before I met Katy at Meg's, I'd asked him to pull the file on Santo's/the Python for me.

"Santo's?" he said. "That dump on Bennington Street?"

"I see you've been there."

"You know what I'm always looking for when I'm running for office?" Of course—a bullet. Slip ran at-large. Every voter got to cast ballots for up to four candidates, because there were four at-large city councilors. But a vote was worth a lot more if it was a "bullet," a single vote. A second vote, for somebody else, meant that you just broke even with the other candidate. Anybody who voted for four candidates . . . well, there weren't all that many voters in Boston that stupid.

"East Boston's one of those places," Slip said, "where I always think twice about asking somebody for a bullet. Don't want anybody to take me literally, you know. And let me tell you, I would never, ever ask anybody in Santo's for a bullet. Not unless I'd made a good Act of Contrition first."

"They call it the Python now."

"A rose by any other name . . ."

"What do you know about Santo's?"

"It's been a bad place for forty years."

"East Boston's changed a lot in forty years."

"The language, maybe, but Santo's is still a magnet for assholes."

"Can you find out who owns it for me?"

"I can find out who's listed as the manager."

"Do the right thing, Slip."

21

WHEN HENRY MET SPIKE

I was holding court at my Allston outpost, Grogan's Run. Believe it or not, some guys don't like to go into either Somerville or Roxbury. So I was negotiating with a couple of tailgaters from Southie. They wanted to know how many cases of cigarettes I could take. I asked them how many could they get. Every time the legislature jacks up the tax another dollar an extra pack my bootlegging business goes up another thirty percent. Cigarette smuggling is a bigger racket now than it was in the sixties.

It's gotten ridiculous, how much smokes cost. After all the taxes, a carton of cigarettes now costs around $100 in Massachusetts. In New Hampshire, it's "only" $56, and of course it's even less in the tobacco-growing Southern states. The local taxes were so onerous that the five-mile zone just south of the New Hampshire border was starting to look like Syria, with nothing but abandoned convenience stores, gas stations and packys, none of whom could compete with nearby New Hampshire's lower prices.

Every time the legislature hiked the cigarette excise tax yet again, the DMZ would creep another mile or so south. The state economy was withering away, but for cigarette smugglers, it was boom times.

I was haggling with the Southie crew over price before rather than after the "heist" because the drivers read the newspapers too, and they understand their loads are suddenly worth a lot more dough. The Southie hijacking crews know better than to ask me to front them anything, but they wanted a number on how much they could expect from the job.

None of these were what you'd call real "hijackings," of course. The driver just turns over the load to his friends, and they pay him off. That's why they were asking about money. I'm positive the truck driver had other crews putting bids in too. Hell, he wouldn't be much of a Local 25 Teamster if he couldn't get at least a little auction going. The guys I was dealing with, I offered them top dollar because the profit margin now was too great to risk losing a load over a few hundred bucks. They were satisfied with the price and all I asked in return was that not all of the Marlboro Lights and Newports go missing before the truck got to my warehouse in Everett.

I don't mind a few random cases of Parliaments and Merits and Alpines thrown in with the popular brands, but please, don't piss down my back and tell me it's raining.

We'd about wrapped up our business when my cell phone rang. It was Hobart.

"Spike Tierney's on his way over to see you," he said, and I groaned. Spike Tierney was a hothead, a loser, a drunk. I motioned to the Southie guys that we had a deal and that I'd catch up with them later. I kept the phone to my ear as we all stood up and shook hands and then I sat back down to talk to Hobart.

"I thought he was still in on that weapons beef," I said.

"I guess he got out."

"He looking for work?"

"No, he's looking for his girl."

"His girl? What am I, fucking Craigslist?"

"His girl is Dottie. She was over here drinking the other night, remember?"

"What's she look like?"

"She looks like every other skank hanging out here."

In other words, twenty-five going on fifty-five.

"So he just got out," I said, "and now he's trying to run her down because she sent him a 'Dear Spike' letter. Is that it?"

"Something like that, I guess. I thought you might want a heads-up."

"You didn't tell him where I was, did you?"

"Fuck no, are you kidding? He just walked out. I told him she'd been in here, but I guess maybe he figures you know something I don't. He's working the circuit."

I hung up and considered the possibilities. Spike was a real red-ass, just what I didn't need. But then it occurred to me that for once in his life, perhaps Spike could do something worthwhile for me.

About five minutes later, Spike Tierney swaggered in. Gone five years, and he was acting like he'd never left. He sauntered over to my table, a big smile on my face. He thrust his hairy paw out and I stood up to shake it.

"Bench, it's been a while." He sat down, uninvited. That was a bad habit he had picked up in the prison mess. "Listen, I need a favor." Who didn't?

"Remember my girl Dottie? I been looking for her all over town since I got out. I can't find her nowhere. If I didn't know better, I'd swear she's giving me the swerve. But I hear she's at the Alibi the other night, and I am wondering, do you talk to her?"

"Dottie?" I said, furrowing my brow, pretending to give it some real thought. "Dottie Ballou, right?"

"That's it, Bench. Dottie Ballou. A real doll."

If he thought Dottie was a real doll, then she hadn't been visiting him much down at MCI-Norfolk. She'd put a lot of miles on that chassis of hers during the five years he'd been away. Whatever Liz McDermott was guzzling, Dottie was drinking double.

"Dottie?" I said, laying it on thick. "The night she was in my place, I think she was with Henry Sheldon."

"Henry who?"

"Henry Sheldon. He's a loan shark down Weymouth. Big fat fuck." I grimaced. "I don't mean to be the bearer of bad tidings here, Spike, but I thought they were an item, you know what I mean?"

His lips curled into a frown, more than a frown, actually, more like rage.

"Henry Sheldon, huh?" he said. "Where's this motherfucker's office?"

I had to tell him. What are friends for? He stormed out of Grogan's Run. I got up and watched him climb into an old, beat-up Dodge, of all things. It looked like about a fifty-fifty shot Spike could make it as far as Weymouth in that POS. I was also watching to make sure he hadn't forgotten the quickest way to Weymouth. He turned right and headed north on Market Street, toward Storrow Drive to the Turnpike Extension. Poor Henry. I figured he had about forty minutes to live.

22

THE MOTHER'S MILK OF POLITICS

God, I hate to park downtown. I don't care if I'm running a cheat sheet or not, it still pisses me off to pay thirty dollars for a couple of hours. But I had a stop to make at City Hall. By the time I got to the seventh level of the Government Center garage, I was dizzy from going up all those flights in circles. The elevator smelled of urine, but that was better than the only other thing it could have smelled like.

City Councilor Slip Crowley was sitting in his fifth-floor office, feet on his desk, watching a rerun of *Charlie's Angels* and smoking a Kool.

"Take a load off, pal," he said, motioning toward a chair. "I don't know how much good this is going to do you, but I pulled everything in the file on Santo's."

The folder was fairly light, but I didn't have much time.

"Gimme the CliffsNotes version," I told Slip.

"Last year, month of February sticks out," he said.

"And why would that be?"

"They didn't get closed down once that whole month." He crushed out his cigarette. "You may remember, that was the month there were three blizzards. Or was it four?"

"Owner of record?"

"One Domenic Gargiulo. Does the name ring a bell?"

"No, should it?"

"He's a probation officer, East Boston District Court."

"No shit," I said, standing up and walking around Slip's desk. "Does that computer of yours work?"

"How the fuck would I know?"

It worked. Slip got up from his desk and went around to the couch and again put his feet up. It wasn't an election year. Things were slow. Correction: things are always slow at City Hall. They're just slower in the even-numbered years.

I quickly got on to the website of the Office of Campaign and Political Finance. Life is so much easier with the Internet. I clicked on "Candidates" and typed in the name Donahue. Then I clicked on "Contributors" and typed in the previous year and the name Gargiulo. I got just what I was looking for.

He lived in Revere with a woman named Donna, and a couple of kids, all of whom were deeply committed to fulfilling their civic responsibilities, namely, handing cash to politicians who could return the favor, in spades.

Their favorite statesman was none other than Donuts Donahue of Worcester.

"Find what you were looking for?" Slip asked.

"Tell me something, Slip," I asked. "Why would a probation officer in East Boston and his whole family be giving money to Donuts Donahue? I mean, I know the connection to Donahue through his cousin, but why not one or two of the local guys too?"

Slip lit up another Kool. "You're lucky you're asking me these questions, and not one of your marks up in the State House. People might start saying you've lost your fastball."

"C'mon, Slip, don't bust my balls."

"It's simple, pal. There's too many guys in Boston, splitting up too few jobs. Unless he's in leadership, a rep in Boston gets one or two probation jobs, if he's lucky. Out west, less competition for the slots.

More Republicans for one thing, and even they have to get a few. Eventually, one of them probation hacks out in the 413 area code picks off a deputy commissioner's job. That makes it a lot easier to get somebody in, if you don't have to call the commissioner in Boston, like everybody else does. Think of western Mass like baseball. They're not in Fenway, they're in Pawtucket, but when you're going after a P.O.'s job, what the hell does it matter who gets it for you?"

"So Donuts maybe got Domenic Gargiulo his job?"

"More'n likely."

"And the introduction came in the usual way."

"If you mean Benjamin Franklins, plural, the answer is yes."

I asked Slip if he remembered Santo's from his old days on the Licensing Board.

"I do indeed. It was an In Town joint. Course, what wasn't over there, back then? I read over the police reports before you got here, they're celebrating diversity now, if you know what I mean."

I knew what he meant. Knives, machetes even. Still, Slip didn't use the old slurs like "spic" anymore. Too many cell phones recording everything. One bad video on YouTube and your career could be over.

"Why would Donuts be going to the Python late at night?" I asked.

"I'd find that hard to believe."

"Believe it."

As long as I was at City Hall, running up my parking tab in the Government Center garage, I might as well save myself some time later and take care of another errand. I got back on Slip's computer and punched in the name of a pay site I'm a member of, where you can run DOBs and phone numbers and addresses. This time I was looking for DOBs—of Mr. and Mrs. Gargiulo. Odds were, they'd been born in Boston, and if they had been, their birth certificates would be on file in the city clerk's office on the mezzanine.

I got the dates I was looking for and headed downstairs. As I expected, the line was the usual new-Boston Tower of Babel, ninety

percent illegal aliens queued up to pull their anchor babies' birth certificates. They were only taking the welfare Americans couldn't be
bothered taking, as George W. Bush would say. The birth certificates they needed to prove that one of them was at least technically
an American citizen, which entitled the entire family to the full
Tsarnaev, as we now called the panoply of welfare bennies avail-
able to every Third World freeloader who could drop a baby here in
the Live for Free or Die state.

I finally got to the window, and asked for the birth records books
from 1965 and 1968, the years the Gargiulos had been born. Normally, that's a bit of a pain in the ass, because you may be there for
a while, but the clerk was so happy to be waiting on a fellow Amer-
icano that there were none of the usual dirty looks. Plus, I had the
birth dates.

Mrs. Gargiulo's maiden name was Zenna, and her mother's
maiden name was Palermo. Neither of them rang a bell. But when
I got to Domenic, I saw that his mother was the former Carmela
Marzilli.

Marzilli—as in Blinky Marzilli. I wrote down the particulars and
then asked the clerk to make me a copy. Now that I was actually
asking her to get up out of her chair and do something, her attitude
took a turn for the worse. It improved when I handed her a twenty.
I wanted to have something to show Bench McCarthy the next time
I saw him.

23

JUNK IN THE TRUNK

In the morning, the story about Henry Sheldon was all over the all-news radio station. The manager of a loan company in Weymouth had been gunned down in his office, but no cash was missing. Robbery did not appear to be a motive. The police were baffled. I love it when the police are baffled.

Poor Henry, I'm sure he never saw it coming. But then, how could he? I began to wonder, what other loan sharks might be willing to loan an upstanding character like me some dough? Next time, why not go for fifty, or even a hundred large?

It was about 7:30 in the morning, and the first thing I did as I walked into the bar on Hancock Street in Quincy was make eye contact with the bartender. I knew him vaguely, and he recognized me and nodded. Ditto Foley had told him to be expecting me. He motioned silently with his head toward the back of the bar. I'm sure he noticed the billy club I was carrying in my right hand. I'd left my car in the alley behind the bar, in case I had to leave in a hurry. Then I'd walked around and entered the bar through the front door.

There were already a couple of working men sitting at the bar, but they didn't look like cops. For one thing, they appeared sober, like they'd just gotten off the overnight shift at the nearby Stop & Shop warehouse. But everything about the guy sitting by himself in a booth in the back of the darkened, dirty room screamed cop—bad cop. There were three empty highball glasses in front of him, and a half-full one. He was holding a smartphone. Twenty years ago, it would have been a *Racing Form*. He looked like the kind of guy you used to see at Suffolk Downs in the afternoons. Now he probably owed twenty large to some offshore gambling outfit run by a congressman's on-the-lam brothers-in-law.

I slid into the booth across from him, keeping the sap low so he couldn't see it as I laid it down next to me on the pockmarked, slashed plastic that covered the bench.

"Are you Tim Fitzpatrick?"

He looked up, somewhere between shit-faced and legless. I doubted he'd drawn a sober breath in at least five years. "Who wants to know?"

"That's not important," I said. "What's important is your son."

"My son?" You couldn't say he bristled exactly, because he was too far gone to bristle. Recoil was more like it.

"Listen carefully," I said. "Your son is threatening to file a criminal complaint against the son of a friend of mine. This friend of mine gave you $5,000 yesterday, which seems more than fair under the circumstances, namely that your son came out on the short end of a barroom brawl."

"Who are you?" he said blearily.

"Believe me, you don't want to know. Now listen, I can't stop your son from filing a complaint against my friend's son, but if he does, I've got a guy who's going to file a complaint against your son for starting another fucking fracas in a gin mill."

"Bullshit."

"This guy I know, he's going to swear that your son sucker-punched him, not in Quincy, but in Boston. Boston, you understand. Where you don't have any clout, but this friend of mine does. He knows the clerk/magistrate, and he knows the judge. And we have witnesses. And your son has a record, I've checked his CORI. He won't get much time, but he'll get thirty days in South Bay, and my friend's got friends of his own in South Bay, and some terrible things've been known to happen in South Bay, most of which don't even make the papers anymore. But guys inside there are getting shanked all the time. Or maybe they get a hot shot, you know what I mean?"

He squinted at me. "Do you know who you're talking to?"

"I'm talking to a motherfucker who oughta be very happy with his five grand that he can now proceed to blow on stupid fucking bets or give it to his son so he can stick it up his nose. I'm talking to a drunk-ass loser who ought to be giving a good talking to to his son about trying to shake down people who've already beat the shit out of him once. *Capisce?*"

His nostrils flared. "I don't have to take no shit off no guinea hood from Boston."

"I wouldn't know about that," I said. "But I do know you do have to take shit off me. This is your one and only warning."

Out of the corner of my eye, I saw the bartender glancing over at me. He was shaking his head. Perhaps I'd spoken too loudly. Like me, he didn't want any trouble. I nodded, to silently indicate to him I'd keep my voice down so that the two guys from Stop & Shop wouldn't notice anything amiss. I'd have bought them a drink except I didn't want them looking over this way to thank me. Then I turned back to the cop.

"I'm going to tell you just one more time: you've been paid five grand, now you better quit while you're ahead. You won't be hearing from me again. Neither will your son. But if my friend or his son hears from you, you're going to be in a world of hurt, and I don't mean maybe. Some guys can fix things in Quincy, and some guys can fix things in Boston, and the ones who can fix things in Boston, those are the guys you have to watch out for."

His mouth was half-open. He'd be pissed when he sobered up, as much as he ever sobered up, that is.

"So you're Ditto Foley's muscle?"

"I'm just a friend of his—and yours," I said. "Let's keep it that way."

"Fuck you," he said, and that's when I realized he was one of those guys who just wouldn't listen to reason. Sometimes you get more with kind words and a billy club than you get with kind words. So I grabbed my sap, gripped it tightly, rose from the booth and reached across to slug him squarely across the side of his face. Luckily, he was so drunk he didn't cry out, just slumped out of the booth and thudded loudly onto the floor, unconscious. The two guys at the bar heard that and turned around, as did the bartender.

"Guy can't handle his booze anymore," I yelled. "Wet brain, like Ted Kennedy there at the end. It's a tough way to go."

The bartender had come back to check on things. He wanted to do something, but I told him, "Just give them a round on me, Sully, and put it on my tab. I'll get him out of here."

Free drinks! That's usually all it takes to make a concerned citizen lose interest. I leaned over and grabbed Fitzpatrick by the collar of his jacket. For the first time I noticed the gut on him. He was a real load. I dragged him out to the back door, then out into the alley. I was out of breath by the time I dropped his dead weight onto the pavement. I fumbled for my car keys and then unlocked the trunk. I gathered him up again and grunted as I pushed him against the open trunk. He fell back heavily, still unconscious, so I grabbed him by the legs and lifted him up and into the trunk. I slammed it down and went around, got into the car, started it and drove off.

A drunk ex-cop passed out in the trunk of my car, and it wasn't even eight in the morning. This day had nowhere to go but up.

My next stop was Sally's headquarters In Town. It was on Prince Street, and everyone called it the Dog House because Sally's mother used to sell hot dogs out of it. I pulled my car up in front of the sign "Reserved—Valet Parking." The valet had taken the day off so I just got out of the car and walked up the steps that led to the front door.

There were two guards posted outside the door. One of them was Cheech, in his usual overcoat. His brother Hole in the Head wouldn't even be buried for a couple of hours, but for Cheech the mourning period was over. On the other side of the steps was one of the younger guys in his crew, a kid named Blur, wearing a Bruins jacket over a large handgun, maybe a .44.

I saluted them and bolted up the steps. There were two more guys just inside the door, and I walked past them and headed into Sally's back office. His son Jason was sitting there, his legs crossed. Usually this time of day, Jason would be pumping gas himself at the gas station Sally had bought him on Cambridge Street, at the bottom of Beacon Hill. That station was Jason's pride and joy, maybe because his father left him alone there. This morning Jason was looking sheepishly at his father, who was screaming at somebody on his cell phone.

"No no no no," he was yelling. "Don't you even think about it!"

He slammed down the cell phone and looked up at me.

"That fucking broad Liz. She gets arrested again last night, and now she wants me to send a lawyer up to the first session and bail her out."

"Drugs?" I asked.

"Not directly," he said. "Common nightwalking. Turning tricks on Marginal Road. She claims she was set up, but I've heard that before. I give her at least a grand at the wake—you saw me—and now she's locked up again."

"Poor kid," I said.

"'Poor kid'?" Sally said, incredulously. "Whose side are you on? I got people shooting at me, and now I got this here to worry about."

He grabbed another cigarette and lit it. I sat down heavily.

"Hi, Jason," I said but before he could answer, his father cut him off.

"Never mind the small talk," Sally said. "What have you got for me?"

"Nothing new," I said. "You think anymore about that friend of ours that we were talking about last night."

Even though Jason was Sally's son, he wasn't one of us. He didn't need to know about Peanuts and Blinky. If he ever got called before a grand jury, he'd be in a jam—he'd have to either implicate his father (and me) in a murder conspiracy or commit perjury or take a contempt citation.

"You got a plan yet?" I asked.

Sally took a long drag and methodically blew out a series of smoke rings before he spoke again. "You know, I got my own sources too. I'm hearing the same shit you're hearing, I make a few discreet inquiries, I'm satisfied I ain't got a problem."

"So why'd they take our friend's nephew out of general population?"

"You'd have to ask them. I only worry about me."

"You're not worried about our other friend there?"

"No more'n I'm worried about anybody else." He didn't include me with Blinky, in or out, not that I expected him to. I felt the same way about him. That was one of the main reasons we got along. It was strictly criminal. That's also why he didn't shoo Jason out of the room while we were talking. Being Irish, I wasn't a threat to some day muscle Jason out of the line of succession and succeed Sally. What I would be taking over, and why I would want to be taking it over, I could never figure out. But Sally and the boys cared about this thing of theirs, or at least pretended to.

"That kid from City Hall ever find out anything?" Sally asked

"I haven't talked to him lately, but he's got a couple irons in the fire," I said.

"Cripes, I hope they're hotter than yours."

The phone rang again. Sally looked at me glumly and then down at the phone. He must have had a premonition it was more bad news. He was right. He picked up the receiver and listened for a few seconds.

"Noooooooo!" he screamed. "He can't be dead! He owes me $13,000."

I'd been ready to leave, but now I had to know who'd bought the farm. I sat back down again as Sally kept yelling, until he finally slammed down the phone without saying good-bye.

"Remember Camel?" he said. Another morbidly obese half-a-wiseguy, ran a cheese shop on Richmond Street, a degenerate gambler, a barfly. "Took a fucking heart attack last night at Mohegan Sun, keeled right over in front of a slot machine. Deader'n a mackerel. I'm out another 13 g's. I can't fuckin' believe it."

"Gee, Dad," said Jason. "I mean, what did you expect, the way he smoked? After all, his nickname was—"

"Shut the fuck up, college boy!" Sally snarled.

Death cancelled all debts. That's just the way it was. Henry Sheldon could tell you that. I stood back up to leave. So did Jason. Sally looked up at his son with disgust.

"Sit down, college boy," he said. "I want to talk to you about these Las Vegas nights."

He looked at me. "Where you goin'? Sit down—I want you should hear this too. This kid of mine don't believe nothing I tell him. But you—he thinks you walk on water."

I sat back down.

Sally ran Las Vegas nights for some of the local Catholic churches. It was short money, but it kept guys working. Jason had been promoted to boss, but unless you've worked your way up, you'll be lost running a Las Vegas night, or anything else.

"I hear you're using cards more'n half an hour," Sally said to Jason, his eyes narrowing in rage.

"Dad, I tell 'em to keep changing the decks, but sometimes they forget."

"They forget?" he said. "Do they know whose money they're playing with?"

"Gosh dad, I thought you told me to keep that on the q.t."

"What I meant was, tell them it's your dough, but come on tough, like you're the wiseguy. Make 'em fear you!"

Sally looked over at me. "Right, Bench?"

"Explain things to them, Jason," I said gently. "Tell them how card sharps don't need any time to mark the decks, that's what you say to them, so they understand. Just explain it."

"Explain nothing! Say that's a fuckin' order! Change the goddamn decks!" Sally pointed a fat finger at his son. "And that's a fuckin' order 'cause you're a fuckin' idiot. And by the way, I also heard some of your friends are letting these motherfuckers bet up to $300 a hand. I told you, twenty-five bucks max."

"They forget sometimes."

"They forget? Then you tell them you got some guys who might forget not to beat the shit out of them."

"Gee, Dad, it's not as easy as it used to be. I got people coming up to me now, they don't like the odds in the game. They tell me they're being ripped off."

"Ripped off?" Sally jumped up, supporting himself with his two hands on the desk, leaning forward into his son's face. "All you gotta do is tell them, 'It's for charity, you fuckin' asshole!'"

He slumped back down into his chair and glared at Jason for a few seconds longer before turning to me.

"You doin' anything for dinner?" Sally asked me, before looking back over at his son. "I'm talking to Bench, not you, college boy."

I shrugged. Sally wasn't much for formal invitations.

"Come on by the Café Ravenna tonight around six-thirty," he said. "I got some shit we need to talk about."

"We can't talk about it now?" I said.

"Nah," he said, giving me a dismissive wave with his cigar. "What I want to talk about, I'll know more tonight."

"Okay," I said, warily. Jason looked over at me plaintively.

"Can I get a ride with you back up to the station?" he asked, and

I said sure. I felt as sorry for the kid as I felt for Liz. It was that kind of day.

I stood up and walked back outside. Cheech and Blur watched me coming down. Both of them were smirking, which I didn't understand, but when I reached the pavement, Blur pulled me over and leaned in close to whisper in my ear:

"You got somebody in the trunk, Bench?"

I'd forgotten all about the drunk cop. I looked at Blur and nodded without saying anything.

"Has he been yelling?"

"Crying's more like it," Cheech interjected.

"I'm sorry, guys, I apologize." When it's called for, I believe in admitting my errors. "Now, if you'll excuse me . . ."

I went around to my front passenger door, opened it and picked up the billy club off the seat. Then I walked around to the trunk and slammed the club down on the hood. Hated to do it, more body work for Rocco, but how else could I get his attention without opening the trunk? I loudly banged on it, putting two big dents in the trunk.

"Hey, you in there, shut the fuck up or you're in big trouble!"

"Are you going to kill me?"

What a stupid question to ask. This guy was a moron, even by cop standards.

"I told you, shut the fuck up. Now listen to me. Take off your pants and tie them around your eyes, you got that?"

Cheech and Blur were now standing close to the car, cracking up. This was going to be the highlight of their day. Jason just looked confused.

"Are you gonna kill me?" the voice came from the trunk.

"Listen *gavone*"—I threw that in for the In Town guys, and now they were laughing even harder—"if I was going to kill you, why would I need you to blindfold yourself?"

Then I asked Cheech to get me a bottle of the cheapest booze Sally had in his liquor cabinet, and when he returned with a fifth of

Lechmere gin, I hopped in the car with Jason and headed for Government Center.

"Thanks for the ride, Bench," Jason said.

"No problem, kid," I said.

Traffic was crawling, as it always is around Quincy Market. Jason cleared his throat and I had the uncomfortable feeling he wanted to get something off his chest. I was the wrong guy, for this kind of thing I'm always the wrong guy, but sometimes you don't have any choice.

"Bench," he said, "can I ask you something?"

"Sure," I lied.

"Do you think my father's disappointed in me?" It wasn't my place to say anything, and even if it was, I like to keep things strictly professional. It was an awkward position to be in, especially stuck in traffic, all by ourselves.

Jason said, "I mean, I know he's disappointed in me, but I just . . . I don't know, sometimes it's like, it's like you're closer to him than I am."

The light turned green and a big fat female Obama voter sauntered across the crosswalk, oblivious as she talked on her Obamaphone. I leaned on the horn, she turned to give me the evil eye and I responded with the finger. The light was turning yellow as I finally made it around her fat ass and across the intersection.

"C'mon Jason, you're his son, his flesh and blood. I'm just another guy from Somerville who knocks around with him."

"No, no, it's more than that, and you know it."

"Look," I said, "your father just wants what's best for you. He loves you, he really does."

"Yeah, but he wishes I'd turned out like you," Jason said, staring straight ahead.

Some guys are cut out to be wiseguys, and some aren't, it's as simple as that. The kid grew up in Nahant, so the odds were against him—or for him, if you prefer—from the start. He was a nice kid, polite, not a fag, what more did Sally want? I never could figure out what bothered Sally most about Jason, the fact that he was happy running a gas station, or that he'd gone to college for a couple of years.

College, probably. I think Sally figured as long as Jason was running a gas station, even on the backside of Beacon Hill, maybe some day he'd straighten out and start buying loads of hijacked merchandise from his truck-driving customers.

Then Sally would have something to be proud of.

Sally had a nephew, a real nephew, his brother Louie's kid. Jesse James, they called him. Now there was a fucking chip off the old block. Kid was twenty-four, twenty-five years old, grew up in Eastie, dropped out of the tenth grade, a real bad-ass. He started ripping off drug dealers in Chelsea, passing himself off as an undercover cop, pulling out a badge, yelling "motherfucker this" and "motherfucker that" like a real hard-on.

For the record, Sally was appalled, told Louie to cool the kid off. Off the record, he was proud as hell. He was living up to the Curto name. Then one night he tried to rip off a dealer who turned out to be an undercover DEA agent. Cop pulled a gun, Jesse James shot him in the leg, and now he's doing like five hundred years in ADX Florence, the fed's "supermax" prison out in Colorado.

I had to go out there with Sally and Louie last summer to visit Jesse James. I signed in as "Jason Curto." If you think Lewisburg or Devens is depressing, check out Florence sometime. No wonder John Gotti got cancer when he was at the old supermax prison in Marion, Illinois. Dying was the only way he could get out.

"Look, Jason, it's none of my business, so you can tell me to shut up anytime—"

"No, Bench, you're the only one who's close to my dad that I can talk to—"

"Well, what I was going to say is, stop feeling sorry for yourself. Besides, look what happened to Jesse James. Was he a success? Do you think your dad wishes you were locked up like your cousin, for life?"

"Of course not, but sometimes I think he wishes I were what he'd consider a success." He paused. "Like you."

We were at the gas station now. I turned off the ignition and looked over at Jason.

"Jason, let me tell you something, off the record. Guys like your father and me, we're all done. I'm a fucking dinosaur, I'm the last of the Mohicans. Someday something's gonna happen . . ." My voice trailed off, and Jason nodded. It didn't help his own personal predicament, but he knew what I meant.

He shook my hand and got out of the car. I was just getting ready to take off again when I heard a tapping on my window. I looked around and it was Liz fuckin' McDermott. This really was my lucky day. I'd have to remind myself: don't play the numbers tonight. No way I could win today.

I rolled down the window.

"Bench," she said, "I got to talk to you."

Her and everybody else. From the trunk I heard more noises. It sounded like he was kicking the trunk. I sighed, grabbed the club off the backseat where Jason had thrown it, and got out of the car.

"Excuse me, Liz, I'll be with you in a minute."

I went around to the back of the car and this time I really slammed the billy club down on the trunk hard.

"Shut up!" I said. "I'm not warning you again!"

"Where are we?" came a terrified voice.

"It's not where we are, it's where you're gonna be if you don't shut the fuck up! Do you hear me?"

A few seconds later, I heard, "Ye-ye-yesss."

"Say 'yes, sir!'" I ordered.

"Yes, sir!" he said.

I turned around and walked back to the front of the car. Now Liz was laughing.

"Oh, Bench, you're such a card."

"What do you want, Liz, I'm busy today."

"Can you drop me off someplace?" she asked. "I just made bail."

"Who put up the dough?" I asked.

"The Weeper," she said. He was a notoriously tightfisted bail bondsman. I was surprised he would spring for a drug addict like Liz.

"Is the Weeper going soft?" I asked.

"I told him you were my collateral," she said.

She was lying. She knew better than to say something like that. And the Weeper knew better than to believe her.

"Tell me what really happened, Liz?" I asked.

"Okay, I had a watch."

"Did you steal it from those yuppies?"

"No, I borrowed it."

The fog was lifting. There was only one person she could "borrow" a watch from expensive enough to hock to the Weeper for her bail.

"You stole a watch from Sally?" I asked, incredulously.

"I borrowed it," she said. "And I wasn't robbing that other place either, I was just taking a nap. I mean, why would I need to steal anything more if I already had Sally's watch?"

It was junkie logic.

"Let's get in the car," I said. "We have to get the watch back. Who's got it, the Weeper?"

She nodded and wiped a tear from her eye. Then she went around and got in the passenger's side.

"I'm sorry, Bench," she said.

"I'm sorry too," I said. "For you. Did you really tell Sally you were going to tell Rosa?"

"Maybe, I can't remember, but so what? She doesn't know about me? Jason knows." She waved at Jason as he came out of the station to a fill-up some hedge-fund manager's Mercedes.

"Liz," I said, "you're not supposed to flaunt it, don't you understand? Sally's going to want you . . ."

"I know," she said, as we headed south on Cambridge Street, toward the Common and the South End. "He wants to have dinner with me, and I'm afraid. I told him I wouldn't come unless you were there."

Oh, now I understood my late invitation. I was the bait to lure Liz to the Café Ravenna, and from there . . .

"How'd you know where I was?" I asked.

"I called Cheech and asked if he'd seen you, and he said you'd just left with Jason. Are you going to have dinner with Sally tonight?"

"Yes," I said, "but don't go inside until you see me." Now I had another problem: how to avoid going to the dinner where Liz was supposed to get set up.

"Is Sally going to miss the watch?" I asked, but before she could answer, I heard more banging in the trunk.

"Let me out of here!" he was screaming. "I didn't do nothing to you!"

"Shut the fuck up!"

In spite of herself, Liz was smiling.

"I can't believe what you do sometimes," she said.

"Believe it," I said. "Now, is he going to miss the watch or not?"

"Never," she said. "I know where he hides it. It's in—"

"I don't want to know. Just fucking get it back from the Weeper. How much was your bail?"

"Three thousand."

"Jesus Christ," I said, reaching into my coat pocket. Henry Sheldon's money was going fast. I handed her a wad of hundred-dollar bills and told her to get the watch back and we'd worry about putting it back later. I pulled over on Columbus Avenue and let her out.

She came around to my side of the car and tried to kiss me but I brushed her off. No teeth and I could only imagine what her breath must smell like after a night in the lockup and then some cheap hootch to cut the D.T.'s after she made bail.

"Thank you, Bench," she said, looking down at the money in her hands.

Odds were she'd use the money for more coke, or something, but that wasn't my problem. If anything happened, I just wanted to be able to tell myself later that I'd tried to do something. I'd never say it to anyone—that would make me seem weak, sentimental. I just wanted to be able to rationalize it to myself. Maybe I do have a conscience after all.

Nah, probably not.

———

I still had one problem, and he was in the trunk of my car. But as I drove south into Roxbury, I knew exactly what I was going to do with him. I drove into Franklin Park to the old Mattapan State Hospital and found a young tree, not too wide. I parked the car out of sight of the road, went around to the trunk and slammed the billy club down again.

"Are you blindfolded?" I said.

"Yea—yea, yes," he said.

"You better be." I opened the trunk and sure enough, he was.

I pulled him up by his collar and then dragged him to the tree. Then I opened the glove compartment, put on some fresh gloves and took out a pair of police handcuffs I'd picked up somewhere along the line. I used the cuffs to handcuff him around the tree. As fat as he was, it was a tight fit. Then I went through his pockets, found his wallet and extracted Ditto Foley's $5,000 check. He had put me through a lot more than five grand's worth of aggravation. Then I took the bottle of cheap gin from the Dog House and poured it all over his head. Finally, I pulled his underwear down around his ankles. I wanted him to be found seemingly drunk and the victim of some homo hijinks.

"Where am I?" he said, his eyes still covered by his pants.

"Welcome to the jungle, baby."

24

NOT JUST ANOTHER PRETTY FACE

I knew getting the lieutenant governor's cell phone records was going to be a bitch of a job, and I'll tell you why.

The problem was, the State Police had custody of the phone records. The staties are like a different world. I'm a Boston guy, out of City Hall, ex-BPD, heavy connections to the State House through my years as Mr. Fix-it, or Mr. Fixer, for the old mayor.

The State Police cover all of Massachusetts, including even a few parts of Boston, like the airport. I would never think of calling them hicks, but that's exactly how a lot of city guys see them. Whenever they try to expand their footprint in the city, like right now in the Seaport District, there's a major-league turf war. Which is a long way of saying, the BPD and the staties are wary of each other at best, and I'm still a Boston cop as far as the staties are concerned. That makes it much more difficult for me to extract usable amounts of excrement from my erstwhile rivals, especially at reasonable prices.

Typo Rivard, my liaison in the attorney general's office, understood the bureaucratic morass I found myself in. Fortunately, the A.G. has his own cadre of State Police investigators. These are usually very well-connected guys. After introductions from Typo, I had started working with one, a Lieutenant Paulino, who had explained that this case was even thornier, because being from Worcester, the lieutenant governor was very tight with C Troop, who were the first responders to his, ahem, accident. Everybody in C Troop was with the lieutenant governor, at least in the Office of Campaign and Political Finance reports. Well, almost all of them. Which was why we figured that, given enough time, we could find the weak link.

"There's always a bad apple," I told Lieutenant Paulino at our first meeting at the Red Hat, on the bottom of Beacon Hill, just down the street from his twenty-first-floor office in the McCormack Building. "Even Jesus had a—"

"I found Judas," he said with a smile. "It's all lined up."

At this point I wouldn't have been surprised if Typo had told me my services were no longer required, and sent me on my way with a grand for my troubles. But these guys didn't want any fingerprints—always a good policy, but especially when you're dealing with sodomite dynamite here in the Gay State, Sodom and Begorrah.

"I don't have to meet him in Worcester, do I?" I asked.

"Good Christ no, that would be asking for trouble," he said. "It's all lined up for tonight. Eight o'clock. Brian Boru's in Lowell."

These Irish names crack me up, like any of the local harps know who Brian Boru was, any more than they've ever read Flann O'Brien, or Brendan Behan, both of whom also have pubs named after them. There's only one Hibernian name that means anything to American turks—Guinness on Draft.

The pick-up went off without a hitch. At 8:00 p.m. I was sitting in a booth in the back of the Brian Boru under an ancient framed portrait of Eamon de Valera, another Irishman nobody in the bar could pick out of a lineup. With me in a plain business envelope were twenty-five of my closest friends, all of whom were named Benjamin

Franklin. The off-duty statie, wearing a Harley jacket, sidled in across from me and pushed a folded-up edition of that evening's *Lowell Sun* across the table. I reciprocated with a copy of the morning's *Boston Herald*. He got up and left without saying a word. I did the same five minutes later.

I consider myself a professional shit excavator. No need for a written contract, I work on a handshake. I follow my clients' instructions, obtain the political feces that they require, and after thoroughly washing my hands, move on to the next assignment. But this time my curiosity got the better of me. This might be a real game changer. There was a very good chance that the governorship was on the line right here. Like everybody else in the state, I wanted to know who Crash had been calling that morning at 5:20 when he was driving at 108 mph on I-190 in his footy pajamas.

I'd known I couldn't resist the temptation, so I had bought a throw-down cell phone earlier, in the Acre, at a store that had hand-lettered signs in six languages saying "WE ACCEPT EBT CARDS." Outside Brian Boru's, in my Oldsmobile, I ran my finger down the list of phone numbers until I got to 5:22, just after the crash. It was a 508 area code. I picked up the burner phone and dialed. It rang three times before someone picked it up.

"This is State Senator Lisa Mulcahy, how may I help you?"

I hung up the phone. Lisa Mulcahy, oh my God.

The ugliest woman at the State House, maybe in the state. What did the *Herald* always say about her—a whale of a candidate? Not just another pretty face. Tons of fun.

Then I went up the phone bill's list of numbers. He'd started calling the same number at 10:56, probably about the time his wife turned in for the evening. He'd been lining up a session of bury-the-brisket at the local hot sheet no-tell motel.

He wasn't queer after all, just blind. Who knew? This was even better news for the A.G. His foe the lieutenant governor couldn't trump the exposé by coming out of the closet and saying, "I am a gay American."

I immediately called Typo with the good news.

"Turns out he was playing doctor with the shades drawn with the senator from the Third Worcester," I said.

"That sow?" he said with a laugh. Glasses were clinking. As usual Typo was in a bar. "He must have been so horny he'd have fucked the crack of dawn."

The lieutenant governor's career was over.

"I didn't know they were still running Pig Nights at the State House," I said.

Typo Rivard laughed. "Good work, my boy. I'll see you at Foley's in an hour."

My brother Marty has seven months to go on his latest bit, or so it says on the Bureau of Prisons website. He's up at Devens, a federal medical center, a nice place to do time, if you have to do time, which my brother does, because somebody traded him up. He was driving another load of stolen cigarettes, and the cops got a "tip." That makes twice now he's gone away on a load of stolen cigarettes.

It's not easy to get to the phone up there, or so Marty tells me. Not as bad as in some of the higher-security pens, like Otisville. Weekends are the worst, of course, because the cons can call their girlfriends who have jobs, even though in my experience most of them are on the dole, at least lately. Marty tells me Saturdays are quite a show, guys stroking themselves off in front of the payphone. I'll spare you the rest of the X-rated details.

This was a Tuesday. He had the phone reserved for ten. I'd handed over the cell-phone records to Typo Rivard, had a quick hihowahya with him, pocketed my own bulging envelope and then excused myself. I only live two blocks from J.J.'s. The call from my brother came through right on time.

"Commissary account's starting to run a little low, bro," he began. I guess I don't blame him. Gotta be quick, we never talked much longer than four or five minutes. He'd gotten into the Internet, and now he was complaining that the BOP was robbing him blind, a dime per e-mail, everything censored on top of it all. It had to be the only part of the federal government running in the black.

"Can you get up here?" he said. It was the money he wanted to see, not me.

"As soon as I can," I said. "Listen, you hear anything?"

"It's easier to talk in the visitors' room." Pause. "Safer."

"I understand, but I'm in kind of a rush. Anybody taking the bus?"

"Funny you should mention the bus. Remember a guy named Mikey Tickets?"

"Mikey Tickets from East Boston?" I said. "Mikey Tickets from City Hall?"

"Yeah, him. He always talks about how when he worked in Transportation, you used to send over the reps' parking tickets from the State House and it was his job to fix 'em."

Yeah, Mikey Tickets, after the old mayor left office in a photo finish with the grand jury, the same grand jury I was running neck and neck with, Mikey Tickets backed the right guy in the next mayor's fight. He got a promotion, handing out urban redevelopment grants, only he started handing them out to himself, which was why he was riding the bus now.

"Shouldn't he be out by now?" I said.

"Contempt of the grand jury," Marty said. "Another eighteen months, on and after."

"What?" I said. "He was working solo. What's he got to give them?"

"He's from East Boston."

"He was never in the rackets that I know of."

"You sure about that? I repeat, he's from Eastie."

I thought hard. To me he was just another hack from Ward 1, a guy who started every other sentence with "Not for nothing . . ." I think he used to tend bar at Junior's Trolley. Maybe sold a few pills, but . . .

"No, it ain't pills, at least I don't think so. He told me these were DOJ guys came to see him, prosecutors, with DEA and the State Police."

"DEA?"

"They handle organized crime in Boston now, don't you know anything? FBI's been cut out of the loop since Whitey." He chuckled. "Are you back peepin' through keyholes again? You have to call me to find out what's going on?"

He loves to do this to me. He's inside and I'm out. The one time I got in a real jackpot, I was nolle prossed, and yet he's the smart guy, Mr. Three-time Loser.

"Just tell me what happened."

"Okay, okay," he said. "This was about three weeks ago. First they run him through the wringer up here, they drag him out of population and make him sit there in some closet for three hours, you know what I mean? I've told you how it works."

What the feds do is, if you're not cooperating, they throw you in a holding pen for hours at a time. Then they bring you in and you say, I'm not saying nothing until I see my attorney, and they say okay and drive back to Boston. After which you are returned to population, and everybody's giving you the fish-eye look 'cause they think you've been ratting them all out these last three or four hours.

If you're lucky you might not get shanked that same night in the shower.

Next morning, you're calling your lawyer, and the feds are coming back, and this time you are answering their questions, you are ratting, and next thing you know, you're in WITSEC—

"Are you listening?" my brother Marty said. "Mikey fucking Tickets could talk a dog off a meat wagon, so he's okay, he explains to everybody what happened. Once the feds realize he ain't cracking, they put him on the bus."

Diesel therapy, they call it. They drive you around the country, you and a bunch of other cons they're trying to crack. The windows are covered over, so you don't even know what time of day it is. The only thing they feed you is sandwiches with cold cuts, and I don't mean Boars Head Black Forest ham either. So you get constipated. Every night, the bus stops at a different lockup and you file off, but you can't buy anything at the commissary or make phone calls outside, because you don't have an account there.

This can go on for months, or so Marty tells me.

"Is he back yet?" I asked.

"Fuck no he ain't back. There ain't no round-trip tickets on that bus. They either crack you or you end up in some state pen in the south that's ninety percent jig. And that's when you flip. Most guys figure, who needs that? They crack quick once they get on the bus."

"So you haven't talked to him?"

"I just told you, he's on the bus. Or was. Next time I see Mikey Tickets it'll be at Santo's."

"What did you say?"

"He used to tend bar at Santo's before he got hired at City Hall."

I was suddenly anxious to end the conversation. "Thank you very much, Marty. Anything else?"

"Just don't forget me," he said. "You told Ma you'd look after me. The way I interpret that, it means you never let me get under a hundred bucks and, brother, I'm getting close."

I told him I'd see him Saturday. Maybe.

25

I'D RATHER BE LUCKY THAN GOOD

Sooner or later, you get caught flat-footed. To quote somebody, there comes a night when the best get tight—and when it happened to me, I wasn't even tight. I just wasn't paying enough attention as I pulled up into a parking space a few doors up the hill from the Alibi. It was dusk, and there was nobody on Broadway—Somerville has gone from working class to non-working class. It wasn't like the old days, when people at this hour would be getting off the bus and shopping for a few groceries or a six-pack before walking home. Now it might as well as have been midnight.

Suddenly I heard the squeal of tires. That was what saved me. If they'd just driven up at a normal speed they'd have had me cold. Instead, I had time to hit the sidewalk rolling, toward a dented-up minivan with a roof rack for ladders, something that belonged to a tradesman, probably a painter.

As I rolled I could see the front plate-glass window of the Winter Hill Barber Shop explode. They were using an automatic rifle. And I was unarmed. If they knew that, my reputation might still precede me, but it sure wouldn't save me. I'd be the next guy laid out in the front parlor at Rossetti's.

But it was just dark enough, and I was just low enough to the ground. They didn't even know where I was as they next raked the front of the Alibi, but nothing gets through those steel plates. I heard the squeal of tires again, and I raised my head just enough to see the taillights of an SUV, a big one, maybe an Escalade. Stolen, undoubtedly. It was headed east, toward the McGrath/O'Brien highway. I figured I had only a few seconds before the crash car pulled up and opened fire, so I jumped up and bolted for the Alibi. As soon as the boys had heard the shots, they'd locked the front door, and I had to bang on it for a few seconds before Hobart cracked it open, 9 mm Glock in hand. I pushed him back inside, then grabbed the gun from him and relocked the door. Finally I hit the deck, just in case. Outside, they opened fire again. This was car two. They couldn't get to me now, and they knew it, which must have pissed them off, because they fired off a few more angry wasted rounds, which we could hear bouncing harmlessly off the steel plates outside. It only went on for a few seconds, but it seemed longer, much longer. Finally, it was over.

"Call the cops!" I yelled to Hobart. The few customers all started getting off the floor, dusting themselves off. Occasionally customers—civilians anyway—asked me why we'd boarded up the front window years earlier and put steel plating where the glass used to be. I always made some lame joke about being allergic to sunlight. I had a feeling no one would be asking me that question about steel plates again for a good long time.

The cops were there instantaneously, so quickly I barely had time to hand the Glock back to Hobart, who stashed it behind the bar. I knew the TV crews would be here soon too. I called Sam, the owner of the barbershop next door, and told him I'd pay for any deductibles on his insurance policy. He sighed and asked me if we had any plywood or two-by-fours at the Alibi that he could use to board up his place. He was driving in from his home in Arlington.

———

I get some respect in Somerville. God knows I should, I spread enough cash around. When they arrived, the uniforms left me alone and let the captain handle the perfunctory questions. His name was Paul Vitagliano, Paulie Vitt we called him. Two years ahead of me at Somerville High, or would have been, if I had stuck around long enough to graduate.

"What's going on with you guys lately?" he asked me casually.

"Would you believe me if I said I didn't know?" I said.

"Probably not," he said. "I read the newspapers too, you know."

"Well, don't believe everything you read."

After a while the reporters and TV crews arrived. I retreated upstairs to my club—I don't feel like giving every wannabe in the city a good look at me. Rather than block the front door and look like an asshole on the eleven o'clock news, Hobart let the crews inside long enough to get a few wide shots of the bar, sans the few customers who hadn't screwed out the back door when the shooting started. After they got their videotape, Hobart told them to beat it and they all took off for headquarters in Union Square and the official statement from Captain Vitagliano.

There were still a lot of cops around and I knew eventually I'd have to go downstairs and at least make an appearance. But first I wanted to call Sally on his cell phone. I'd stood him up on our date at the Café Ravenna. I was just hoping Liz had done the same.

"Where the fuck are you?" he said, his voice slightly slurred. "You were supposed to be here three hours ago."

"I got ambushed outside the Alibi," I said.

"What? Are you okay?" He sounded sincerely concerned, maybe because if I were gone, Cheech would be his top gun. Hell, maybe his only gun, if he couldn't convince Salt and Peppa to come work for him.

"Yeah, I'm okay, watch the eleven o'clock news."

"Get any of them?"

"Jesus Christ, Sally, I'm lucky to be alive. Remember when I put in those steel plates over the front windows, and you told me

I was wasting my money? Those plates absorbed about a hundred rounds."

"Whatever happened to revolvers?" Sally mused. He sounded like the old man, Tommy Callahan.

"If a guy's got a machine gun," I said, "a thirty-eight's worth about as much as a knife at a gunfight."

"But you're okay, right?"

"I'd rather be lucky than good, Sally."

Now that he knew I was all right, he suddenly seemed a lot more relaxed. Maybe it was the dago red he'd been swilling all night.

"Hey," he said, "I heard on the news tonight, somebody dusted Henry Sheldon."

"Yeah, I heard that too. The police said they're baffled."

"They are, are they?" he said with a chuckle. "Tell you something else I heard. I heard somebody just borrowed some big dough off him."

"Is that right? Got any names to go with that?"

Sally started to say something, then thought better of it. I had a feeling he was going to say something about karma, only karma wasn't his kind of word. What he'd say was, "What goes around comes around."

As if I didn't know.

26

LOVE ON WINTER HILL

As I drove up Winter Hill, the first thing I noticed was the police cruisers in front of the Alibi. I thought about just heading up the hill, turning left on Medford Street in Magoun Square and then heading back into the city.

But my curiosity got the best of me. I parked across Broadway and then crossed over, just as one of the police cars was pulling away from the curb in front of the little barbershop. I saw a slight, older guy standing on the sidewalk. There were shards of glass everywhere, and he was nailing up boards over what was obviously a shot-out window.

I kept walking, and opened the front door of the Alibi.

"We're closed," somebody yelled. Then I saw Bench, sitting at the big circular table with a couple of what I took to be plainclothesmen. He saw me and nodded to the guy who'd yelled at me.

"He's okay, Hobart." He looked back at me and pointed to the bar. "Make yourself a drink, I'll only be a couple more minutes."

The cops didn't ask who I was. That would have been impolite. I grabbed a stool and just sat there. The bartender was apparently taking the night off, and nobody had been called to fill in. Not that I was particularly thirsty. After another ten minutes or so, the cops stood up and shook hands with Bench—I was watching everything in the mirror behind the bar. They made their way out and shut the door, and Bench locked it behind them. Then he turned to me.

"Just another night in the All-American City," he said.

"A drive-by?" I asked.

"What else?" He pointed toward a booth in the back. "Let's sit down. You sure you don't want something to drink?"

I shook my head and sat down. "I found out who owns the Python."

His eyes narrowed. "Anybody I know?"

"You know a guy named Blinky, right? It's some cousin or some other relative of his."

"Be specific."

"All I know is, the owner of record is a broad named Gargiulo, and her mother's maiden name is Marzilli."

He just sat there, staring at me. I took the folded birth certificate out of my coat pocket and handed it to him. He read it silently, shook his head, refolded it and pushed it back across the table to me.

"Anything else?" he finally said.

"Yeah. You know a guy named Mikey Tickets?"

He shook his head. "Tell me about him."

"He used to be one of the mayor's fixers at City Hall. He's from East Boston."

"So?"

"So he's been in the can for a while, mail fraud, wire fraud, the usual shit, he was taking kickbacks to steer federal grants—"

Bench grimaced. "Let me guess, they've brought him back to testify before a grand jury?"

I waited for him to say something else, but he could hold his mud, as my father used to say. Bench McCarthy never said anything that might come back to haunt him in, say, a grand jury proceeding. He never volunteered any information, not to me anyway. Suddenly I heard knocking on the front door of the Alibi and a woman demanding to be let in. Hobart, now sitting at the round table with an automatic in front of him, motioned one of the younger guys sitting at the bar to open the door.

A beautiful dark-haired young woman in a micro-miniskirt rushed in, looked quickly around the bar and made for our booth.

"Bench," she said, throwing her arms around him. "Thank God you're okay. I just heard."

"It happened two hours ago," he said coolly.

"I was getting my hair done," she said. He looked over at me, then back at her. "Patty, this is—" I realized, he couldn't remember my name.

"Jack," I said.

"Bob," he said. "Bob Smith."

"Pleased to meetcha, Bob," she said, then turned back to Bench, real anguish visible on her face. "Bench, why us? Who's doing this?"

"Somebody who doesn't like me would be my best guess." He managed a slight smile, then stood up and hugged her tightly. She had an even better figure than I'd noticed at first glance. "Listen, baby, the good news is they're not very good shots. And the better news is that this time you weren't with me." He kissed her on her forehead. "I'd never forgive myself if something happened to you. You know I love you, baby."

Patty's eyes grew wide. This had to be a very rare occasion, judging from her expression and Bench's reputation as a hard guy. And I was a witness.

"Bench," she said, tenderly, "this is the first time you've ever said you love me."

He reached over and brushed a lock of her long black hair out of her face and around her ear. "I'm not a heart-on-my-sleeve kind of guy, am I, Patty?"

Boy, was that the understatement of the year.

He reached into his coat pocket and came up with a house key, which he handed to Patty. "Hobart'll drive you to Brighton, and you wait for me there. I may not get back 'til late tonight."

All this was right out in the open. I guess Bench didn't keep a lot of secrets from the boys, at least if they didn't involve something that could lead to something that would land his ass in a document that began, "The United States of America versus . . ." Patty stood up and they did another major lip-lock, like it was prom night at reform school. However, the timing didn't seem right to tell them to get a room. So I held my own mud.

With Hobart behind her, Patty sashayed out of the Abili, every male eyeball in the house following her. Obviously Bench didn't mind; she was yet another confirmation of his status as the alpha male in these here parts.

After Patty and Hobart were gone Bench told the just-arrived fill-in bartender to turn the outside lights back on, including the flashing beer light in the smaller, side front window that wasn't covered by steel plates. It had somehow been spared in the fusillade; Central American armies have never been renowned for their marksmanship, or anything else for that matter.

"Never let 'em see you sweat" were apparently a few more of Bench's words to live by. But Bench wasn't taking too many chances. Just inside the door, out of sight from the sidewalk, he had one of his guys in a captain's chair, a sawed-off shotgun on his lap, covered by a beach towel. Of course you may be thinking that possession of a sawed-off shotgun is a felony in America. But we weren't in America, we were in Somerville. And Bench apparently hadn't gotten the memo from the Bureau of Alcohol, Tobacco, and Explosives.

On the other side of the front door from the sawed-off shotgun, on the last bar stool in the corner, sat another guy. His stool was turned toward the door, and on the bar in front of him was what looked like a pregnant *Herald*. It bulged out because it was on top of a 9-mm Glock. The odds of the East Boston crew reappearing tonight were slim, but like the Boy Scout he'd never been, Bench preferred to Be Prepared.

He walked over to the booth and noticed where I was sitting, looking north, toward the door.

"Mind switching over to the other side of the booth with me?" he asked. "I like to be able to see the door—it's just one of my little, uh, peccadilloes."

I stood up and made the change. Bench slid into the other side and then slapped a .38 revolver on the table. "You understand?" he said and I nodded. I understood.

"Tell me more about this Mikey Tickets," he said.

"I don't know much, just that he's on his way back."

"Is he on the bus?"

"I'm not sure, but my understanding is, they're not trying to bust his balls."

"If you're on the bus, they're busting your balls." He took a deep breath; he looked quite beat, which was understandable, considering. Watching him, I noticed something small and shiny reflecting in his hair. It took me a second to realize it was a tiny sliver of glass. I averted my eyes quickly before he spoke.

"You know there's more than one grand jury," he said. "What's your interest in this hack?"

"He used to work at Santo's."

Bench nodded. "Seems like all roads lead to Santo's. But what's this got to do with me?"

"What's this got to do with you?" I asked. "How about, you don't get shot."

"Too late for that. They've already been shooting at me."

He wasn't exactly a font of information, but there were certain steps that Bench could take to put an end to this that I couldn't. So my job here was to provide him with enough information to get the ball rolling. How he got the mission accomplished, that really wasn't my concern, or my clients'. So I didn't think I had a lot to lose by leveling with him, at least up to a point.

I asked him if he'd known who owned the Python, and he shook his head. He was tapping his fingers on the table, as if he were try-ing to recall something or somebody else.

"It's interesting, that name Marzilli," he said, "but sometimes one and one don't add up to two, they add up to three, or four. I can't take anything for granted. Could be instead of the way you're laying it out, somebody's out to knock off me and the other guy and the casino bill is the decoy, instead of the other way around. You follow me?" He rubbed his eyes, as if he'd been up for twenty-four hours, although I doubted very much he rolled out of bed before noon.

"What I can't figure out," Bench said, "is why wouldn't all of these casino people want this bill to pass? Way I got it figured is, if you have to post a bond to build a $500 million casino, there has to be plenty of money to go around. More than enough for everybody. Am I right?"

I shook my head. "Not everybody gets a license. In fact, most of them don't. The problem is, there's only three casino licenses up for grabs, one of which is set aside for the Indians. They cut the state into three districts, and if the law's passed then the new Gaming Commission decides which applicant in which district gets the license."

He nodded. He still read the newspapers. "Seems like it'd be a lot cheaper, not to mention less trouble, just to bribe those guys for a license. How many are there?"

"Five, but they all answer to the politicians who appointed them."

"In other words, they're bagmen is what you're telling me."

"That's one way to put it, I suppose."

"Is there any other way to put it?"

"Not really," I said, "now that I think about it."

He smiled weakly. "This has to end, one way or the other, and as far as my friends and I are concerned, it only ends one way."

"That's the way we feel too."

"Well, we feel it a little stronger, if you know what I mean. This thing is costing your people a lot of money. But you can always get more money. They're trying to kill us." He took a dog-eared business card out of his shirt pocket, turned it over and wrote a number on the back, then pushed it across the table at me.

"Memorize that number," he said. "You need to reach me, that's the number to call."

He let me watch it five or so seconds longer, then pulled it back and returned it to his pocket.

"Do you want mine?" I said.

"Nah," he said. "I have a feeling you'll be needing to call me before I need to call you."

27

SALLY SINGS THE BLUES

I met Sally at Carson Beach the next morning. I came by myself. After last night, he was again accompanied by a driver/bodyguard, a guy I'd never seen before. I explained the situation to him, as it had been explained to me. He was not happy.

"So Blinky's cousins or some such shit own Santo's, and you think he should get hit over that?"

"I'm just putting the facts on the record, Sally. It's your call."

I didn't mention my theory about how Blinky was going to blame me for killing Sally, which would set me up for my own Rossetti's send-off. I wanted Sally to regard me as a disinterested observer.

"Are you telling me some fuckin' assholes are usin' me for target practice to kill a bill?" he said, his voice rising. "This ain't even about the rackets?"

"Don't take it personally, Sally. It's just that people recognize our names. If they want to scare off the legislature, they need names that the public will recognize."

"Fuck the public," he said. "Two more killed last night in Maverick Square. Spics. Spics killing spics, not usually one of my big worries. It's on the metro front of the *Globe*." He yelled over to his driver, who brought over the paper, which I thought Sally had said he didn't read. The guy passed it over to Sally, who handed it to me. I scanned it quickly—two guys in a parked car. No IDs, no licenses, no plates on the car. They weren't any of our guys, that much was for sure.

"Coulda been anything, Sally," I said. "Drugs, most likely."

Sally shook his head. "Do you believe in Santa Claus too? Look, if what you're saying is true, they need more bodies. I'm totally shut down. I finally told everybody, fuck it, go to Florida 'til this thing blows over. Of course, they'd already fuckin' screwed anyway, so I might as well stay ahead of the curve. It ain't as much of a problem for you. The spics look more conspicuous in your areas."

Except for Castle Island here, Sally hasn't been to any of my areas lately, or if he has, he hasn't been paying enough attention. The whole world is turning into Greater Chelsea. Revere is tottering. Shirley Avenue looks like Dot Ave, which looks like Saigon.

"Here's what I wanna do," he said. "I'm gonna tell everybody to come back from Florida. We're gonna start taking these people down. They wanna war, they're gonna get a war."

Yeah, and I knew who was going to be the one to fight it. To quote Sally himself, his guys couldn't find their way off Hanover Street. Steroids, cocaine, cannolis—they were as worthless as tits on a bull. A war was just what I didn't need. There were too many conspicuous spics, and only one of me.

"Sally, let me explain it to you again. These people that killed your nephew, that killed Hole in the Head and Vito, that have tried twice now to kill me—these guys want a war. You start one with them and they win."

"Hey pal, I got news for you. They kill us, they win too." He took a cigar and a small cutter out of his topcoat. He tried to cut off the top of the cigar, but his hands were shaking. He looked up at me in embarrassment, pocketed the cigar and cutter and pulled out a pack of Marlboros. He lit one, and after a couple of puffs, he started talking again. "Besides, I been thinking, if this 'war' so-called kills the casino legislation, maybe we can cut ourselves in next year."

"Sally," I said. "Are you fuckin' nuts? I thought we agreed on this. This isn't Vegas 1965. The Rat Pack ain't walkin' through that door. We can get some short-money shit, but nobody's cutting us in on a counting-room skim, and you know it. These are publicly traded corporations. They got security, they got surveillance cameras, they got lawyers, this ain't like shaking down a bookie. We'd have better odds going back to robbing banks."

"That was your thing," he pointed out. "You were the stick-up guy."

"And you know why I quit—'cause everything had changed. Cops can scramble too fast. Takes big balls to walk into a bank, always did. Now it takes big balls and small brains—it ain't worth it. Twenty-five, thirty grand, and they hit you with thirty years on and after just for the machine gun."

"We ain't talking about robbing banks, we're talking about being shot at," he said. "They're using us as, whattayacallit, props, in their own fucking movie. We gotta fight back."

I shook my head.

"Sally, you're not listening to me. Somebody put these people up to this. Me and this kid from City Hall, we seen Denis Donahue, the senator, he's gonna be the president next year, we seen him over on Bennington Street in Santo's there."

"So we hit him too."

"Are you crazy?"

Sally sighed and threw his cigarette over the seawall onto the beach. He sagged, then walked over and slumped onto a bench. I followed and sat down beside him.

"I just got so much on my mind." He closed his eyes and shook his head. Something had to be wrong, because he wasn't screaming at me, telling me to tell myself to go fuck myself. I knew better than to ask him anything. Whatever he wanted to say, he'd get around to it, in his own way. Finally he did.

"It's Liz," he said. "She's been coming 'round the Dog House yel-
lin' at me—in front of the boys. You can't slap a broad around no
more. Look how many State Police get busted these days. If a statie
can't slap a broad around, who can? I just have to sit there, taking
it, and she fuckin' yells."

He tries to use me to set her up, I can't make it because I almost
buy the farm, and now he's singing the blues, to me of all people.
But I had to keep up my end of the conversation.

"What's she yell about?"

"How the hell do I know? It's shit that don't mean nothing. She
thinks I was talking to some other broad, I forgot her birthday, one
of the boys didn't take her car in for a tune-up, before her car got
repo'ed that is. Who the fuck knows? It's a different thing every
day, all married-type shit. You think I need two wives? One is too
many. Way too many. And since when do you have to remember
your girlfriend's birthday? They must have fuckin' changed the
rules on that one too."

I thought about Patty. Someday she was going to put the full-
court press on me.

"Anything I can do?" I asked, then realized I didn't mean that.
"You know, talk to her, something like that."

"Nah," he said, finally looking up at me. "This here's something
I gotta handle on my own."

I told him I'd make my rounds and report back.

"Okay," he said. "I'll see you tonight at the Café Ravenna. Eight
o'clock. I still owe you dinner."

Jesus, I'd thought I was past that land mine. Sally was giving
Blinky a pass, but he still wanted to whack Liz. I wondered how I
could get out of the dinner tonight, and tomorrow night, and the
night after that.

28

A BUG AT B.B. BENNIGAN'S

I was in the waiting room in Caulfield's office on Park Street. The old man was meeting with another group of clients, this time Chinese. Finally they left, bowing all the way out the door, and I was ushered in.

"Global economy's working out for you?" I asked him.

"They pay more than my . . . traditional clients, let's put it that way, young man," he said sourly. "The problem with my American clients is, they actually expect me to deliver."

I filled him in on what I'd learned. I told him about Bench McCarthy, and about the probation commissioner, and their trip to the Python in East Boston.

"You actually went to East Boston," he said. "I'm impressed, Mr. Reilly. That's what I call legwork."

"I can't remember that going to East Boston was ever a box of chocolates, Mr. Caulfield. But it looks pretty shady, the next president of the Senate, in that barroom."

Against my better judgment, I mentioned the grand jury. There's always a grand jury sitting, somewhere. So if you act like you're passing on some inside information, you just sound stupid.

We used to make jokes at the State House about grand juries being empaneled "on spec," but they really aren't. Whatever grand juries are currently in session just handle anything that comes along. I'm talking federal of course. The state attorney general doesn't do grand juries, unless he's going after a tree warden somewhere in Franklin County, or maybe a car dealer suspected of trying to turn back odometers, which is impossible now anyway. I think it's in the state constitution—the state A.G. never goes after anybody who can fight back—i.e., the legislators who control his budget.

Not that I cared—these days, the A.G. was my very good friend. He was my candidate for governor, at least until somebody else came along with more money.

"I'm not sure what this grand jury is doing, or even how many there are," I said to Caulfield, already regretting my decision to mention it. "Maybe two—one going after the Mafia, the other going after the State House."

Mr. Caulfield looked bored. The only thing in East Boston he cared about was the airport. "Do you have anything for me to report back to my clients?" he asked.

"Stall 'em," I said. "I can't put it together yet." I thought for a while. "You think I could get a bug in Donahue's office?"

"A bug?" he said with a smile. "In Denis Donahue's office? He has the place swept every weekend by the State Police. He's so paranoid he's installed motion detectors in his office. That's off the record, by the way. But the point is, forget about it."

"Help me out here, Mr. Caulfield. I don't know this guy. He's gotta have some habits. There must be some places he likes to hang. How about the Twenty-First Amendment?"

"You mean the Golden Dome?" he said, using the Bowdoin Street bar's old name. "I'm sure he hasn't been in the Golden Dome since Keverian was speaker." He paused. "Okay, I just thought of something. He has a table at B.B. Bennigan's, goes there every afternoon around five, meets people."

B.B. Bennigan's was a lunch-trade pub on Tremont Street near where Dini's Sea Grill used to be, with food that was just about as forgettable. It also attracted a pretty good cocktail-hour crowd, but was closed by nine at the latest. Who the hell would want to be walking around that part of Tremont Street after dark, given the sort of riffraff that hangs out on the Common and in Downtown Crossing?

I asked Caulfield, "What kind of people does he meet there?"

"Bagman people. Connected people."

"Have you been there with him, Mr. Caulfield?"

"Certainly," he said. "If I hadn't, what sort of a 'connected' person would I be? Do you really think you could drop a bug in there?"

"Have you got any better ideas?" I asked.

He said nothing but leaned across his one-acre mahogany desk and sighed, which I took as a nonverbal, deniable-if-need-be-later acknowledgement that he was in for a penny, in for a pound, sort of, at least as long as I didn't get caught.

He told me that as you walked in the front door of B.B. Bennigan's, there was a bar on the right, and on the left, maybe ten to twelve booths. In the middle were tables, foursomes. Denis Donahue had the last booth in the back, and they always kept the second-to-last booth vacant, to prevent eavesdropping. Donuts always sat facing out, toward the door and Tremont Street.

"Regular bartender?" I asked.

He nodded. "One anyway, two at the most. Suffolk Law students, the usual."

I stood up.

"Are you going to make a run at him?"

"Do I have a choice?"

"Be careful," he said. "If you're caught—"

"I know, I know. The secretary will disavow any knowledge of my actions."

29

SANTA'S LITTLE HELPER

There are places so down-and-out, or corrupt, or most often both, that even wiseguys can't make money out of them anymore. Chelsea is one such place—the old Winter Hill gang pulled out back in the eighties because so many people had their hands out that even Whitey and Stevie couldn't turn a profit. East Boston is getting to be almost as bad.

Now I was back in Eastie for the second time in two days. I'm used to people delivering money to me. In Eastie, I'm the one making the deliveries, this time to the family of another one of my guys who's doing a bit, in Allenwood. His name is Ricky, and he made the mistake of taking a machine gun on his last armored car robbery. I tried to warn him, I try to warn them all, but what do 213,091 inmates of the Bureau of Prisons have in common?

They didn't fucking listen.

I still called Ricky occasionally, for information, because he might be rubbing elbows with a different crowd down there than Bobby Bones. The problem was, if I didn't want to drive down there again, and I didn't, I always had to go to his mother's house to talk to him. She was on the BOP's approved list of callers, and I wasn't.

The drawback with using the relative of some jailbird to make the calls for you is that they expect something in return. I told you about Bobby Bones' sister in Charlestown. That's like going to the Cotillion at the Myopia Hunt Club compared to visiting Ricky's family.

Their hands were always out, they were lucky they weren't charged with impersonating the illegal aliens who'd taken over Ward 1. Not that I blame the cons' families—usually the guy in the can was the family earner, for better or for worse, and don't believe any of that bullshit about wiseguys' families being taken care of by the benevolent Godfather while they're away. If there are any flies on Sally, they're paying rent. I have to take care of some of the families of the In Town guys who ran with me out on the street, not because I particularly want to, but because somebody's got to do it, and it sure as hell ain't going to be Sally.

With these eighty-five percent federal sentences, sometimes I feel like I'm paying child support, or alimony. They lock guys up now and throw away the key. Career criminals, they call us at sentencing. Which we are, but nobody's perfect. Used to be, I'd be taking care of Ricky's family for maybe seven years. Now it's twenty.

Believe me, I didn't run for the job of Santa Claus. It's just one of my chores, a very expensive chore at that. I hadn't even been looking to talk to Ricky, but one of his cousins sent me word that he was desperate. What could I do? So now I was in East Boston, making a delivery.

I parked my car two spaces down from another low-rider with the hood open and two fresh-off-the-boat illegals peering into the motor. Drug lookouts, just like the ones outside the Python. This is what passes for Neighborhood Watch in Eastie. God, I felt like an asshole. I'd had to hook up with Peppa again to pick up methadone for Ricky's junkie brother so he'd have some for his trip to Florida, and here he was, living in a neighborhood where you would literally trip over drug dealers if you walked out your front door. I'm sure his excuse was, he didn't *comprende español*. Bet he'd learn to *habla* pretty fast if he didn't have me as his gringo mule.

And by the way, Ricky's brother ain't worked since the Johnson administration—Andrew Johnson. Where the hell does he get the money to fly off to Florida on "vacation"? Vacation from what?

Plus, I'd been buying so much shit off Peppa lately, I figured he was starting to wonder about me. I wouldn't be the first boss to start dipping into his own wares.

I walked up the steps and almost broke my ankle when one of the rotted wooden steps gave way under my left foot. The buzzer didn't work, so I rapped on the door. About a minute later, Ricky's mother limped to the door and let me in. It took about ten minutes for her to gimp her way back into the kitchen with me following behind her. She let out a long sigh as she collapsed into a chair covered in plastic, which someone seemed to have used for a little knife-stabbing practice.

I sat down on the other side of the ancient kitchen table and removed an envelope from my coat pocket. It contained $3,000 in $100 bills, what she claimed her junkie son had stolen from her. I know that's a lot of dough, but this wasn't strictly charity. Ricky and I had done a lot of work together—wet work, during the Charlestown thing—and in addition to being charitable, it was only prudent to try to keep him as happy as possible, and quiet.

Maybe the cops wouldn't have any witnesses, and it would be his word against mine, but why roll the dice? An indictment is always a disappointment.

"You a good boy, Bench," Ricky's mother said in a thick Italian accent. "You always take-a care of Ricky. You didn't have-a to go In Town for this, did you?"

"Nah, Ma, I'm doing okay." Better than Henry Sheldon, that's for sure. That was the silver lining. At least I wasn't parting with my own money. Easy come, easy go.

"Matty, he stole-a my jewelry, even my wedding ring from Santoro—you remember Santoro, don't you, Bench?"

Ricky's father. Yes indeed I remembered him. He gave me my first pinky ring as a bonus after I hijacked a truck carrying TVs for him.

He was a miserable fucking human being, pinky ring notwithstanding. The way Ricky told the story, Santoro had been a prizefighter as a kid, the cham-peen of East Boston. But apparently the only times he ever successfully defended his crown were outside the ring, against Ma. I wondered how much Ma remembered of the real Santoro. She'd been as soft as a grape for a while now, which I'm sure was why her junkie son Matty figured he could steal her valuables.

Anyway, she was babbling on about her wedding ring. Knowing Santoro, I figured she was lucky the ring didn't leave third-degree burns on her finger when he slipped it on.

"It was bee-you-ti-full, four carats. Oh sure, he heisted it, he never told me, but I always knew. You know how you can always tell things like that, Bench."

"I certainly do, Ma."

"But you know, what's it matter? I always say, it'sa the thought that counts."

"It certainly is."

"Matty, he stole-a all my Hummels too, and my Lladros. Santoro give me them too. Most of 'em he gotta from a house he knocka over in Concord. I had a couple hundred of them. First I noticed a few of them missing, then I went to my sistah's in Providence two weeks ago, and when I come back, they was all gone. Them and my jewelry."

"Ricky told me," I said, looking across the table at the envelope full of hundreds. "If I were you, Ma, I wouldn't keep the cash here. Not as long as Matty's around."

She quickly reached across the table, grabbed the cash and shoved it into her apron.

"You a good boy, Bench," she said again. "I always told Ricky, stick with Bench, he knows how to handle himself, he can straighten a thing out."

"He'll be out soon enough," I lied.

"Bench," she said, "about that other thing, for Matty."

I nodded and pulled out the ten packs of methadone I'd gotten from Peppa at $25 apiece. I don't like putting myself in needless jeopardy, and yet here I'd been driving around all morning with a Class A controlled substance, a narcotic. It was insanity. We don't even sell this shit, as a matter of policy, so Peppa had to get some as a favor to me. I'm his boss, but it was still a favor, a favor for an asshole named Matty, and I hate to waste favors, especially on ungrateful assholes. I pushed the packets across the table, but these she didn't immediately pocket.

Instead, she reached for her cane. "I wana Matty should thank you." She slowly stood up, gripped the table with one hand for support and tapped on the ceiling with the cane. "Matty," she yelled. "Come down here, Matty. I want-a you should say thanks to a friend-a your brother's what done you a favor."

I shook my head. "No need for that, Ma." I leaned across the table and took the cane and tapped on the ceiling again. "You can stay up there, Matty." There was no response. He'd probably nodded off. I didn't want to see him, because if I did, I'd most likely slap him around. And that was Ricky's job, not mine.

I stood up and walked around the table to kiss Ma on the cheek. Her breath smelled of garlic and cheap wine. God, what a madhouse.

"Remember, Ma, get that cash outta here, or he'll grab it for sure."

"I know, Bench," she said, nodding her head. "Nona this would have happened if Ricky was still around. I don't know how many times I tell him, Ricky, no more stickups. Cops now, they got too many cameras, radios, red-dye packs. Stick to the drugs, I says. Find some spics-a sell it for you. God knows we got enough of 'em around here now." She waved her arm in dismissal. "You was always smarter than him, Bench."

I said my good-byes and made for the door. I was out on the sidewalk when my cell phone rang.

30

. . . AND YE SHALL RECEIVE

Bench had given me the number of one of those cell phones with an area code you never heard of. He probably changed phones every couple of days. That way by the time any cops could get a warrant to listen in, the phone would be gone. So I called the cell phone du jour.

"Yeah?" he said.

"You know that party we saw over in Ward One last night?"

"Ward One?" he said, obviously puzzled. Sometimes I forget, not everyone is into city politics the way I am.

"Eastie," I said, and he said "Yeah" again. Bench McCarthy, I had come to understand, was a man of few words.

"I got a plan, but I'm going to need some help."

"So why you callin' me?"

"I mean, we're after the same thing here, aren't we?"

"Are we?"

This was going nowhere fast. He wasn't going to say anything over the phone. Maybe he wasn't going to say anything, period, but I had to try.

"How about we meet somewhere?"

"How about we run into each other somewhere?"

"Please, this could pay off for you too."

"I've heard that before."

"Look, I'm coming over to the Alibi. Okay?"

"It's a free country," he said.

A half hour later, I was sitting at the bar, watching a guy behind the tap that everyone in the joint called Hobart. Bench McCarthy wandered in about fifteen minutes later, walked over to Hobart, whispered something in his ear, and then motioned for me to follow him into the back of the bar. We sat down in the back booth.

"Okay," he said without much interest, "what's going on?"

"The senator has a booth in B.B. Bennigan's—"

"—On Tremont Street?"

"Yep, right down from the State House. He doesn't hang at the Twenty-First Amendment—"

"—Can't say as I blame him. I was in there once, had to pick something up. I never seen so many front-runners and ass-kissers in one place."

I wondered what he had to pick up. Funny, on the phone getting a word out of him was like pulling teeth. Now I couldn't finish a sentence.

"Anyway, I can drop a bug in the booth, that's no problem—"

"—So you're not going to try to put a wire in the Python?" He had a slight smirk on his face.

"Listen, I want to try it this afternoon, I don't have much time here. I need someone in that booth in front of Donuts'. So the bartender can't see me."

"And you don't have anyone else who can help you out except me?"

"I usually work alone," I said.

"I guess the fuck you do, if you have to come to me." He paused and thought for a second. "Can this second person, could it be a broad? A good-looking broad? A young, good-looking broad?"

"That would actually be perfect," I said. "You got somebody in mind?"

"Yeah," he said. "Her name's Patty Lamonica."

31

BAITING THE TRAP

Like Sally says, it's not easy. Not with Patty, anyway. I called her at my lawyer's office where she "works" and told her to get down to the Alibi. I explained to Patty what I needed from her, and you would have thought I had asked her to start turning two-dollar tricks in Grove Hall.

"You want me to sit in a fucking booth in some old-fart dump on Tremont Street with a 'private eye,'" she said. "I've never even seen a private eye, except on TV."

"Lotta things you never seen except on TV, but that doesn't mean they don't exist. Besides, I never knew you not to like sitting in some bar pounding down the Hoodsies on the arm."

That much was true. She usually wouldn't drink anything without a little umbrella in it. And I don't think she'd ever drunk anything except on the arm. I'd told her to dress "for me," and at least she followed those instructions. She was a born cockteaser. Patty looked like one of those teachers that're always getting fired when somebody drops a dime to the school superintendent that they used to be in movies with titles like "Big Sausage Pizza." She sashayed into the Alibi wearing her usual short, short skirt and porn-star pumps.

And around her neck, of course, a necklace featuring a cross. Who doesn't appreciate that de rigueur fashion accessory, the crucifix? Nothing says "devout" like a twenty-four-carat gold cross dangling down around your cleavage.

"You look great, babe," I said.

"Damn right I do. And flattery will get you nowhere."

The Alibi is always dark, even at mid-afternoon, but Reilly's eyes widened as he took in Patty—a good sign. The only possible problem would be if the bartender were gay, a not unimaginable scenario nowadays around here.

I couldn't remember if they'd been introduced on the night of the shooting, so I went through the formalities again, after which he got right down to business.

"So Patty," he said, "did Bench explain—"

"I wanna change the plans around a little," I interrupted. "I want to plant it. I just bought some new gear I want to test out. Maybe you didn't know, I'm a master electrician."

"You are?" he said.

"Yeah, when I was in Lewisburg, I figured I might as well learn a trade."

Better than taking some bullshit creative-writing classes from some chump from WBUR who was trying to save the world from George Bush. Came in handy too, a few years later, when we were hunting down Beezo Watson and the Townies. They were very careless on the phone.

Jack Reilly was trying to remember something. "Didn't I read something about you, during the gang war?"

"Don't believe nothing you read in the papers, Jack. But the fact is, I do keep up with the technology. I'm a jack-of-all-trades you might say. Let me handle it."

"Who's gonna sit on it?"

"That's your thing, Jack, I'm not big-footing you on that. Just let me put it in, I'd feel better if I did it. You can sit with Patty in the crash booth."

He smiled. Reilly liked the phrase "crash booth." Then he checked out Patty again.

"You think you can keep the bartender interested?" Reilly asked her.

"If he's got a pulse I can."

I'd brought my kit with me downstairs from the office. I grabbed it off the floor and put it up on the table. It was the signal to leave.

"What's the range on your gear?" Reilly asked.

"About two hundred yards."

His eyebrows went up. "Wow, that must have set you back a little." He glanced back at Patty; he couldn't keep his eyes off her. It was lust at first sight. Patty instinctively knew he was checking her out, yet she still looked bored. He was just another jerk-off twenty-plus years older than she was, which was bad enough, but even worse, he didn't look like he had a lot of dough. Jack of course knew where he stood. He was just taking in the scenery. It was like a free trip to the Super Bowl.

"C'mon," I said. "We'll put the receiver in your car. You're a cop, you find a parking space down there in one of those alleys off Winter Street. You and Patty drive down there together, get settled in the crash booth, and I'll come in about five minutes behind you. I'll sit in the last booth, the one behind you—that's the one, right?"

I turned to Patty. "And Patty, Jack is the boss. No lip. Just follow instructions."

She looked over at him with disdain, and I felt sorry for Reilly, because I was afraid he was going to have to deny that he had been checking her out. Instead, she just said, "I hope this is worth it."

"Oh yeah," said Jack Reilly, "it will be."

32

MONKEY BUSINESS

It was about a fifteen-minute drive into the city. Patty wasn't exactly a sparkling conversationalist, and she smoked like it was still 1975. She didn't even bother to roll down the window. I found a spot in a fire lane in one of the alleys near what used to be Locke-Ober. I leaned across the front seat to the glove compartment to grab my ancient Official Boston Police Business placard and managed to brush her knee first with my hand and then with the placard.

"Watch it buster or I'll tell Bench," she said.

As we walked into B.B. Bennigan's every head turned to the door. Fortunately, there were only about three of them, and they were all sitting at the bar. Even more fortuitously, one of the heads that turned belonged to the bartender. Which meant he was straight. I led her to the booth and motioned her to the side where we could see the front door, and the bartender. Then I slid in beside her. She hit me with a withering glance.

"Keep your hands to yourself," she said.

The bartender was about thirty, looked like a Suffolk Law student-type, just as I had expected, the kind with a no-show job at the State House, second or third generation hack from Milton by way of Dorchester. Someday he'd be a clerk/magistrate, begging cases right and left. He sauntered over, his eyes lingering on Patty's legs. Patty ordered a Long Island iced tea, I went for a beer, bottled. They didn't have anything on draft; it was that kind of place.

The bartender brought the drinks and, having nothing else to do, stuck around to check out Patty some more.

"You two new around here?" he asked.

"Buzz off, Junior," she said. He was mildly taken aback.

"That's no way to treat somebody who didn't card you," he said.

She reached for her purse, which was between us, and her hand brushed up against my thigh and lingered maybe a second too long. I hoped Bench got here fast.

The bartender waved her off. "Don't bother," he said.

"She didn't mean anything by it," I said.

"Who asked you?" she said, and then looked over at me and smirked. Now I was in on her jokes. Bench apparently hadn't impressed upon her that this was business, monkey business perhaps, but business nonetheless. The bartender, confused, wandered back to the bar. I'd wanted him to be our friend, but it was too late for that now.

"Leave him alone from now on, okay?" I said, as the front door opened and I saw Bench stroll casually in. He was wearing a dirty old white Red Sox hat, a windbreaker and carrying a medium-sized Macy's bag. He looked like a workingman on a very late lunch hour. He stopped off at the bar, spoke to the bartender and motioned in the direction of the booths. The bartender nodded, and Bench slowly made his way back toward Donahue's booth, nodding casually at us. He put down his shopping bag and then pushed it back to the wall. Then he sat down heavily in the booth, facing out to the door, and then the bartender was walking towards him, shaking his head.

"This booth's kind of reserved," he told Bench.

"I didn't see a sign," Bench said.

"No sign," the bartender admitted. "It's just . . ." He turned around to check out the clock behind the bar. "Look, this booth, there's one of my regulars who comes in, usually just after five. It's four-thirty now, as long as you just have one drink, it's okay, but then you gotta find another place to sit, and if he comes in early, you gotta move. That okay?"

"Sure," I heard Bench say. "I appreciate it." I wondered if he'd duked the kid a sawbuck, or maybe a twenty, then decided no. That would have set off alarm bells. Then I heard him order a Bud Light. He was trying to be as inconspicuous as possible, and he was doing a pretty good job of it. In his line of work, it paid not to stick out.

Then the bartender noticed us.

"You guys will have to move too when this party arrives," he said. No "sorry" for us; Patty had taken care of that.

The bartender returned a minute or so later with Bench's beer and went back to the front. He was taking care of his handful of customers, but I didn't like the way he kept glancing back our way.

I pulled out a twenty and handed it to Patty and told her to go get us another round.

"Why don't we just wave to him and get him over here?"

"Because your boyfriend doesn't want him seeing what he's doing?"

"I don't need another drink," she said.

I leaned over, picked up her Long Island iced tea, two-thirds full, and drained it in one gulp. I almost immediately felt a warm glow inside from the five or six shots of booze.

"Wow," she said. "You got a problem?"

"No, but your boyfriend does if the bartender sees what he's doing back there. Come on, shake a leg." I stood up to let her out of the booth. She moved slowly, languidly, but I was no longer fantasizing about her in the sack. I just wanted to get this over with. I glanced back at Bench, both his hands under the table. I'm sure he was wearing gloves, so he had to make sure no one noticed. When Bench saw me looking back at him, he smiled and nodded. He was good. It looked like he already had the bug attached underneath the table and was just trying to find a way to attach the microphone to the wall so that it wouldn't be seen.

"Five more minutes," he silently mouthed.

I watched Patty leaning over the bar and suddenly I was checking her out again, just like everybody else at the bar. I didn't realize they made dresses that short anymore, or ever, for that matter. She and the bartender seemed to have patched things up. They were enjoying a good chuckle together now. I had a feeling this next Long Island iced tea was going to be even stronger.

As I watched them flirting, the door opened once more. It was still a little early for Donahue, but what I saw was even worse than Donuts. It was Katy Bemis, with a chinless, emaciated fop in cuffed trousers and wingtips and wearing a bow tie—a *Globe* colleague, obviously.

She spotted me, smiled and waved, and began walking back to the booth, right past Patty. I had a funny feeling I wouldn't be feeling funny very long. She walked right up to me, Ichabod Crane lingering behind, and kissed me on the cheek.

"Jack," she said, "what are you doing here? Can we sit with you? This is my editor, Alexander Chauncey Giles."

He stuck out a cold dead fish of a hand and said, "Call me Sandy."

"Of course," I said. They always call themselves Sandy, those Alexanders. I smiled. "I'll bet you like balsamic vinaigrette on your arugula, am I right, Chaunce?"

His smile was as weak as his handshake. "Right-o! How did you guess, old chap?"

Sometimes you can see disaster thundering down on you, but there's nothing you can do to save yourself. This was one of those moments. Katy was waiting for me to invite her and Sandy to sit down, but I was watching Patty shaking her ass at the barflies on her way back to the booth, her drink in one hand, my beer in the other. Katy couldn't see her, but she noticed my eyes drifting off and then she turned around. She said nothing, but if looks could kill . . .

"Hey, Jack," Patty said, putting the drinks down on the table. "Who's the old bag?"

Katy's jaw dropped. Sandy seemed utterly befuddled. I had a feeling this was his natural condition. I was a little thrown off myself; she'd said no more than ten words to me all the way over from Winter Hill, and now she was trying to start a catfight. And she wasn't drunk either. I'd guzzled most of her first Long Island iced tea. I glanced back at Bench, his two arms still underneath the table, but he had a faint smile on his face. This was apparently a variation on an act he was quite familiar with. Patty slid past me into the booth.

"Jack," said Katy, with ice in her voice, "why don't you introduce us to your new friend?"

"Oh sure," I said, "Patty, this is Katy and Sandy."

"Pleased to meetcha," she said, putting on a heavy Somerville accent. I was still standing, facing Katy, when Patty grabbed me by the arm. "C'mon, Jackie, sit down with your Patty and have a drinkie-poo."

"By all means, Jack," said Katy, "sit down and have a drinkie-poo."

"Look, Katy, Patty's just putting you on here." I pulled myself loose of her arm and took a step toward Katy. That, I immediately realized, was a mistake. She swung her pocketbook directly at my head and the metal clasp hit me square on the left side of my cheek. It hurt, and I knew it would leave a welt, in just about the same place as the one she'd laid on me at the Eastern Standard.

"Please, Katy," I said, and this time she kicked me in the shin. Just my luck she was wearing boots—pointed boots. My eyes widened in pain, but what could I do?

Now the bartender was walking rapidly toward us.

Suddenly I felt someone brush by me. It was Bench, bag in hand, smirk on his face. I'd done my job perfectly, and so had Patty. The difference was, Patty had known what she was doing, and I hadn't.

The bartender walked directly to Katy. "Is this creep bothering you, ma'am?" he said, directing a dirty look in my direction.

"Not any more he isn't," she said, turning on her heel and walking out, Alexander Chauncey "Sandy" Giles following meekly behind her. The bartender gave me a withering look.

"I knew you were trouble from the start," he said. "I want the two of you out of here—now."

"Gladly," I said. Now I was the one grabbing Patty by the arm. She got up and as she walked by the bartender toward the door she snarled, "You didn't put any Triple Sec in that last Long Island iced tea, motherfucker."

33

NEVER SPEAK WHEN YOU CAN NOD

I was waiting for them outside the Burger King, one door down. I put the bag down and grabbed Patty and gave her a kiss on the lips.

"That was beautiful," I said to her. Then I looked over at Jack. "How about that? Couldn't have gone any smoother. What a break."

"So are my ankles," he said.

"Your face is gonna be a mess too," I said. "Who was that nutty, stuck-up broad?"

"My ex-girlfriend," he said, and I laughed again.

"If she wasn't your 'ex' before," I said, "she sure as hell is now."

Reilly looked over at Patty. "Did you have to call her an old bag?"

Patty smiled sweetly. "It got her attention, didn't it?"

"Yeah, it sure did." He rubbed his cheekbone where her purse had struck him. He shook his head sadly, as pedestrians moved around the knot we had created on the sidewalk.

"What's it to you anyway?" Patty said. "I thought you said 'ex.'"

"Yeah, but . . ."

I said, "There's 'ex,' and then there's 'ex,' right, Jack?"

"Exactly," he said, and then his eyes widened. "They're coming," he said, looking across Tremont Street to the Common. "It's Donuts and the probation commissioner. We gotta get back to my car."

I grabbed him by the arm. "There was another bug under the table. Tiny, even smaller than mine. Has to be the feds—they're the only ones that have state-of-the-art shit like that."

"No shit!" Reilly said. He seemed almost happy about it. "Great minds think alike!"

"Something like that," I said.

His shitmobile was around the corner back in the alley. No ticket—his old police placard apparently still worked. My original plan had been to give him another cell phone and then drive back to Somerville with Patty. Let him monitor the pols' bullshit. This whole thing was a long shot anyway, and we didn't all need to be sitting in a cramped car listening to two assholes dropping names and bragging about how tough they were.

But we'd run out of time, and now we'd all have to listen together. Plus, maybe the feds knew something we didn't. They could have a bug in the State House too small and sophisticated for Donuts' state cops to spot. Reilly and I got into the front seat and Patty climbed in the back, muttering about the junk—old newspapers, fast-food bags, empty GIQ bottles of Ballantine Ale. That's what my father and uncles used to drink; until I was sitting in the backseat myself at Anthony's the other night, I hadn't even known they still brewed that panther piss. Patty was still grumbling loudly as she threw everything onto the floorboards or pushed it aside.

"Shhhhh," I told her, as I turned on the receiver. All we could hear was the usual barroom noises, laughs, clinking glasses, an occasional shout.

"Hope we got the right booth," I said.

"You did," he said. "My sources are pretty good on this sort of thing."

"Will the ex put two and two together?" I asked.

"You mean, assuming she ever talks to me again."

In the backseat, Patty giggled. A cloud of smoke floated into my face. Patty never read the warning labels on the cigarette pack. But then she never read much, period.

Suddenly, I heard a clear voice. "Two VOs and water, Sean."

"That's Donuts," Jack said.

"VO and water?" repeated Patty. "Jack, do you know anyone under sixty?"

"You mean besides the old bag?"

"Shhhhhh," I said again.

"We can't afford any more fuck-ups," the senator said. "I thought you told me those cons at the Python knew what they were doing."

"They killed Sally's nephew didn't they? And that other wiseguy there."

"But none of the Somerville guys. You wanna push a war in the news, you need casualties on both sides."

"How 'bout those two McCarthy killed up the Hill?"

"I meant, white casualties. How many times I gotta tell you, Drew, nobody gives a rat's ass about spics getting shot. Or crooked hacks like your shooter there from probation. Your average citizen cheers, actually. Nobody thinks those guys are going to take over a casino. You gotta hit some of those guys over at the Alibi."

Reilly looked over at me. I don't know what he was expecting me to do, wet my pants maybe. But I played a dead hand. Talk is cheap.

"Tonight," the commissioner said. "They're at the Python, just waiting for the word."

"Normally, I wouldn't want to know the details, but I haven't been very impressed with your performance so far."

Then there was nothing, except glasses clinking. Their VO and waters had arrived.

"Thanks, Sean," I heard the senator say, as another cloud of smoke drifted up from the backseat.

The commissioner was talking. "The problem is, the only way my P.O.s run into these guys is if they get caught." P.O.s—probation officers. Like they were some kind of professionals, rather than run-of-the-mill payroll patriots. "If they get lugged, maybe my guys can recruit them. Problem is, the best ones never get caught, they learned inside, like McCarthy there. That's why we're having trouble. We're using second stringers."

"Nobody like Bench McCarthy, eh?" the senator said.

"You're a legend," Reilly said.

"Shhhhh," I said again.

"He did time, Bench McCarthy," said the commissioner. "They all do time, sooner or later. I pulled his jacket. He had a spotless record with DOC, except of course for the boog he shanked in the shower for Sally Curto."

"Let's just make sure you and I don't end up with our own jackets," the senator said. There was an awkward silence for a moment or two before the commissioner spoke again.

"I guarantee we'll get somebody tonight, maybe not Bench, but some of his guys. The plan is, we bust into both of the places he might be at, shooting. The Alibi and the garage in Roxbury. He's gotta be one place or the other, he's never in Allston at night, and he keeps that garage open most nights 'til midnight. They're just waiting at the Python for me to call . . ."

"These guys I'm with, they want to see some results."

"Results? The bill's dead, isn't it?"

"Gotta keep it that way," Donuts said. "That's what they're paying us for."

"I understand," the probation commissioner said. "But the feds are closing in on the department. They subpoenaed a whole bunch more today; my people are absolutely fucking scared shitless. They're not used to this."

"And you are?" asked the senator.

"You tell me I'm going to get taken care of, I figure I'm going to get taken care of. Your word is your bond, right?"

Reilly glanced over at me. I didn't know what he was thinking, but I was picking up major rat vibes from the commish. If this thing went south, the race would be on. The fact that they were cousins meant nothing, not when the Graybar Hotel loomed on the horizon. My money would be on the commish to beat feet to the feds first, because he had more to trade up—his cousin, the next president of the state Senate.

The commissioner was still talking.

"See, my problem is the guys at the Python are getting antsy. It's one thing to knock over a check-cashing agency on the Lynnway, it's another thing altogether to make a run at Bench McCarthy."

Fucking right it is, pal, and don't you forget it. This is what they mean about your reputation preceding you. It really can save a lot of wear and tear on your ass.

I stepped out of the car and took out one of my burner cell phones. I called Hobart at the Alibi. I told him to get two cars over to the Python and have them tail whoever left the bar, as long as there were at least two of them inside the car. Then I told him to find Salt and Peppa and tell them that I wanted them in Roxbury on the roof of the building across the street from the garage with sniper rifles. Then I told Hobart, get my Bushmaster .223 out of the garage at the top of the hill and make sure it was loaded. I stepped back into the car.

"Did I miss anything?" I asked.

"Nah," Reilly said. "Just some tough-guy talk. People getting whacked, hit, clipped, the usual B-movie shit." He looked over at me. "They haven't called the Python yet, if that's what you're wondering."

Then they mentioned Sally, and it was time to start listening again.

"What about Sally?" said Donuts. "We gotta get him too. That's part of the deal with your goddamn guinea friends, that we clear the decks for them."

"Don't remind me."

"So is our guy working on that?"

"Yeah, he says he's got it all figured out. He's—"

"I don't want to know. I just want it to happen."

"How about your boy on Morrissey Boulevard?" the commissioner said. "Is he ready to run with this tonight?

The senator chuckled. "Yeah, he told me he's hearing that something might be going down tonight. That's what his 'sources' are telling him."

Now it was the commissioner's turn to laugh. "His 'sources,' huh?" He laughed. "You think he's ever even met a gangster?"

"Not unless the hood lives in Lincoln. That guy, I don't think he ever leaves the *Globe* building, except when he's going down to Newbury Street to buy some sixty-dollar socks."

"How's he get all that great dialogue?" the commissioner said, his voice cracking up. "As if I didn't know—"

"I'm sure tomorrow's piece will be full of on-the-scene reportage, cinema verité of the printed page. Maybe Bench McCarthy's last words—"

I took that as my cue to hit the road. I glanced over at Reilly. He looked like he wanted to say something, probably about what his girlfriend would think if she could hear this. I'd gotten the feeling she was one of these people who thought everything was on the level, or at least that the *Globe* was. Why else would she hang around with a fruit like the one she'd dragged into Bennigan's? But whatever Reilly wanted to say, he thought better of it after listening to those State House coat-holders running off at the mouth about killing me. Sometimes you just leave the patter to the guy who's calling the shots, which was me.

"I gotta get going," I said to him. "Can you sit on this, let me know if anything happens? I especially want to know when that commissioner asshole makes his call. Just call me and say 'They're in the air.' That's all, nothing else. Then hang up. And don't call me again tonight." I turned toward the backseat. "Patty, I'm gonna be tied up the next few hours. Jack'll take you home, or you can call an Uber."

"I'll stick with Jack," she said.

I should have leaned into the backseat and kissed her, and I should have shaken Reilly's hand. But I was already running late.

As I closed the door, the last thing I heard was the commissioner telling the senator, "Just makes sure McGee spells Sally Curto's name right this time. It always cuts down on the verité of the cinema if you're claiming to be a street guy yourself and you can't even spell the Mafia guy's name right."

"It's the *Globe*," the senator said. "What do you expect? It's not like they're writing about somebody important like Harvey Milk."

I was barely listening now. I felt it coming on, the tingly sensation I always get when I'm looking for somebody, and I don't mean looking for somebody who owes me money. I opened the door of Reilly's car, got out of the front seat, slammed the door and headed toward Tremont Street to pick up my car behind the State House.

I knew what I had to do, and I only had one question. Who was this guy who was coming after Sally? I was pretty sure I knew, but I had to be sure. Damn, if only they'd dropped his name. Stupid fucks, name-dropping left and right like the civilians they were, but on the most important one, the real turd in the punch bowl, the snake at the garden party, they dummy up.

I could feel the goose bumps on the back of my neck.

34

BEYOND A REASONABLE DOUBT

Patty had moved into the front seat and was listening to the conversation, which had descended even further into inanity and pseudo-machismo.

"Jack," Patty said, "are these assholes as slimy as they seem, listening to them?"

"Slimier," I said.

"They like to sound tough, don't they? But they really aren't, are they?"

"They're not going to be in that car driving to the Alibi tonight, if that's what you mean."

"I wouldn't want to be in that car tonight, would you?"

"No, Patty, I wouldn't."

The conversation dragged on for a few more minutes. I was afraid they were going to order another round, but I got lucky. About twenty minutes after Bench left, the commissioner dialed his phone and said, *"Dónde está Toro?"* The Bull indeed. In English he told Toro it was time to move, and Patty looked at me.

"You want I should call Bench?" she said.

I shook my head and dialed his number.

"They're in the air," I said, and he replied, "Okay," and then hung up.

"Wanna go somewhere and have dinner, Jack?" she said, and the temptation was great, very great. But I needed her kind of trouble like, well, like a hole in the head. Plus, I did have an appointment in Dedham, thank God. I told her no and she said, "Is that snotty bitch from the *Globe* really your girlfriend?"

"Used to be," I said.

She regarded me closely. She was interested in me, not physically, thank God, but in a gossipy high school who's-dating-who kind of way.

She asked me, "You think you're going to make up with her?"

"I don't think the time is exactly right," I said. If the time was ever right. Patty seemed calmer now, a different woman almost. But she was just a kid, no matter how Hollywood she looked, or how long she'd been running around with Bench.

"Are you pissed at me?" she said, touching an old-fashioned metallic cigarette lighter with her engraved initials to a Newport.

"Nah," I said, truthfully. "What happened was bound to happen, sooner or later."

"You getting anything on the side, Jack?" she asked.

"Not really," I said evasively. The truthful answer would have been no, period. But no guy wants to look like a loser, especially when you're sitting next to someone who looks like Patty Lamonica.

I started the Oldsmobile and headed over to Ball Square. Normally I would have gone straight up Winter Hill on Broadway, but that meant passing the Alibi, and I didn't feel like getting caught in any cross fires, so I took Medford Street through Magoun Square—a name I've always considered particularly appropriate, given the high percentage of goons in the neighborhood. Then I turned left onto Broadway.

"Can I ask you another question, Jack?"

"Sure. I don't know if I can answer it, but I'll try." Good Lord, I was sounding almost fatherly.

"I couldn't quite follow that conversation," she said. "Why do these people want to kill Bench and Sally?"

"As best I can tell," I said, "it appears that some big casino company with more money than brains got aced out on the action—there's only three licenses up for grabs, and one of 'em's for the Indians. So this company—I don't even know which one it is, just that it was one of the losers—decided to try to kill the bill until next year when everything would start over, on a level playing field. So they went to Donuts, and somehow he sold them on this insane idea of killing Bench and Sally. Maybe his cousin came up with the scheme, I don't know. Anyway, Donuts figured that if he could make it seem like the local element was already fighting over the spoils, the pols at the State House would get cold feet. His cousin, the commissioner, is about to get indicted, and he's already got a bunch of crooked guys he had to fire looking for work, so they had plenty of talent warming up in the bullpen, or so they thought."

"But they really didn't?"

"No," I said. "The guys they sent out, the cons and the crooked P.O.s, they could fuck up a wet dream, pardon my French."

She laughed at that. They're not making Catholic schoolgirls like they used to, if she'd ever been one, which I doubted.

I said, "Whatever, they couldn't close the deal."

"Because of Bench?"

"Because of Bench."

"Why are the feds after the Probation Department?" she asked.

"Because the P.O.s—the probation officers—they all paid off pols to get their jobs, and now the feds want to know who they paid, and how much, so they're terrified of going to prison, the P.O.'s. And the commissioner there, he's talking tough, but usually, the tougher they talk, the faster they fold. He's got to be in the crosshairs. Did you hear Bench say there was another wire under their table? That's got to be feds. And from what I heard, it sounded like the commish was telling Donuts—the senator—that he expects to have Donuts taking care of him."

"What do you mean, 'taking care of him'?"

"That means he gets his end, even if he goes down."

"And if he doesn't?"

"Then Donuts goes down too."

"How'd they get hooked up, those two?" she asked.

"Cousins, and birds of a feather," I said. "The senator had some walking-around money from the casino company. And he knew the commish was all jammed up with the feds and might have access to wiseguys—make that, wannabe wiseguys—who might be talked into trying to take out your boyfriend."

She considered that for a moment. Then she asked me, "They really aren't good people, are they?"

"No, they're not," I agreed.

I pulled the car up in front of Bench's condo in Ball Square.

Patty said, "Did you hear that guy saying that somebody was trying to set up Sally?"

"Yes, I did."

"Who was the guy they were talking about?"

"I think Bench knows, but it's a big shot, a made guy probably, Mafia, and with guys like that, it's like proving something in court."

"You mean, beyond a reasonable doubt?"

"Exactly," I said. Maybe she wasn't as stupid as I'd thought she was. "But right now, Bench's gotta deal with these guys from the Python."

"And then Bench will hit the other guy in the head."

She said it, not me.

Before getting out of the car, Patty gave me a kiss on the cheek. Then I was back on the road, an hour of bumper-to-bumper traffic to get to Dedham during rush hour.

I'd set up the meeting a week earlier, before I'd even stumbled into this mess. At the time I was just doing a favor for a friend of a friend, talking to an amateur who wanted to run for an obscure county office. Short money at best, assuming he even decided to run. Now I knew I'd have trouble keeping my mind on my end of the conversation. I would have canceled it but this was the kind of guy who'd keep calling and calling and calling until I finally sat down with him. Besides, what else was I going to do tonight? My services were not required for the kind of task at hand. Even if I'd wanted to get involved, Bench McCarthy would have told me again to screw.

So I was sitting down with a guy named Robert O'Mara, one of those perennial candidates who keep running for the same office over and over, in his case county register of deeds. I guess somebody has to be the register of deeds, but for the life of me I couldn't figure out why, unless it was the pension. Come to think of it, that was reason enough for most guys, and then some.

I walked into the 99 in Dedham and he was immediately waving at me, trying to get my attention. About fifty-five, wearing a loud sport coat, a wide tie and double-knit pants. His gut hung over his belt; if ever a man was meant to wear suspenders, it was Robert O'Mara. He was wearing a large campaign button, green lettering on white background: "O'Mara Register of Deeds."

I wondered what Bench McCarthy was doing at this moment. I suddenly realized that I was now providing myself with an alibi, in a different county, a long, long way from Somerville. In other words, this meeting was not going to be a total loss.

After the customary small talk, O'Mara told me why he was running for register of deeds—for the third time.

"I can't believe we still have county government," he said.

And I can't believe anyone still cares.

"I need some work done on the campaign, but I don't have a lot of money."

Somehow they always go hand in hand, needing some work done on the campaign and not having a lot of money.

He told me a long, involved story about how the Registry had had a bindery for deeds since at least the eighteenth century, but that now it was much cheaper to just subcontract the printing, not to mention even simpler just to scan the deeds and put them online. So, with excitement in his voice, as if he had stumbled onto a major scandal, O'Mara told me how the county commissioners had done away with the bindery department and moved the single remaining hack employee out to the parking lot out in back of the courthouse, which had always been free, and now he sat outside in a little booth, charging five bucks per car.

"Isn't that outrageous?" he said.

I nodded, trying to feign interest. His next story was about how if you wanted a copy of a deed, you had to go to a room where another ancient hack would get it for you, unless of course he wasn't there, which was most of the time, in which case you could just wander back into the stacks and grab the book yourself.

"In other words, they don't need this guy," he said. "Why is he drawing a salary?"

"Maybe," I guessed, "he lives on a corner in Quincy and puts up a yard sign for the Register every election."

"And if you want to make a copy," he continued breathlessly, oblivious to my little dig, "they don't have copying machines. Well they do, see, but what you have to do is, you have to pay a buck—a buck, instead of fifty cents, like in Middlesex! And then they make out a receipt, and you have to take the receipt down the hall, and there's three or four of these hacks just standing there, unless it's lunch hour of course, when the entire office is closed, and you have to give them the receipt, and that's when they make the copy for you. If they feel like it."

I wanted to get back outside to the car and turn on the radio to find out if the shooting had started yet.

"Can I ask you something, Bob?" I said.

"Shoot," he said, and my mind was immediately back in Somerville.

"How much does the register of deeds' job pay?" I said.

"One hundred ten," he said.

"How much were you planning to spend on the fight this year?" I said.

"I'm hoping to raise thirty thousand," he said. "But to be honest, most of that will be my own money. I came into an inheritance this year. My mother passed away. You wouldn't believe how hard it is to raise money for a county race, unless you're selling jobs of course."

I sighed. "Can I make a suggestion?"

"Of course," he said. "They say you're the best at what you do."

"Thank you," I said. "I don't like to see anyone throw his money away, so I'm going to make a recommendation to you, Bob, a free recommendation—can I call you Bob? If you take your thirty grand and get it out in cash, I'll personally introduce you to the register of deeds—what'd you say his name was?"

"O'Connor, Kevin O'Connor. He's from Quincy."

"Of course he is," I said. "I guarantee you, Bob, that for thirty large I can get you a job at the Registry that pays eighty grand. You want to be assistant register? Associate register? I'll bet I can even line up a job for you as deputy register. And everything on the level, so fucking legit I'm not even checking to see if you're wearing a wire."

I smiled; I wanted him to think he was one of the boys. "This O'Connell—"

"O'Connor."

"This O'Connor, he's got a business on the side, right. Lawyer?"

"No, insurance agency." Of course it was an insurance agency. It was Quincy. Lawyers starved in Quincy, unless they were public defenders.

"How's that sound, eighty grand?" He seemed puzzled. It was just now occurring to him that I was more like O'Connor than I was like him.

"Once you're inside, on the payroll," I said, "you can start working on reform from the inside. It's always better to be on the inside, believe me."

Six months at the courthouse, and he'd be a union steward. And he wouldn't be bothering me—or anybody else, except maybe

O'Connell, er O'Connor. But if O'Connor wanted to pocket O'Mara's thirty large cash, and I knew he would, then that was the price he'd have to pay.

"Let me think about it," O'Mara said, running his hand through his greasy, thinning brown hair.

"You do that," I said, "and get back to me. Right now, though, I gotta run. Give me a call when you make up your mind."

"Deputy register," he muttered, more to himself than to me, a far-away smile in his eyes. "Deputy register of deeds . . ."

35

BEEZO BAFFLES 'EM

I suppose I could have called the Somerville P.D. and had them make the stop. Their guns obviously wouldn't be registered, and probably most, if not all, of the shooters were illegals. But this was my problem. I had had it with these people. Trying to kill me was bad enough, but trying to kill me not for any particular reason other than to stop a casino bill that Sally and I had absolutely nothing to do with . . .

I never figured myself as "collateral damage," just as I'd never expected to be an extra in somebody else's movie. Sally and I had turned the other cheek for far too long. It was time for some payback. I knew just what I was going to do. I was going to shoot out the stoplights at the intersection of Broadway and the McGrath/O'Brien Highway. Back during the Charlestown gang war, I'd considered it, to the point of spending some time with the engineer from the Traffic and Parking Department at City Hall. I could have used a guy down below at the lights to turn them off, but that was one more witness, and I've always been a believer in the old axiom, if you want something done right, you'd better do it yourself.

I knew I could knock the lights out with a couple of shots. That would stop traffic, and then the people in the cars would be sitting ducks. Back then it was going to be Charlestown gunsels, now it would be illegals from East Boston.

I'd even picked out the building I was going to shoot from, a four-story office building on the southeast side of Broadway. Hobart still had the keys to get onto the roof of the building. I parked my car behind the Alibi on Marshall Street. Hobart was waiting for me in the stolen hit car—the boiler, as we called it. He'd picked a non-descript gray Chevy that looked like a million other gray Chevys.

There wasn't much time, but I told Hobart to keep the car running and wait while I ran upstairs. I told you I had a small freezer built into the floor in my office upstairs, but I didn't tell you what I kept in it. A few years back, before I buried the rat bastard cocksucker who ran the Charlestown crew, Beezo Watson, it occurred to me to chop his right hand off and save it for just such a moment as this.

Talk about baffling the cops—this one would drive them crazy, if they found Beezo's prints on the rifle I was planning to use. If the Bushmaster was good enough for the D.C. sniper, it was good enough for me. As for Beezo's hand, I'd had a lock put on the freezer, and it had been a while since I'd shaken hands with my old rival. He was cold, very cold, and stiff. Dammit, I should have taken him out to thaw a few hours earlier.

I briefly considered taking Beezo downstairs and putting him on "defrost" in the microwave behind the bar. But I didn't want to take any chances on "degrading" the quality of the fingerprints, as the forensic pathologists say. I slipped Beezo's hand into a white plastic CVS bag, ran back downstairs and jumped into the boiler.

Hobart had the Bushmaster under an Army-surplus blanket in the backseat, along with a silencer and a pair of gloves. I called our guy who was trailing the Python car and in as few words as possible filled him in on what was going to happen. The shooters were driving a dark green Toyota Celica; for some reason illegals just love Toyotas. My guy said it was banged up, again just what you'd expect in a typical illegal mobile. They'd just passed the Mount Vernon Restaurant on the Charlestown line. They were about four minutes away.

Hobart dropped me off outside the four-story building, and I slipped on my gloves, unlocked the door and then started climbing to the roof. All the while I was talking to our guy trailing the green Toyota Celica. I told him to let me know when he was within a half block east of the McGrath/O'Brien intersection with Broadway. That was when I would shoot out the stoplights. Once the Python car was stopped, my guy was to flash his lights, and then pull a U turn and get the hell out of there.

He understood perfectly.

It was sunset, with just enough light left to make the first shot easy. As soon as he told me how close they were to the lights, I fired four shots at the signal box. It wasn't a difficult shot, but I had to make sure. I reloaded as traffic halted in all directions, and then I saw my guy flash his lights, pull a u-ie and take off back toward Charlestown.

The Toyota from the Python was the second car at the lights, just where I wanted it.

I drew a bead on the Python driver's front side window. I'd take him out first, so that the others would have to get out of the car and start running. Actually, they probably would have had a better chance of surviving if they had just stayed in the car and hit the floor. They would have known that if they'd been in the military, but I very much doubted they covered this point in Guatemalan basic training. They were going to panic and make a run for it.

I fired at the driver's window. It exploded, and so did the driver's head. He was dark, wearing a baseball cap. I could see the guy in the shotgun seat, snapping his own head around in wild panic, trying to decide what to do. He didn't quite make his decision in time.

I blew his head off. He must have already had the passenger door open to escape when the bullet struck him, because as the force of the shot hurled his body against the door, it flew open, and his corpse tumbled headfirst out of the car onto Broadway.

Next I aimed the rifle at the back window and started firing. The guy on the passenger side was quick enough to get out and take off running. He got away. The one nearer to me slumped over, so I kept firing through the door, just to make sure. The silencer had cost me a grand, but it was really coming in handy. Nobody else stuck at the lights was panicking because they were too busy honking their horns, as if that would make the traffic signals flicker back on more quickly.

I reached into the CVS bag and took out Beezo's hand. It had thawed just enough. I pressed his dead fingers around the trigger, then made a couple of palm prints on the stock of the Bushmaster. Maybe I was overdoing it, but I had to make sure there were enough prints to get the cops' attention. I figured that once the cops saw whose prints were on the trigger, they'd be too busy running around like chickens with their heads chopped off to worry about any other clues. I left the rifle on the roof but kept my gloves on. I dropped Beezo's hand back in the plastic bag. He had one more job to finish tonight. Then I ran down the four flights, taking the stairs two steps at a time, and jumped into Hobart's boiler.

"We got time to get to Roxbury?" I asked.

"Wow, you're on fire tonight," he said.

"Why should Salt 'n' Peppa have all the fun?" I said, turning around to see what else was in the backseat—an AR-15. I called the trail car on the second vehicle out of the Python. There'd been an accident in the Sumner Tunnel and it was total gridlock—beautiful, I'd have plenty of time to beat them to Roxbury.

Then I called Peppa, who was a better shot than Salt. He was already in position on top of the abandoned old factory building across the street from our garage.

"They're in a minivan, black," I said. "If they pull up in front of the garage, don't start nothing. A gray Chevy is gonna roll past."

"I'm just backup?" He sounded disappointed.

"Anybody makes it out of there onto the sidewalk, they're all yours."

He laughed. "I know how you work, boss. Looks like a slow night for me."

"They also serve who only sit and wait."

"Thanks, Mr. McCarthy." He only called me Mr. McCarthy when he was trying to give me the needle.

"Just let me know," I said, "when they pull up in front of the garage."

By the time we got to the garage the sun had set. It was perfect hunting weather. Nobody was out. Nobody is ever out after dark in Roxbury, unless they're in the mood to commit suicide or homicide. It had cost a lot, having to put up new barbed-wire fencing around the garage, but otherwise the place would have been looted within days, maybe hours. Still, I liked having a place over here. I needed a garage somewhere, and the police couldn't ever stake it out, that's for sure.

"Cops gonna be confused tonight," Hobart said. "Two shootouts, one on the Hill, one in Roxbury."

I smiled. "Do you think they'll be 'baffled'?"

"Not for long," he said. He didn't know about Beezo. Hobart wouldn't have thought of asking why I was carrying around that little plastic bag. "The reporters, they'll be baffled for sure, but the cops'll fill them in." He tapped on the steering wheel. "Will this be the end of it?"

"I hope so, but I got a feeling not quite. I think this is just what those bastards are looking for, a gang war, quote-unquote."

"So why are we giving them ammunition?" He smiled. "Bad choice of words."

"They keep trying to kill us," I explained patiently. "You know my policy. Do unto others before they do unto you. No exceptions. They were going to machine-gun the Alibi tonight. That would make twice in four days, three times in a week if you count the other time. What am I, a fucking clay pigeon?"

We had pulled over outside an abandoned Catholic school a couple of blocks from the garage. Hobart's cell phone rang. He said "okay" a couple of times and then hung up.

"They're just sitting there, in front of the garage. Our guys broke off and are heading back to Somerville."

"Anybody left in the garage?"

"No," said Hobart. "Rocco was the last to leave. Salt 'n' Peppa turned on all the lights, then locked the doors and went up on the roof. There's two guys in the car, they're just sitting out front, like they're waiting for somebody to come out."

I shook my head and reached into the backseat for the AR-15. I released the safety and told Hobart to pull up alongside them, without lights.

"Simple fucks, just sitting there," I said. "Let's take a look." Without lights, Hobart crept up to the corner. The van was there in front of the garage. Its lights were off too.

I took my phone and called Peppa. "Be prepared," I said, and hung up.

Then I looked over at Hobart: "Go for it," I said, and he floored the boiler, bringing it to a stop just in front of the minivan so I could fire through its front windshield. All I could see were shadows in the front seat. When the windshield disappeared in the hail of bullets, so did the shadows. I racked the entire vehicle with fire until I was out of ammo and then we sped off toward Warren Street. As we put some distance between ourselves and the garage, I heard more shots. Rifle shots. Peppa was getting in a little target practice too.

I took out Beezo's hand and wrapped it around the trigger of the machine gun. Hobart looked over.

"Is that whose hand I think it is?" he said, his eyes wide with awe.

"You was there when I chopped it off, weren't you?"

"Yeah," he said, "but I just thought it was some kind of sick demented Whitey Bulger shit."

"I'll bet you were too freaked out to say anything, right?"

"You ain't kidding."

"Well, what do you think now?"

He smiled. "I think this is gonna baffle 'em to no end."

Still wearing gloves, I quickly disassembled the AR-15, then had Hobart pull down a side street with another abandoned warehouse. I put the gun in an old canvas bag, zipped it up and threw it into the doorway. Then we headed back to the Expressway south, got off at Gallivan Boulevard and as we crossed over the Fore River bridge into Quincy, I took Beezo's hand out of the bag and tossed it into the water.

As Hobart turned around in the rotary on the Quincy side of the bridge, I took out one of my throw-down cell phones, called 911 and told the cops about the bag that had been dropped in the doorway. I didn't want any concerned citizens of color or otherwise stumbling across the gun and later using it for something I wouldn't approve of, like sticking up one of Sally's gambling offices. As we crossed the bridge back into Dorchester, I hurled the phone into the water.

I had a pretty good idea what was going to be leading the eleven o'clock news tonight. It'd been a while since I'd topped the local TV news.

"Let's go back to Somerville," I told Hobart. "I think I'm going to take a vacation for a couple of days."

36

"BOSTON IS A KILLING GROUND"

I sat down with Slip Crowley at J.J. Foley's around nine, but I had actually arrived there much earlier, as soon as I'd gotten back to Boston from my meeting in Dedham with O'Mara. I didn't figure on getting any visits from the cops, but in case anybody had seen me with Bench McCarthy over the last couple of days, I wanted an alibi for the whole evening. I made sure to buy a round for the house as soon as I arrived, so if necessary I would have two or three cops to speak up for me, all that I'd need.

In the meantime, I was shooting the breeze with Slip in the Berkeley Room.

"I got an e-mail today," I said, and he nodded, without interest. "You know what it said."

"You're going to tell me, right?" Slip said.

"It said, Albert Crowley has sent you a message on LinkedIn."

"What?" he said. "What the fuck is LinkedIn?"

"I was gonna ask you the same question," I said. "Actually, I know what it is, it's some kind of business website, supposed to keep you in touch with the other young Jaycee types, shit like that. I was just wondering, how'd you decide to get onto LinkedIn?"

"I got this intern, good-looking kid from Emerson, about twenty years old, she tells me, I gotta get into social media. I have no idea what she's talking about. She tells me, all her friends are on Facebook. Everybody 'friends' each other. I told her, anybody wants to 'friend' me, they can 'friend' me a C-note at my next time at Anthony's."

I laughed.

"So did you accept my message?" Slip asked.

"Are you kidding me?" I said. "Only message I ever get from my 'friends' is, can you lend me a C-note?"

Slip took a long sip of his 7&7. "You know, I can't even remember how I ever got along without a cell phone. Them fucking phone booths reeking of piss and junkies breaking into the change boxes—remember? It's fucking great not to have to worry about that shit anymore. Then e-mails came along. I hated them at first, but I actually don't mind them anymore either. It's quicker than a letter, plus I don't have to talk to those cocksucker reporters anymore. Even the *Globe* can't misquote an e-mail. But anything beyond that—texting, twittering—"

"Tweeting," I said.

"Twittering, tweeting, it's for twits, okay. What do they say—TMI?"

"Too much information," I said. "That's very good, Slip."

I looked at my watch. It was almost ten. I got up and walked over to the widescreen HD TV set. There was a little panel built underneath the set where the Foleys kept the remote control. I grabbed it, switched to Channel 25 and turned up the sound.

Slip looked at me, puzzled. "Since when did you start worrying about whether or not you have to take an umbrella with you in the morning?"

"Just watch," I said, and then the news came on.

"Tonight," said Maria Stephanos, the anchor cupcake, looking simply smashing in her boots, "Boston is a killing ground."

Slip leaned forward. Unlike the weather, he'd need to be able to offer an opinion on this at City Hall tomorrow. They first went to

Somerville. Usual B-roll of police tape, uniforms, detectives, blue lights flashing, ambulances and EMTs—the same old same old.

The liveshot reporter, a blonde who looked and dressed like she'd come to work directly from her high school prom, said, "Police said the killer or killers apparently shot out the traffic signals with the same type of rifle that was recovered from the roof, a Bushmaster .223. Police found three men dead in and around the car, as well as a large cache of weapons and ammunition in the Toyota, which had been stolen in Malden two days earlier. The massacre occurred about two blocks from the Alibi bar, an alleged organized-crime hangout on Broadway that was the scene of a drive-by shooting just two days ago. According to police sources, the Alibi serves as the headquarters of a reputed gangland chieftain whom Somerville and State Police are describing tonight as a 'person of interest.' Less than an hour after the first nine-one-one call in Somerville, another bloody shoot-out erupted in Roxbury, where Biff Buffington is reporting live—"

"Biff Buffington!" Slip sneered. "Are you kidding me? That guy's so light he carries rolls of dimes in his coat pocket for ballast so he doesn't blow away in a stiff wind."

"Shhhh," I said. "I want to hear this."

"Maria," the wide-eyed reporter said, his voice cracking, "Boston police are baffled tonight by a second one-sided shoot-out in Roxbury—"

This time it was a slow-moving car with someone firing a machine gun into another vehicle that had just parked in front of a garage frequented by the same unnamed "gangland chieftain." One of the three men in the parked car had survived the initial blast and jumped out of the car, but was then immediately cut down by a sniper apparently firing from the roof of the building across the street. He was reported to be on life support at Boston Medical Center with a bullet wound to the head.

Boston police had recovered the long rifle, but there appeared to be no fingerprints on it, just a pair of gloves next to it on the roof.

Police sources told the reporter they doubted the owner of the weapon used in the roof shooting was in possession of an FID.

"As in the Somerville shooting, the Roxbury death car was found to be full of weapons, all fully loaded. Police said the vehicle had been reported stolen from a Peabody mall two days ago."

Slip shook his head. "I grew up three blocks from there. St. Patrick's parish."

"If you see St. Pat, tell him the snakes are back," I said, motioning to one of the young Foleys for another round.

I kept watching, but the rest of it was mostly speculation. Channel 25's crack investigative reporter, who looked like Clark Kent, had put on his best tam o'shanter and trench coat, and was quoting some more unnamed sources to the effect that the gang war had really heated up now. So much so that Clark Kent had decided to stay put in Channel 25's safe suburban studios in Dedham.

Finally it was time for the weather, so I turned down the sound, walked back over to our table and took a long gulp from my new beer.

"I'd like to know who was in them two cars," Slip said.

"Remember that place I had you pull the Licensing Board records on?" I asked.

"Santo's?" he said.

"Now they call it the Python."

"Well, if they're from the Python, and there's six of 'em shot, five dead, I'm going to say the over-under on the number of EBT cards they'll recover is fourteen."

"I'll take the over," I said.

My cell phone rang. I looked down at the number—the main line of the *Globe*.

"You've heard what happened tonight, right?" Katy asked.

"No," I said. "I've been in the Christian Science Reading Room with Mary Baker Eddy all evening."

"Cut the bullshit, Sonny," she said. "I know who that woman who was with you today was—Bench McCarthy's girlfriend."

"I believe he pronounces it McCar-tee," I said. "The 'h' is silent, unless you're a Protestant."

"I don't have time for one of your runarounds, Jack. I lost my temper today; I admit it. I apologize for hitting you."

"You kicked me too, remember?"

"I apologize for kicking you too," she said, although I got the distinct impression she wasn't sincere. "But now that I know who the girl was, I know you must know plenty, and you're going to tell me all about it."

"I accept your apology, apologies."

Slip silently mouthed "Katy?" and I nodded. He stood up and waved a dismissive good-bye, muttering something under his breath about "Little Miss Muffet." He figured it would be a while before I was free, and I figured he was right.

"Maybe you forgot," she said, "I was with you that night at Fenway when we saw the probation commissioner in Donuts Donahue's seats?"

"And that has to do with me how?"

"Two of the people shot to death tonight were probation officers. Suspended probation officers. With their cons—their clients, whatever you call them. What were the cons doing with crooked P.O.s in stolen cars loaded to the roof with guns?"

"That kind of question is above my pay grade." I tried to keep my voice steady. Five or six was a lot to take out at once. And the fact that some of them were cops, sort of, even if they were dirty, was going to make the story that much bigger.

"For starters, you could tell me how you and Bench McCarthy's girlfriend"—she pronounced the name properly this time—"happened to be sitting in the booth in front of the senator's, a couple of hours before this happens."

"How do you know that this woman, this—I know her as Donna, by the way—how do you know that she's Bench McCarthy's girlfriend."

"The FBI takes surveillance photos of guys like him, as you well know. They got about a million of him and Sally Curto at Castle Island—no sound, but a lot of pictures, and video. They also got some in Somerville of McCarthy with a girl who looks a lot like— what did you say her name was?"

"Angela."

"I thought you said it was Donna."

"Donnaangela," I said. "You know how the Italians do it. Combine the first names of the two grandmothers."

"Really? I didn't know that. Anyway, her name, as if you didn't know, is Patty. I think that's how you introduced her, but I was so angry with you at that moment that I'm not sure now, and neither is Sandy. So I'm asking you now, were you at B.B. Bennigan's this afternoon with Patty Lamonica? Somerville High dropout. FYI, as if you didn't know, she's practically been living with Bench for three or four years now."

"You don't say," I said.

"You didn't answer my question."

"The answer is no."

"Liar," Katy said, not even trying to hide her disdain. "She's nineteen! You do the math."

I ignored that. She only cared about one thing right now—her story.

"There's something else here that doesn't make any sense," she said.

"Do tell," I said.

"Enough with the hick affectations too," she snapped, then lowered her voice to the traditional reporter's I-know-something-you-don't-know tone. It was something I'd become very familiar with during the time we were an item.

"I don't know why I'm telling you this," she said, "but there's something very strange about that Somerville shooting."

I waited for her to continue, but she didn't say anything.

"Well?" I finally said.

"Just wanted to see if you were still awake," she said. "The State

Police already ran the prints on the gun that was used in Somerville. They found it on the roof of a building at the corner of Broadway and the McGrath/O'Brien Highway. And you'll never guess whose fingerprints are all over it."

"Jimmy Hoffa's?"

"Close, actually. Remember Beezo Watson?"

"No shit! He's been dead for, what, three years?"

"Not dead, missing."

"Dead," I corrected her.

"So how did he shoot those guys tonight?"

That "fact" left me speechless for a moment. Bench McCarthy was good, even better than I'd thought.

"What do the cops think?" I asked her.

"About Beezo? They figure they'll catch up to him later, if he's really surfaced. The working thesis is that Bench has somebody in this East Boston gang, and they tipped him."

Good. That was a theory I could live with.

"But how does Beezo fit into this?" I asked. "I thought he and Bench hated each other."

She again ignored me. She was working out her own theory, and she just needed somebody to bounce it off, somebody not named Chauncey or Josh, the two most popular male names in the *Globe* newsroom.

"What I'm wondering," she said, "is whether somebody dropped a wire somewhere. See, I remember seeing the probation commissioner in the senator's seats at Fenway. They're cousins. And now you have probation officers, dirty ones, in this gang, or crew, or whatever you'd call it. And then I recall, I saw my old friend Jack just this afternoon at Donuts' favorite bar with Bench McCarthy's girlfriend. Coincidence?"

"Two problems with your theory," I said. "Number one, everybody knows Donuts has his office swept for bugs every week by the State Police. And number two, you just told me Beezo Watson's prints are all over the gun."

"Oh, please. That's obviously a red herring. The Westies down in New York used to do the same thing. They'd chop off the other guy's hand, freeze it and save it for a future moment just like this."

"They really did that?" I asked her in surprise.

"Jack, the booze is destroying your brain cells. Don't you remember, I read that in one of your true-crime books," she said. "Remember how you told me I should read some and I might learn something?"

"Since when did you ever do what I told you to do?"

Katy is so good-looking that sometimes, usually to my detriment, I forget how smart she is.

"But how do you put a wire into his office?" I continued, trying to deflect attention away from B.B. Bennigan's. "Someone told me he had motion detectors put in."

"Maybe they dropped a wire somewhere else." She paused for a second. I probably should have said something, but I couldn't think of any witty repartee.

"You still haven't told me," she said, "how it is that this afternoon you happen to be in the same bar Donuts frequents and you're with Bench's jailbait, Patty Lamonica or Donnaangela or whatever you're claiming her name is. And don't tell me you had to find a new gin mill because they were painting Foley's. Could be it was you who put in the wire. It wouldn't be the first time you planted a bug."

"Perhaps you've forgotten," I said. "Massachusetts is a two-party state." Meaning everyone has to know they're being recorded or it's against the law. "So you see, it couldn't be me who did it, if anybody did that, because I would never do anything that wasn't strictly legal."

She laughed out loud at that.

"You're good at wires," she said. "I can testify to that."

"Katy," I said, "you know how much I hate that word 'testify.'"

"Do you prefer the word 'attest'? Because I can 'attest' to your prowess. With wires, I mean. But the more I consider it, if you're sitting there with a hot babe, maybe you were the decoy, so to speak, while someone else dropped the bug in."

"Is that another one of your theories?"

"Could be. Were you the decoy?"

"If I was, then who planted the bug, again assuming there was such a thing?"

"That's the sixty-four-thousand-dollar question, isn't it?" she said. "But I'm reading the jacket on McCarthy, and it says he's a master electrician. Took all the courses when he was doing that eighteen months for contempt at Lewisburg. Says he's even got a license from the Board of Registration. Bet he works fast too."

"He worked fast tonight, if you can believe the news stories."

"Oh, you don't believe them?"

"I'm one of those innocent-until-proven-guilty sticklers. You may remember, Katy, I had my own photo finish with a grand jury. Turned out to be much ado about nothing."

"Turned out, the feds couldn't prove it, is what you mean."

"Like I said, there was nothing to it."

"I think either you or McCarthy put a bug in B.B. Bennigan's, and because of it, five people are dead, maybe six."

"And how many would be dead if they'd shot up the Alibi and Bench's garage in Roxbury?"

"You don't get to decide who lives or dies. That's not your call. Or Bench McCarthy's."

"No, it's not, but it's not the decision of some crooked hacks and illegal aliens either, is it?" I paused. "You know what you should do? You should call the majority leader right now and ask him if he and the commissioner sat in that booth today and discussed sending over a couple of cars full of gunners to Somerville and Roxbury to take out Bench McCarthy and his gang. That'd give you all the confirmation you need to run your story."

"How'd you like it if I put in my story that you and Bench McCarthy's teenage girlfriend were seen in Senator Denis Donahue's favorite watering hole on Tremont Street two hours before the carnage started?"

"That's not even a good bluff," I said. "So what if you saw me with somebody, how does that connect the senator, or me for that matter, to the shootings?"

"I saw the probation commissioner in Donuts' box seats at Fenway Park, and two suspended P.O.s were killed tonight."

"And who else was sitting with the commissioner in those seats? The future Pulitzer Prize winner, Ted McGee. You want to drag him into this too? And then there's the fact that I'm sure some people saw you with me at Fenway that same night. So using your guilt-by-association standards, you must be mixed up in this too, if I am."

I had her. She couldn't put me in the story, and she knew it. I was of no further use this evening.

"Good night, Jack," she said. "And say good night to Patty—I mean, Donnaangela."

37

ON THE LAM

I keep a room on the third floor of an old one-family house just outside Medford Square. I rent it from an old Italian lady, and keep a change of clothes there. It's strictly a hideout, and most years I don't use it at all. No TV, no Internet, just an old AM tube radio that the old lady found in the basement and brought upstairs for me a couple of years back.

Nowadays, though, I have an iPad, and my cellphone has a WiFi hot spot, so I was able to read the early editions of the newspapers shortly after midnight, while sitting on the lumpy old mattress of my bed. I wasn't exactly gripped with remorse—after all, they had been trying to kill me. Still, I admit that to the squeamish must have seemed over the top, five people shot to death, another on his way out. It was like a Blackfriars, or Sammy White's Brighton Bowl, one of those massacres from thirty-five years ago that I'd always heard about.

But what exactly are you supposed to do if somebody sends six or eight guys after you? You can't take any prisoners, that's for sure. Not in this line of work. Nobody gets read his Miranda rights, let's put it that way. If the situations had been reversed, they wouldn't have read me mine.

It was hard to see how they'd be bothering either me or Sally again, but on the other hand, it looked like this guy Donuts and his hack pals had gotten what they wanted. Nobody in the legislature was going to vote for a casino now.

The next morning, right at 6:00 a.m., my cell phone rang in Medford.

"You hot shit you! That was fucking awesome!" It was Sally. "I'm almost afraid to meet up with you after last night."

"Sally, ix-nay," I said. "See you in Winthrop?"

I hoped Sally remembered the code. Winthrop meant Winchester. The cops would never figure us meeting in Winchester. Even though it was in the same Senate district as Somerville and Medford, it seems suburban—safe.

Which was probably why Sally's driver was George Graft. I hadn't seen him since the troubles started. He was more Sally's friend than anything else, a wiseguy, but with an asterisk. Sally must have figured the war, such as it was, was over.

In Winchester, we meet outside Piantedosi Bread Shoppe downtown. I got there first and was leaning up against a mailbox when Sally pulled in behind my car. He jumped out and ran up and hugged me and kissed me on both cheeks and then grabbed me by the arm. I waited until George Graft got out and then I went over and gave him a hug and said "Welcome back." Then Sally grasped my arm again and started walking us both toward the train station, so we could talk alone.

"I was expectin' you again last night at the Café Ravenna," he whispered. "You don't show up, it ain't that big a deal, except that Liz stopped by, and she likes to see you, but then I'm home, waiting for a call, only it's not you, it's George Graft, telling me turn on the late news, there's been a shoot-out in Somerville—"

From the way he was telling the story, I could see that he'd thought I'd been hit. Maybe he would have been broken up about me sleeping with the fishes, but that was something he would have gotten over. After all, he didn't seem to miss Hole in the Head. What he would have missed about me was my muscle. One thing about Sally—he played all his cards face up. He wasn't devious about anything. Damn right he was glad I was still alive. He still had somebody to protect him, and through me he had avenged his nephew, and his street boss.

He had gotten it done, that's what he'd tell everybody down in Fort Lauderdale next winter. I've got this kid, this Irish guy—and his goombah pals would say, we heard you cut the kid in on everything, fifty-fifty, he's your partner now, he's practically a made guy. And Sally would answer sure, he thinks he's my partner, I let him have all that shit in his own neighborhoods, but that's all it is anyway, shit. And the goombahs will say, I thought all the new shit he split with you, fifty-fifty, and Sally will say, sure, sure, that's the deal, but there ain't no new shit, you know that, everything that's out there now, low-hanging fruit, just begging to be picked, it's always feds pretending to be wiseguys.

And you know what, if Sally was saying that, and he probably was, he'd be right. But still, being his "partner" was better than always having to worry about getting whacked, or snatched, because most of the time it's the same thing. They grab you off the street, they hold you for ransom, and when they get the dough, they cap you.

For me, being with Sally means not having to replace all the plate-glass doors at my next apartment with steel plates, so I don't get picked off when I'm eating breakfast with Patty at the kitchen table.

Don't get me wrong; I know I could get clipped at any moment. It's almost happened three times in the past week alone. Sally might even decide to take me off the board, or try to. Believe me, I have no illusions about Sally. But I've got a skill set none of his guys have anymore, which cuts down the odds of getting hit in the head more than somewhat.

"Do you know how this'll look to New York?" Sally was saying, gesturing with his cigar as we walked past a bus stop with parents standing with their kids, to protect them from any random killers who might be out for morning constitutionals. "After last night, nobody's gonna fuck with us for a very long fucking time."

"Sally, watch your language," I said, lowering my voice. "They're not used to guys like us in Winchester."

Sally shrugged, but didn't speak again until we'd put thirty or forty yards between ourselves and the school-bus contingent. I spoke first.

"Sally, remember a couple of months back, you told me our problem was we hadn't been shooting enough guys? Discipline's all shot to shit and everything. Remember when you said that?"

"My poor nephew," he said, nodding. "Them dirty motherfuckers—I can't tell ya how great I felt last night when I seen it on the late news. That nice neat row of machine-gun bullet holes in their fucking car in Somerville. It was just like the old days. Larry Baione would have been proud. I seen him once, down Shawmut Ave, he was firing a machine gun while he was hanging off the running board of a Packard. He left rows of bullet holes all up and down the street."

He was telling me the same story old Tommy Callahan had told at Hole in the Head's wake. Only then he'd said Tommy was going senile.

Sally was still waving his cigar around. "You don't see shit like that no more!"

"That's the effect I was going for, Sal. The retro look."

"The beautiful thing here is all them weapons in their cars. They were fuckin'"—he caught himself this time, even though there were no matrons on either side of the street—"they were trying to kill us, no question about it. These here weren't no innocent bystanders, these motherfuckers had it coming, and they got it, in spades."

Man, he loved taking credit for something he had nothing to do with. Then something occurred to me.

"You were waiting for a call?" I said. "Since when do you wait for a call, especially late at night? And since when does George Graft or Cheech or anybody ever call you after they go off duty?"

Sally stopped and then threw his arms around me and gave me another bear hug.

"Man, I trained you good. I just say one thing I shouldn't, make one simple mistake, and you pick right up on it."

"I get it now," I said. "You were still planning to use me to set up Liz, even after I told you to knock it off. She wouldn't have come to the Café Ravenna if she didn't figure I was going to be there. Did you do something to her—you better tell me now, Sally, I'll find out."

He waved me off. "Nothing happened to Liz."

"But something was supposed to, wasn't it?"

"What are ya talkin' about? I'm crazy about Liz. You know that."

"What was the play?"

He stopped walking and turned around to face me directly.

"Look," he said, "this Liz problem is personal business, you understand, and I'm only gonna tell ya 'cause you're a beautiful fuckin' guy after what you done last night?"

"Save the Vaseline," I said. "Tell me what you were gonna do."

"You know that fucking cowboy hat? She was wearing it again last night. I knew she would be. I told her, I had some guys I had to meet, but I'd see her later at the Nite Lite on Commercial Street. I told her, wait for me there. I was gonna send in two guys. You know 'em. Spucky and Jimmy Lynnway. They never come In Town, nobody knows 'em."

"You bastard. I'm out taking care of business for both of us and you're sneaking around trying to cap a friend of mine."

He nodded. "Friend, huh? Ya know, I been meaning to ask you about that. What's up with you and Liz? I know it ain't her magnetic sex appeal."

"I feel sorry for her."

"What the fuck, I know you all these years, I never hear you say you feel sorry for nobody. How about Henry Sheldon, you feel sorry for him? Or them five guys last night, you feel sorry for them too?"

"Liz ain't trying to kill you, Sally."

"The fuck she ain't. She says she's gonna call Rosa, I call that try-ing to kill me."

I stopped on the sidewalk. I had my hands on my hips and was shaking my head. This guy really bugs me sometimes.

"Sally, that's nothing but the drugs talking, and you know it."

"Then I gotta kill them drugs."

"Look," I said, "I'm serious here. Let me handle Liz. I'm gonna make her disappear."

"Now you're talking!" He clapped his hands together. "The old Bench is back! If you say you're gonna make her disappear, I'll pull Spucky and Jimmy Lynnway off."

"That's not what I mean and you know it. She's not gonna bother you anymore, okay?"

"She's out on bail, you know that, right?"

"I'll settle up with the Weeper. It's only a couple grand. I'll get her out of town. It won't be a problem. This ain't like you and me going on the lam."

The deal with wiseguys is, you have to move fast once you get that target letter from the grand jury. If you're not going to stick around, you take it on the lam before the indictment, not after. Then later on when you come back after you see what everybody else in the so-called conspiracy got for time, you can claim you didn't know there was a warrant out. That way, they can't charge anybody close to you—say, in my case, Patty or Hobart—with aiding and abetting a fugitive.

God forbid they actually lug you, because then you have to post bail. If you jump after you post bail, then you're out fifty or a hun-dred grand, probably more now for me and Sally being career crim-inals and drug kingpins and all that shit. They throw everything but the kitchen sink at guys like us. It's all boilerplate; down in Lewis-burg, we used to pass around the indictments against ourselves for everybody to read, and the plagiarizing cocksuckers used the exact same language in every one of them. "On or about," "racketeering enterprise," "parties known and unknown to the grand jury." At this point I think I could write an indictment in my sleep.

But these days I don't think they'd even give me and Sally bail. They'd call us "flight risks."

Damn right we would be.

I finally said, "Please Sally, leave Liz alone, okay?"

"You say you're gonna handle it, you're gonna handle it. Calm down. I know you had a busy night but this here is my business. I didn't say nothing to you about Henry Sheldon, did I?"

"What do you mean by that?

"What do you think I mean? You think I don't know what happened?"

"I don't know what you're talking about."

Sally smiled. "Please, Bench, you think I fell off a turnip truck? I know what you done. So don't give me this holier-than-thou routine with Liz."

"Well, you don't have to kill her."

"Did you have to kill Sheldon?"

"I didn't kill him."

He looked at me. "I'm through talking about this. Look, I didn't come here to get in a beef with you, I just wanted to tell you, good job last night wrapping it up."

We were approaching a convenience store. "Sally, the problem is, it ain't over. Let's go in here and get a *Globe* and I'll show you."

"Fuck the *Globe*. I wipe my ass with the *Globe*."

I walked in, grabbed a *Globe* and gave the Indian behind the counter a buck and a quarter. It breaks my heart, every time I have to buy a *Globe*. It only encourages them. I read the main story quickly and saw mention of a "person of interest" that police in Somerville and Boston wanted to question but could not find early this morning. That was to be expected. What I was really looking for was on the front page, right underneath the main story, which was headlined, "Five shot to death, 1 wounded in Somerville, Roxbury/Indicted probation officers included in toll."

I was looking for Ted McGee's column. The headline read, "The Scourge of Casinos." It began:

"The simmering underworld war for control of the state's new casinos last night flared into a fiery crescendo of mobster mayhem not seen anywhere north of the Rio Grande since the St. Valentine's Day massacre."

North of the Rio Grande? Who knew that Ted McGee was a foreign correspondent on top of everything else?

As we walked back out onto the sidewalk, I handed the paper to Sally and pointed at McGee's column. He read it quickly and handed it back.

"Total bullshit," he said. "And by the way, if this was the St. Valentine's Day massacre, that makes you Al Capone."

"That's not the point," I said. We were walking back toward our cars now.

"When I see a headline like that," Sally said, "I know it's time to fly to Florida for a month. You oughta get outta town too. And I don't mean Medford."

"Not yet," I said. "There's still loose ends. They're still trying to deep-six the casino bill by saying we're killing each other. We're just lucky they can't shoot their way out of a paper bag, or they would have."

"So what? That's better for us, if they don't know what they're doing."

"I'm just saying, there's been plenty of money spread around to get this casino bill passed, and now not passed. A couple of weeks from now, this blows over, the votes are back. The people shooting at us may make another run, just to close the deal."

"That reminds me of something," Sally said, "who is behind this whole thing? I ask you again, who are these people? We gotta get them next."

"Too dangerous," I said. "It's pols—I'm not even going to tell you who."

"You don't have to tell me who. Just put a rocket in their pocket."

"Sally, it ain't 1963 anymore."

"You're talking too much to this private dick, is what I think.

You're starting to sound like him, like some State House fuck that goes to law school nights and thinks he's a half-a-wiseguy."

"Listen, Sally, I don't need Reilly or nobody else to figure this out. They have to make it quote-unquote underworld. The cops like me for these jobs but there's none of our guys dead. Maybe it was Beezo Watson."

Sally snorted at that one.

"Don't laugh," I said. "That'll be in tomorrow's paper, maybe on TV tonight. Beezo's fingerprints are all over those guns."

Sally put up his hands. "I ain't even askin' . . ."

"I'm just telling you, Sally, these hacks may have one more run in them."

Sally stopped again. "So how come we're standing here?"

"You're standing," I said. "I'm walking."

He picked up the pace. When he tried to walk fast, Sally waddled like The Penguin in Batman. He couldn't keep up the pace—any pace—for long. Lucky for him, our cars weren't far away.

"What's their next play?" he asked, breathing heavily.

"All I know is, we were listening in on them yesterday—don't ask me how. And they said they had somebody 'inside.' "

"You mean, like Hobart?"

"C'mon, Sally. Have they been hitting my places? Not until the other night, and even then they went after places everybody knows I own. They've been going after your rackets, the barbooth game, the check-cashing front, things only someone inside would know you had a piece of."

He pulled to a full stop right there on the sidewalk and grabbed me by the arm. His nostrils flared, his mouth contorted with rage. I knew what was coming next. He was going Sally.

"Listen up!" he bellowed. "When you see that kid of mine"—this was me he was talking about, not his own son—"you tell him he better find that no-good yellow rat, and then I want him dropped, right where he stands, I don't care if it's on the corner of Hanover and Commercial Streets in front of eight million fuckin' tourists.

Ba-boop-ba-bing-ba-boo. Hit him in the head! You understand American? Too many fuckin' rats, we gotta Orkin-ize the whole out-fit. You tell him I said that."

Yes, Sally, I will. He closed his eyes and started breathing even more heavily. He was coming out of it. Thank God it was a short one, or one of the Mommy brigade here in Winchester would be calling 911 for sure. Finally, when he was calmed down, I tried to resume our conversation. Nothing I could do now anyway. I knew what my plans for the day were—lay low in my Medford pad until the senator arrived at B.B. Bennigan's to wet his whistle.

"I was you," I said to Sally, "I'd keep under cover today. Have somebody with you. I should know something by evening."

He nodded at George Graft. He was standing beside the Cadillac. George Graft clicked the key to unlock the door and they both climbed back into the car. I walked over to the passenger's side and tapped on the window. Sally hit the button and it went down.

"Do me a favor," I said. "Don't hit Liz without telling me."

He stared straight ahead and nodded without saying a word. He didn't like being spoken to this way.

"I mean it," I said.

38

IRRECONCILABLE DIFFERENCES

I was lucky I had this casino piece of business because otherwise, I was rolling nothing but snake eyes. Sure, I was getting business from my regular customers, the long-time incumbents, the real hacks. A lot of them had primary opponents, but I'd noticed a disquieting trend. The people trying to take them out tended to be older, over sixty, sometimes closer to seventy. Historically, the kind of people who usually ran for the legislature against incumbent reps were younger. They were small businessmen, third-rate lawyers, town hacks, mamas' boys living at home, empty-nest housewives.

But those were the people pulling up stakes in Massachusetts and fleeing. When you get your future hacks calling it quits and heading south to Florida or Tennessee, one of those no-income-tax states, you know you've got a long-term problem, and the problem is you just can't make a living here anymore, period, unless you work for the government.

These political hacks I work for, they've really wrecked the state.

Which is a long way of saying I needed more jobs, and beggars can't be choosers.

Still, I had a bad feeling about this guy I was meeting. Not so much bad as despondent. I couldn't imagine he was a paying customer. I'd been referred to him by another of my former clients, a state rep from Norfolk County, which meant he used to live in Boston. He told me a guy he knew was getting a divorce, and needed some sneaky stuff done.

I met the guy in my office at J.J. Foley's and bought him a beer. Then I started in on my usual spiel about no-fault divorce, about how a guy is always screwed one way or the other. How if she catches you with a gal pal, you owe her a million bucks. And if you catch her with a boy toy, you owe her a million bucks.

Then I asked him if he knew why divorces were so expensive. He didn't.

"Because they're worth it," I said.

He was better dressed than I'd expected. Sometimes, when guys are out of the house, they start to get sloppy. Collars fray, pants don't get pressed. The clothes don't fit as well. They put on weight, or lose it. Depends on how much they drink, which depends on how many nights they're out hitting on nineteen-year-olds, which depends on how much money the lawyers and the ex have or haven't sucked out of them yet.

This guy's name was Kevin.

"I want to get the bitch," he said, and I tried to remind him that if she catches you with—but he waved me off.

"I wanna take her off the board," he said.

"I don't do hits," I said. "And if you want a little free advice, don't even talk to anybody else about shit like that."

He shook his head. "I don't mean 'hit' like that. I just want her to lose the kids. I could give a shit less about her. I just want my kids."

I nodded. Guys never get the kids. Co-custody is as big a farce as no-fault. He had obviously figured that out.

"Here's what I want you to do," he said. "I want you to plant cocaine in her car, and then call the cops."

"No way," I said. I didn't even have to think about it.

"I'll pay you a grand. For ten minutes' work. I'll even supply the coke." He was reaching into his coat pocket before I shook my head and he stopped.

"Why don't you save yourself a grand and plant it yourself?" I asked him.

"What if I get caught?"

"You know, that was exactly the same question I was asking myself."

"I heard you were good."

"The key to being good is not doing stupid stuff, and this is as dumb as it gets."

"I don't get it, I offer you good money for an easy job, and you're not interested."

I sighed and looked him in the eye for a few seconds before I spoke again. "Let's say she gets busted, and she's all hysterical, and she calls you to bail her out, and one thing leads to another, and there's this great big reconciliation between the two of you, and don't tell me it can't happen. So eventually there's some, what did they used to call it, pillow talk, and you tell her what you did, that you had the coke planted on her."

"Why the hell would I do that?"

"Why the hell wouldn't you? I don't know you, and you don't know me. So let's just operate on the assumption that you would eventually tell her what you'd done, and when you do, she says I can't believe you would hire somebody to do something like that to me, the mother of your children. And you tell her, you know, honey, you're right, I was way out of line doing this, and I'm going to get you out of this jam you're in, this coke-possession charge. And how do you suppose you'd do that, get her out of it, I mean?"

"Turn you in?"

"Bingo." I didn't even mention the fact that he probably wanted me to plant the shit in some mall parking lot somewhere, one of those places that are totally covered by surveillance cameras now.

"You won't do it?" he asked.

"I won't do it," I said.

"Do you know anybody who will?" he asked.

"Find yourself somebody who won't think it through, or can't." I paused. "I'd suggest maybe a junkie."

"A junkie?" he said. "You want me to give a bag of cocaine to a junkie?"

"You begin to see the problem with your plan now?" I said. "If I were you, I'd try to make up with her. Like I said, it's a lot cheaper."

I stood up and walked back to my car. Inside, I dialed Bench Mc-Carthy's number.

"I'm going back to that place this afternoon," I said. "Any interest?"

"Can't make it," he said. "Call me if you hear anything. Gotta run."

"Want me to pick up your stuff if I can?" I asked.

"Don't take any chances," Bench said. "I think we can surmise who has the other one there."

"Good point, I think you should just take a write-off."

"I think I will," he said.

39

THE LOCAL CONSTABULARY

I couldn't talk to him, I was in the Alibi, and it was full of cops from Somerville and Boston. I'd gotten tired of lying on top of the bed in Medford, listening to the same stories over and over on the all-news radio station. I knew I had to talk to the cops eventually, so I just drove back to Somerville and waited for some apprentice rat in the neighborhood to drop a dime to 911. I always talk to the cops, at least the Somerville cops. I'm a local boy made good. Or is it bad?

The cops didn't want to be here, unless it was lunch hour and they were drinking free booze, or heading down into the basement for an on-the-arm shopping spree. But they had to be here—they had their own shooting to "investigate," plus it was police protocol to accompany their fellow flatfeet from Boston. I personally didn't think I'd gone overboard last night, and neither did the cops, when you got right down to it. Those guys had been trying to kill me. No civilians got taken out. It was all very clean, both here and in Roxbury. But they had a warrant.

I was standing near the Alibi's front door, my arms crossed. A couple of the plainclothes Boston detectives were questioning me, and the uniform Somerville guys were prowling around in the back, and down in the cellar, in case I'd left any of the murder weapons in plain view.

"So you weren't here last night?" one of the Boston plainclothes cops asked me. His name was Evans. He had a bad comb-over and his clothes were threadbare and cheap, even by cop standards.

"For the third, maybe fourth time, no, I wasn't. I didn't feel so hot, so I went home early."

"Where's home?"

"Last night, I think I spent the night on Sparhawk Street," I lied. "In Brighton."

"Boston?"

"Last time I checked it was. I send the property tax check to City Hall, if that's what you mean. Always check the box to give an extra dollar to the mayor's college scholarship fund too. He's a helluva guy, Mumbles. Sorry he's leaving. And I like to help the youth of America, even if they're not from America anymore, most of them."

"What are you, a wise guy?" Evans said.

"I never thought so, but the papers say different."

One of the Somerville guys, Captain McKenna, stepped between me and the Boston guy, Evans.

"C'mon, Evans, you got nothing on this guy and you know it."

Evans shot him a withering glare. "I don't need you to tell me anything."

"We're just here to assist," McKenna said calmly.

"Thanks for the 'assistance,'" Evans said, his voice thick with sarcasm. "Five people killed last night, in front of this guy's hangouts."

"Businesses," I corrected. "I'm a businessman."

"Nice business you got here," said Evans. "Same business as those dead guys. Between Somerville and Boston, we found two revolvers, three machine guns and four sawed-off shotguns and approximately two hundred rounds of ammunition in the two cars. What do you suppose they needed that much firepower for?"

"You'd have to ask them," I said, and Evans stared right back at me.

"You wiseguys think you're so tough," he said. "But the other guy never gets a chance to fire back at you, do they? You kill 'em in cold blood, as far as I can see."

I looked over at McKenna, to see if he wanted to correct the record, but he just lowered his eyes and stared at the floor.

"Captain Evans," I said, "I got shot at just the other night, right outside this door here."

"So I heard," he said. "And a few days earlier you killed the two guys who were firing at you further up on Broadway."

I looked at him carefully. He wasn't as dumb as I'd thought he was. He was trying to get me all hot and bothered enough to admit to shooting the guys at the top of the hill. A real long shot, but he got points for trying.

"I don't know what happened there in Ball Square, only what I saw on TV."

"I'll bet," he said.

I made a mental note to myself to make myself some more friends on the BPD. You know what I mean by friends. In Roxbury, I had a few uniforms from B-2 on the pad, but that was more for on-street parking outside the garage—keeping the meter maids at bay—as well as the occasional "tip" to the building inspectors from City Hall. But a few envelopes at Christmas don't even begin to cover handling a drive-by machine-gun shooting.

"Where'd you say you spent the night again last night?" Evans asked.

"Sparhawk Street, Brighton," I repeated, yet again.

"Anybody with you?"

"Nobody you know."

Evans glanced over at McKenna, who spoke up. "Answer the question, Bench."

"My girlfriend, Patty."

The Boston cop looked over at McKenna. "You know her?"

"If he says she was there, she was there."

"You mean, she'll say she was there." Evans really didn't like me. This was not an act. "How old is she?"

"Nineteen."

"Nineteen," he repeated, "and you're what, forty-five?"

"Forty-four, thanks for asking."

"How'd you meet her?" he asked.

"Babysitting," I said.

40

... NEVER NOD WHEN YOU CAN WINK

I really didn't hold out a lot of hope that I was going to get anything more out of the bug at B.B. Bennigan's. For all I knew, either management or the feds had already found it, and yanked it out. It was about 3:30 when I parked in the alley around back from the barroom. I thought about going in and checking it, but the bartender might recognize me. Didn't seem worth the risk. Who knew who was in there now? Somebody might be waiting for me.

I halfheartedly turned on the receiver, and much to my surprise I picked up the sound of muffled voices, from nearby booths. I'd gotten lucky. I had batteries enough too, so I settled in for a wait until—knock on wood—the senator and, if I was really lucky, the commissioner arrived. A meter maid came by a half hour or so later, but she lost interest in her quota from City Hall after I gave her forty bucks. It was cheaper than a ticket, and I could put it on my cheat sheet.

Around 4:30, I heard a voice clearly ordering drinks. VO and water. It was the senator. He ordered two, which meant the commissioner was on the way. He arrived about five minutes later.

"I got the letter today," the commissioner said.

"The letter?"

"The target letter." He sounded exasperated. "From the grand jury."

"I thought they'd told you you were okay," said Donuts.

"I thought they did too. You can't trust these motherfuckers."

They continued on in that maudlin vein for a couple of minutes, the commissioner bemoaning his fate, the senator futilely trying to change the subject. He wasn't getting indicted, so why should he care about anybody else? I could have told him, he was playing with fire now. The commissioner would soon be needing someone to trade up, and the next Senate president would make a nice catch for the G-men, much more impressive than a crooked commissioner appointed by a lame duck governor. The more I listened to Donuts, the dumber I realized he was. Whoever he was working for, Donuts was so eager to please them that he wasn't thinking straight, which involves looking out for number one.

"Listen," Donuts said, "my people still want some results."

"Christ, Denis, I gotta handle this other thing? I gotta get a lawyer, a real lawyer."

"You need money for a lawyer, and the best way to get money is to fucking finish the job."

"Finish the job? You wanted some bodies; well, you got some bodies now. Them guys aren't as over the hill as we thought they were. Two of them that got killed were my guys."

"Two fewer witnesses against you. Look on the bright side."

"Easy for you to say." He paused. "I got another problem too. That guy, the one that's been feeding us the info on Sally, he says we still owe him. And you know what his end is: we have to take out either Sally or the other guy."

Name, please, I need a name. But there was silence. I would have bet that the commissioner was doing the math in his head—how many years would he have to do if he reeled in Mr. President? Could a suspended sentence still be in the cards? House arrest?

"That's one guy I guess we can't afford to cross," Donuts said. "You said on the phone that he'd come up with a plan."

"I don't like talking here, I don't trust this place after what happened. Let's go outside."

Oh, let's not and say we did.

"What if they got a wire in here?" the commissioner asked.

"Are you fuckin' soft? You got a target letter today. I oughta be worrying about you."

Crooks starting to turn on one another. Who could have ever predicted this?

Donuts said, "Do you have a plan, or do I have to find somebody else?"

I could hear the commissioner chuckle, but not happily. "Good luck with that," he said. "And thanks for your sympathy. But anyway, yeah, I do have a plan." He paused for a second. I was on the edge of my seat. So was the senator, I presumed. "I had to get some real shooters this time. Cost me a bundle too."

"Put it on my tab."

"Damn right I will. Anyway, you know Sally's got a son, the kid's about half a retard, to keep him busy his father bought him a gas station down on Cambridge Street, back side of the hill, about two blocks from MGH. You know the place?"

"Wrong side of the hill," the senator said, archly.

"Whatever, the kid parks every day in the alley behind the place, leaves around five, I don't know where he goes, it ain't important, because he ain't going anywhere tonight. These guys I brought in, they ice-picked one of his tires, they're watching, waiting for him to come out. When he's on his back jacking up the tire, they shoot him."

"We need the old man, not his nitwit kid. Besides, it's a gas station, he'll have one of his guys change the tires."

"Listen to me—all we need is ten seconds. We don't kill him, we just wound him, grab him, hold him down and shoot him in the kneecaps, that's what I told them to do. It's two blocks from Mass General, that's where they'll take him. They'll call the old man, and he'll come running. You know the circular drive there, that's the emergency entrance. When Sally jumps out of the car, we're waiting for him."

"At Mass General? You're gonna plug Sally Curto right there at the hospital?"

"Is there a better place? You wanted headlines, this'll get you some headlines. Ted McGee can go crazy in the paper. Crime out of control, brazen gangsters, one of the greatest hospitals in the world—"

"How you gonna know when Sally gets to MGH?"

"Leave that to me, okay?"

I listened a couple more minutes, but they had downshifted into innocuous conversation, innocuous to me anyway. I'm sure the commissioner was worried about his target letter, but he'd have to find himself a quarter and call somebody who cared.

I had to find Bench McCarthy real fast.

41

JASON TAKES ONE FOR THE TEAM

I got to the garage in Roxbury around five. As I'd anticipated, the District 2 uniforms assigned to the "crime scene" weren't giving us nearly as much attitude as the plainclothesmen from headquarters. The uniforms had been around with the local detectives in the morning before I arrived, and now Rocco was going to have to refill the beer machine.

"Boy, boss, them guys sure know how to drink," he said.

"As long as they pay," I said. That was my own little joke, cops paying.

"One of 'em wanted to know when you was gonna put 'Gansett back in there."

I laughed. "Must have been an old-timer. A detective, right?"

"How'd you know?"

"Who else remembers 'Gansett? I heard that's what Wimpy used to stock the cooler with when he owned this place."

"Wimpy Bennett." Rocco said it wistfully. "You got a mighty early start, boss. Especially for a guy who ain't even from Roxbury."

"Wherever I am," I said, "is Roxbury."

I walked back to my office. Just outside, some of the boys were playing hearts. I like that, at least they aren't on their fucking iPhones or some such waste of time. I'm old-fashioned that way. I asked Peppa if I could see him alone, and he turned his hand over to one of the younger guys, an Italian from Hyde Park. I closed the door behind him and turned on WBZ, the all-news radio station. It's always harder to pick up voices if there are more of them in the room, instead of music.

He sat down across from me and I pushed the humidor across the desk and offered him a cigar. He shook his head.

"Nice piece of work last night," I said.

"That's what Uncle Sam trained me for," he said.

"How come you didn't put in your twenty years?" I asked.

"You pay better," he said.

Just then my cell phone rang. I looked at the number. For a second it didn't ring a bell, but then it did. The private dick. No introductions, the way it should be. Just start talking.

"Does Sally have a son with a gas station?"

I sat straight up. "What about it?"

"They're gonna shoot the kid, and then when the old man goes to MGH, they're gonna hit him as he goes in."

I stood up. I was already trying to figure out the quickest way into the city.

"Who are the shooters?"

"I don't know. The commish said he had to pay a lot more for them."

"You sure about this?"

"I'm just telling you what I heard on that thing. One other thing. Donuts asked him, how's he gonna know when Sally gets there, and the commish said, 'Leave that to me.' What's that mean?"

I thought of all the people who might be driving him. It could be any of them. Sally had become a Mafia Macbeth, those he moved moved only in command, nothing in love. I'd never trusted any of them. I couldn't prove anything, but I had to let Sally know what he was walking into.

"You got a piece with you?" I asked Reilly. "Just say yes or no."

"Yes."

"Can you get down to the hospital and hang around the emergency room?"

"There's gonna be at least two of them and only one of me." He didn't sound scared, he was just figuring the odds in his own head.

"Is it a throw-down?"

"It's registered," he said.

I decided to change the subject.

"They always got hospital cops there, you know, making sure nobody blocks the emergency lanes for the ambulances. These shooters are going to stick out like sore thumbs. Once you make 'em, you can tell the cops they're packing."

"I don't know." He sounded doubtful. Again, not scared exactly, just dubious. Probably figured the rent-a-cops wouldn't give a shit. They might roust him instead of the shooters. He would know better than me how they would react, being one of them. Come to think of it, one night about a month ago, I was coming out of Ox Kennedy's taproom in Quincy Market when I saw a gangbanger aimlessly wandering around with a knife in his hand. A plunging knife, the kind that you wear like brass knuckles, only you've got a three or four-inch blade in your palm. Push daggers, they call them. Only good for one thing, stabbing somebody. You have to understand that the fucking knife people are crazier than gun nuts. The reason they carry knives is they're so far gone they can't get a gun permit. Those knife people scare the shit out of me. You never want to get shanked, believe me.

Anyway, this night at Quincy Market, I saw a cop and told him about the gangbanger with the knife. He gave me a dirty look.

"What the fuck you want me to do?" he said.

Reilly said, "You still there?"

"Yeah, I'm thinking."

"Think fast," he said. "Why don't you call him? You must have his cell phone."

"I do, but he's got a big mouth—that's off the record." Why was I worried about dissing Sally? Odds were he'd be dead within the hour, unless I could figure something out. I asked Reilly, "You wouldn't happen to have a ski mask in your car, would you?"

"No, I only rob banks on Thursdays. Listen, I'm leaving right now for MGH. I'll try to stop the car when they come in and get him outta the car and we'll make a run for it. That's all I can do."

He'd be lucky to pull it off, and he knew it. He needed backup.

"How soon can you get here?" Reilly asked. "Where are you?"

"Roxbury," I said. "Listen, you gotta watch it when you approach the car. His driver has to be the finger man. He'll be armed for sure. You come walking up to the car and he'll cap you and then deliver Sally right up to the door. I know Sally. He'll figure you had the contract."

I hated talking so openly on the phone like this, but what alternative did I have?

"What kind of car's he got?" Reilly asked. I liked that he hadn't asked any follow-up questions about getting shot.

"A white Cadillac Escalade. Unless he's in the Lincoln Town Car, dark blue."

"You really can't call him?"

"Nah, he sits in the front seat. The driver'll make the play for sure if I call."

"How about texting him?" he asked.

"Sally? Are you kidding? Look, I gotta get going. Keep in touch, but watch the driver."

"Is Sally carrying?" he asked, reasonably.

"Doubtful," I said. Yes, he'd been packing at Hole in the Head's wake, but other than that, I hadn't seen him armed since about 1992.

I got up and walked over to the corner of the room and opened up a floor hide that dated back to the Wimpy Bennett days. Marty Hide was working steady even in those days. He was what you'd call a survivor. I threw off a greasy old blanket and picked up an AR-15. God, I love the AR-15. It's basically a stripped-down M-16, thirty copper-jacketed rounds per clip, great for a bank robbery, a small massacre or just plain going out in a hail of bullets, à la Jimmy Cagney in *White Heat*. I wasn't planning on checking out today, so I loaded it quickly, covered it with the blanket and put it under my arm. Peppa watched me, but he didn't ask any questions. I'd trained him well. Finally I walked out to my car, threw the gun on the front seat and started the engine.

I had a bad feeling I wasn't going to get to Mass General in time.

42

SCRAMBLED EGGS

By the time I got to the gas station, the hit on Sally's son had already gone down. At least there were enough cop cars around to indicate something serious had happened. But no ambulances—they must have already taken him to MGH. I could see the back alley where they'd shot him. It was teeming with plainclothes cops. I wondered if the shooting had been recorded by any surveillance cameras.

There are so many goddamn surveillance cameras these days, everywhere you go, and not just in the cities either. I wondered how many videos of the famous old gangland hits would have ended up as video on the late news if someone tried them today.

I parked next to a fire hydrant in front of the branch library on Cambridge Street and crossed first the street and then the police line at the gas station, flashing my old BPD badge. As soon as I made sure Sally's kid had survived and was on his way to the hospital, I called Bench.

"The kid's alive," I said.

"Good," he said. "I'm just crossing Mass Ave. Can you hang on 'til I get there?"

I told him I'd do my best. I pulled out and headed back down Cambridge Street towards Mass General. I didn't want my car anywhere near the hospital entrance, so I parked in a bus stop two blocks south of MGH on Cambridge Street.

If it got towed, so be it.

I reached around into the backseat and rummaged through all sorts of crap. I used to keep the Olds relatively neat when I was going out with Katy, but since we'd broken up, I'd fallen back into my old habits. Yellowing newspapers, fast-food bags, Styrofoam Dunkin' Donuts cups . . . Patty had had every right to complain. Finally I found what I was looking for—a navy blue ski mask. I pulled it down low over my forehead. I'd figured it was there all along, but I didn't want Bench pissed at me if I'd lost it somewhere along the line.

Then I reached into the glove compartment and found a cheap old pair of sunglasses I'd bought at the Walmart on Route 9 in Framingham on a surveillance job a year or two earlier. That was the best I could do for disguises, but it would have to do. Gloves would have been nice too, in case I had to open the door to Sally's Town Car, but I didn't have time. I made sure I had my "disguise" on before I got out, just so the cameras wouldn't catch a before shot of me. But I couldn't be sure another one hadn't already caught me inside the car, checking out my new look in the rearview mirror and making sure I had the safety off my .38.

I got out of the car as casually as possible for a guy in May wearing a ski mask and sunglasses. I locked the car and then began walking toward the hospital. Another thing it would have been nice to have: a phone booth to duck into, somewhere I could stand and not stick out like a sore thumb, but when was the last time you saw a phone booth? I finally found a mailbox to lean against, right on Cambridge Street, on the same side of the street as the hospital, about a block east.

If Sally's car was coming from the North End, I'd be able to see it a few blocks away. If Sally wasn't driving, which I assumed he wasn't, I was going to jerk open the front door, gun drawn, and tell

Sally to get out. If he were in the backseat, which Bench had said he wouldn't be, I'd still tell him to get out.

Once I did that . . . well, I wasn't sure what I was going to do with the driver. I wouldn't even know his name. But I didn't have any time to ponder my decision, because I saw the Town Car about two blocks away. If it was the wrong Lincoln, someone was going to get a surprise, but there was nothing else I could do.

I continued leaning against the mailbox until the Lincoln got closer, and finally stopped at the traffic light just before the hospital entrance. The fire station was across the street, but it wasn't quite warm enough yet to have the hero jakes sitting out front.

I stalked toward the car as I removed my gun from my pocket. I grabbed the front door handle. It wasn't locked. Sally looked petrified as I opened the door, gun in hand, wearing a ski mask.

"Sally, out," I said, waving the gun at the driver as I addressed him. "You, keep going, right to the hospital, and wait for us there."

"I'm not getting out," Sally said.

"You better," I said, putting the gun to his head. "Bench sent me."

"Bench?" he said, in surprise.

"C'mon, we ain't got much time." I grabbed him by his arm— very flabby, I noticed. "And you, driver, don't try to be a fucking hero. Just keep driving to the emergency room entrance."

Sally looked back as he stepped out of the car. "Do like he says, Eggs."

"Throw your gun out," I told him.

He had it under his left leg. First he slowly told me where it was, and then what he was going to do with it.

"Very good, Eggs," I said. Obviously Eggs didn't want his brains scrambled. Now he was holding the gun gingerly, by its grip, with his fingertips. "Throw it out, away from the car. And then drive straight to the emergency entrance."

Then I pulled Sally out of the car. I kept a good grip on his arm and started walking him very fast back up Cambridge Street toward City Hall.

"Shake a leg, Sally, they were going to put you on the spot back there."

"At the hospital?" he said. He was already starting to get winded.

I was walking fast too, but I took time to turn back around for a moment. Eggs, whoever he was, had not followed instructions. He was backing the Town Car out so fast onto Cambridge Street that he slammed into a bus that was heading past MGH toward the river. Eggs jumped out of the wrecked car and started running and then I saw why—two swarthy guys, automatic pistols drawn, were running toward the car. They were closing in fast on the Lincoln Town Car.

"Don't look now, Sally, but your car's about to get air-conditioned."

The first shots hit the Lincoln, and Sally and I both took off running. Then there was more shooting. Seemed like a lot of shots for a simple hit, especially considering nobody was even in the vehicle. But I didn't feel like establishing my eyewitness status, and neither did Sally. We were going uphill now, and Sally was panting even more. But I wanted to make it to the alley next to the North End branch library, which would put us out of the line of fire.

When we turned into the alley, I stashed the gun back in my coat, ripped off my mask and sunglasses and threw them down. We took off running. I thought we were going to make it, but suddenly I heard the voice behind me.

"FBI," a voice yelled. "Halt, drop the gun."

Sally grunted. He wasn't sure. I was, though. If they'd been wiseguys they just would have shot us without any TV theatrics. When I skidded to a halt and put up my hands, Sally did the same.

"Don't make any sudden moves, motherfuckers!" the guy said, and I ventured a glance back at him. He was a kid, about twenty-eight, and he was wearing one of those blue FBI jackets.

"Both of you, on the ground with your arms out." Both of us followed instructions. He said you, not "youse." Now I was positive he wasn't a wiseguy.

43

AN EXECUTIVE DECISION

I was driving down Cambridge Street just in time to see Reilly and Sally cut into the alley. Then I saw the FBI agents following in after them, guns drawn. Both those guys have been around; I figured they weren't going to do anything stupid. I knew I wasn't going to. There was no way I was going to stop to vouch for my pals, not with that AR-15 under my coat on the front seat.

Up ahead, Cambridge Street in front of MGH was already blocked off. Sally's Lincoln was up on the median strip, its back end demolished by the collision with the T bus. I saw Benny Eggs spread-eagled on the ground, his hands flex-cuffed behind his back.

On the other side of the car were a couple of perforated bodies. They looked brown, or tanned. Them, I didn't care about. But Benny Eggs? Now I knew who was trying to whack Sally. It was Benny Eggs' boss, Blinky Marzilli. Benny didn't have brains or ambition enough for something like this, delivering the boss to a gangland assassination in front of a million witnesses. I wondered if it had dawned on Benny yet that he was supposed to go out with Sally, not to mention the two killers. The FBI had been listening in, just like we had. They had the hospital staked out too.

What a clean sweep it would have been, Sally gone and everyone who knew anything about the hit gone too. Sometimes, though, dear Blinky, the fault is not in the stars, but in ourselves, that we are next on the Hit Parade.

I made a U-turn and doubled back around through the West End and went around the Leverett Circle and past the Science Museum and Lechmere Station and onto the McGrath-O'Brien highway.

Somerville, my hometown. I parked in back of the Alibi, walked in and told Hobart to get me another boiler from the top of the hill and a sawed-off shotgun, and that I'd be waiting for him around back in fifteen minutes.

I knew what I had to do. I should have done it long before it got to this point. But Sally had said no. Well, now Sally was out of commission for at least the next few hours, and I was going to have to make an executive decision in his stead.

I sat down in a booth, picked up a burner cell phone and started making calls. I needed to get an address for Blinky.

44

ANOTHER BEAUTIFUL FUCKIN' GUY

They took us back to FBI headquarters at One Center Plaza, and questioned us, separately of course, for more than six hours. Same questions, over and over again. In the three-block drive from where they grabbed and cuffed us, up the hill to FBI headquarters in Pemberton Square, I decided I would rely on the "gag" defense. It was all a big joke, a gag, me pointing a gun on Sally and dragging him out of the car.

"You pulled this gag just after his son had gotten shot?" an agent asked me.

"How the hell did I know?"

"Did you know your gun was loaded and the safety was off when you pointed it at him," he said.

"It's gotta be realistic for the gag to work."

"I think I'm gonna gag," the agent said.

I found out later, Sally gave them the same general routine. He didn't put it across as well, I'm sure, probably because he was still frantic about his son, at least for the first couple of hours, until they let him make a phone call to find out he was going to survive.

They asked Sally if he knew me.

"Of course I know him," Sally said. "He's a beautiful fucking guy."

"If you know him, what's his name?"

"Mack," he said. "I call him Mack."

"Do you know your driver's in custody. Ben Cristofaro."

"Is that his name? I always meant to ask him."

"The guys that were going to shoot you, they were from New York. Do you have any idea why they would want you dead?"

"You'd have to ask them," Sally said.

They didn't tell us then, but they'd also arrested the commissioner and Donuts a couple of hours after we were taken into custody. So that was the feds' mike under the table. They'd heard the same conversation I had, they'd gotten to MGH a little late, just in time to take out the shooters. Now they had the senator and the commish not just on racketeering and conspiracy, but also for murder. And in one of the shooters' cars, they'd discovered a couple of grenades, each one of which is, as Bench McCarthy never tires of pointing out, a weapon of infernal destruction and thus another thirty years on and after. Tough break, especially for the man whose word was his bond, Donuts Donahue.

The feds cut me loose just before midnight. I took the elevator to the ground floor of One Center Plaza. My car was about three blocks away on Cambridge Street and I started walking toward it, hoping against hope that it hadn't been towed. Now I was less worried about feds, or shooters, than I was about the City of Boston's Traffic and Parking Department. As I walked, I called Katy Bemis on her cell phone. She'd been trying to reach me all night. Of course she had.

"I need a statement," she said.

"Why should I tell you anything?"

"Because they think you're still my . . ."

"Here's my quote," I said. "It was all a gag."

"You pulled a gun on Sally Curto right before two professional hit men from New York opened fire on his car and it was a gag?"

"Am I under arrest?" I asked. "They must have believed me."

"Senator Donahue and the commissioner got arrested tonight too. What's the connection?"

"Listen, Katy, why don't we do lunch tomorrow? After a good night's sleep, maybe I'll remember more."

"I've got a deadline right now. It'll be too late then."

"It's never too late, Katy." I hung up on her. It felt good. The phone immediately rang again, so I turned it off.

Walking down the hill, with the Athens Garden on the other side, I spotted Sally Curto. He appeared to be waiting for a cab, which didn't seem right for The Man, even though he was obviously not the prototypical Uber customer. He must not have had to hail a cab very often, because if he did, he'd have known enough to make his way to the Omni Parker House or Quincy Market, where there are always plenty around.

"Sally, you need a ride home?" I said, and he jumped. He was still skittish. He'd had a very close call.

I introduced myself, and asked him why he was standing out here.

"Didn't you have a lawyer in there?" I said.

"Fuckin' right I did," he said.

"And he couldn't give you a ride home?"

"For another seven hundred bucks an hour? No, thank you."

He said he'd have rather gone back to the hospital, but it was too late to see his son, and Jason was out of danger anyway.

"Thanks, kid," he said. "You really saved my ass. They told me your name's Reilly? You don't really look that Irish."

"My mother was Italian."

"I knew it!" he said. "I knew it!"

"She was from Richmond Street."

"I knew it!"

From then on, we were buddies. We walked back to my car—amazingly it hadn't been towed, but there were $300 worth of orange tickets under the windshield wiper.

"Fuck them meter maids," Sally said, grabbing the orange tickets out of my hand. "Give 'em to me, I'll fuckin' show 'em who's boss."

Which meant tearing the tickets up, and me getting them sent to me a second time, with surcharges. I grabbed them back and said I had an in at City Hall. He nodded and passed them over to me. I asked him where he wanted to go.

"You know the Alibi?" he said.

45

BLINKY SLEEPS WITH THE FISHES

I figured Sally would be stopping by. He hardly ever did, but tonight, he'd want to be filled in. He and Jack Reilly showed up about 12:30 a.m. Sally tried to make a John Gotti-esque entrance, but he was too tired to pull it off.

Sally gave Patty a peck on the cheek and his usual line about how she ought to find herself a nice Italian boy. He shook hands with Hobart and hugged him. Then he just shook hands with a couple of the other guys who were a little lower on my organizational chart, which was why they didn't rate a hug. Finally he motioned to me. We went to the booth closest to the restrooms. No one was going to need to relieve himself for a while.

He even tried a little small talk.

"You got yourself a good girl there," he said of Patty. "I don't know how many times I tell my poor Jason, always marry an Italian girl. They won't go runnin' to the cops on you when you slap 'em around."

I nodded. I knew the small talk was over.

"So how'd you know what they were doing?" he said.

"We put a bug under the table in their bar," I said.

"Who's we?'"

"Reilly there. I told you about him. He was working for some people up at the State House."

"Them motherfuckers shot my son. I want 'em dead."

"I think they already are, Sally. The ones we could get anyway."

"That cocksucker Benny Eggs, I want him hit in the head. And Blinky—it had to be Blinky."

"Blinky's gone," I said.

"He run away already? To Florida?"

"I mean, gone. Blinky ain't coming back, Sally. Somebody hit him tonight when he pulled his car into the garage. He had some fucking punk kid with him too, a 'bodyguard.' He had to go too."

Sally stared at me silently for what seemed like ten seconds. Then he leaned across the table and without saying anything gave me a big wet kiss on the cheek. A tear rolled down his cheek.

"Did he say anything?" Sally asked.

"Sally," I said, "you know I don't do, 'did he say anythings?'"

Besides which, the only time anybody ever says anything before they get hit is in the movies. Famous last gangster words—there aren't any. If you give a guy time to say, "You dirty rat," you're also giving him time to pull a two-shot derringer out of his sleeve. The only time a guy ever said anything to me was when we were sitting in a car by the Bunker Hill Monument and he laid out a couple of lines of cocaine and asked me, "Do you want a line?"

Those were his last words. I'll leave it at that.

"Is this it?" Sally finally asked. "The end of the war?"

"Yeah, if you want to call it a war."

"My nephew got killed, my son got shot. Hole in the Head is dead. Yeah, I'd call it a war."

I reached over and patted him on the arm. "Sorry," I said. "You need a new driver too."

He sneered. "I never trusted that cocksucker Benny Eggs."

"I hope not," I said, "because I got a hunch right now he'd be willing to tell the feds he shot Kennedy if he thought it would get him into the Program, or at least keep him locked up so's we can't get to him."

"And all along I thought it was Cheech," he said.

"I told you Blinky was a rat. He thought he could slip in and be the new Stevie, or Whitey. The guy on top ratting out everybody underneath."

Sally waved me off. "Nah, Cheech made more sense as the rat."

"After his own brother got killed?"

"That's why I suspected him. You know how many times Hole in the Head tried to cap him?"

Now, he said, he was going to have to promote Cheech. We'd have a big dinner tomorrow night at the Café Ravenna, he said, and afterwards, down at the Nite Lite, with only the made men present, he'd make the big announcement. It was fine by me. Let the guineas have all the fun burning Mass cards and pricking their fingers. Like all good drivers, whether in organized crime or politics, Cheech was finally going to get a soft job. And now that the war was over, Sally wouldn't be needing any more tough-guy chauffeurs.

"George Graft is okay," Sally said. "I know him since Tech High. He's the last guy I got left who don't get lost in Roxbury. Maybe I'll use my boy, too, after he gets out of the hospital."

"Be a while, huh?"

"Yeah, he needs rehab on his legs, they said. They really did a number on him, these motherfuckers."

I didn't say the obvious. They could have killed him. This is what happens to your kids, or your nephews, if you're in what they used to call the life.

"You want a drink?" I asked him.

"Yeah, a double Drambuie, on the rocks. And don't give me any of that cheap-ass Lechmere coffee brandy either. I ain't one of your mick hod-carrier customers who can't tell the difference. *Capisce?*"

"One more thing," I said.
"Whatever you say," he said.
"No more Liz," I said. "Leave her alone."
"Right hand of God . . ."

46

AVE ATQUE VALE

The next night we all had dinner at Sally's place on Hanover Street—the Café Ravenna. Bench McCarthy called me in the morning and told me I could bring a date, but not that daffy bitch from the *Globe*. Briefly, very briefly, I thought about asking him if Patty had a sister, but I was afraid what his answer might be. What if he said yes?

I asked him if it was really wise to have everybody assemble in one place, and he said it was the best thing to do, to allay any lingering suspicions the feds had about a gang war.

I called Katy and talked to her for about a half-hour, without mentioning my plans for the evening. I gave her some warmed-over human-interest stuff, as she calls it, not that any of it seemed very interesting compared to the real story. But for some reason she was in a good mood, maybe because she'd already had a front-page exclusive on the *Globe* website about the formerly missing Beezo Watson now being a "person of interest" in the five murders. Despite the fact that she knew it was bullshit, she'd played it straight, and the story had already been picked up by Drudge. That meant hundreds of thousands of extra hits. And there was another bit of news that she passed on.

"They posted a job listing this morning for a new metro columnist," she said.

"It took them this long to get rid of McGee?" I asked.

"You always said there's a lot of inbreeding over here."

"Yeah, but I was talking about the fact that they don't have chins anymore."

"The brains are the second thing to go," she said, "after the chins."

"Is it going to be held against you," I asked, "that you seem to know a lot of Roman Catholics who were actually born in Boston and who don't celebrate diversity?"

"They already think there's something wrong with me, running around with you."

"Present tense?" I asked.

"Don't get your hopes up," she said, and hung up.

I had to get to the courthouse to attend the preliminary appearances of the senator and the commissioner. It was my last assignment for Mr. Caulfield. They were already wearing the orange prison jumpsuits issued by the Plymouth County Correctional Facility.

I didn't say anything to them, but I recognized the senator's lawyer; he'd been mine when I had my little problem at City Hall all those years ago.

He came over to where I was sitting in the second row, behind the cops and the assistant U.S. attorneys and the reporters, most of whom didn't recognize me, thank God.

"Have your ears been burning, Jack?" my old lawyer whispered with a smile.

"I don't know why they would be," I said.

"My client says you put a wire under the table in his booth."

I leaned in even closer to him. "Tell your client there were two wires under that table—and that's off the record. I'll deny it if you call me as a witness."

"Don't worry, it's in the feds' statement of facts."

"Not my name?"

He smiled and shook his head. "They don't do that. The way they see it, it's free advertising for you. They don't do any favors for anybody, as I think you'll recall. Besides, there were no fingerprints on your wire."

These initial hearings never last very long. The defendants always look distracted, at least if this is their first time getting lugged, which it was. They're doing the math in their heads, how much time, multiplying it by eighty-five percent, trying to remember what they've already been told down in the joint about how the sentencing guidelines work.

I wondered if anyone had yet mentioned the grenades in the car. Thirty years on and after is always a disappointment.

The senator looked back and smiled at his wife, who sat stone-faced. I'll bet she'd told him this was going to happen. I'll bet she'd told him over and over and over again. Or at least that was going to be her story now. If I were him right about now, I might prefer the House of Correction to the old homestead.

Back on Beacon Street, I reported back to the Caulfields, the old man and his son. We sat down in the office and his son Terry poured drinks. A lot was happening at the State House too. The Senate president had accepted his floor leader's resignation "with deep sadness"—appropriately so, since it was also going to end his campaign for governor. The commissioner had been suspended—without pay. I guess he wasn't in the union anymore.

"They're moving the casino bill out of committee tomorrow," Terry Caulfield said. "They want to make sure there's no appearance of impropriety."

We all got a good laugh about that one and poured another round all around.

They were so pleased with how everything had turned out that they wrote me a bonus check for $2,000. I almost fainted, but I had to get moving. Before dinner, I had to meet a guy at J.J. Foley's who wanted to talk to me about the $500 million worth of paintings that had been stolen from the Isabella Stewart Gardner Museum.

I'll tell you about that some other time.

47

SALLY DELIVERS A SPEECH

Sally usually sat at a table in the back of the main room at the Café
Ravenna, with no one allowed to sit at any of the adjoining tables.
He didn't want any eavesdropping. But tonight he took over the
entire back room, which was usually reserved for parties. He had
two off-duty Boston cops sweep the place for bugs, not that any
crimes were going to be committed tonight, at least we weren't planning any.

It was a small gathering. Patty and I and Hobart from Somerville. Jack Reilly showed up with Slip Crowley, the Boston city
councilor who was a friend of Reilly's and, more important, had
done Sally a lot of favors back in the old days when he was on the
Boston Licensing Board. George Graft was there, and Cheech.
And a few others—half-ass wiseguys from Sally's social club and a
couple of their wives. I also noticed Spucky and Jimmy Lynnway,
the wiseguys he'd been planning to send after Liz McDermott.
They were apparently coming aboard full-time. It was like a Mafia
wedding.

On Sally's orders, they had a bartender on. We were all getting a
good buzz on when Sally called the meeting to order.

"First," he says, "I would like to offer a toast to all of youse. Youse are all a beautiful fucking guy."

He'd been into it, all right, all afternoon. But nobody was going to say anything. He went on at some length about his son's condition—improving. Then he mentioned Slip Crowley's ancient machinations for him with his old Combat Zone liquor licenses at City Hall—some of which were pretty amusing. About twenty minutes in, Sally got to me.

"This guy Bench," he said, "not many people know it—"

"And I'd just as soon keep it that way, Sally."

That got a few laughs, and gave a couple of people a chance to get up and get drinks or go to the bathroom. But of course it didn't stop Sally.

"I meet this kid, I'm doing a bit in Norfolk, on a bullshit state gambling beef. And I run into this kid, and I mean he is a kid, he's like seventeen years old. In the can with all these hard-core criminals like me, they called him something, in-something, what'd they call you, Bench?"

"Incorrigible." I could see this all ending up on the front page of the paper someday.

"Lemme tell you how incorrigible. I got some problems back then with some wiseguys in Revere, and they thought with me in the joint, it'd be a good idea to hire this big fucking—"

"Sally, please," I said.

"I know, Bench." He paused, then looked out at the gathering. "You know what Bench likes to remind me of, and I ain't kiddin' here. He always says, 'There's no statute of limitations on murder.'"

At this point I decided an intervention was in order. I stood up and pushed back my chair.

"Folks," I said, raising my wineglass, "what the olive-oil importing business gained, the criminal bar lost. You would have made a helluva criminal lawyer, Sally." I clinked my glass with Patty's. "Here's to Sally, our pal, we're glad you're okay, and Jason's gonna be okay, and I'm okay, and everybody's okay. *Salud!*"

Sally was winded, thank God. He sat down heavily and George Graft brought him another drink. The Café Ravenna is a traditional North End tomato-sauce place, which is to say, nothing memorable. But this night I swear they must have ordered out from one of the good joints, maybe Bricco.

Everything was top notch. The antipasto, and none of that wilted iceberg-lettuce salad as the second dish. Perfect eggplant parmagian, and then veal saltimbocca, exquisite, which we were chowing into when suddenly Liz McDermott came barging into the back room, the maître d' in hot pursuit. She was wearing her ten-gallon hat again.

"Sally," she said, "I've got to talk to you."

Sally stood up and waved off the maître d'. Then he looked over at George Graft, who was also getting up, and shook his head. Sally would handle this one by himself. Patty leaned over to say something to me, but I shushed her. I knew Sally would be speaking too softly for me to hear much, but I wanted to try to catch at least a few words of what he was saying to her.

He was gesticulating wildly, and then he reached into his coat pocket and came up with a wad of cash, which he threw at her. Then he flicked her hat, which gave the play away, if I'd had any doubts. He turned back around and nodded at Spucky and Jimmy Lynnway, who were standing at attention, more bodyguards than guests.

As Liz staggered out, I stood up and walked out of the room. The men's room was behind the bar, so it didn't look suspicious. But instead of going to the head, I ducked out the emergency exit in back and dashed back around the building out onto Hanover Street. Then I stepped into the doorway of Mike's Pastry next door and waited for Liz to come by. She was still counting the cash Sally had given her as I grabbed her and pulled her into the bakery.

"Liz," I said, "I thought I told you to get out of town."

"Ah, Bench, it's just one more night." Her words were slurred, she was swaying. I wondered how much of Henry Sheldon's money she still had left. "Give Liz a kiss—"

I pushed her away, but not before I smelled her breath. Whiskey. Rotgut blended rye no doubt. Good Lord.

I grabbed Liz by the shoulders and shook her as hard as I could without attracting attention.

"Liz," I said, "whatever you do tonight, don't go near the Nite Lite. He told you again to come down wearing the hat, didn't he?"

She frowned at me through rheumy eyes. But unlike Sally, she wasn't drunk. She was stoned to the gills.

"You must think I'm stupid, Bench. I know he wants to get rid of me. If I'm wearing the hat, they'll know who to shoot when they walk in."

"You know that, Liz, and yet you still went in there looking for him, in front of all those witnesses?"

"Witnesses? Those are his friends in there, like you. He's not gonna have me hit in front of his friends. The Nite Lite, that's where he wants it to happen."

Her voice was rising. She was angry. I glanced over at the people behind the counter. Thank goodness, I didn't recognize any of them. Still, I put my finger to my lips and shook my head. I reached into my pocket and came out with about a grand in hundred-dollar bills.

"Do me a favor, Liz, get the fuck outta town or you're gonna get killed tonight."

"I know that, Bench," she said, grabbing the bills. "I already bought my ticket. I'm going to see my sister in—"

"Don't tell me, I don't wanna know."

She took off her hat and handed it to me. "Got any molls you wanna get rid of, Bench? Give 'em this hat and drop 'em off at the Nite Lite around midnight." She laughed so hard she finally started coughing—a real smoker's wheeze. "That's what time Sally says he's going to meet me there. He's happy again, Bench. His son's alive, he's got you, the war's over, and he figures he'll never see me again." She suddenly burst into tears.

I walked over to a table in the bakery where two young touristy couples were finishing their cannolis and cappuccinos. I held out the hat and asked if anyone wanted a $350 hand-tooled genuine leather headband chapeau. One of the women giggled and grabbed it and they all started laughing. The girl put it on and they all started taking pictures of her with their cell phones. She and the other woman posed and then the first woman put the hat on the second one's head and they all started taking more selfies to tweet out. . . .

I walked back over to Liz and gave her a hug.

"I gotta get back to the time," I said. "Please Liz, take that money, don't put it up your nose or stick it in your arm. Get the fuck outta Boston. Catch a plane tonight. Go anywhere; just get out of town. I'm serious."

She turned to walk away, but before she could get very far on Hanover Street, I called her back. I held out my right hand, palm up. I pointed at her with my left index finger, smiled and shook my head.

"Almost forgot something, didn't you, Liz?"

She tried not to smile. "What do you mean, Bench?"

"Sally's watch," I said. "Let's have it. I know you got it back from the Weeper. I called him and he told me you got it out of hock."

"Ah, Bench," she said, "that watch is my grubstake."

"That watch is your death warrant," I said. "Sally'll send someone looking for you if he knows you have the watch. Guess who'll get the contract."

She sighed and reached into her purse. The watch had apparently been there all day; she had to take at least three full nip bottles out of the bag before she finally came up with the watch and handed it over. Then she smiled as sweetly as she could.

She went up on her tiptoes and kissed me on my lips as I did my best to hold my breath. "You're a good man, Bench."

"No, I'm not," I said, "and you know it."

She laughed again, and I pointed my finger at her once more.

"Be missing," I said. She nodded and walked out of the bakery and I went back to the party. I never saw her again.

Within the week, the story had been thoroughly aired out in the newspapers, except now it had become a political scandal rather than a gang war. Once the heat died down, the casino bill rose from the dead, Beezo-like, and came out of committee. It passed both branches of the legislature overwhelmingly and was signed into law by the lame-duck governor. The Gaming Commission then officially designated the company Reilly had been working for as the licensee for the Boston casino, which was really in Everett.

I asked Reilly if he'd supplied the info that had so obviously been used to shake down the commission and the legislature. He just laughed and said, "Who wants to know?"

I guess I had that one coming.

A few days later, Sally invited me to dinner at the Café Ravenna—a real dinner, not a let's-set-up-Liz supper. Just him and me, with Cheech on the door. Cheech seemed pleased with his promotion. I noticed he had even bought himself a new raincoat. I assumed he hadn't changed sawed-off shotguns, because he still listed to the right.

This time I was happy to go, because I'd given the watch to Jason at the hospital and told him that when he got out he should leave it somewhere in the Dog House where Sally would be sure to find it, and would just think he'd had a senior moment and misplaced it.

After dinner, Sally took a fat envelope out of his breast pocket and pushed it across the table.

"I appreciate what you done," he said. "I know we're partners, but you had expenses. This here's for your troubles—fifty large."

I smiled in gratitude.

"Now," he said. "I got a business proposition. You know I know some people in Everett." I nodded; they call the pols over there "the Common Council," as in, common thieves.

"I ain't told you about this," Sally said, "but when it looked like everything was goin' south, I bought a liquor license on a joint one block from the casino. Got it cheap too. Under the table of course. We're gonna have hookers, shylocks, bookies, you name it. You want in?"

Does a bear shit in the woods? Of course I wanted in.

"Good," he said. "We'll go halfsies. Now you owe me fifty grand."

I looked down at the table with my money bulging out of the envelope, then up at Sally. He smiled and swept up the envelope and put it back in his pocket. What the hell, though, it still seemed like a real steal, getting in on the ground floor of a gin mill around the corner from a "resort destination" casino, even if the resort was Everett. I was already considering names—for some reason, I always liked "the Horseshoe," a very popular name in Nevada, just like you see a lot of joints named "the Paddock" around racetracks (or in the old days, in Somerville) . . .

Sally interrupted my daydreaming: "I just need one small favor of you, Bench."

Obviously. Fifty large was too good to be true. My eyes narrowed.

"Kiss me, Sally," I said. "I always like a kiss before I get fucked."

He waved me off. "What's wrong with you? Only you could look a gift horse like this here in the mouth."

I puckered up my lips. "I'm waiting," I said.

"Okay," Sally said, "since you asked. You know, we—that's you and me, partner—we're gonna need some muscle in this new joint, to keep out the element, the element that ain't us, that is. I was just wonderin', I been watchin' how some of these guys of yours handle themselves. I need guys that can straighten a thing out. So I'm comin' to you, everything up front and on the record, partner—"

"Please, Sally, get to the point."

"Okay, the point is, do you mind if I ask them guys you got with you at the garage, with the card game in Andrew Square—"

"Salt 'n' Peppa?"

"Yeah, them two. You mind if I ask them if they'd like to come in on the joint? With us, I mean, because we're—"

"Partners, yeah, I know, you told me once already. Partners." I paused as he awaited my response. He was rubbing his hands together, a sure sign he was anxious.

"Sally, you do understand, Peppa is . . ." I paused.

"I know, I know, I regret all them things I said about him now, I truly do. Don't tell him what I said, I mean, but I'm just telling you, I'm a fucking changed man. If I can just get this thing off the ground, I'm going so fuckin' legit it's ridiculous. Will you send 'em over the Dog House to sit down with me?"

What choice did I have? He's my partner.

The final problem we had was when the lawyers for Donuts Donahue filed a motion in court demanding to know how many bugs had been under the table at B.B. Bennigan's, and who had placed them there.

I asked Jack Reilly to handle it, since he'd had the same lawyer as Donuts. That way he could have a confidential chat with his old mouthpiece and if anything went wrong, both of them could claim attorney-client privilege. Jack sat down with him and the lawyer got all huffy, like he was rehearsing his lines for the trial. He said that if the feds had acted expeditiously, as he put it, and warned everybody about the plot, nobody would have gotten killed and his client would now be the president of the State Senate. He mentioned that back in the eighties when the FBI put the bug in Jerry Angiulo's headquarters, the G-men had given a heads-up to at least two guys that Jerry and the boys had been planning to put to sleep.

Jack listened and then went to see some guy he knew who worked for the A.G., an old reporter who owed him a favor, and this guy put him in touch with someone high up in the U.S. Attorney's Office. I don't know exactly how that conversation went down, but Jack pointed out to the fed that because the FBI hadn't alerted certain parties to the threat, the way they used to do, it wasn't just five people who ended up dead—it was three illegal aliens of color. Jack told him that if Eric Holder and Barack Obama ever found out that the DOJ office in Boston hadn't warned these undocumented Democrats that evil white American gangsters would be using them for target practice, that would not bode well for the U.S. attorney, who was already under suspicion, on the grounds of being a white heterosexual Roman Catholic male.

After due consideration of about ten seconds, the consensus in the U.S. Attorney's Office was, what can we do to make this go away, Mr. Reilly.

Jack told them he thought maybe he could make Donuts' motion for disclosure disappear. But first he needed something to bring back to Donuts's lawyer, and really, was it fair to tack another thirty years on and after his conspiracy sentence for those grenades in the shooters' car at Mass General that he knew absolutely nothing about?

I guess that after all my complaining about it, that new statute came in handy for me, because once Jack put the deal together, that was the last either of us heard about the second bug, or Donuts' thirty years on and after.

One final thing. In case you were wondering, after his spectacular return, Beezo Watson immediately vanished back into the mists of time. Every lead was a dead end, you might say, and his disappearance went back into the "cold case" file—get it? A month or two later, Jack Reilly's girlfriend wrote a Sunday story in the *Globe* about how the cops no longer considered themselves baffled by Beezo's fingerprints on the murder weapons, having concluded that it was all a cruel ruse by a cunning culprit.

"This was like something Whitey Bulger would have done," one of the cops was quoted as saying.

Now that pissed me off. Being likened to Whitey Bulger, that's a low blow. What have I ever done to deserve being compared to a sick treacherous fuck like Whitey?